] *Partitions of Unity*

ALSO BY JENNIFER MASON

The Oddball Gypsy Raconteur

Valedictorian

Sebastopol

Tors Lake

Partitions of Unity

] A NOVEL [

Jennifer Mason

Exponential Press, Santa Barbara, 2018

This is a work of fiction. Characters, places, and events are the product of the author's imagination or are used fictitiously. Any resemblance to real people, companies, institutions, organizations, or incidents is entirely coincidental.

] [

Published by Exponential Press
Post Office Box 3643
Santa Barbara, CA 93130

ISBN 978-0-9980221-0-9 (hardcover)
ISBN 978-0-9980221-1-6 (paperback)
ISBN 978-0-9980221-2-3 (e-book)

Book design: Studio E Books, Santa Barbara

for Laurie

"A strange disturbance took hold of me: to be strange people."

—Anonymous

"There was room enough there to place any story, depth enough for any passion, variety enough there for any setting, darkness enough to bury five millions of lives."

—Joseph Conrad

$$1 = \varphi_1(\tau, p) + \varphi_2(\tau, p) + \varphi_3(\tau, p) + \ldots$$

] *Partitions of Unity*

] *One*

A LULL HAD SETTLED OVER THE MARKET. A move in the direction of an early summer high was detected in its day-to-day variations, but a quantitative theory hedging an upward trend in the current conditions lagged. Instruments of bearish speculation were exercised. Caution was playing its role. With no evidence of where the resistance was coming from or why it would weaken, theory had supplemented the explanations provided at the close of each session for the breakout that hadn't happened. Risk aversion, quantified in the mechanism of utility indifference valuation, provided the long perspective. So that no one source of uncertainty should shoulder the entire responsibility for a narrow trading range, theory was re-supplemented. Astrological vapor trails were consulted—the South China Sea crisis, dry weather, self-reflexive commodity markets, that stuff: drama. It was the easier pill to swallow, the comforts of a plot unfolding, life goes on, as opposed to EOTWAWKI, the end of the world as we know it, which nevertheless fit better the stagnant model. The market had a snowball's prayer is where the theory found an idea of itself.

In short, I'm out of here.

That was the phrase that inhabited the many rumors that followed Alix Sociedes—a Greek at birth—and her demons—Greek gods at heart—as far as the police cared to make any use of it. There was no last person who testified credibly to having seen her. There was the treasurer of the Rainbow Charities. A mixed package of denominations had rolled out of his beach cabana in a suitcase on wheels. Alix was in toreadors. God, she left a beautiful memory. She was laughing. It's what the cops wrote. The state of mind thing. In that perspective her disappearance had all been too foolish to go to the authorities with in the first place. She was where the Rainbow Charities' money was, and that was like trying to read the market or silence or the electromagnetic spectrum. Wherever Alix was, that's where the scam was.

] *Two*

EVERY EVENING OF the first two weeks of May I'd been setting aside a moment on an upper patio to watch the tip of the sun give off a green flash as it slipped over the edge of the ocean off Maui. You were warned: don't blink. You did or did not catch it as the light took itself around the world. Let the night begin either way. The sun will be back. Another day, another green flash.

A back-and-forth with a legal group in Madison, Wisconsin, had introduced Ada Tomek, an Oakland investigator who would be contacting me. She didn't want to get into anything like a detail online. She volunteered to meet my return flight to San Francisco. She'd be crossing the Bay Bridge on Giants double-header day was how she chose to explain how thoroughly motivated she was to use up her afternoon for a few minutes in private.

We fixed our signals. I'd be the tall blonde with the blue bag over her left shoulder and the pet turtle on a gold leash.

Ada Tomek waved me into a black Jeep at the curb.

I'm a professional dominant in San Francisco. Clipped to her visor was a picture from my web page. The image advertises an intimacy I provide at my place of business, the English Department. I am displayed contemplating an open book supported flat in my hand. My hair is up in the style of an Edwardian governess.

The outfit is appropriate to a thin slice of the world of kink—what those for whom it matters call old-fashioned discipline. A dressage whip is held under pressure of my upper arm. This frees my right hand to arrange itself in the service of make-believe. My fingers hold time still as a conductor brings an orchestra to a rehearsed surrender to the outpouring of a performance, the willing submissive predicament.

She hauled a valise from the foot space under her seat to her lap and set the emergency lights while opening an envelope. In the envelope was a passport-style photo of a man shown above the second button of a dress shirt. I had never seen him, convinced enough to turn my hands up empty.

"It's nice to be home," I said. "In a month I'll start thinking how much I miss the islands. I returned the photo. "You've been to Hawaii?"

"Once in a while, business. You have a library. You stamp your books: Elizabeth Cromwell, English Department, San Francisco, 94109. You sell them?"

"My librarian could tell you. I don't think so. The man in the picture; who am I supposed to know?"

"Burleigh Polk," she said. "Three of your books are on his shelf."

I transferred a roll of keys to my right hand and gave the bats in the belfry a stare.

"If he were a client, I wouldn't tell you."

"Integrity. Catches my interest. Misplaced, however, as things stand with Mr. Polk. He lived on a steep rise in the Piedmont. He walked a sack of groceries to his front door, got the key in the lock, got the door open, and fell sideways over a stone balcony. They think he was top-heavy, tried to hang on to his bags and went over with them. He must have thrown a can of peas to the side on the way down, twenty-three feet. He was airborne to the bed of roses. Might not have been the last thing he saw. A heart attack was the official cause of death. Massive. He was forty-eight years old."

"As I say, I can't recall him. They don't always use their birth names. Maybe a long time ago he asked for a service I don't provide. That would lead to a suggestion that he look elsewhere. So if he was a client?"

"I can ask you questions and you'll know the answers, and you'll make a dollar even if you don't."

"When did he die?"

"Second of March."

I sifted the recent past with that lifted eyebrow that explained to me what it was supposed to explain: three to four months and I didn't miss him? I was saving her a dollar. "He would have been a no-show."

"Make no lemonade," she sighed.

"Come again?"

"A phrase, my father's. I passed the bar, worked six months on an antitrust case, slept four hours a night on a cot. I quit. It wasn't the hours. It wasn't the cot. It wasn't the case. I hate working with people in person. I'm always making lemonade, sinking my teeth into things, going it alone. It's expensive being me. Some of it's my money that lands in the sewer. I say the most innocuous things and upset people so naturally."

She took 380 to 280, up and over Potrero Hill, cutting east off the intersection at Divisadero and Haight, the back door to the English Department. She had no patience with the lane she was in. A car passing triggered a shift, not that it advanced position between stoplights. It lost ground, it gained ground. It didn't matter. It was a principle. Shift or die. She knew where to stop.

In certain periods of portraiture, she would have been a classically perfect plump, a girl of the olive-drab dungaree sector of the culture—an outfit, I imagined, discovered at the age when she was deciding the ways Ada does what's right for Ada. It was still right for her. She gave a good impression, a hire who got the job done. An orange thigh pocket might have held a pair of pliers. It was the money pocket. She unzipped it and put an envelope in her hand and moved it at me, the kind of motion that money moves my hand to meet. My eyes did the motions: I didn't want it.

"I would appreciate fifteen minutes," she said.

"Whose hard-earned money are you offering?"

"Polk worked at Lawrence Livermore. Livermore had a note in Polk's file, that in the event of his death or injury the person to be notified was his beloved mother. Sort of a trope. They're not related. In a timely fashion she produced personal correspondence that to her mind clearly reads like she should have everything. She hired Harrison, Fleet, and Stone in Madison. They hired Remnick and Dyer, an Oakland firm. They pay me."

"Who else wants everything?" I asked.

"The other woman who calls herself Polk's mother. They tracked Polk's father to her. Tough break for her: she hadn't married the biological father. He died. The biological mother is not known to be alive under any name. Harrison, Fleet, and Stone work for the good mother. It's how he wrote to her: Dear mother...etcetera, etcetera...as ever, your loving son. A judge would have to weigh the value of his sentiments. Polk neglected to formalize his wishes. We'll see. The despised pseudo-stepfather, a Mr. Gus Winifred, came out and looked over the estate. Reading body language, he's a fighter. He can dream a bit, if Polk's letters don't constitute a will. The ones that apply read like Polk's intentions, but they're nothing till a judge rules."

"Polk never married?"

"Not on the books. A multigenerational family habit."

"Any other mothers?"

"California. There are no statements in Polk's hand as to who was in line to receive a portion of anything he possessed. California is looking good."

"Who accepted the remains for burial?" I asked.

"The beloved mother. Harrison, Fleet, and Stone suggested this would show her love."

"What is the estate?"

"Polk had two domiciles. He lived in the Piedmont house.

His girlfriend lived in the other one, up in Montclair. Three bank accounts. Defense stocks way outperformed the market. When they opened the safety deposit box a fellow representing Lawrence Livermore scooped it out. His eyes only. California couldn't find hidden assets. I'm paid to look harder. If I can forge a real will and don't mention it, I get a bonus."

"Who gets my books?" I asked. "What are they?"

"*Plutarch's Lives. Speak, Memory. The Glass Key.* Who gets them is up in the air—not fiercely contested."

"What if I want them?"

"You hire me, I can get them back for you. Incidentally, how would Polk have them on his shelf in the Piedmont house?"

"Nothing's come to me yet. What's your answer?"

"In the Montclair house is a floor-to-ceiling oil painting. Not a bad likeness of you in boots and whip."

"Oh, God. Anything covering my ribs?"

"All bare terrain. California will sell wallet sizes in food marts. If you can prove the image is you, the courts can get you a cut."

"Suppose we cut out the courts?"

"The painting disappears?"

"Didn't the Mona Lisa disappear?" I said.

"If you can do it, don't tell me. Anyway, I walked Mr. Polk's photo in your neighborhood. I'm not a cop, so I can't flash threats. Making ends meet on a shoestring, I can't afford the privilege of lining the bank accounts of a dozen neighbors for how I might reach their comfort zone for the honest truth. Nobody recognized him, answering for free. If the two of you were playmates, you're good at keeping it to yourselves."

"I've taken you into my confidence, Ms. Tomek. Never met him. You could pay me to say I did. What would that get you?"

"Square zero. The people who recognize you never heard of Polk. If he gets his inspiration where he gets his thrills, it's not a lead I can run down. You and Polk don't connect. In his neck of Oakland the butcher, the baker, the candlestick maker said he dealt in cash. He was remembered for his hunk of manhood, overshadowed by the number of fifties he passed. They recall a lot of fifties. Nobody saw you."

She grabbed a wadge of papers out of a pocket and circulated a colored drawing to the top of the heap. It was a floor-to-ceiling life-size oil of a whip in a dark room that should be in a castle. The face of the woman holding the whip was me at about the age the man who commissioned the painting wanted me to be to stare at. She could have been me twenty years ago, even ten.

She shuffled the drawing to the bottom. On top now was a photo.

"Polk whipped himself once in a while," she said. "The coroner says the variations in his scars make it impossible they all came from him, and he'd bet most couldn't. Polk was a regular, a high-frequency practitioner. In his scrapbooks are photos of women who would put them there. His house had a playroom. There was equipment. His desires were facilitated there at least some of the time. Who in particular he played with? Some would guess you, the woman in the painting. But not me. I'm merely confused by the books."

"I suppose neither of Polk's mothers is fighting California for these treasures. Foul play?" I asked.

She rubbed her lip. "The heart is a lonely hunter, I think I heard. His heart broke. Nobody could come up with darker implications. The postman saw a can of peas on the lawn. Otherwise Polk wouldn't have been found for a day or two. The house keys were still in the lock. Died alone."

She tapped a photo of a long-limbed college-aged girl born to stretch her limbs for the greater glory of art. A second photo was the same face, but it caught her with her jodhpurs riding under her cheeks, a hand massaging a hip like it was pretty valuable. She was smiling back at someone in pyrotechnically strict allure, her blouse open, lit with the slow burn, fun on her mind. She was in a lean, about to give it a try.

"Polk had a woman who needed free rent," Ada said. "The couple across the street said she left in the morning, returned in the evening. Her hair was not always the same maroon, but they said they could only think of that one word for it. She had a UCB book bag. They assumed she was a student at Berkeley. They overheard her answer her phone: Mavyn."

"How much is Mavyn asking for?"

"Her car is licensed to a woman of her appearance with an address in Paso Robles. I left a message. Haven't heard back. She didn't come forward to ask if she was in a will. She wasn't in a written rental agreement. I'm not sure what I'd be following up on if I dropped in for a visit to Paso Robles."

"You don't know if she cried when she heard the news? Sometimes all we have is blowing our noses, hemorrhaging sincerity. It's worth a try."

"If she tried, whoever gave her his hankie didn't tell me."

I didn't move. The still me acted as though I had asked out loud if that was all she needed.

"One more book," she said. "*Der Mann Ohne Eigenschaften.*" It was candy-sucking German. I'm not sure how many words it was.

"Never owned it," I said. "I don't think. My name in it?"

"He had a shelf of science books in the Montclair house, not popular science, technical books, an overflow location, it seemed, for books he'd used in college courses. Some were French, some German. A volume one and volume two of this *Der Mann* were stuck together in a fancy box container. A couple shelves lower was another two-volume collection. Same author. Some wear and tear, separate from each other. The first collection looked expensive, specialty work.

"I was hired to find out what Polk had that was worth anything, so I pulled a chair over to look at the publication date, and didn't find it. The crafted volumes were hollow. Inside was a statue of a woman. The statue was heavy. At first I thought she was gold. Your name was on the base. She could have been modeled on your professional image."

She shuffled a photo of a bronze-looking statue of a woman,

naked to the waist, flimsy crafty peek-a-boo below, two hands holding a riding whip behind her bottom.

"You have the statue with you?" I asked.

"I couldn't sneak it out. There was a lady with me, an agent of the State of California. I pilfered some filings. Not gold, but the statue is maybe worth more than all the books on the shelf sold at distressed auction."

"You didn't tell California that Polk put a statue of me in a book. Why keep that our little secret?"

Her eyes smiled with a bloodhound's tender gravity.

"I'm not stopping anybody doing their job. You ever see an employee of California pick a book off a shelf?"

"Actually, I have," I chimed in a mock gravity. "Comes up in sessions. Start with a book and see where it takes us."

"They're thoroughly punished for misunderstanding the author's purpose, I assume?"

"That's one way it can go," I said.

"An address for a storage unit was in *Plutarch's Lives*," she said. "A key was taped to the inside front cover."

"So?"

"So I went to the storage unit."

Another photograph came to the top. A woman in Roman sandals and toreadors was walking away from the artist. A narrow wood-chip footpath disappeared into a wood that didn't look like the California around here, trees shocked with oranges and reds, more like maple syrup country. She was a full six feet as measured against a well-developed hedge, straight light yellow hair a good few inches layered on the shoulders, dressed as you would encounter a fine shape out and about on Valencia—not many, but definitely, yes, one a day if you were looking for the real San Francisco. A canvas carry bag was over each shoulder. A cozy similarity to me was evident in selected particulars.

A second drawing was an answer to what was in the bags.

An office setting, swivel chair and desk, was just inside a glass wall. The willow and pond garden beyond would have dominated my attention for the wow factor of how some people turn their backs to nature during the working day. A stack of currency on a desk had a teaser packet of bills flopped against it. The visible bill was a fifty. There might have been a hundred of those in rubber bands just leaning on raw cash. The woman in the chair was me, descriptively. I had a pen poised over a pad, a hand in my lap, and a look in my eyes: counting all this was all so unnecessary. I was taking someone's word for it.

I wasn't the woman who had her picture taken. "She's not me," I said, "even if I can lead you to it and get half the reward."

"The elusive dualism," she said. She stuck a question in her cheek, like a marble, but kept the question a mature discreet consideration.

"You need to find someone who knows her Spinoza," I said.

"The woman going in the woods is Mrs. Spinoza? But where is this room? Where is this office, this garden? This money?"

I heaved a shoulder, and put my hand on the door latch. I had a foot on the street when Ada swatted the steering wheel with her envelope. It was a thick swat, a reminder of much good that would come of a transaction.

"There's a box of Polk's videotapes in the trunk," she said. "At your leisure, I would appreciate you having a look at them. They require an expertise I don't have."

"How many tapes?"

"Could I just not say? However many you look at is how many. How many dollars you remove from the envelope is how many that is."

I wheeled my bag to a locked gate. Three of my books had wandered off to Polk's house. I didn't want to wonder how long it would take to go to sleep adding it all up. I had reached an age knowing a lost thing, once lodged in calculations, is never finished.

I tapped on the car window and said, "Let's look in the trunk." I stepped behind the car. It saved her the trouble of smiling. The trunk popped. Things you owned a car to carry here to there, over and over, easiest left in the trunk, were there, things I carried around, all that and some boxes. One was the metal kind you could pick the lock of with a dime. The other was a traveling filing cabinet with handholds. She asked if she could bring them both in.

I had her drop them in a corner in the office. She made a meaningful quarter turn to the door. I walked her back to the street. She put her right hand out, "Thanks."

"I'd love to retire," she said, "but not like Polk did it. Can you imagine yourself looking at a map of the Golden State and you draw a line from Death Valley to Mount Whitney and advertise a fun run along that line? You heard of the Pikes Peak Ascent? It's a marathon. Polk was one of them, an ironman, had plenty of time someday to never consider the need for a will, is how he would calculate. He'd live forever. His mother would be dead. California would be dead. It must have surprised him. I mean, on the way down, realizing he was dying, if he had time to realize. Not likely he did, but not for sure.

"Livermore was a good job. Extreme training soaks up a good deal of work conflict. Polk had a life that was working. Polk is every estate manager's good lesson. That's their lemonade."

I lowered the windows in the kitchen, and went to the corner store, and spoke about the green flash at sunset off Maui with the owner. He was glad I'd caught sight of it. I'd missed it a few nights, too, and we shared that experience, wondering how that could happen. Fog is what we ended on. I was home.

I dumped my elbows on the bathroom sink and washed my face and had a sit and a groan and said hello to the four kitchen walls I missed terribly. I cleared my throat, drawing attention to an old, tired traveler waiting for water to come to a boil.

] *Three*

IN THE MORNING my hair felt like it was making its own yoghurt. I showered and set a place at the office desk. I had a pot of coffee and refrigerated crumb cake. I had a hard oak chair. I cleared a couple square feet of mess off a reachable section of desk and put the cup to my lips, the doyenne of the English Department, all proper formalities.

A ten-thousand-dollar check wasn't a new experience, but appearing infrequently, as a sentimental reverie, I always had the pleasure of rapidly blinking for a few seconds. I set the envelope on the table and the check on top of it and took some time out with the comma they put among the zeros. It's standard punctuation. It takes the blur from a number, and you think, well, they didn't say something they didn't mean. The thought I was worth it flustered me pleasantly, but it wasn't money till I exercised the critical faculties. See what might come out of a talk with Harold Hall.

It was time for the day to acquire a little hustle. I dialed Mr. Hall and gave my name and waited in the empty space to find out what made me expensive.

"Your appointment is Thursday," the voice said.

"What would the appointment be about?" I asked.

"That would be the reason for the appointment."

"Who am I talking to?"

"I'm the cook. At the moment that's not what I'm asking you to notice."

"Is Mr. Hall available at the moment?"

"He will be available Thursday."

I wasn't yet tired of earning a living. It was the business. Dominance and submission arrives in the first breaths. It was a job if I wanted to keep it going, helping people understand the nature of the courtesies appreciated when contacting a professional dominant.

"Reviewing all that has transpired between us, I am Elizabeth Cromwell and you are, if I understand you correctly, the cook. Hi, Cook. That puts us pretty far up on the food chain. The question now is, what's cooking? You may or may not want that to be a surprise. Your choice. I have your check," I said. "I'll put a note on it: 'Please don't tear me up.' Your turn."

"You've used, 'transpire,' barbarically."

"So I have. Mr. Hall and I might be able to make something out of it. At the moment, you're in the way."

"In ten days it will be July fifth. He's where he always is in late June. Shaping the battlefield."

I could hear the tune: Beach Boys—help me help you help Harold Hall. Awkward phrasing, missing a "Help me Rhonda, help me get her out of my heart."

"Start with the planet," I said. "Is this battle on earth?"

"You indulge too much thinking."

"Dang, there I go crossing wires. I was trying to be funny, which is a cue. I like you. I don't know why. And that's a cue. The best, really—I don't have to explain it to me. I think I'll just go on trying to be funny. We were on earth, or where?"

"July fifth is the seventy-fourth anniversary of the Battle of Kursk."

"Mister Hall is in Russia?"

"Mr. Hall reenacts the battle on the property. The scale is three-fourths of a unit to a thousand."

Most of my calls were for the purpose of dotting and crossing times and places and investing a chunk of hope that the party of the second part will show up per all the conditions prearranged in the kind of conversation we are not having at the moment. I didn't hang up. I still liked her.

"Please go on," I said.

"A suggestion. You might pay attention. Thursday, Miss Cromwell, is July first. On that day the Soviet general staff received a final communiqué from the Russian spy network, Lucy. When that was received, the waiting was the war. The main attacks would be on the fifth."

I thought about it briefly. "With all this commotion, how is it Mr. Hall can see me Thursday?"

"They're in a lull. The Russian mines are touchy. Russian sappers are out digging up German mines, replanting them on the invasion routes. Mr. Hall can see you a few hours on Thursday. A buffet will be available."

"Well, Cook, I am hearing a yes. This devotion I am hearing in your voice is fascinating. I almost want to say yes out loud. I don't know why...but...that's good. I am interested in what it is in my web page that suggests a connection in Mr. Hall's thinking between me and a lull in a battle. At some point, however, you should tell Mr. Hall no to any buffet. Can he accept that?"

"Would a second check cover emotional twinges?"

"Checks are much appreciated, but less and less the coin of the realm in this instance. These reenactments. Who normally attends? Not professional dominants, surely."

"Mr. Hall will explain. Mr. Hall is a very impressive man. I have yet to meet his equal. Do you know Los Altos?"

"Sort of. But I won't need to think about it. When Mr. Hall gets around to that moment when he knows he wants to see me, he will call and we will arrange an appointment. He will receive my directions. Please remind him thereafter that if he has a reason to change his mind, he should give me twenty-four hours' notice."

The line went *click*. On their side, I know these people are wounded souls. They have been hurt. The trauma does the talking. On my side, the job was to remember that.

A good cook. She left us in the deep-freeze. Nothing spoiled. My fingers strolled my check around the desk. Two miles above Tintern Abbey was about where a searching mind would have a look at what the spirit is missing. Life swelled beyond the dull balance of money. I spread the little black book open to *Notes* and put some of my views of fate into the ledger: "Spoke to Cook, Harold Hall, maybe? Weird and worth a try."

———

I INTERSECTED Harold Hall and the City of Kursk online and found nothing at the crossing point and no mention of his name in a few pages of war refinements.

It's ridiculously easy to get deep into Halls. There are more Harold Halls than James Halls, as a casual impression of the historical record. I got one hit with the Soviet Union, an ambassador, Philip Hall, with a quote that people kept current for a generation: "If the United States doesn't have a war with the Soviet Union by 1953, it never will."

A string of Halls connected to the beginnings of white ownership in California. They had died on the land they owned, names and dates on a plaque that had some space at the bottom for a few more names. The plaque was in a pre-World War II *Life* magazine montage from when there must have been more land than I ever heard of registered in the Hall name. A couple of lost Hall hubs had been here and gone within a day's reach and return of San Francisco, connected by a vanished Hall Road. At the south end was mentioned a Hall Hill, the "Acropolis of Los Altos," a hit on the Wikipedia, but not there on Google Maps.

Harold Hall of Los Altos was unaccomplished for the purposes of biography, and kept his middle initial to himself.

Four

THE MWCR ON MY CALENDAR in my twenties was the Montclair Women's Cultural Retreat. Angela Foley was a prodomme in Berkeley and a poet, and the Poetry Gang read here, which she organized along the lines of AA meetings. We all went to the podium and declared: "I am a poet." After that the floor was yours for fifteen minutes. You possessed the crowning privilege. Whatever you said was poetry, and you took the declaration into yourself as an article of faith that you would always be a poet. It was a solution to what I needed. A client of Foley's was the groom here some ten years ago—nine years? Eleven? Foley had been, or was then, currently, a tutor of some of the guests. The subject of servitude in marriage was in the air. A round of burlesque limerick caught on after the cake was served, which set off some post-ceremonial activities not to my taste, and that's all I can use for any deeper analysis as to why I hadn't been back. I'm sure that wedding is when I was separated from three of my books.

My car rolled a few lengths along the top of the grade and hesitated to go any farther toward the house on the hill. It would have had to violate instructions at the base of the drive:

THINK ABOUT IT
ALL YOU WANT
DON'T DO IT

The sign was a tilted square, lettered in two colors, no rhyming scheme, but catchy, the point of the thing, but overdone somehow, urges a regression to get some paint and mess with it.

I had always parked on the side street and walked back down the hill as far as the three oaks in the middle of the block, where a path from the street had been worn in two directions onto a trail along the upper edge of the property. At a gap, I had taken a jump through the growth to a sundial. I tried it again.

It was a leafy shortcut of too many years ago. I could still bushwhack the straight line of the main footpath, but the gaps in the hedges had grown closed, and hard thicket shut off the connecting tracks. Anything that had once been familiar had taken refuge in the years. I kept at it but only managed to reach a clearing at the corner of four backyards.

The breeze had struggled along with me as far as lower Piedmont and given up. No punch left in it these days in June, not like the old days in June before the jet stream looped through Alaska and shifted the seasons. It was hot up here, but when you broke into one of those panoramas that occasionally flowered in a broad space between houses, you could see you were a long way above the bay, and the shimmer in the view was spectacular. I liked the weather up here generally—and lately it's been a plus in my retirement thinking. It's probably why I'm here today. Three books? Who cares?

Downslope was the shape of an old lady in a straw hat kneeling on a pillow in a corner garden. I didn't heave a pebble into the tomatoes to get her attention. I didn't want to know anything that much. I didn't want to startle her. If humanity had a best image of itself it would be a woman left alone to her memories tending her garden.

I backed out to the street the way I'd come and went around and up the members' drive to four pale plum-purple columns that evenly broke the glowing white front of a Williamsburg.

A catering van was unloading from the turn of a roundabout

onto the walk. An old green crate was all done up as a guard-house/ticket booth. Whatever it had since been up to, it had grown out of direct light and lodged under bougainvillea. The foliage was cut out in front. Two parking spaces were assigned, "Belle Hogan" and "Ann Wimberton," at eye level on a board that was made to lift easily off a couple iron rings but hadn't needed to be. Belle's spot was occupied.

I thought about calling, leaving a message, asking who wrote *Larks in the Popcorn*. It was as good as leaving my name. That would warm her up and let her cross her wires on the everyday heroism in the out-of-nowhere encounters of middle age, recalling someone you haven't seen for...what? Ten years? Was it that long? Longer? No? Don't say yes.

The sky was full of a plain blue in pretty nice territory long after the end of an era. A fountain was shooting a high spray. Water flowed over the lips of bird feeders around an arc of twittering color. A burnt lawn lit up a peaceful morning, and I joined in with the tune coming out of the open doors to the Montclair Women's Cultural Retreat. I knew the words.

"*Sh-boom, sh-boom...ya da da da da da da da...sh-boom, life could be a dream, sweetheart...hello, hello again...sh-boom, sh-boom...*"

Big flat orange pavers took over from three red brick steps up to lacquered hardwood strips that ran off diagonally from the entrance to cover a room about as large as would have been expected of a man who wanted to dance in his spare time and put a house on top of a dance hall. When he passed on, the size of the room sold the house to Ann and Belle. They needed a room for all kinds of parties.

An easel advertised a themed event: A sock-hop, Friday, 50s tunes, door prizes, two dollars. Bring a girl. The music was coming from the direction of five women on risers, a college group, or in that age group, a guitar, clarinet, trumpet, piano, and a microphone, and quick on the uptake. I was new circumstances. The singer pointed at my sunglasses and they all hit it:

"Lollipop, lollipop…oh lolli lolli lolli…lollipop, lollipop, oh…"

A gray-haired housemother was at a desk at the opposite wall. One of those standing fans that give you an understanding of propeller planes and why they can get off the ground was making life respectable. Life was still hot. A few two-fingered swipes across my forehead collected what was thinking of dripping. I waved to the band and kept up against the flow of air to the desk. The old lady was working figures off scraps into neat columns on larger lined sheets, her arms covering her business, or lose it in the gale. Diverted, she looked at my waist and thought that was enough conversation, and got back to wiggling her pencil.

I caught my breath in a plastic bucket seat and watched her pencil a second. It wasn't wiggling. It was getting twisted in a plastic sharpener. I was thinking to ask her something when the music stopped. When it stopped, a brunette in a French roll and Swedish shorts was gripped with a mission of joy. She stepped from a row of music stands and walked undeviatingly at me with a vigorous hump in her hips. She reached a hand from a strong young shoulder. She had a good-looking upper half on a superbly super lower half. I lay my hand on her tender waiting hand. As I gave my name the hand got my hand to its feet and pulled me into the middle of the hardwood. The band had something ready.

"Oh when the saints…go marchin' in…oh when the saints go marchin' in…I want to be in that number…when the saints go marchin' in."

I lip-synced, "I don't know how to do this." She jiggled past my left hip, bumped it on her way, then passed my rear backwards, butt to butt, bumpity-bump, then backwards past my right hip, and locked eyes like we'd had three drinks and time for bedroom moves. We did that three times. The third time she lost control. She kicked her shoes to the wall and let her hips do the propositioning.

I guess all that to-do was too much for the guitar player. The woman at the microphone quit making music for the second team. She edged her friend out of my zone of attention. She lifted my arms over her shoulders, pulled me into her gravitational field, locked a pelvis on mine, and took the wheel.

"Blue, blue, my world is blue; blue is my world now I'm without you. Gray, gray, my life is gray; cold is my heart since you went away..."

I went this way and that, occasionally thrown into a sweeping turn and sudden backward embrace. Small miracles, two out of three swoops I made it back to my senses on my feet. When the music stopped, her eyes wanted this to go a step further, but I encouraged her to clap along with the rest of us and keep her shoes on.

My partner shook hands and bowed. I didn't deserve it, but I squeezed her hand and said, "Elizabeth," and poked her tummy. "And you are...?"

"Brett. You want to remember me when you want to slow-dance."

"What comes next?" I asked. "What do I take off?"

"Anything you want. You want to do it to music, we can do that. You want three of us, we can do that. Life is young. Life is sweet."

I pointed to the bookkeeper. "She doesn't get any fun?"

"She's not a producer. You look like a producer. Are you?"

"Not in this life," I said.

Her hair fell both ways off a path along the side of her head that took a lot of care to look like it parted of itself in the shower naturally. We kind of looked alike. She asked in the longing in her eyes if we had something eternal in common.

Brett snapped her fingers, that "oh, dammit" snap, blew that one. "She's not a producer. We wasted our best stuff."

The woman I'd danced with first bobbed her head at Kay at the piano, Rayne on clarinet, and Trish on trumpet.

"Waste?" the first dancer disagreed. "I'm Jillian. We all fell in love. You coming to the dance?"

"I'm out of practice," I said. "I don't need to tell anybody."

Jillian grabbed my hand and left a message: "You have no excuse to be lonely the rest of the day. You could get it all back. Tender loving guidance. We don't usually get an audience. What brings you to rehearsal?"

"I was here when dinosaurs roamed the earth," I said. "It was a wedding."

"A man and a woman?" Brett asked.

"It happens once in a while. It happened here," I said. "Look it up. I left some books. I dropped by to check the lost and found."

"You brought books to a wedding. A gift, and you want to see if they left them here?"

"I was early. I was sitting in my car getting content with a book. A woman parked ahead of me. She asked if I could move my car slightly back to let her get the front of her car out of the curve at the corner. We talked a bit. I talked about the groom. She talked about the bride. She was from Manhattan. She lived down from the mayor's place, not far from Central Park. That ended that. I had some books on the front seat. She asked if she could look through a few. I didn't think she would be interested, but she had a look at the titles and didn't hand them back. When I locked up I said to leave them on the curb next to the car. She sat across the aisle during the ceremony. We were at different tables at the reception. I don't recall I checked the curb when I drove off. They're not there now."

"You haven't been back since?" Brett asked.

"You cannot believe how out of it I've lived," I said.

"The healing power of lost books. It can work. What do you do?"

"This and that," I said.

Brett had had the inward directedness of someone working on an association. A smile flashed, half filling a vacant expression. She had caught on. "Sex work. I tried it. My heart will go on."

"It's work of a sort," I said, "not horizontal."

"The English Department!" A deference broke through in the slow phrasing, more than I expected anyone in her place in life would accord the practice. While she had been thinking, her body had been stiff. The intensity magnified her presence. In other circumstances I would have tossed a question or two at her to see what's on her mind.

"The English vice," she tossed over her shoulder to Jillian.

"When it's slogan driven," I said. "I try to avoid anything that can be described in a short sentence."

"Belle is upstairs?" I asked.

"Ann is. Belle is in Vancouver. What would you like to hear?"

"You wouldn't know it." I drifted off in a gust. "The Chipmunk Song."

"Technically," she said, "it's the Chipmunks' witch doctor song."

A smaller room with a fireplace was on a line with the entrance to the grand ballroom. It could hold a fair crowd, too. I had eaten cookies in it and advertised my interests in the news of the day with guests who stayed out of the sun. I was dancing on my way up the stairs.

"Oo, ee, oo, a, a, ting tang, walla walla bing bang, oo, ee oo, a, a, ting tang, walla walla bang bang...oo, ee..."

Ann was waiting for me in a big relaxing lean in a big black chair in a big office in the light of a big window. The chair rolled forward, not enough to roll her onto her feet.

"I heard what you said. I was piping the music up here. You made their day. They threw everything into this group in high school. They call themselves Nowheresville, sort of casting out a hook to Margaritaville, stay busy, stay remembered, meet who they need to meet, play where they need to play. They're popular here. It gave them a name, but no God particle. They need their Margaritaville, not his. They thought you were the ticket to the stars when you walked in and looked their way.

She said all this while she placed two hands flat on the blotter, pushed off, and came around the desk and gave me a big hug, in the middle of which I was told I was still nice to look at. After which it was suggested it would not be bringing too much thinking to the occasion to suggest I plant it on the sofa and let's us get out the libations. It looked like I was looking for a woman at a wedding. Ten years ago. We might have to sit and close our eyes.

"You said you want your books."

"I know where I last saw them."

"And you looked there and they weren't there." She put water in a glass and put the glass in my hand.

"We're getting big numbers in our birthdays, Elizabeth. You want to know what happened to the dinosaurs. The grooms come and the grooms go. How many, I couldn't tell you. People can't find things and wonder if they forgot them here. If they're right about that, they go on a shelf in the storage room off the kitchen—if they go. A guarantee, your books aren't there. Otherwise, how can I help?"

"How's Belle?" I asked.

"Seeing her dad."

"I don't want to take up time."

"Can't recall you've taken up much. One wedding and no reason to grace the premises since?"

"I didn't know I'd forgotten my books."

"I don't know what you're talking about. You're too sharp not to know what you're talking about. You don't want to tell me. You want to tell me you lost some books ten years ago. I almost think you think you need a reason to say hello, but it's not like you beating around the bush. It was in your hug. There was something mental in it. So we're going to do it your way. If you find this woman who took your books she isn't going to know what you're talking about. She didn't steal your books. You don't believe that. Am I thinking you two had a moment? You'd like to see where the years went?"

"I gave her a book. She brought it back. Not interested. Then I let her grab a bunch. I think she did take them, not with a guilty conscience. Taking books is not stealing, not if you have a condo on the East Side. Otherwise she'd leave them on my car, or on the curb. Or else she'd have to pack them for the return flight.

She may have been flying out the day she arrived. That's not unreasonable going east to west."

"Maybe she read them on the flight and left them for the cleaning crew."

"The only problem is, how did they get back to Oakland?"

"You want to get into how the cleaning crew read them on the flight back to Oakland?"

"That's an otherwise," I said.

"And you lost interest. Why now?"

"Just learned now. An Oakland fellow had them in his library. He wasn't a collector. He collected a lot of pictures of me. I could have met him. Ten years in a man's thirties can erase anything I might remember."

She held a foot of air between her hands for two seconds. She held more and then less, like we were done when the space was gone. She pushed her chair back and put her glass in a sink. I put my glass in her hand and watched her swirl what I'd left in it.

"Let's look at it this way, you're here now, my mind is open." She was reading some sparkle coming from the water. "Let's get nefarious. Leave the woman out of the nefarious part temporarily. She meets a guy. He asks about the books in her hand. They speak highly intellectually. It's fun. They get around to names, and she tells him they had a good time and this good time comes to an end. But he gets the books. They're on a chair after she leaves. He looks inside and sees the name of the owner, and that's you. He looks you up and thinks this is fate. He calls you, perhaps to meet and return your books, but, given the circumstances as you're presenting them now, you two don't pair up. He downloads a few pictures and moves on. There are other fish in the sea."

She gave me a hug and a wink. She was close. At the door I looked back. "You had a sundial on the back lawn. Still there?"

"We did. We do. You need the time?"

"I may at that."

"Drop by for the dance. Women meeting women for spontaneous combustion."

The upstairs was air-conditioned. The machinery was working hard. I'd been here before in the private kitchen in the next room, on a July day when it hadn't been on. She crossed an imported rug to her desk. She wrote a name on a card and handed it to me.

"If you know someone who needs a band, call Brett at this number."

I put her card in a pocket. I hadn't mentioned the stack of money on the table and the woman on the other side of the stack. The man with my books had put my image on the body of the woman. I hadn't mentioned that either.

I unlocked my car and left it partially hooked. I started up the street looking at how much room I had between me and stupid. The books were at Polk's house. They could no longer be anywhere else unless...God in heaven, give it up. The sundial had its meaning. I was running out of the most important day of my life. I looked up Polk in the directory, verified the address Ada had given me, connected the address to where I was and let the Voice tell me the quickest route.

I did what I was told. I swung through a U at the next intersection and went down the hill to where the road divided twice, one quick split right after another. At the second split I pulled to the curb, breathing through my mouth, confused, but not sure it was confusion. Something just wasn't right in this heat. The name of the street where I'd made the U had caught up with the brakes. It wasn't sudden. The whole damn day was bogging me down whenever it wanted. I let out the brake and shut off the Voice and went back up the hill. I stopped where I'd parked before and started all over. Relax. Think through the steps.

The thinking went the way it went before. It stimulated a fiddling with the door handle but no ingathering of resolutions to get out. But I got out anyway just to shake some bones. The impulse to turn my head in the direction of the name of the cross street occurred just as I knew I didn't need to look—Beatrice. Polk's other house was on Beatrice street.

The corner house wasn't it, but the address was even. I could see ahead for a block to a barrier where Beatrice narrowed to a T, and between me and the T perhaps five or six places on either side. Polk's place was not far. I kept going.

At the second house the hedge was waist high. Polk's address was black numerals on a trash barrel on a stone rise next to a slatted box with exposed asphalt shingle, the gray roofing stuff. It was a silent neighborhood at this hour. Naptime. You could see all the intelligent design, but the whole region was in hibernation. It put you back at the scene of a mass extinction, except for insects, the ultimate survivors. They had the upper hand, possessed above in that strange buzz in nature that gave the air a mountain silence holding the fullness of death that carried from the Polk house.

Raw planks laid across cement platforms formed descending steps over ground cover, some strain of ivy and weedy clumps. At a front window, double hung, not curtained, the steps joined a walk from the front door to a side gate that had no latch and couldn't be pushed or pulled open. I got on my toes. Twenty-some feet off was a high wooden barrier built flush to the neighbor's fence. A gas meter, the well of a crawl space, and some yard barrels were what there was there.

On the other side of the property was a dirt run between the house and a high fence. It was open space as far as a chain-link gate at the rear of the house. The backyard was different hues of brown and sporadic green shoots. Beyond the chain fence was where the old woman I'd seen earlier had been working her garden, a good sharp drop below Polk's backyard. The roof was what there was to be seen of the house from here.

I started back to the street and glanced in a side window that allowed a line of sight to follow through the inside to a second window at right angles to it. It was another way to see the Bay Bridge.

At the front window I leaned in over a trash barrel and cupped the glass between palms and got my nose in the dark space. An open living space had the sole function of a projection room: one chair, a table next to the chair, bare wood under a floor lamp and footstool. Instead of a projection screen, the chair was facing a life-size painting of a woman, whip and boots, trimmed in fur. The variant of Venus in Furs had captured a humorless alienation. She was an undraped me, stripped and dolled up as I never advertise, and it pissed me off.

The chair was empty.

I slipped along the side of the house back to the fence and leaned around the corner. This back ten feet of house was an addition. A vertical crack in the stucco showed where it joined, not past patching. The window on the back was open. I could reach around and stick my fingers in. Then the thought came to me: don't stick your fingers in. I took some snaps in the direction of where I had been earlier. That was my lookout point. I took a few pictures of Venus in Furs through the window, and jiggled the front door on my way away. If the door had been open I could keep that to myself and get closer pictures.

He had the Bay Bridge and me on the wall. Polk never knew he was having a last look at a chick in furs, life's grand design.

They had a machine at a one-hour photo in Montclair that I could stick my chip in and get some blown-up images as fast as I could stick the bills in. A sandwich shop had arched windows and mahogany tables and skinny sandwiches that fit a mouth with civilized eating habits. I had a beer and composed three texts, crossed off two of them and sent the third to a woman with a position at the downtown library.

"A wedding. Eight to twelve years ago (best estimate) at the Women's Retreat in Montclair. What was the name of the groom? Desperate. You were there."

A half-sandwich came with three potato chips and two pickle slices and a purple paper napkin. Between nibbles I gravely obsessed over links to some distant connection with Polk, and wiped the corners of my mouth. The woman in the painting didn't have to come from anywhere. Men perfect their own dream babe, a part here and a part there, and sweat those details, but they need a real woman to flee from. They need the details that need to be fixed.

I didn't have a reason to walk around Montclair. I returned to the parking structure that bordered a wooded area and passed time on a shaded bench.

A message to me: "Will call—wait."

I pressed the answer button and said hello and listened.

"Elizabeth. How bad do you want this groom?"

"He's peripheral. I'm in Montclair, digesting a brew before I take to the freeway. Before that I was looking through a window at an Andy Warhol masterpiece. A chair was arranged to view a painting of a woman in leather boots. She looks like me. It was on purpose."

"What's the name of this gallery?"

"It's a house."

"What's artistic?"

"The empty chair."

"Is this an art object? I mean, a person does not actually use the chair for viewing pleasure?"

"He did, I would guess…until he died."

"I see it. This empty chair is a death representation."

"The State of California has a lock on the front door. I'm the only one thinking of breaking in to steal the painting."

"Was there sawdust on the floor?"

"Sawdust?"

"Kidding. I saw an oil very much like what you describe over a bar in Central City. Tourists come from all over to drink to her health and beauty. They say she's Alma Mahler, but the fact-checkers say that's all part of our frontier legend. Which brings me to the question you posed. The state keeps records of these unions, you know, two hearts joined for life. They make it official. If you have the date it can't be too much work."

"I don't need his name. I said I did, but I don't. I have the name I need. Do you remember a man who would have introduced himself at the wedding as Burleigh Polk?"

"Why?"

"There could be a fortune in this for you—and for me. If you don't make me explain this, I'll tell you why."

"Could you not explain this, even if I didn't want you to?"

"I don't need you to remember him. Wasn't the bride from New York?"

"For conversational purposes, what would you prefer, a yes?"

"I met a woman from Manhattan at the wedding. She might have been with Polk. She must have been with Polk for some of the time. This question is important. What is her name?"

"It might take a few minutes out of my break to run that down. Then I'd need dinner and drinks and cab fare, and I wouldn't want to hear about this anymore."

"The woman looked like the bride at the wedding," I said. "I don't know why I think this, but if I hadn't seen the painting where I saw it, I never would have caught that."

"The woman in boots? You're being lame."

"Stretching for it. Anywhere out of this context it's a total nothing. Polk knew where an awful lot of fifty-dollar bills were. Did I say he's dead? The bills might still be where the bride left them. The woman in Manhattan will know something."

"I thought about two and two and how easily the pieces go together for you, Elizabeth. You leave me no easier choice. I just blocked your phone number."

That saved me dinner and drinks and cab fare, and I might have caught on to something.

I parked in front of Polk's house, his other house, the one down the hill, where I'd been going two hours before, like it was still a step in a plan I was on that had been worked out. Like I was in history, and the mystery of Polk was just some mood I hadn't got out of my system. The phone call had made the experience of the mood intellectual, as it had had to be explained, so it had a tug, almost a motivation to wonder what the hell I was up to, not enough to block my own number, but I was getting there. I took a minute, scouting the premises.

The house was a standard copy of a suburban style, the two-story Spanish fortress, a floating castle high off the street. The windows were protected by iron grates cemented into the walls. Castilian crosses kept the devils out. The bars on the upper windows had two crosses for extra protection. Zigzag brickwork climbed a steep front yard to a landing that connected to the other side of the property by a walk that continued around the house. A short set of stairs went from the landing to a wide porch. A huff and puff had reached me up onto the porch where Polk lost out on the longer life.

The door had the massive construction of five hundred years ago, when a door had to be what Moorish invaders thought twice about. Parallel columns of square bolt heads emphasized hardwood panels bolted to a door behind. Kicking the door to gain entry would give the inhabitants plenty of time to grow old and die natural deaths. Facing the door I swayed some, getting a feel for what it would take to lose my balance and heave sideways over the balcony. The top of the ledge was low on my hip. If I were falling that way I could see it. Over you go. A life-and-death event that wiped out equilibrium would seem to fit a heart attack.

The punishing regimen had hardened his heart. He suffered for his God—a life lived in a reverence of suffering.

] *Five*

B Y FRIDAY EVENING I'd decided I'd made up my mind as far as getting out of the City into the out-of-doors for a view from up in the hills. Something had been building. Since Hawaii I'd had a post-holiday addiction to making sure the sun was going down without getting caught on the edge of the ocean. I followed the roads up the hill again and hung out on a café patio in Montclair Plaza. The pastel strip beyond the land was losing out to the fog on schedule.

The server had cleared my place. I had turned down a second helping of the house luxury. The server gave it the old college poetry reading. *Orgy* rhymed good with *chocolate.* Comes with a free extra hot water and some chat. I was the last customer. She asked if she should leave me alone. She had heard me talking to myself.

"I've been waiting for dark," I said. "I'm an overly disciplined person. I talk to myself."

"I thought it was a new kind of phone," she said.

"I've assembled a workable plan to break into a house. I was running it past my conscience. The details look doable, no totally obvious obstacles. And you? What are you doing tonight?"

She smiled that smile that knows I never have any fun, and have fun at it. It's a gift. She wasn't interested in keeping this going. "Hanging out with friends. We're closing. How does a half-hour work for you?"

I finished my tea, erased a circular stain on the table and carted the pot to a service ledge and went back to check what I'd left in the dark space where the sun went down. I never entertained the standard countervailing moral doubts in Polk's case. Guys who lasciviate over something they have taken of my image have opened a door. He was dead. His house was deserted. I had no fewer doubts, but I had a decision. Which exit.

I overshot my destination by one exit and reversed to an intersection, and started the upward crawl back to the lanes above Montclair. Each street dumped you into a narrower street with more fences. Banked light coming around voluminous bushes was good enough to tell you the colors of the recycling barrels. I had the window down, but couldn't be sure I was seeing even a part of a house, yet the numbers were right out close to the street, large and all one font.

At the crossroads where Dane Circle kept going and Manzanita Terrace sloped off to the right was the final checkpoint, and I set the odometer and counted off .2 miles of asphalt that had gone gritty and crunched under the tires.

The mind plays tricks in the hills. When I got to the balloon-shaped opening at the end of the road I knew which way I was pointing but couldn't reconcile it with my mind's sense of what the grade of the road indicated where I had gone down. I locked up facing Angel Island. It didn't seem correct, but that was what it was. I'd dropped some distance into a canyon that bottled the air. It wasn't moving, and the quiet carried the sound of voices in movies from open windows. Crossing a footpath it was still hot in the dark, and I'd soaked up heat driving with the window down and wasn't losing it. The other side of the bridge became a ledge with houses on the high side, and then it was a named lane that got a little wider but wouldn't be wide enough for an alley in a city. Straight ahead would put me at the intersection near Polk's house. I could hear the band at the Women's Retreat.

Entering the alley I was alert to a challenge from anyone who would see I was new to the area. I had an answer. I was going to the dance. But it was a funny way of doing it, and I couldn't say I'd made a wrong turn, I was lost, I was using the stars. By the time they thought about it, I was gone.

I was passing a row of garages. In a driveway were two legs sticking out from a beach chair. The owner's hind end was placed in a stable position near the ground. The legs were forgotten in the alley under a table—a warning system. A car would have to knock a bottle off a table before the tires would run over her legs.

The silhouette of a glass refracted colored motion in little circles. I had been gearing up for a quick pass, not stirring up conversation with the neighborhood watch, but as I flitted in the line of sight between the woman and a motorbike, she cleared the frog in her throat.

"Have a pleasant evening," she suggested.

A voice competently in command of a complete sentence, not all words in one breath, uneven enunciation, careful on her syllable separation. The last word did her in. It took flight on a cough. For a cough it was possible to go wrong in many ways if she tried another sentence. I'd have to pass her on the way back or take the night off getting to my car, but by then she'd be down to blinking goodbye, another sheet to the wind. It was that kind of nice voice in a nice evening.

"You, too," I said. I felt like scratching my back. I kept my ear to the ground.

At Polk's street the curbs around the corners were painted red. It gave open access to the dark walking space inside cars parked tight, two wheels on the dirt. I had an eager stride, like a woman with an honest purpose on my way to a dance, but once I had passed inside the three oaks I slipped into cover, stopped and watched, caught sight of nothing, and backed off slowly several steps, convinced there was nothing. I had been here. In the dark it was, and was not, the same. It demanded new ways of putting a foot in front of another while thinking. I wrapped a flashlight

under a cloth and kept the glow down low in tall grass. I'd kick
a foot around and take a step. I didn't remember anything to
worry about. I was fine to the corner where the four properties
came to a point.

I could see the bay and the lights on in the old lady's house,
but I couldn't see a face at a window. I swayed some at "Wake
Up, Little Susie," and pulled my socks up. I knew the layout.
I checked again. The side fence between Polk and his neighbor on the corner was high, wide boards. The lady's fence had a
two-by-four running waist high on studs. The horizontal beam
was old and splintery, but I had gloves to keep from leaving fingerprints. Nobody had left a stepladder. I got a foot on the top
board and a grip on the high fence to haul the other foot up. I
took a step and hurled into space and landed upright in Polk's
yard. From there I kept as close to the ground as possible on two
feet. I'd seen escaped cons do this under searchlights.

The addition built onto the back of the house had used up a
back porch. The entire rear of the house was a flat face elevated
on cement blocks. It had about that much appeal. There were
two steps to a back door, and, why not, I tried turning the knob
and pushed and pulled and went back to the window idea. I got
two hands under the open window. It went up to the cool strains
of "Have Some Madeira, M'dear?"

The step here was the fly in the ointment I had considered
all through dinner. The blocks under the house were pyramid
shaped, two set close together at the corner, two more close
together every few paces, the pairs evenly distributed. The two
near the window were not under the window, but they had a flat
section, which offered a foothold.

I braced a tennis shoe on a block and pulled my chest to the
sill to get the other shoe on the other block. It was a detail I had
tried already in my head. The gain in height was not enough to
get my elbows over the sill. When I got my tits over the sill it was
all over. I was in. All I had to do was fall forward on my head. The
blocks didn't get me there.

The red brick borders of tree plots along the fence came loose with a push inward. I got a tree's worth out, stacked them, and walked around to get a feel for what could make a platform. Their advantage was clear. I could assemble the standing place away from the wall, but I had to push off. The bricks had to stay put. I had to get more to make the structure solid. It's where breaking and entering had stopped being fun.

A three-foot box of bricks was enough to put my waist at the opening. I wiggled in on my stomach between a table and a washing machine. On the table was a stack of towels. I doubled one over the sill and planted two hands on the sill and bounced up. I walked my hands along the table and washer till most of me was in. Rotating sideways I put two hands on the table and pulled a leg inside and lay a knee on the washer. I rotated flat and pushed up on two hands and a knee. This took all the pressure off the leg on the sill. I picked that leg up, put that knee on the washer, took the other foot off the washer, dangling it to where a toe settled onto the floor.

Then two toes, and I was shaking out mangled nerve ends through the final swoon of "Unchained Melody." The places that hurt needed a minute. While I rubbed an ear there were cheers.

There wasn't any finishing school that prepares you for this escapade, but I was in. Let the Ringling Brothers put this in their circus.

I bent and massaged two-handed an ankle and a calf, and put a knee together like it used to be. I went across to the other leg and heard a creak and listened, and then heard a follow-up creak, and stopped breathing. It wasn't coming from me. I lifted my eyes. Over in the vicinity of two men's shoes was a thick shape in illumination. The shape of a man connected to a shadow on the wall.

Heaven bless the American laundry room. At hand was a pair of safety scissors, blue handles, blunt at the ends but, wielded with determination, capable of trimming his nails. I put a hand

out and drew the scissors into a grip and stood aggressively defen-
sively. I brought them low to my side in a confident motion, as if
I were sure I wouldn't need them. He could think about it.

He was a bit under my height and lean in the face, and in the
stillness he occupied, he was a bastard, utterly a happy bastard.
He had me where he wanted me. He was finding the smile hard
to let go of. He had watched me the whole time. He could have
opened the door, but it would have punctured his fun.

He had on a jacket and tie. This rape would be a formal affair.
I could have said there were men waiting for me. I made it less
formal.

"Get out!"

He nodded up and down in the manner of getting something clear, getting clear of it, getting it clear to me. He wasn't
intending to bother with me. A thought took a while pulling
the door open. He didn't shrug or indicate a resolution, but the
slow act of leaving silently dragged a secondary intention out the
door.

Outside he started diagonally for the corner, then stopped,
walked back to the window and stood sideways to me, facing the
fence, as if making a note of some private reaction to the yard,
or the music, or the stars.

"Watch me leave," he said. "Watch what I do. Do what I do."
His eyes wandered along somewhere over there where the music
was coming from. He gestured at the back door. "Make sure the
latch is locked. Pull the door shut until you hear the click. Shut
the window. Replace the bricks around the tree."

He was behind schedule, now obviously in a hurry, but he
stopped and accented the occasion in French verse. He looked
around in the sky and found a French phrase to describe the mystery of love and beauty sent one's way in the night. He pointed at
the house. It was mine now.

"What you are in search of is in the next room. One right,
one left, and then on the right in the shelves at eye level. You will
be looking at it."

He took a few steps back the way he had been going and said, "I will be at the Grandstand. It's a bistro on Grand. I'll be there an hour. It is a great night. You will be the third person to know how great."

He pulled a plank away from the fence, and stepped a foot through the gap, and slid the rest of himself sideways after it. He held his index finger up a second. Follow that finger. He put the base of the plank flush to the fence. The finger pulled it into place from the top. That's the last I saw of him, the outer knuckles of a hand.

I was accustomed enough to the light that I could see the other end of the addition. Outside the window was a fence. I had a hand on a clothes dryer, wall shelving to my right. Ahead in a kitchen was a telescope on a tripod that stuck out from behind the far side of a freezer.

I hesitated to make a sound, thinking there couldn't be more like him in the house, but I hadn't counted on him, and the odds on all kinds of foul weather in this place at this hour were elevated over what could be guessed. I shouldn't be here. Some sort of atonement would be justice.

I put the scissors ahead at where something might come at me. That nothing did at any moment meant nothing for the next. I went to the back door, opened it, and put my back to the screen for a quick get away. I counted off four beats of "String of Pearls." I spent time collecting what he said—exactly—the right off the hall, the left, and the smile? What did that mean? He had the parts of me put together as soon as he saw me. I had dropped right into a slot.

It started fitting a big tingle. Somebody knew something. Not like all those tingles that had launched no connections listening to Ada Tomek. There might not be any *Plutarch's Lives*. On the other hand, there was *Plutarch's Lives*. I didn't know how it came to be where it was found. Was it the hook, the straw in the breeze? Why me, a busy businessperson, why would she bother that I bother? One man, encountering me out of nowhere, tells me that me being here tonight now makes all the sense in the world. So I don't know what I know. That explains why I'm here. Does it?

He did say where he would be. I couldn't get from anywhere to there. Money always puts a there there. There was money in this madness minding its p's and q's.

Straight ahead from the back door you're in a short hall, five paces between a hall closet on the left and on the right a blind corner, a break in my vision. I didn't like the jumping out of nowhere geometry. I took the longer way around through the kitchen to stay out of the hall. From the dining area there wouldn't be a blind corner.

I edged past a long window over the sink and counter. Everywhere in the addition the floor was a simple repetition of flowery linoleum. I listened for something distinct from what I could associate with the dance. I couldn't hear my own steps. A footfall behind me would be inaudible. I stopped often to catch a sound that had popped out of stealthy doings, a sound not to notice. So far, no such sounds. A kitchen table was the dining area. From here I could see the tops of the houses across the street and light from the front windows. I left the kitchen cautiously in a slow, sliding motion onto hardwood that squeaked. The same stuff went into the hall and beyond the corner down into the little hall into a viewing room in moonlight.

The woman in the painting was a good copy of me. She was arranged in boots and gloves, frozen in time in that designed period of suspense when she is about to happen. Her arm was extended to the side and back, waiting in a velvet curtain before driving off her right leg, untwisting her back and shoulders, throwing her weight in an arc with the arm ending full forward. The curve of the whip would follow through an uncoiling bow, and when the traveling bow ran out of leather, all the energy would be released in a carefully controlled collision, how soft or hard depending on the ground rules, rehearsed or not, the lucky guy out there in the target zone taking his chances. More chancy if he's getting it for free from a perfect stranger. The great aphrodisiac: risk. The long life option is to buy pain. As a professional, it's a bias.

The artist, it's safe to say, got points for effort. The woman was what Polk wanted to put a chair in front of and pop his cork to…or who knows? Suppose you were sailing along and your ship sank, and you and you alone swam to a deserted island that just happened to have all of life's necessities wrapped up waiting for you. As the ship went down you had just enough time to fill a bag with the elements of civilization that would nourish you the rest of your life—a Beethoven symphony, a Rembrandt, a Shakespeare play, a croquet set, a bag of marbles. Polk grabbed something he wanted in childhood, something he didn't get and had to go back and get, got it and wanted more; or he wanted to fix what he got, and get it the way he wanted it. That was the subject of the painting. Exactly what that was in his mind I meet year after year. The subject is no longer camp. It's agreed, it was never culture. There was too much fun in it done in the shadows. It gets thumbs down as a variety of religious experience. I stay away from it, and I would be the one to call to get some of it. Somewhere after the reign of Emperor Norton the City lost interest in blowing clowns out of a cannon on the Embarcadero. The whip is still here in the art of the divided self, not as easy to explain as rap.

A wraparound headset was draped over the back of a chair. I plugged it in to a table socket and held it up to my eyes to mobilize a total experience. That seemed to be what it was for. It boosted illumination in a hologram capability. Suddenly I was in another room, but it looked familiar, and when I took the headset off and looked behind, I was in that room, with a small green point of illumination coming from a crystal on a platform, as it was in the hologram. I went to the crystal and bent to see what powered the thing, but didn't touch it. As I did it went out, and when I stood up it came on again. I did this a few times until I realized the contraption operated off some signal coming through the window. I could cover the crystal and move the dot on my hand. I bent in that direction and sighted to the hill just up the grade and above the road into the mass of the mountains, but saw nothing. When I looked back the crystal was dark.

The painting was a load for a mule, thinking up close as to what I was in for hauling it out of here. Working alone I would cut it out of its frame and roll it up in two or four sections. The overall tonnage was maybe fifty pounds as a guess, calculating a pound a square foot and six by eight feet of canvas. Suppose it was two pounds. What was two pounds? I had a long way to lug it at an odd hour, and I couldn't tell how long it would take to get it into transportable condition. I'd already fooled around on the problem through two songs. There weren't that many left. The noise laws up here might cut the band off within ten minutes, and then what do I run into? That's all the time I wanted to use on this. I backed up a step, not sure tonight was the night to carry this off. Another step decided it. I could come back. I still wanted a look at the statue. I could carry that in a shopping sack.

I'd circumvented the short hall from the kitchen to the one right and the one left. I was done poking around in the open area of the painting. I'd postponed the statue. I could do it another time. Visceral uneasiness had lost power over the power to concentrate on real fears. Anything coming at me from there, I could see it coming. Now it was just down to how likely it was I was getting trapped in that hall. Then it was not knowing what was waiting in the room.

It turned out it was an unoccupied room of ordinary size. The bathroom on the other side was empty. The windows were sliding windows close to the ceiling. The top of the bookcase covered half the window. I got the flashlight following along the shelves to where the guy said I would find what I wanted.

The upper shelves were hardbacks, a section of thrillers. A collection of Auden essays was the end of English. Then *Lehrbuch der Algebra, Gesammelte Abhandlungen, Einführung in Funktiontheorie*, a dozen feet of it, mathematics and physics in

French and German, and then *Der Mann Ohne Eigenschaften*, two volumes in a slipcase. I turned it face-down on a desk and let the insides drop out. The two volumes dropped together, and they didn't come apart. I turned the set flat and opened the cover. There was a statue wedged inside. I hefted it one-handed. It weighed like gold. It had my name on it. A governess with a two-handed grip on a cane behind her back, peekaboo, the way we do.

I picked up the statue and gave it a turn. It wasn't something I wanted on my desk. The things I say and do are gaudy enough. If I were inclined to toss her out the window crossing the bridge, I needed a reason to shake off the one clunker that had obstinately been kicking back at me. Getting even with a dead man, traipsing over everything he had lost, would be more than an undignified use of laws broken. But the boorish element at the moment had its kick. I took the statue. At the back door I wondered. This would solve itself once I wrestled the other problem into shape. I put it back. On the way to the car I didn't feel better about it. At the car I was relieved. I wouldn't return. I don't think.

I entered Grand in the upper reaches of apartments with numbers that went in the right direction as I went down the hill. Coming around the bend some blocks along, a place where people went out for drinks was on the right. There were flashing lights in the street, like the circus was in town, but the familiar oscillating pattern of an ambulance indicated trouble, the ever-constant risk of worshipping Friday nights out. The ambulance had backed into the space next to a side flight of steps. Two cruisers were double-parked in the south lanes. Flares had been set along the median. The opposing two lanes were divided into single-lane traffic. I got into my lane and waited until a cop gave the go-ahead.

The Grandstand was a converted two-story house with an outdoor drinking-dining area where the front yard used to be. The indoor part of the business was up steps. I caught a sudden rush of activity in the doorway as I passed, medical people bent over a stretcher coming out. I couldn't park for two blocks. I found a spot and locked up as an ambulance went past.

A cordon of yellow tape went around the trees, the trash cans, the sidewalk, the parking area. A gang of ex-patrons and events-watchers were hanging around waiting for the cops to finish up and go away so they could stop watching and go to another bar. The cops were interviewing a huddle of folks where the ambulance had been. I didn't see my Frenchman. Two cops in the street at the side of a cruiser were talking to each other, not too concerned with time passing. I could ask them how long it might be until we could go inside. There were other ways to learn nothing.

Two women, recently girls, were each carrying a teddy bear. To my left was a narrow walkway that ducked past an apartment complex to steps up the hill perpendicular off Grand. The women knew the area, but not as the crow flies. They were debating their next move as I arrived. They took the steps. They passed a man on the front steps of the apartment. He was lit up and waving a cigarette and evidently expecting conversation. What he said to them didn't get any for him, but what he said kept him talking. He said he would show me how to stick my head under the tape and get a drink: "Ack Nashural."

A man in a bow tie and wingtips and plaid jacket was in a plastic bucket chair leaning against a wall.

"It makes you think," he said. After an interval he said, "It makes me think, I should say. You can do what you want."

The nothing happening marched on.

"I was out for a smoke. I know the rules. I bring my chair over here. Fifty feet away. Two dudes come flying out that door. Right behind this lady hotfoots herself down Grand. Then the ambulance. A woman officer runs in and her partner throws them flares in the street. Two more cops go in, and nobody come out. Two minutes, my count. I didn't hear shots. They could have pistol-whipped the cashier. They were treating somebody for ten minutes, my count. It makes you think. It makes me think. They bring him out feet first. A kiss before dying. Black dudes. Oakland's toughest. Work for Lava over at the motel on MacArthur. I meet my ladies there. Lava has a crew. Not all black. A Chinese, or a close cousin, drives an old-time Karmann Ghia. I drive away in complete safety. They make sure."

I dialed the Grandstand. I let the phone ring for enough rings if anyone was bothering.

"Wrong number," he said. "Call Sharon. It's her night. She's in." He gave me a number. I called Sharon's number. A woman's voice answered. A bad atmosphere made a bad connection.

"I'm supposed to meet someone," I said. "He didn't come out. I was wondering when I could come in?"

"Are you a relative?"

"We're good friends. He's French," I said, thinking on the move. "Born in Paris."

"I can't say anything. Sorry."

"I'm outside," I said. The line broke.

I went home.

] *Six*

TWO WEEKENDS HAD PASSED and no Ada Tomek. I'd watched a few tapes in the box of Polk's material that she'd left with me, enough to call it quits. I left a message for her to pick it up. I left a second message saying she should let me have a day by which she would pick it up. In the absence of a return call, the day I had in mind was mine to choose. That was today. I turned off Grand at Perkins, filled up at the service station, and got permission to lock my car up at the back wall for a minute.

I lugged the box to the cleaners across Perkins. That was the address of Tomek Investigations. I set the box against the wall next to the P.O. boxes and wrote "P.O. Box #12" on the top flap and didn't think I had to say why I was leaving a box at that P.O. box. The woman at the counter came around the counter and had a look. She had a suggestion.

"You call Tomek."

"I called her," I said.

"Yoocalltootime."

"I called her two times. She's not picking up. She live here?"

She went in the back room and returned with a claim check. On the back was what wasn't in the directory. Tomek lived in apartment 3B. It was a number up Perkins. I'd left two messages at the phone number. I entered the address in my directory and checked that I was matching box #12 with the right slot. It was empty.

"When was she here last?" I asked.

"You take box."

"If Tomek isn't at home I'll leave her a note that she can pick up her box here."

I operated on the impulse of a mind convinced of the rightness of the stronger case. I had made the right decision till I unlocked my car. I communicated with a nagging thought. I ran my fingers through my hair two times. I backtracked to the cleaners and looked inside. The counter was vacant. That was a tip-off. I was leaving a flaw in my wake. Somebody would make that box go away and figure how to make a dollar off it to cover expenses and inconvenience. My picture was in the box for just such purposes. In just such circumstances I could cut out troubles, the ones I could imagine and all the rest. That was it. I lugged the box across the street and dumped it in the trunk. I did the hair thing again.

I could leave a message for Tomek via the legal bunch in Oakland, but I forgot the name. I could look up legal offices in Oakland and it would come to me. Remnick and Dyer of Oakland came to me as the approach that would end with me holding the box and the weaker case.

I drove around the corner and parked a block down at a coffee cafeteria. In line I located a commercial shredder. They could toss the whole box into Godzilla for $22.95 and bury the shreds free. I fixed a concoction to my liking and took a chair. Mitt the Mutilator was another option. He converted the box to dust. Nobody can reconstruct dust. $39.95. I had a win-win to sip and think about. I was weighing the peace of mind the extra cost would afford when the call came in to my private number. It wasn't a name that had my permission to call that number.

That was unusual, too unusual. It contained a reason I should know about. "Yes," I said quietly. It was a man's voice in a hurry.

"I want the laptop that belonged to Lavoisier."

"I don't know anyone by that name," I said.

"You said you were his friend. You knew he was born in Paris. He wasn't, but close."

"How did you get my number?"

"Robaire," he said. Then he translated, "Robert." Then he said, "I don't know what name he says to you people. There's a reward. It's of no value to you—to anyone. You can't get in. You can't sell anything on it."

"It's not with me."

"If you give me a number, I could go higher. Probably."

A drop of coffee jumped out of the sipping hole on the cup I was swirling and hit my blouse. I dabbed that up with a finger and stuck the finger in my mouth and sucked. I left the phone on the table. When I picked it up he was still doing a deal with himself.

"What happened to Lavoisier?" I inquired.

"I just want the laptop."

"I told you already."

"Fine." His voice was a high-speed logical calm. "One of you took it. Call me when you can tell me who has it. Ask around. Tell her to call me. Call this number. It better be soon, or I give you to the cops."

I went to the bathroom and pinched my stain with several applications of cold water. I pinched the stain wet, and held paper on the spot. I rolled the windows down in the car and tilted the seat back to put my head where it could rest and do some good. The caller knew my number. The rest added up in his head. I should get a second shot at that in case the cops were in this somewhere. I couldn't leave an irate citizen stewing in his juices as if nothing had happened. I pressed a button.

He said, "You did the right thing."

"Okay. I like your attitude. Cut out the threats. Let's do some business. Here it is. You get what you want. I get what I want. We start with what happened to Lavoisier, or you can hang up. I don't care."

"What do you mean, what happened? You were there."

"I was where?"

"At the bar, where he died."

Now there were two pieces that fit. I reconnected with the last French man I met. I remembered.

"I was outside," I said. "I can't see through walls. An ambulance took somebody away. He died? I didn't know. How did he die?"

"He was poisoned."

"In a bar? In Oakland?"

"Bad gin. I don't know. They didn't say what poison. They keep that to themselves."

I said, "I have no knowledge of this." I said this to myself. It didn't work with me if I was arguing my case. I had a better line. I listened to that one and wasn't any more interested. It ran me out of ideas. I was stuck.

"There's about sixty bucks where I am now," he said into a silence. "I can have more. Where will we meet?"

"Lavoisier was murdered?" I said. I suddenly sounded serious to myself.

"I'm not saying you. You said you were outside. The laptop was not with him. You have it, or you know who does."

It had been on my mind for at least a minute to bring the Oakland P.D. into this. They hadn't been to see me. So why didn't he tell them that I had the laptop or knew who did? Wouldn't that be part of the investigation? That was a good question.

I hung up. I returned to Perkins and got a spot close to Tomek's place. I pressed the button on 3B. It rang once. The second ring was where I finished testing it. I went back to the car and rolled the window down. I had found a spot of shade to think in. This was the new base of operations. What had been important did not look so important now.

Lavoisier had been murdered? Killed himself? Either way, if the guy who called didn't tell the cops about me, they would tell him they didn't like it. And I had a lot more to tell them. And I had a reputation. It was worth something. I told cops things they might want to know in a timely fashion. That would mean accounting for the interval between the time I had heard Lavoisier was murdered to when I said I would like to make a statement. Somewhere in there we would be discussing my encounter with Lavoisier in the house of a dead man, and how I was entitled to be there. I would need legal guidance.

And this might all be a dream. I couldn't just forget it. I wanted to see what I could forget. I called my guy.

"Where are you now?" I asked.

"I can be wherever you want." His voice was less agitated. I'd come to my senses.

"Suppose we talk," I suggested. "You might get what you want." As I was hearing him, this was an option open at the moment, and he wasn't arguing. He knew it. What he didn't know was he was operating from four stupid assumptions—that I knew of.

The pause seemed to be overly involved for a thinking pause. Definitely not clear thinking. I had to do that for both of us.

I repeated, "Where are you now?"

"I made a mistake. I can't leave. It's not possible," he said. "His wife moved out. I have to get the place cleaned up."

"Let's try again. When people give you a 'yes' what goes wrong? Just say the first thing that comes to you. Don't think."

"Just a minute. Fifty-eight bucks and two dimes. There's another twenty in the glove compartment. Come on over. I'm good for the rest. I can get it today."

"You want to call me back? I'd like to know what kind of person you think I am. Take some time. Come up with a few options."

"You're wonderful. You want another option? It'll take a while. In the meanwhile, see if you can find Linden. The house is on Linden. You enter Linden off Chaucer. The fifth house on the left. Might be the sixth. Huge purple jungle in the front yard."

"You have an address?"

"I already dumbed it down."

"I see it," I said. I had the satellite on. "The drive is on the right. The sixth. You are Andrei Andreyev," I said. "There's one of those at Berkeley. He's in the math department. Are you using his phone?"

"I pay for it. Why not?"

"I don't care whose phone you pay for. I don't know who you are."

"Call the math department."

"Not good enough, Andrei. What would I say that would get an answer that says I can be sure you are who you say you are?"

"I don't know how smart you are."

"I dropped out of school in the eighth grade."

"Call the department. Get anyone. Give them a name. Call me. Give me their name. I call them and get the name you gave them. I call you and give you the name you gave them."

"I can't follow all that."

"Oh, fuck. How did Robert get mixed up with you people?"

I knew it. He lied. A Berkeley professor would not use language of that sort with a lady.

Linden was one of those narrow two-way streets that should have been a footpath. Parking was two hours without a permit on one side. Overgrowth was the state of affairs, a rental culture, or just the culture. Cut it, it grows back. Skip a year. Forget about it. The sixth house on Linden had a shade-making monster that left a little room for a noon sun to graze the corner of the porch. I took a place on the street and took a few steps on dead grass to an unswept walk.

It was a peaceful summer neighborhood with the day very hot now, and not yet noon. The car in the drive had a UCB sticker on the driver's side. Off a few steps from where a stone walk turned right to the front porch, a canvas chair sat on a square of bricked paving put there for a nap. A drinking glass sat on a napkin. The chair was next to a section of sawed-off tree stump that put a chess set where you could reach the pieces from the chair. A glass dirtied with concentric stains was by the leg of the chair. A chain of rings, different hues, counted the number of days a liquid had been evaporating. A banana peel folded into the glass had turned black and shriveled. The junk that falls out of trees had joined a chess game where the game had stopped.

The porch was a lot of maintenance neglect kicked down the road. The boards had sprung their nails. Some kiddie cars on three wheels were at the top of the steps in front of the door.

I moved them. I didn't knock. I went in, shut the screen gently, and listened. There was a living room on the right with well-worn furniture pulled into the center of the room. A stairway had shoes and odd containers on many of the steps. A room to the left of the steps had a bucket and mop. It had a table and four chairs. The floor had been mopped. It was dry in streaks. Along the outer wall of the stairway was a passage to a rear window. I went along to a door from which came the sound of something clumplike being dropped into boxes.

At the door the smell of bleach was strongest. To the left a man was pulling things out of a refrigerator and apparently operating on a sorting scheme getting items placed compactly in boxes. He had on a pair of cut-off jeans and wool socks that had the shade and vigor of dead grass. They had lost elastic and bunched up at his ankles. He knew I was there. I had broken his concentration. He was stumped by an open sack of flour.

He stood and looked at me. He was tall, dark and more confused by a sack of flour than he would have been if I weren't noticing he had nothing on above the jeans and no trace of underwear.

"You should go to the police," I said.

"We talked already. I'm their focal point."

"What are you planning with that sack of flour?"

"Put a rubber band around it."

"Then?"

"Fill this box here, and that one, and let it sit here till I can get it to the food bank." He looked in the fridge. "Where's the laptop?"

"Why haven't the police asked me?"

"How would I know? What do I do with all this garbage?"

"Throw it away? Take it home? Whatever you think those boxes are for."

He took a long step and reached a load of small half-empty glass containers in a heap, sandwich fixings.

"I don't know what you're doing," I said. "Evidently a dead man's laptop is missing and you're on record offering me money for it and not telling the cops. Was he murdered? I mean, poisoned, in a bar on Grand Avenue? I never heard of that."

"Who are you? Your name is blocked."

"A general in homeland security."

He pushed the fridge shut and looked at me, not to know me. "You can't sell it to the police. What are we negotiating?"

"I'm in good with the police. I'm not going to lose it for a laptop. I don't have it. I don't know where it is, but I know a great deal more than you know, and I hope I know how you got my phone number. I hope I know it's Sharon. She's a server at the Grandstand. She gave you my number. Why didn't she give the number to the police? For that matter, why would she give the number to you?"

He kicked a few boxes into a row out of his path. He pulled two thumbs upwards on his pants. He had a build. It made him nicer to talk to in the abstract.

"I asked at the bar," he said. "They know it's not a heart attack now. They don't believe poison. The cops informed Robert's wife yesterday. I would assume they've had the results a while. They searched the house. They came to his office, but all his stuff was moved here. The department assigned someone else to his office. It's not a shrine. I told the police about the laptop. They wrote it down. There was no laptop when his body was taken away. This woman I talked to remembered you. Your number was in her log."

"Why would I call Sharon to reach Lavoisier? It's a question you could think about."

He had thought about it. "He didn't have his phone with

him. You knew Sharon to call. You knew Robert was in the bar. He always had the laptop with him—or very near. So you had it."

"Do you ever listen to yourself? I asked Sharon if he was there? I'm bringing his laptop back to him and I'm what—blackmailing him after he's dead?"

"I have a class at two, a seminar at four. His wife is taking the children home to France." He caught sight of a speck drifting in air and concentrated. "And how would you know to call Sharon at the bar? How do you know her number? She never heard your voice before."

"You want to know? Or do you just want to ask?"

He didn't look at me. He looked like something was getting through, not what he was liking, but he was looking at what was actually there, a lot of mix-up in his head. He was getting the hang of it, chewing gum and pulling stuff off shelves. And sneaking looks here and there, looking for something near where I was.

"His wife called me the night she heard. I came over. The next day the cops found his car a couple blocks from here. His wallet and phone were inside the seat. He was alone in a bar in Oakland without his laptop."

The last fact widened the circle of strange circumstances.

"I saw Robert an hour before he died," I said.

He looked at me like this was not far from the missing piece of the whole truth.

"This morning, before you called," I said, "I knew none of this. I came over here to find out how I got into the middle of it and where the middle was. I don't know who drove him around. I can tell you he had a black carrying case when I saw him. He put it through a space in a fence and climbed through after it. It's the last I saw of him."

He didn't look up, but he was looking at the floor like I'd told him to mix the flour with mustard and ketchup, dump the walnuts in the mix, glaze the loaf of wheat bread with it and put a candle on top. He wasn't sorting now. He put a foot on a box and pushed it as far as a push would push it. He lined up three other boxes with it, end to end. It didn't look like an accomplishment. There were twenty boxes to go. He'd gone wrong somewhere and didn't feel like describing the state of confusion that went with it.

"I have to call the police," I said. "I will tell them everything I know. I don't think it's a good idea to talk about any of it with you now. Later, if you like."

"I don't think it was you," he said.

"Don't tell me who you think it was. I'm leaving."

He followed me to the front door and down the steps to get the model of my car and the license, which wouldn't do him a bit of good for the laptop. Too much had been dumped on him not to know it. He stuck his hands in his back pockets, one in each. It was a very quiet manner of holding his hand out. Thanks. I had some pity for him, sort of. He had a dead friend and a grieving wife and children to carry around. He had a house to clean up. And he was a suspect. And there was a missing laptop that could be in Escondido.

I unlocked my car and thought about what I shouldn't say and said some of it.

"I had thirty seconds of contact with Robert Lavoisier before he was killed. We were in a kitchen. He was leaving. I was arriving. This and much more will come out. You'll find out. I hope you get the laptop. He was carrying it when I last saw him. It's what I'm going to say I saw."

] *Seven*

THERE WERE SIX OF US, six women, at the Alameda courthouse, the same bunch as before, positioned at the same table in an upper floor. We had met a week earlier, two detectives assigned to the Lavoisier investigation, Grey and Herring; an assistant district attorney, Sarah Crane; a woman introduced by first name only; my attorney, Patricia Ferenci, the one with a ponytail; and myself.

The ADA told me and my lawyer where to sit. She sat opposite us. Her detectives sat next to her, not too close. The other woman had the end of the table. She hadn't had anything to say at the first gathering. My attorney guessed the federales had an interest in the case—Lavoisier was a French citizen—and wanted a second opinion of goings-on at the interview. A cop in San Francisco had made a call on my behalf. He underlined my help to the SFPD. If I had crawled through a window in the night and stolen a Rembrandt, he'd take my side. Ferenci had a document that said my unauthorized presence at Polk's former residence could go away if I avoided contaminating the truth in the full explanation of the break-in. No break-in is innocent, but I was starting with innocence to lose.

The first get-together had gone well. I was looking good. And feeling like a good citizen.

My attorney had gotten her two cents in. I had come in on my own sense of civic responsibility.

Today was different. There was a lot more paper on the table. Nothing was said about how much help I was providing, no greeting, just the bare question: Are we all ready? My attorney had me practice how to stick to business. I'd been advised. Nothing is funny. Nothing is innocent. This was a murder. I knew how to read faces. Don't be clever. Crane was opposite me for real this time. She was the only woman at the table with a wedding ring. She had kids in school, upward political trajectory, on the move, higher ambitions, keeping her eye on her interests. Follow her example.

She opened a folder and slid some papers to both sides and got the questioning off on an unexpected start. The folders were fat with ammunition. They wanted my back to the light.

"Ms. Cromwell, *Der Mann Ohne Eigenschaften*—am I pronouncing that correctly?"

"I don't know German. I couldn't say."

"You said Ada Tomek said the phrase to you."

"Yes."

"And did she pronounce it the same way I did?"

"I can't remember."

"It's an unusual phrase for someone who doesn't speak German. You heard it once, you said, and didn't think much of it, yet a week goes past and you walk into a dark room and pick it out of a row of books. And under a certain degree of fear for your safety."

"I was afraid," I stated.

"I would be too. I wouldn't climb into a dark house. You identified Professor Lavoisier as the man who confronted you. You told him to get out. Might he not have been the owner?"

"The owner was dead."

"Yes. Let's say he was the caretaker of the late Dr. Polk's estate, appointed by the State of California. We can stipulate it's an unusual hour to be there, but what we might also stipulate is that he was authorized to be there. You were not. But you were afraid. Let's move on."

She had an eight-by-ten photo, Lavoisier at a table, at a restaurant. She turned it in my direction to refresh the initial claim that this was the man at Polk's house to a high degree of certainty.

"He didn't confront me," I said. "He was on his way out. I was on my way in. He was amused."

"You said he knew what you were looking for. How would he know what you were looking for?"

"I have no idea."

"Did he say anything that indicated he knew Ada Tomek?"

"No."

"And yet he knew exactly what you were there for?"

"As far as the statue, it would seem so."

"Ada Tomek steered you, with Professor Lavoisier's timely assistance, to the statue."

"I wouldn't say 'steered.'"

"She told you where it was. A man you had never met happened to be at the same place and at the same time as you. One might say exactly the right place at exactly the right time. As if you were meeting to coordinate a transfer of property. How would you explain the coincidence?"

"Unusual," I said.

"And you had not, to your knowledge, met Ada Tomek before your return from Hawaii, or since?"

"No."

"Nor Mr. Polk?"

"No."

"Yet he kept a statue with your name on it in a book. And you went there to look at it? Why go to all that trouble and then, when the coast is clear, you put the statue back where you found it?"

"It had to do with the fact that he was dead. The fact came alive to me looking at the painting in the den."

"What came alive?"

"An appreciation that I was about to make a mistake. It's the kind of statue that lacks a balance I value."

"It's how you advertise."

"I hear from many men like Polk. He might have called me years earlier. If so our interests hadn't meshed. I saw that in the painting. The statue was a significant interest in his life. It's distinctly opposite to how I advertise. Except for my hands, I'm never exposed below the neck or much above the ankles. As for the painting, it advertises an activity I have never engaged in… not in business."

"He put your image on his wall. Then he put many hours into the simple act of staring at it. That's a lot of devotion without trying to meet you. It's a lot of devotion even if he did try."

She smiled, and got it out of sight poking in her files. When she looked up she had an answer. "There's no indication Polk was an artist. It seems reasonable his art was purchased. Then he put the statue in a book. I understand art on a wall. I don't understand art in a book. Or is that the art of it?"

I looked at her till she decided I had looked long enough.

"Do you want to think about that?"

"I couldn't tell you what Polk's relationship to art was. He bought the statue and put it in a book."

"He hid the statue and hung the painting. Agreed, he couldn't put a painting in a book, but he could hide it. Of course, small items are more easily stolen. To the point, though, how would Professor Lavoisier have known where he put it? He had directions on hand ready for you. It made sense to him that the same thing was on your mind."

"I didn't know what he knew. It didn't occur to me to wonder. I told him to get out."

She searched around on a page for a cue.

"You decided to speak with Professor Andreyev. You spoke at length with him."

"I don't recall 'at length.' Five minutes."

"He remembers a longer conversation."

"I don't. He was busy. He had things on his mind."

"He was cleaning the refrigerator," she said. "Does that help?"

"He had a pair of shorts on," I added. "He was attractive. I was under the influence. What did he say I said? That might help."

"He said you were not what he expected. You called him to warn him you ought to go to the police."

"He called me. He wanted a laptop. He thought I had it or knew who did. I understood immediately. I was slotted in a particular place in his thinking. I was a Lavoisier evening companion. He had a reason to think I would go for a reward. He threatened to sic the law on me. When I heard Lavoisier was dead, I knew enough to know not to try to brush this under the carpet. The laptop was important. It occurred to me, Lavoisier had been carrying a satchel. I saw him set it on the other side of a fence and crawl through after it. It seemed to have gone missing. So I'm saying he called me first. I called him back."

"You went to the Grandstand to see Lavoisier. Why?"

"Polk was dead. I had someone I could ask how it was that Polk had my books. It was on the way home. I was interested how he knew what I was looking for. That was interesting additionally because I believe my appearance surprised him."

"Books are a significant feature of your practice. Does that help you match wits with customers?"

"The short answer is highly misleading."

"Mislead me, if you would, please."

"Early in my career I was tutored by a wise lady who said to stay out of hospitals and stay out of courtrooms, and know when you can't."

"That a 'yes' to what question?"

"I have a regard for what I do for a living. I don't like talking about it casually. If the occasion necessitates, the significant features of the profession as I practice them can be unwrapped, but not in a word."

Ferenci put a closed hand on the table. A finger flicked out of a fist. It pointed at Crane's folder. "What would you like to know about Ms. Cromwell's profession? How do you see the question relating to Professor Lavoisier's death?"

"She crawls through other people's windows for three books she didn't know were missing for ten years."

Ferenci pointed a finger at Crane's file. "We've covered that territory." Ferenci added a second finger. "She didn't drive him to the Grandstand." Three fingers. "She doesn't know how he got there." Four fingers. "Do we need to go over this again?" A thumb was all there was left. Thump. Case closed.

Crane held her point. "He knew why she was there." She counted off one pause. "We can assume he knew her profession." Another pause. "He took an instant shine to her. Why offer her a safer exit from the scene than hopping over a rickety fence?" Third pause. "He invites her to the Grandstand. He wishes to initiate a professional arrangement over drinks." Last but not least. "She accepts."

Nice symmetry. I wouldn't recognize my symmetries.

Ferenci patted the table and let the hand flop there. This could go on. "How do these statements connect to Lavoisier's death?"

"Books are her connection to the home of a dead man. Lavoisier knew the book she was looking for. Then he died shortly after he invited her to meet him. It just seems there are too many books involved. I was hoping Ms. Cromwell could shed some light here."

Ferenci danced her finger, like a needle in a little earthquake. "We can assume books were not the topic he had in mind speaking to Ms. Cromwell through the window. I still don't see Ms. Cromwell's profession as it impacts Lavoisier's death."

Crane's hand played a little Bach. "Lavoisier was not killed at a railroad crossing."

"This didn't become a murder investigation until it was too late to decide where the poison was administered?" Ferenci looked at Grey and Herring. She let the hand rest. "He was alone? Sitting by himself. Suicide was not indicated?"

Crane moved a piece of paper. "It hasn't been ruled out. Would Lavoisier invite Ms. Cromwell to join him to witness his suicide?"

"I wouldn't think so."

"So we are back to books and Ms. Cromwell's profession. Is there still any objection to answering my question?" Crane was a tired mother. "I'll ask it differently if that would help you with a yes or no."

"Are we back to 'matching wits with customers'?" I said.

"Was Polk a customer?"

"Ms. Tomek asked me that. I don't recall him. He might have been, but it would have been a long time ago."

"You keep records?"

"There would be a phone record."

"Are you familiar with *Plutarch's Lives*?" I asked

Ferenci brushed my shoulder, not enough to knock me off the chair. "If the connection could be made, however tenuous it might be so made, between Ms. Cromwell's profession and the death of Professor Lavoisier, we would be eager to join the discussion at the point of that connection. So the answer there is yes. But I would recall that we've discussed this matter at length in private. Ms. Cromwell's use of books in the purpose of matching wits is off the subject."

"Two men are dead. A professional dominant is not associated with either, professionally or otherwise, except by books. Books take the whole statement she's provided to the edge of parody. I am trying to understand what is being parodied. It just seems too breezy. Is there a better word?"

"Typhoid Mary," I said.

Ferenci said, "Look. The laptop is what you're looking for. Who has it has a great deal to reveal. Professor Andreyev brought Ms. Cromwell into this investigation. You want a word. There it is, 'laptop.'"

"Computers can be located. This one cannot. This one doesn't even exist. People would like to understand that. And Ada Tomek hasn't been seen for a month. Why did she drop her investigation and go missing?"

"What about the two black guys?" I asked.

Grey looked at Herring in a wide-angled look, not directly, but they stopped breathing simultaneously. Crane looked at Grey and Herring, disguising the surprise in her face with a lot of difficulty. Crane looked at Ferenci.

"What two black guys?"

Ferenci shrugged.

"The two black guys who ran out of the Grandstand after Lavoisier had been poisoned," I said. "And the black lady who took off after them. Ask them about the laptop."

There was no point poking her papers, but that's what you do after you rub the knuckle of a thumb on your lip. Crane let her reactions get themselves under control.

"Two black guys ran out? Ran where?"

"I wasn't there. The man who told me said he told two officers. They told him they would take his statement later. You can get the information from them."

"You spoke to the officers?"

"They were telling us to cross the street if we wanted to go up Grand. There were two girls with teddy bears. They took the walkway."

"Teddy bears? What girls? With Lavoisier?"

"I don't know. They were outside. They were there when I arrived. They were talking to themselves. A man out for a smoke told me he recognized the black guys. He called them 'Oakland's toughest,' but I didn't feel he was saying they were cops."

"You didn't feel this would be evidence?"

"I just remembered. Wait a minute. I did mention it. He gave me Sharon's number. I told you. It's there in the statement. I forgot. Yes, I did tell you. Maybe I didn't. He said he knew who they were. They worked for a woman named Lava at one of those motels on MacArthur. Lady Lava is at a motel on MacArthur. He said he went there for his ladies. These guys were in her protection detail."

"He saw Lady Lava run out of the Grandstand? He said 'run?'"

"I think so. He told the officers. I'm sure he told them more than he told me."

She blinked a bit grimly. "Anything else you might have missed earlier that might have slipped your mind?"

"How did Lavoisier get to the Grandstand? Maybe the keys to the car he was driving were in the satchel with his laptop. Two black dudes and a theft go together fairly naturally. You don't write that down, but they do."

"You said the man out smoking just said there was an African American woman, not that she was Lady Lava."

"Black woman…hotfooted it…down Grand…toward the freeway. Could have been a gang."

"You didn't get this man's name?"

"Why should I have it?" I tried my first serious frown.

"What's the problem, Ms. Cromwell?"

I shook my head. "It's as important as my books. It doesn't work. Black people don't poison people."

Crane nodded. "I hadn't thought about it that deeply."

"I can help," I said. "Black kids might drive French people to white bars. They run away when they die."

"He said that?"

"He would have said they take laptops in white bars. It's where the poisoned white people are—if this is how this fact routine works, which, as I'm trying to explain regarding my books, no way it does, not in my experience. The facts don't point. It's what bothered me, thinking about coming over here and giving evidence. For a time Professor Andreyev thought Lavoisier had died of a heart attack. Up to then, *comme ci, comme ça.* When he called me he had heard from the wife it was poison. It made me realize he had evidence he didn't know about. He thinks the mathematics in the laptop is valuable. He doesn't believe the police can solve this murder. He didn't say that. I believe he believes it. He's not naïve, and he didn't kill anybody. I knew that in a minute.

"I warned him in so many words that what he didn't think he had to tell you, what he didn't think was pertinent to the case, was what he had to worry about. He had to tell you. I knew when I came in here it wouldn't be pleasant. Every person blames their rough edges on the job. When I listen to you, I hear something of myself I don't like. It's why I didn't take the statue. It's why you don't have the statue of a gallows on your desk."

"What am I doing wrong, Ms. Cromwell?"

"I'm this way," I said.

"I wouldn't want to be questioned by you."

"You're not asking the questions I would ask. If Lavoisier was poisoned, somebody did think deeply. It was time-release. I don't know if you can determine the mechanism. If you can, you'll get an idea when the stuff got inside him. Where was he then?"

"Suppose he took a pill he thought was safe to take? The release was immediate."

"I would look at the wife, then," I said.

The a-ha moment. "Thank you, Ms. Cromwell."

Crane collected her file and looked around, but not for questions, just a formality up in the air before we all went out and faced the shifting weather in the afternoon.

"If there's nothing else? Well, I would like to thank everyone."

Crane was on her feet when she asked Ferenci to meet briefly in her office. I went downstairs by the stairs. On the street Ferenci said I had convinced them I had blood on my hands. But nobody they cared about. They would get me on something else, like Lavoisier rode a bike to Grand and I stole it.

I didn't answer. It was a bit embarrassing to take murder seriously. Hell of a dysfunctional annoyance all around.

Eight

I GOT THIS NOTE out of the P.O. box, a Berkeley postmark, on pastel blue, half-size paper:

"If you care to meet, I'd like to. —Andrei."

Evans Hall on the campus of U.C. Berkeley was a pea-green gray to blend with dead grass on an overcast afternoon as the four horsemen of the apocalypse dropped in for a seminar. I took the elevator to the tenth floor. You either put the classrooms around the outside with windows and the faculty offices inside without, or the other way around.

I found the numbered windowless cubby and took a chair against the back wall. I was ten minutes early. There were four fellows already staked out, catching up, or counting holes in the ceiling. I was old enough to be a professor. I was odd enough to make it look like I was lost, or the room had been changed.

Andrei came in talking to a tall kid in the year of his growth spurt, maybe halfway through junior high. He was in a purple shirt with PRAGUE in white letters. They talked in words I had never heard while Andrei erased the blackboard. When he was done erasing the kid said he'd work it out and let him know when he was done, and left the room. Somebody close to the door shut the door.

Andrei pulled a new stick of chalk from a box and broke it in half. He had started thinking as the one half was thoughtfully laid into a chalk tray. The other half he twirled in his fingers one-handed. He put it behind his back. He was in a brown T-shirt, tucked into jeans, no socks, and sandals broken in already three years back.

There were nine of us for the fifth lecture in the summer series. The official notetaker was called on to formalize that we were on Theorem 3.2.2.

Professor Andreyev looked at me, and as if for my benefit he summarized where the lecture of the previous week had left the subject. We had the proof of a theorem all to ourselves for the hour.

He began to dissect the coming resolution of the problem as a careful peeling away of layers. There were the easy parts and the tricky parts and stuff called modularity and the functions that had modularity. There were two aspects of it coming up in the proof that had to be distinguished. If we ignored this distinction we were up the creek about everything.

The prime player in the distinction was a thing called a parameter. His name was *kappa*. His essence was that he was elusive. He was the solution of an equation, the largest real solution in fact, and Andrei apologized for wasting time on that, but the fact had to be included.

The equation was also elusive. To get at it you had to consider a sequence of equations. Andrei wrote down the first equation, specifying its order in the sequence with the subscript 0, and he showed how the next equation, with subscript 1, was related to that one. He noted that he would waste more valuable time doing the equation with subscript 2, because it clarified how the *kappa* with subscript n, in the nth equation related to the *kappa* in the previous equation. The goal of this part of the proof was to show that the sequence of *kappa*s tended, in the limit, to our *kappa*. The *kappa*s were not monotonic increasing. That was one trouble. They went up and down unpredictably, but the equations followed patterns according to "residue classes," and the trick here was to focus on a particular residue class and to note that once one of these *kappas* was larger than 2, they all were—in that residue class. We would ignore the rest for a while.

I was amazed I was keeping up. I could see the whole picture. And then he said something about primitive roots, and it was like I had known nothing. From there I was lost till the end. So far we were just proving a lemma, which is a side result, a helper theorem that feeds a necessary statement into the proof of the theorem. At the end of the lemma, Andrei dug for an analogy:

"Life is good."

I guess it was for me. I didn't have to take the final exam.

Then he said he had lied, and he went back to a place in the lemma where he had skirted a complication. He cleaned up an omission. He thanked everybody. They had been too polite to call him on it. He used the filling-in of the complication to launch the proof proper, but I never did catch up after the primitive roots arrived on the scene. I know a fact I will never forget: 5 is a semi-primitive root of 16.

The lecture went over the hour. It was the end of the day. Three people took off during the mopping-up. The last few minutes harbored a gathering at the board. One guy had a core trouble, which worked out, but when he spoke it through to be sure, he lost it and said he'd figure it out. He was gone in the middle of it.

At which point Andrei looked at me a second time. He put his stub of chalk in the tray and got the dust off in his pockets. I remained seated.

"I had some free time," I said.

"I'm glad you have some. I'm afraid I used it up on all that baloney."

We had become acquainted. We had the room to ourselves. He put his back on the wall by the door.

"So," I said.

"I didn't expect this. I'm surprised."

"I'm surprised I'm here. Why did you want to see me?"

"I don't know. I just did. I didn't think I would, though. You have to be somewhere?"

"No. How about you?"

"Not till day after tomorrow. I'm glad you're here. Want to get something?"

People compressed in travel said good night to us and hesitated but didn't stop. We crossed to a coffee shop on Bancroft and joined a line, and used the close quarters to pry some. It felt right, not backing into a question. Go in. Noise was the pleasant surrounding for casual intimacy.

"Your friend," I said, "You were cleaning his house. His wife left?"

"His wife had to go home." He went through thoughts. He put his hand out at the doorway to the street, as if pointing to the building far away we had been in just past. "He lectured there, where we were. Deep thoughts in a shallow subject, he called it. I owe him."

"You used the word, 'owe,'" I said.

"I don't know why he worked with me. Out of my league. I'll always owe him."

"I wanted to talk about him," I said. "When I saw you at his house I had the feeling you did, too."

"We have different reasons, I would venture to guess."

"I'd venture to say I appreciate the opportunity to compare reasons."

He laughed. I laughed at his T-shirt. He had changed to a solid royal blue. Evening wear. He had lost weight. His hair was longer. He might have shaved yesterday. He hadn't bothered with socks. He might always look like he didn't care how a woman saw him. We jittered in tight spaces to a table. He put his elbows on the table. I crossed my legs. We had a sip and settled into casual waiting.

He relived an experience. His eyes went proudly spacey and he looked out of where we were, as if out a window. "I had worked a long time on a problem. I had several false proofs. I was really down, and then there was a strange feeling one minute, looking at the way certain expressions came out of something Robert had said at lunch. I hadn't seen them before. I stopped eating a few days. I knew it was done, but I was very scared."

I narrowed my eyes, my effort at communicating. "Deep thoughts on a shallow subject?"

He saw I had caught on. It prompted a continuation.

"I was convinced I was aiming too high. And I went higher. Always a mistake on my own. For me the natural direction is going into the clouds."

"Professor Lavoisier pointed you to the shallow end?" I asked.

"He could see in deep where it didn't occur to anyone. I think it's why he didn't talk to people. He didn't go to parties, dinners, coffee-and-doughnut soirées. I met his wife before he did. Jacqueline. I told her I liked the name."

"She was a mathematician?"

"An area of finance. She was in grad school at Columbia. I was at Columbia for a year. I met her and a friend of hers at a gathering. They went to parties together. She wasn't easy to reach for small talk."

"You tried?"

"With the friend, yes. The friend was in math. I called her a couple times. After that she was booked up, as far as she and I were concerned. Jacqueline was somebody who dressed up and went out and didn't want to meet anybody. We passed on the quad now and then, two ships in the night. I was talking about her with a Columbia guy I knew at a conference at Ohio State, and he pointed to a table across the room of the faculty club and asked, 'Is that her?' And it was Jacqueline. She was with Robert. They were married. Twelve years this year.

"She called me the night she heard Robert was dead. The police showed her a photograph of a dead man. She could iden-tify Robert in person the next day. His wallet and car keys were not on him. His car wasn't at the tavern. When everybody was kicked out the lot was empty. They ran license plates on the streets all over. They found it the next day, a block over, a block up from where he lived. His keys and cell and wallet were in a compartment in the seat. He must have met someone who wouldn't need to phone him.

"Once the police had the toxicology report, it was police business. They came to my office, my house, they asked me to come in for a formal chat. They hammered the suicide possibility. By then it had gone up in the hierarchy. It fit their idea of a man checking out in a place where he was lost, unknown, abandoned, where he had never been before. They covered territory like attack dogs. I'd say something and they'd change it like I was ducking them. Had something happened that had some pivotal influence on him? Like, was I having an affair with his wife?

"She called me as soon as she heard. The cops were there when I arrived. She wanted me to stay with the kids. She wanted to see Robert. They wouldn't say he had a heart attack. It was all crazy. It's still crazy."

He cut off a piece of cake and dissected it with a knife. "I go to France day after tomorrow."

"How's the house coming?"

"Robert's place? I met the guy who manages it. He asked me where the Lavoisiers were. I asked about the deposit. He wouldn't commit to a number. He was figuring how much he could screw them for. I haven't heard back. I'll have to follow up when I get back."

When the cake was in crumbs he changed the subject. "I can't believe he died in a bar. He seldom drank. He didn't fool around. But somebody drove him around. He had to get from where you saw him to the Grandstand. Unless there was another car he was using. They didn't consider a second car for a week after he died. They can't go back. You can, but they can't, and the people who can won't admit they can. That can't be fixed. And I guess there would have been an unexplained set of keys on him, unless someone took them. But when?"

He mashed cake into the spaces in a fork, and finally got some off the plate for a few seconds. Then he dropped the fork. "I'm glad I'm not a cop. I would lose interest in the misery they have to slog through—very fast. They put me through the killer scenario.

It was easy to be innocent. They tried to get me as the third leg of the marriage. It's maybe what pushed Robert over. Suicide is still a logical possibility, but a lost cause and they don't care. It's something to put in a report at the end of the day."

"A poison time capsule in a bar is a new category of murder," I said.

"It's English, it's not Oakland."

He pushed his cup an inch. He hadn't sipped twice. "Your description of your meeting with Robert, if credited, wrecked suicide, so they had to work you on that if they were going to focus hard on murder."

"My word ought to be good," I said, proudly. "They weren't sure what was good about it."

"You caught Robert, the essence. I could see him from your description. He sees you and he knows what you want and where you can find it. In a half-second he's sifted his knowledge and gets exactly to the right steps without concentrating. Then he suggests how you might help yourself getting around in the dark. And it's all friendly. Any idea what he wanted to talk about at the bar?"

"None."

"See, the cops see a pickup line. I told them he had something extremely important to say that he thought you ought to know once you had found what you wanted in the house. They'll never solve this case. I can't imagine what he wanted to tell you. If I was called on to state God's truth, I would say he wouldn't meet anybody for anything."

"He was gay?"

He lifted his cup to his lips and shook his head with his mouth full. "They think like that. The cops sexualize the concept of motive. You and me, they asked. Would I like sex with you? What's my line with Robert? We did it all, their way. He met someone. Okay, I agree, but not in any way that would lead them to who that is. I've never met you before. I have no axe to grind. I suggested they study very carefully everything you said. We're their suspects, and we're not much. For what it's worth, my reading minds, you're their prime suspect and you're not possible."

I smiled at my cup. "I've had conversations with cops, on good days and not so good. They're looking for a woman in my line of work. The equipment at Polk's place tells them what Robert needed. It's what Polk used it for. It's a fetish where men with imagination can go through dozens of partners in a year. They're showing his picture around my community. They mention a name—mine. They can't believe my story is an excuse to break into a house, and they can't find Ada.

"Otherwise," I said with emphasis, "you add up. Just for kicks they said you're who they're looking at. I said you didn't do it. They didn't ask. I know cops. It's a big clue with them, answering questions they don't ask. They take seminars on that."

He leaned his forearms on the table and gripped his elbows with opposite hands. "I know Robert. I don't know about their seminars. He's not interested in anything people have to say. The case has to assemble itself on that fact. A jealous somebody kills him? Poison? They need a professional assassin from Renaissance times. They need me even to speculate on a hired assassin."

"Well," I asserted, "fortunately we believe in each other. And he met someone who interested him. Or else he rode around nights on a bicycle."

"They thought of that. And take a deep breath. I don't add up. That tends to keep implicating the victim."

We drank up and twiddled our cups a few minutes and twisted our necks thataway at the same time in the same direction, and we went out the back gate to the corner, keeping to the right single file against foot traffic. I was discontented, and yet had what I wanted. Hanging around was asking for a new set of fears that I hadn't the energy to try to put right. He had to explain all this in France to people who cared and were no better at accepting it than cops. They would never believe him. I called a car. We crossed the street.

I got in and turned my eyes. He was walking away, but he guessed when the cab was pulling away and he turned just then and was motionless. "What brought you here, do you think?"

] *Nine*

I ASKED THE DRIVER to survey my block slowly and go around and come back. It's a ritual I take the time to enjoy once in a while. The shadows in the street were deserted shadows. Nothing detectable was moving in the half-lit alley that ran between my street and the next street over. I checked from both ends. When we pulled to the curb I asked him to wait a few seconds. I paid him and moved fast to the high iron gate in the alcove. I had a foot inside the gate when I waved a thank you at him.

Bolting the gate, top and bottom, I stepped onto the platform of a circular staircase that went two full turns down to a narrow passageway that ran perpendicular away from the street about fifty feet to my door. Another five feet and you stand at the edge of a straight drop. Here the passage ends some fifteen feet and a fraction above an alley.

I locked myself inside for the night and sat at the desk and thought about the bottle that used to be in the desk drawer. Cutting it out altogether made it easier to keep the hips sliding into the leather outfits. The extra lettuce and cabbage upped the years of good health, the elusive substance without which life was a bitter reminder you had a choice once.

I checked in with a man who expected my call. He'd seen me arrive. I'd seen him at a second floor window.

"Hello, Ms. Cromwell. Welcome home."

"Thank you, Mr. Liu. How is Mrs. Liu?"

"Very fine, thank you. The man was on the street today. Dark suit today. The Tuesday suit."

Mr. Liu transmitted a video clip of a business-looking number trying his best to amble the streets, like who would doubt he lives at A and works at B and needs to check the lock of the English Department in between, twice a day, going and coming. It looks cool when he's got his phone to his ear. He's following instructions, transmitting the high sign. All is well.

"He parked on Eddy. Mr. Travis got the make and license."

"The touchy-feely thing, it could develop into a nuisance," I said.

"I ask Travis, and Travis leaves a note under the windshield wiper?"

"I would need to think what I would like the note to say."

"What do they want, Ms. Cromwell?"

"What they lost in childhood."

"What he lost is not here."

"It's all in the phrasing. If we did write a note, we would make it instructively coherent, a debate on what we search for when we search for what we can't have."

"He might disagree?"

"Some smart people take his side. A philosophical structure is a life of its own. It creates confusion when he should be watching the road."

"Travis is a great closer. He urges a forceful response, immediate and proportionate. Puncture his tires."

Travis was a worry.

"Let me think about it," I said. "Incidentally, I'm taking my web page down."

"When?"

"Maybe tonight."

The implication slipped by a minute, then turned a corner.

"You're retiring?"

"Life will be different."

"You won't be advertising?"

"I will disappear from the World Wide Web."

"You're looking for what you can't have?"

"Wherever I am, I am there in some connection to the business. Those have been the ground rules since I was seventeen. I'm hoping I can adapt to a calmer style."

"I'm a lucky man. I have a wife who wants me."

"You're the one percent, Mr, Liu. Have a nice evening. Thanks for keeping an eye out. I'll keep you informed."

"It's been a pleasure to work with you, Ms. Cromwell."

A moment of silence fell and continued steadily. I was searching for an appropriate goodbye. The feeling at that instant would be too gushy. The heck with it. I let him inside,

"I've worked with a remarkable man, Mr. Liu. When you say you can do something, you can do it. When you do it, it is done. I will be back. We will meet again. And I may be around for quite a while. Good night, Mr. Liu."

I got into the mail program, asked an agent named Wayles to drop in and see what I could get for the English Department, got out, skimmed world events, drifted off wondering on some faces of the fiftieth or so anniversary of Bob Dylan.

I held a warm cup of tea to my cheek and couldn't think how the output in a field like mathematics would feel, say, in comparison with a medical doctor's satisfactions setting a broken bone or inoculating a kid against whooping cough.

I dragged a laptop off the foot of the bed and looked up Andrei Andreyev and clicked on "Noncommutative Subgroups of SL[2, Z]."

I poured more tea. I slid three cookies onto a saucer and crumpled the bag and dropped it on the counter. I wanted a kid and a house in my name, and I'm sure I'm not off-base thinking I don't know how to do it.

Things I might forget tomorrow go on reminder notes I prioritize on the star system, one to three stars, the last batch of notes before turning out the light:

   *** Schedule. Set up. Get off Internet. Change passwords. Ask Klu how soon I can disappear. Can I?

   ** HF + lunch? Office call?

   * Check basement damage, new window, match?

   * Scarlet, offer: 1.1 million. 08? 09? Get mkt value, then call, still want ED? Was it 1.4? Can she afford? Too much interactive dynamics? Get word out generally.

   * Rolling stock, outfits, donate entry-level dommes?

   * KB likes realtor. Why? Check why. Walk-through soon.

   *** Clients. Forevers: Hendricks, Nicholls, Jim, Colin, Lane? Bryce?
Goodbye, sweet princess party, old school tie. Six of Best. Love in the best places.

   *** Healdsberg? Santa Cruz? Library? Build house from scratch? Where?

   * Ada Tapes. Look again, H. Hall? Burn check? Burn tapes?

   * Andrei

   *** Andrei?

Ten

A BOX OF POLK'S PORN was still riding around in my library. I'd started with three tapes to get the flavor of the collection. I've seen crappy art, but it's not what I think that matters. I'd run across enough titles draped across enough male bottoms to figure the French word for the *unbreeched* is, in its primary trappings, *déculottage*, which helps in its way to let a client give me a clue from the cover alone a style we can explore. Animation puts in front of us the cues to the little necessary frills that stir the juices. I watch reactions, and note especially the unspoken. Why he deserves all this can be too embarrassing to mention. If he doesn't mention reasons, I leave it alone. I avoid tearing secrets out by the roots.

A serious soul might get the ball rolling with some well-formulated declaration that he wants his pants lowered discreetly and then his bottom caned with the utmost elegance. This can be said as if it's the last word on the subject, but as the years have rolled along I've learned to stop and listen. In these solidly boxed-up instructions a great deal is left vague. Between strokes he might think it's wonderful if I know that I should slither lasciviously around to the front and whisper congratulations. I am a mind-reader. I might ask if he wants another. I might want him to convince me. I'm not sure he can take it. We are not neglecting the rapport. I am probing for what is straining for utterance. These intimate in-betweens are rememberings of the forgotten. They are the difference between a heavenly experience and run-of-the-mill.

If the client's worldly predilections open us to literature, there's a splendid panorama and plenty of room to find where we can really click. "God, you're good," means we will be meeting again. Six strokes of the cane delivered under the banner of "six of the best," with all the trimmings of the governess of the manor can connect to what a man might call the real thing. Six times six is a test of stamina that is pushing to exhaust a shame, a fear, a life's continuous weaving of armor. Getting through it is a triumph, and thirty-six strokes is chicken feed in some sessions, but not in mine. I'm not interested in that kind of courage. It's too much like courage from a bottle. Something else is working beneath the endurance, and I'm certain in most cases it's what I call hate wrapped in erotic ready-wear. I'm seeing myself put into a malignant role. And I don't do it. I get arguments that I'm not the one who is getting hurt, but the answer is I am. My profession follows a Hippocratic code. I have to feel as good after they leave as I did before they arrived. I prefer to be used to create fun for both of us. I like two people having fun. I know what that is, and I can define it in particular cases, and it's what matters.

I had set out a half-dozen titles of Polk's stuff and sifted for contents close to my wavelength. The title *Château of Déculottage* was so far off the material it covered that it was just possible I'd opened a classic of the century-old silent genius era.

The initial frames measure the perfectly timed tick of a dripping tap. Small drops of water are disturbing a container of water. The camera is stuck close to the percussion as some reckoning with matter at the misty molecular level. The water is splashing the lens. You see and you don't see, and it might be the tale told by an idiot signifying nothing more than time passes, but unless I'm missing the point, the drip is a lament.

Keep your eye on the drip. Just when you're reaching for your gun to put a hole in the deep and the wondrous, the camera pulls back. The sounds slide over to a rhythmic tapping, a whistle and click. On the left side of the screen a woman is, at the transition, motionless on a throne planted on a coat of arms in an inlaid design. A skirt, slit to the hip, drapes a very relaxed leg in a boot. The heel, stuck to the floor at a point, inherits the burden of carrying the job of allusion. It points to the coat of arms. I don't get a reaction there. I'm wondering where the whistle and the click are coming from. Sounds like a recording of a whip.

The other leg is bent. The knee bulges upward against a wooden arm. Her head has touched a backrest and is rotated upward in a state of withdrawal, not exactly trapped, but not giving off the force of expectation that she is about to leap into a plot. She is looking along the line of her nose. The holding grip and business tip of a whip are drawn together one-handed. The other hand massages the loop. This is not an action show. Relax. She is killing some time. Nothing is unfolding, but the drip keeps dripping, so something is coming, not to a boil, but to an awareness of a triviality that will not be new to her.

A connection is coming. Keep an ear cocked for goings-on in another room. But the hint is a wink. The artistic wink. If you're watching to get off, you might be facing hard truths. You're in the cheap seats. You're the one getting done to. The artist is going to mess with you.

This effort wasn't coding anything in my sweet dark places, but the sweet slowness scored on aesthetic tension. The creator put some brains into this. He was working off his own urges toward some maddeningly misdirected use of time along the lines of eight hours of the Empire State Building sitting there in a thunderstorm. I can argue it's a waste of film. I don't feel I'm out of my mind caring to watch a while.

Three or so paces to the right in front of the throne is a man with an erection that has got up a head of steam and finds itself with nothing to do but show off some splendid posture. He has exercised. He is spiritually hard. He keeps his hands quiet at his side, a pose of honor, or a disability. The man grooves on the woman's boredom.

The language of frozen desire? Could this be it?

The fetish background is a woman's cross-laced leatherette cincher, cream silk blouse, black boots. The taste of the whole business says the man owns the place. He is a man with some money for spending on gear that has a purpose. They are trying out blank expressions in no uncertain terms, a man and a woman recalling something they needed in some stage of development and didn't get and needed to go back and get, or got it once and wanted more, or wanted to fix what they got and needed to get it the way they wanted it the next time. And decided they didn't know how? The man was Polk. I'd seen exactly this madness in the painting and had had already once before exactly this reaction: a man and woman spiffed up to cut loose and get a fantasy out there on the screen in motion. And halfway there, they were giving it a rest.

If the woman had a free hand in all this fluctuating nothing, she didn't give evidence. Of course nobody is required to tremble in a Beckett play. I was looking at Polk from some ten years before, or twenty. It was on display, it was up to him.

Ten minutes passed by my watch and the hard-on hadn't twitched a muscle.

"We will go to the castle," the woman on the throne said.

That swept out that metaphor. This wasn't the real castle. The woman was calling the shots. The man dusted his hair. He gave himself a shake and went to an armoire, opened a hole in a pair of pants, and got two legs in and worked his penis out of the way of the zipper. There were some things he got timed incredibly right, and fast. They sped up the linear narrative. What came next said you'd already missed the best stuff, watching that cock wrap around the front of his leg. He put on a shirt, took it off, and put on another, like, is this on purpose, a wardrobe error?

All the silence went along for a trek up a flight of steps, through a Spanish hall, through a fortress-era Spanish gate, to a dark sedan, one of a matching pair on a rounded stone drive. The woman waited at a rear door, and here I thought we were in for the chauffeur scene as the whip changed hands, but the whip went in first and that beautiful leg after. The camera climbed into the other side of the back seat last. They used a lot of footage on a long drive. If you knew the Bay Area, you knew the cutoffs.

Hills to the ocean side of the 280 freeway bounding Los Altos were all one specimen of fenced-in forest that never provoked an impulse to get out of the office just to see it, but I liked the drive. It was pretty to glance out the window at, though of no particular irregularity to look out for. But I'd look now and then to check if everything was where it belonged out there.

It must have been Saturday. Good day to go fast. The traffic moved along.

Past an S-exit lemons ran along a wide boulevard to a U-turn that swung out of traffic to a stone-columned entrance with its own private signal.

In a close-up the chauffeur punched in a seven-digit code and punched in five more at a prompt, and fixed her face in the mirror while a gate got out of the way. When the gate stopped she followed the go-ahead green arrow. A macadam road ran out of macadam at a dry creek that emanated mysteriously from a tractor that had once dragged spikes to comb the ground. A section of orchard had died off beyond a cluster of rusted junk. Over there was part of a shed. The fording platform looked like the rest of the shed. On the other side of the creek bed the macadam picked up to where it passed a big H stuck in a big bounding ring stuck in a wrought-iron curlicue anchored on two enormous square columns of flagstone.

Bigger than the ranch emblems in the old Westerns, bigger and classier in the manner of two different worlds—this was the Cheops of the breed. It had given some majesty to the ownership of land that had once been everywhere cheap as dirt before the frontier was closed.

The hills weren't much, but too steep to put a shortcut over. A steady twist for a few hundred yards bent through two minor crests, angling away from a prairie peeking through a gap to the east that shimmered in dry, golden grass and slightly browner dirt, hues that still measured the hot season over thousands of square miles of California, but much less of it now locally.

You didn't get land like this in Los Altos except on the big estates. The biggest was the only one, the Hall Ranch. And to get there you would go under a big H and gain altitude on roads that radiate in rising plateaus from its design.

Within days of Ada's visit I had received a check from the Hall estate, on which these limousine lulus are out looking for some same-ol' same-ol' château, and they know the entrance code to the estate. Two people were dead, Ada missing, and I still had a ten-thousand-dollar check under a salt shaker. It hadn't been cashed, but it wasn't a bookmark yet. I am suspicious why I am letting it end up plastered to the desk. Something I had never liked was backing me up.

At times like this I remember there were phone calls to retrieve and messages to read and digest—and I make a living this way. If I take an hour on anything else, I lose it on the bottom line. This is where the logic divided.

I called Cook. I tapped a pencil to a regular heartbeat.

"I'd love to say it's wonderful to hear from you at this hour," she said.

"I'd love to say it's wonderful to call. I could say it in person if we could have a get-together at the English Department. Your convenience, say tomorrow morning?"

"How about now?"

"I want to give you something."

"If I say no to the English Department, then what?"

"There's a restaurant a block over." I gave her a name, and I said eleven o'clock and waited. She hung up. I might just barely have put a foot on the right track for no reason I could think of.

I nibbled on a cookie and couldn't get over it. A triangular crumb of dough separated from a chocolate chip and rolled over once and broke free in a dying fall to the plate. I stuck it to a finger. I licked it off.

Wayles called. He had a place for me when I sold the English Department, four thousand square feet, big wall privacy, prestigious altitude, gourmet view, trees to string a hammock on, Miele dishwasher, Sub-Zero refrigerator/freezer, no dickering price tag. Move quick or look again in two years.

] *Eleven*

THE FIRST THING I learned about Cook was the name she gave the maître d', who called to say a Ms. Kirsten Cook was on her way up. While she was on her way up, I looked her up. There were Kirsten Cooks all over the state, plenty in the Bay Area, plenty all the way to the borders, but no such name listed at the address Hall listed.

The dining area is four curtained alcoves on a covered outside patio—out of hearing of the others, but I heard something going on. I saw a hand, and the curtain parted. Cook dropped a folder on the table and asked for a minute from the server. The server nodded and took herself away. Cook twisted her wrist upwards to shine a watch in her face. I read the gesture. We had said eleven o'clock. She had lean cheeks and some strangeness in her age. Deciding between forty-nine and fifty-one I'd guess forty-nine. If the options were forty-eight and fifty-two I'd go with fifty-two. I don't know what that meant, but that she looked like she lived on lettuce and had some moral satisfaction in the look that gave her. She would die looking fifty.

She crossed her legs rather obviously, not certain of staying, not obvious when she might decide. Her elbow organized itself in a casual position on the parapet. It let her run a finger through short auburn hair. Taking her as she wanted to be taken, she didn't care how she was taken. She and a chair had come together at a right angle to me. Her right hand rested on the table. A moving finger counted, one at a time, four or five, of a set of keys. I had a minute to interest her. If I were a billionaire, I suppose she was what I would be looking for to represent those of my interests that didn't have to be known.

I lifted a videotape from my side of the table and put it in front of her. She rotated the image and didn't bother looking at the reverse side.

"It's why I called you," I said.

"That's what?" she said.

"If you would appreciate a technical term, it's an art film."

"And why do I need to bother hiking up here to look at it?"

"I'm giving it to you," I said. "And I'm confused."

"And you want me to join the video club."

"That's not the way ignorance works," I said. "You ought to laugh at yourself once in a while. Show some self-awareness. You're in the club. We're all in it."

"This is some wisdom documentary? People don't know what they don't know? I already read that somewhere."

I wanted her to get over this. I was contributing to it. I took the step sideways. I collected a breath of preternatural honesty.

"A man died six months ago, a heart attack. His property is up in the air. He died without any written instructions. Among his belongings were tapes of a few of his interests. Images of me are one of his interests. I never met him. One image is stuck behind a stack of raw cash. The image of me is photoshopped. The pile of cash was not found in a storage locker he rented. It indicates that a good chunk of his assets are hidden. I was asked to have a look, see what fresh eyes might see, shed some light."

She had that look: Tell me something I might care about in the next few minutes.

I touched the tape.

"The film begins in a house. I think it's the house of the man who died six months ago. With no possible excuse for taking a drive, four people take a drive to a chunk of land with a big H near the entrance. The driver knows the entry code to the gate. A man appears briefly just as you pass the H. He's leaning on a shovel, a hired hand. But he was also holding a shovel in the tapes I'd seen before. He was a hired hand again and again. So he's a hired hand in the manner of Alfred Hitchcock. He has a role you don't notice, until I noticed I had spoken to him briefly one evening and completely forgotten about him."

"Why would your image be on a woman looking at a pile of a dead man's money? How did you know him? Did you know him? He sounds like an ex-husband. You want your half?"

"He had a statue of me in a hollowed-out book. He was obsessed with my looks."

Her head was positioned on five fingers. They held it from falling over. The fingers did not withdraw. Her attitude rotated in my direction, say fifteen degrees. Her line of sight was still over there, but she reached the tape and put it in front of her.

"This film here, is the statue visible in it?"

"There's a lot going on that's not," I said.

"You want to expand, please?"

"The man with the shovel. I want to know his name, where he is reachable."

"Do you have this statue?" she asked.

I gestured like maybe, but mostly like no. She rolled her eyes, circling her evaluation of how I negotiate.

"You are good at yes and no. Which one is it?"

"There's a picture of it in a box in the office," I said. "It has my name on it."

"Can I see it?" She didn't look around. She watched my eyes, where they looked.

"The English Department is on Stafford," I said. "Next street up."

She crossed her fork at four o'clock and went back to ninety degrees to me.

"I meant to say," she lowered her voice, "I'd like to see the photo of the statue. If you know where a statue can be had, I'd be interested. I'll look at the man with the shovel in the tape. If I know his name, I'll tell you. I'd prefer to do that at home. Regardless, I don't want to eat here. I never did. But these people have a business. It's a restaurant. It's no longer my business."

Some tone of criticism leaked out past the curtains. The server appeared. Ms. Cook stood and opened her purse, dropped her keys in, and snapped it shut. She left two hundreds on the table.

I BROUGHT the VCR from the bedroom to the desk and sped the tape up to the big H part. I wanted to point to the man whose name I wanted.

"That's the guy," I said.

"I can take this tape with me?" she asked.

"It's free," I said, "like my association with Mr. Hall."

"Where did the tapes come from?" she asked.

"Ada Tomek. There's a box of them in my library. The statue is in a book at the home of a dead man, unless the police took it, or unless someone else had some bright idea for it. It's part of a murder case. The man who was murdered told me where to find it an hour or so before he died. That's the part that involves the police."

I rewound the tape and handed it to her. It went in her bag under gravity, and the keys came out.

"The cover is unusual," she said. "More your line of work."

"I get crank correspondence," I said, "but not ten thousand dollars' worth. If Hall wants to run around with his pants down, what's holding him up?"

"The same could be said to you. You didn't cash the check. Money will taint the premises of the holy sepulcher?"

"I can wash my hands."

"In time, Ms. Cromwell, all will be vouchsafed in time. Right now I'll go and sit on a sofa and look at the man and his shovel. We have a bargain. Incidentally who was murdered? If it was the man with the shovel, why is he of any interest to you?"

"A professor. And the man with the shovel is possibly the man who spoke to me outside the tavern where the murder happened. Something connects about him, the posture, the age, the dopey stare. If the Oakland police call on you, you'll be ready."

I took her to the curb. She had clicked her keys as I shut the gate. On the street a limousine was waiting. A man shut the door after her, just like in the art movie.

I had learned something. The check represented a lot of interest in me that I misunderstood and hadn't caught up to. I learned that the invitation to Los Altos had to do with the statue. Beyond that, nothing.

I went inside and put my feet up and took a back lean and let my left hand struggle with the right hand. I had quit reaching into the lower right-hand drawer for refreshments that shut out the dumb, stupid world. It was a new day these days when I put my feet up.

I let the blood go back to where it belonged and went in and put the kettle on and came back and typed the entire H film business in a note. I might need it. I was talking to myself, juggling real long-term consequences if Cook recognized the man in the tapes—more face time with Oakland officials.

I tapped a foot a minute and quit the indoors and waved off a taxi driver. I went back to the restaurant. The woman at the reception stand remembered Kirsten Cook with a man—a week ago, two weeks; she could look it up. She was sure that the man had been in the booth next to me upstairs. He had come down the steps after we left, and then not so sure which way he went. He did come out. He was handsome, like handsome was enough to identify him.

I said not to bother mentioning to anyone that I asked.

] *Twelve*

JUST TO GET THE SPRAWL into a few words, quickly right in magnitude, the Kaiser medical complex in Oakland is the biggest in the world. But how the health maintenance system earns a dollar, whether one business or many in one, that's not a few words. The units on the corner of Piedmont and Sequoia might have been part of it. Suite-looking cubes with designer gaps went together in a toothy arrangement on three levels rising out of one connected structure at the ground floor. Separate stairways offered private access to offices. The majority of these are mental health professionals. The part of the structure on the ground floor facing Piedmont is a furniture store and a bakery.

The building at this location was once red brick, a two-level put up in the 1920s. The name of the business, about where the furniture store is now, was the Moonstone Psychic Glow. The woman who ran that outfit read palms and kept dead loved ones in touch with family. She was there at that address in the early 1950s. She had no husband, no offspring, a high school education, family in Oregon. What's known of her three-fourths of a century later accords with the biographical items of a Renate Flyte-Simpson, a high priestess in a spanking cult, which met in a basement on Piedmont.

A client of mine who dug into this connection debunked the existence of the Renate Flyte-Simpson Society at that location.

The Moonstone Psychic Glow didn't have a basement. That's verifiable. That the owner of the Moonglow was the inspiration for Renate Flyte-Simpson was found in a dedication in a tract in special collections at the downtown library in San Francisco. The author of the tract was certainly the author of the four volumes of the *Minutes of the Renate Flyte-Simpson Society* that began circulating privately in the seventies. So the owner set the author off, knowingly or unknowingly. For whatever that's worth. I have a typed copy of the *Minutes*. I may have the original copy.

What came to light to me in the past day is that a second Renate Flyte-Simpson is currently known at the furniture store where the Piedmont Professional Group is now. It's why I was here. Her gang was into art films. Ada's box of tapes in my office are RF-S Productions. Ask for James at the furniture store when you're into more then furniture is what I was told.

I'd followed a limousine for a block and braked behind it in the entrance to the rear lot. A recently grown-up thing in solid black was let out onto the center of the lot. She waited till the car drove off to look at me, a slow eagle eye to see who was early if we shared a psychiatrist.

She was tall, trim, and terrific in leather; young enough to be new at it, and that trick isn't for everyone right out of the gate. Someone thought so. She was dropped at appointments in limos.

She waited where I would pass within a few steps and said "Mistress Elizabeth," speaking not to be overheard a block away. The blue eyes rang a bell from a movie. The context of the movie was lost. I was stuck. I didn't remember her.

"You were at the Women's Retreat," she said. "I was the singer. We danced. Brett. Two *t*'s."

I relaxed on one leg and nodded. I stuck my finger at the corner of the parking lot, possibly referring to the AOK rental company across the street. Backhoes and wheelbarrows.

"That Jeep over there," I said. "It was on the street. Yours?"

She put in some admiration. "Good memory," she said. "It's how I get around between limo rides."

"But bad on faces," I said. "I remember you at the piano. You were dressed a little differently. You were a good dancer."

"The girl at the piano was Kay. In leather I might look like her. You danced with Jillian. Then we danced. I'm the singer. I thought I stole your heart. We gave you the rush, in case you were a producer and didn't want to admit to it. You were looking for books. You find them?"

"I thought I was looking for books."

"What are you doing here? Or why do you think you're here?"

"I have to answer the same question inside the furniture store. I might as well practice. I'm looking for a woman who took the name of a woman who never was."

"I did that," she said, touching her chest. "Harriet Marwood."

"How about Renate Flyte-Simpson?" I asked.

She tongued a small circle on her lower lip and shaped her Bettie Page wig at a temple to mean she had nothing to say, not about that subject.

"You," I said, high on insight, "dressed in this outfit, in this parking lot, tells me I'm on the right track."

She slouched a little to get personal. "You," she said, high on amusement, "in this parking lot, during business hours, with no interest in furniture, tells me you are looking to hire quality at the English Department. You're on the right track. You're actually there."

"Would that get an answer to my question?"

"There's a card game inside. It never stops. You want to drop in on a friendly game, you can ask anything you want. Suite 206A. It's where I change."

"Any possibility a lady named James is playing cards?"

She fixed the leading edge of her wig again. "May I get personal?" she ventured, getting ready. I wagged my eyebrows, sure.

"If James and Flyte-Simpson don't work out, I'm interested."

"I was thinking of selling," I said. It was the second time I'd told someone. One was enough to start the grapevine rumbling.

"I might drop in and play a few hands. I hate to miss the traffic jam on the Bay Bridge."

She gave me her number on a card with a kitty's face. "In case you want help," she said.

———

I HAVEN'T seen Piedmont two times in ten years, so I can't say how different it is from what it was. The door was open to the furniture store. A bakery next door clung to a memory of whatever occasion I was celebrating long ago. It could have been thirteen items for the price of twelve, when that sort of bonus was a big seller.

There were sofas and chairs and tables and standing lamps and soft carpeting and nobody in the store to share it with. A moment went past. A dark oval stone on a silver chain brushed from a lavender curtain. The woman wearing it asked if there was something she could help me with.

"I would like to speak with James," I said and waited.

The cheeks sucked in a little. The color in her cheeks remained unchanged. I hadn't shocked her. She didn't look confused. The question wasn't beating around a bush.

"If you could wait here a moment," she said. I poked my nose at a few cushions and a few price tags. It was nice quality, a believable operation.

The woman disappeared through the curtain. I heard a door slide twice, then nothing till it slid twice again. Then soft, fast footfalls. She came back in the wake of a woman about fifteen years older, fancier dressed. The older woman didn't mind saying to customers:

"You don't look like James's type."

"That's up to James," I said. I hoped it was, but unlikely I was going to meet James. It was in her eyes.

"I don't recall an appointment," she stated.

"If I call the business number, whom do I reach?"

"If I'm here, me."

"I'd like to call the number when you're not here."

"Leave a message. Does James know you?"

"I don't know who James is to say. I'd like a few moments of his time. I have a couple questions."

"Leave the questions, and leave your number, and I'll see if James will agree to have your questions answered."

"Any way I can hang around and catch James in a free minute?"

"Hang around and think about what I said. There's a dough-nut shop next door."

She hadn't interrupted our talk with a pause or a thought that needed a pause. When she turned, her assistant squeezed sideways out of the way. The assistant had picked up the gist.

"It's a busy world," she said.

"I don't see any customers," I said.

"Might not be a busy world when you're here."

All that unalloyed snotty hand waving was the kind of per-formance to throw at me to minimize follow-up bother. It had the wrong effect. I had a nasty fantasy. I'd sit in the doughnut shop and come in every hour and pester them with furniture terminology with my mouth full and powdered sugar that didn't stay where I put it. It got better. I knew two Oakland detectives, a hard-wired ADA, a federal lady, and a straight line from James to a dead man, and the furniture lady couldn't say I didn't. Then I noticed there was blowback in there, too, just from knowing there was.

I hung around in my car with the door open and a shoe on the pavement working out how much I didn't know could hurt me. I dialed Brett. She told me to come on up to 206A, same as before. It wasn't, but there were two doors.

The door to 206B was unlocked. A reception room was cramped and not a waiting room. Opposite the door to the inside was an open door to a room with mirrors, a dressing table, and clothes visible in the mirrors, mirrors deep in the mirrors. I stepped into the mirrored room. There were six at a poker table in casual naked wear, and nobody cared who walked in. One woman looked at me and then at Brett, like Okay, this the one on the phone? Who's she?

I was introduced.

"This is Elizabeth Cromwell. She's famous."

I met the rest counterclockwise.

Rocco: "I will be famous someday."

Dana: "I was famous in my day."

Sally: "I might be famous. Anybody know my name?"

Sabrina: "My fame is fleeting. I'm holding a shitty hand."

Lou: "I'll never be famous and I don't care. Sit, join, open your wallet. Count out chips over there next to the fridge. You're on the honor system. How do you know Brett?"

"I'm looking for James," I said. "She knows."

Rocco: "I was married to a James. You don't want to find him."

Dana: "I do. I will someday be married to the one and only James."

Sally: "It was a dark and stormy night when I fucked James, and he died delirious."

Sabrina: "James, or James? It matters in Tennessee."

Lou: "I wouldn't know a James. Don't introduce me. You're out of luck with James. You're among friendly sharks. You get to keep the clothes you came through the door in. We'll want the earrings. Those real pearls? I'll give you James for them."

Rocco: "James isn't worth the box he came in."

Dana: "From the box to James ain't up."

Sally: "It was a dark and stormy night when I gave James my box."

Sabrina: "Now we're talking. Love in the afternoon."

Lou: "Great flick. Don't make them like that anymore. Never did. Deal."

———

BRETT AND I left, unknown and unnoticed. She was in orange tennis shoes, white socks, white jeans and a black silk blouse, a young sexy thing currently way above sexy in her age group. She was now a light brunette and still pale blue eyes. Men could think of dressing her up all sorts of new ways, but never get near to anything she cared to want them to think of her in.

"I played poker last month. I left four dollars and fifteen cents on the table and cried," she confided.

"You're not setting me up, are you?"

"Not if you're hiring me. You didn't find James?"

"I don't know," I said. I must not have sounded fully forth-coming.

"What did they say?"

"They played along with the name to see what I wanted to know. Invited me to stick my face in a doughnut, be satisfied on a sugar high, and don't bug them."

"Where did you get the name?"

"A confidential source in my circle who can't be wrong." I felt for my car keys and left them in the pocket. I waved a glance back at 206B.

"How'd you get this gig? As opposed to chief of surgery at the Mayo Clinic?"

"Luck. Sheer dumb luck. We were playing at a party, a large event," she said. "I had gone outside. A woman came up to me and pointed at her throat and mouthed words. Silently she said she couldn't talk. I thought she had throat cancer, and I said we didn't need to talk. She had a performance smile, sad and persistent. She didn't go away. She stood next to me not quite touching, and I expected her to make a move that she wanted touching, and she did. She tapped my arm. I was looking the other way. When I turned she spoke in a raspy whisper. She put her face very close to be heard, or not to be heard too precisely. She didn't want to waste my time. She said I was very attractive. If I wanted to call her there were opportunities for a job. She could give me a num-ber. I nodded. She touched my arm and hoped to see me again.

"I decided there was no harm hearing what she had to say about tuition money. A man answered the phone, which made sense: she needed someone to talk for her. He asked me where

I was in my education, and where I wanted to go with my music. Then he asked if I was busy. I was free, and we met at a restaurant. The first thing, he turned his chair against the wall and leaned his shoulder on it, and said he was a shitty person, which made him mildly interesting in my experience of people. He stirred his coffee a lot, and spooned the surface in tap-taps with casual questions. You know, like did I have any illusions he would grease the wheels for me to get to be a rock star, or any kind of star, like a movie star.

"I said I had hopes. Maybe they weren't realistic, but I had them. I asked about his hopes. He was about fifty. Hopes? He said at the moment his one big hope was that I would let him tell me his life story. He asked. Did I want him to tell me his life story? I asked him what he regretted. That's part of life. He said he took advantage of women, talking at them while making it look like he was opening doors for them.

"Yeah, I looked at him like I wondered how much he regretted it, and we seemed to understand each other. His coffee was cool by now. He lost interest in screwing around with it.

"We went out to his car. He gave me a satchel. There were some movies in it. I should pay attention to the boy–girl interactions. If I felt there was something in there I could do, I should call him back. He would have something for me."

"I called him. I said I could try Harriet Marwood. She was a fantasy governess. I checked if that meant I didn't have to have sex, and he said he would make that a condition with the client, but that I might have to remind the client at a point or two that that was the condition. It could get rough asserting a principle. People who pay other people in great multiples of the minimum wage are used to getting their own way. In fact, that could be the game. I shouldn't have any misconceptions. I might have to walk out of the hotel naked carrying a whip. The agency would back the client *in extremis*. It's good money, and clients see to it you carry emotional scars for life.

"We met for a practice session, nothing physical, just get

the back-and-forth going. He had some outfits for me to do my parades in. He was satisfied. He asked if I was ready. He had a pussycat for me, a guy who comes up occasionally from Altadena. It would be very good if I knew something of the Dodgers–Giants history. The key there was to be a Giants fan, argue for the Giants, but don't be a prick, give ground, sympathize a bit; you have a secret yen to see the Dodgers beat the Giants if they meet in the playoffs. Now, that could happen, even though they're in the same division. It would be wise to bone up there. Know the rotation. Know the bullpen.

"He asked about how much hard work in general I was willing to consider, like learning languages. The better I could speak Italian or Spanish or Dutch, the more opportunities. High-finance elocution was valuable. Better than an advanced degree in economics. As always, provide opposition but go with the prevailing winds. You are the one being paid to make them feel like something is going right in their life."

"What was this Harriet Marwood vehicle?" I asked.

"*The Stairs to the Tower*. It was released before 2000. It's on tape. You want a synopsis?"

"How many stairs?"

"You're good. That's what it was about, a conversation on the way up to the room at the top. A lot of stops and starts. You've seen it?"

"Sort of," I said. "I've done it enough. From the many times on the way up, I've gotten mildly expert on the Dodgers, the Giants, the Mets, the Phillies. I can warn you: Cubs fans. They're not nice. They're the worst. I mean they're the ones who live a birth-to-death failure arc. You get a guy from Chicago, you just hope he likes the White Sox."

"Which reminds me," I said, "you wanted a job. What's wrong with this one?"

"On the ride to where I meet my appointment, I'm blindfolded. No scenery. A whole hour is ruined both ways."

"How's the pay?"

"That's the other thing. Tips. That's it for my services. They're okay, but it means bending over backward."

"You want a cut up front so you don't strain your ligaments. What do you need to take your services elsewhere?"

"What do you get?" she asked.

"That's not the American system of hiring. I get to ask first: what do you hear about Renate Flyte-Simpson?"

"We operate out of 206. There has to be a brain trust. It could be the furniture store. Nobody says, and nobody goes there. I've heard the name Renate Flyte-Simpson. Always sounded like a phony."

"How do you get your assignments?"

"The Starlight Motel. I meet this lady there. No texting, no electronic communication of any sort. I stop by the office and talk to Diane."

"How does Diane tell you when to be there?"

"What do you care?"

"I've been wondering about this problem. Confidentiality. It costs me business. It's getting worse by the minute. Go-betweens are a consideration, but then go-betweens can be for sale. Then you're in twice as deep and you don't know it. The roof falls in and there you are, spitting dust, explaining to a client that nothing's secret."

"They call you directly?" she asked.

"Some of them buy a phone through a stranger. Some buy a stranger. It provides some cover. How do you know when to stop by the office and ask Diane what she wants?"

"I go every other day. I went yesterday. The person at the desk sent me to the office to see the owner, Mrs. Townes. She said Diane had a job for me."

"Diane was at the motel?"

"Sometimes. Not last night. We met at the San Francisco Chess Club. She plays chess with Mr. Townes."

I looked around for something to touch. Get my bearings. Hold me up. "What kind of allegorical talk is that?"

"Loose talk. It's my forte. Diane meets the client first, maybe more than once. She clues me in. She told me when to meet my driver."

"The client contacts Mrs. Townes?"

"Don't know."

"Don't care?"

"Not that I've noticed."

"Mm-hmm, but what if you worked at the English Department?"

"Then I'd know. Will I be working at the English Department?"

I kept pulling my keys out of a pocket and counting them and checking to see if any were lost when I did it the next time. Brett was impatient. She wanted to get going on that career path entertaining men. I liked that. She was eye-catching and quick on the things she had to be quick on. She was quick on getting off topics that didn't move the narrative. She wasn't a natural-born enthusiast. I liked that.

"You'll have to fill out an application," I said. "And I'd want to talk with Diane."

"You have to talk with Mrs. Townes. She'll let you know if Diane wants to talk with you."

I took a stab at cutting out mid-level management. I spoke metaphorically.

"How do I play chess with Mr. Townes?"

She had an easy laugh that let you know that you'd earned an easy laugh. You didn't want to push whatever you were pushing. I felt smaller.

"Don't bother," she said.

We had walked to my car and then moved about three paces this way and that way and come out a few feet closer to my car and right up next to a fundamental insoluble. I was a producer, and I was mulling circumstances. I could see a pathway to bringing an assistant into the English Department. The pathway had been giving me a headache on both sides of the parking lot. She thought I was coming down with something.

"You feeling okay? Sorry for the hard crack."

"I'll survive," I shot back. "What you want to know is, I'm shutting down my business. Not get out all at once, but cut back, get to where I could take an afternoon nap in peace. There are clients who still show up, mostly fond of the premises."

"I studied your web page," she said. "There's a lot to talk about."

She looked at her fingernails and said in a soft tone, "If I read the leaves correctly—if I am reading them at all—we're having a serious talk."

"I took down the web page last night," I said. "I'm erasing myself from the global network. A serious talk means you answer my questions in a serious frame of mind, like I own the business."

She put her lip in her teeth. If it moved it would hurt. We waited for developments. She figured I asked about Mr. Townes, so that's what I wanted to talk about.

"Mr. Townes—Joshua, he wants to be called Joshua, Joshua Townes—I was about to say he is African American, but he grew up in Martinique. When he gets excited he goes into his native language. He plays chess with Diane. It's fun listening to patois. It's the only time I hear her laugh. That's all there is between them. He's at the Starlight sometimes. Once he was with this guy arguing about chess. I think the guy looked down on him. His French isn't French. The guy wasn't trying to be condescending. He couldn't help it. He was in a coat and tie and Joshua butt-kicked him up and down his back. Joshua is a grandmaster. Diane was in a room studying a game. Joshua had gone to the office, and this French guy comes down the hall and just walks in the room uninvited and tells Diane she has a mate in four. She calls Joshua to kick his butt, but they get into a discussion. The man bets him money. He didn't know Joshua is a grandmaster. Joshua tried to talk him out of playing for money, but he was insulting in French, and it got on Joshua's game side. They had a game for a twenty-dollar bill. The guy had a woman at the end of the hall. She kept looking out the door—you know, I'm on the clock here."

I swung my eyes over her face and planted them. That sent the hard signal. Think.

"This French fellow, he wouldn't be a mathematician?"

"Have no idea. I wasn't there. He thought he was God when he spoke French."

"You do me a favor?" I asked. I looked up a picture in the newspaper. I showed her the date of the paper. I showed her a picture of Robert Lavoisier. "Could you ask Diane if this is the guy she saw?"

She looked at Robert as if "why not." She whistled, "Cute. Sure. It says here he's dead, though."

She suddenly looked like she was thinking she had been taken down the garden path and here we were. I was way ahead of her. This was the money question. The basic rule in the escort profession is keep your mouth shut when it comes to what you know about anybody. Maybe you know the year Rome had four emperors and you know their names, and you say something in connection to them, and it will be quoted wrong or, worse, it will get around undistorted, a very stupid thing, something that goes on your tombstone.

She was looking for a job. An opportunity comes along and she puts herself on a back foot. She'd been steered. That's how I saw it in the way she was looking at me. She worked my visage over pretty hard for a while until she got out of it what she was looking for. Then she blew air on her nose.

"You have to go," she said. "Nice meeting you. You have my card."

She headed for her Jeep, and I got my door unlocked and rolled the windows down and decided the insides needed time to cool off. I got out and caught up to her massaging her lip. She was putting some care back into it. She was staring at the space in front of her.

"If you're still thinking about a job," I said, "think about two hundred an hour, linear scale, you keep the gratuity and the gifts—except the books. I get a hundred and the books. If I have to let you go, I hope I have a good reason. You can say yes now or call me and let me know what you want to talk about."

"We'll talk about Orson Welles," she said. She was cheered up. It was the job, or the talk about Welles.

"You know who I'd love to play. I'd never get the chance. I'd love to be Marlene Dietrich when Welles walks into the run-down Mexican whorehouse snacking on a candy bar. I don't want to be that kind of whore. I just want to play Marlene Dietrich in a whorehouse in a movie. I like telling men eating candy bars, 'We're closed.'"

"If you're a dominant, you have that concession going. How do you know about film?"

"I go to Berkeley film festivals with Diane. We're partners. You should know."

"Don't worry," I said.

"I've heard that before."

"Not from me."

] *Thirteen*

I PUT THE CALL ON speakerphone. I was coming off the bridge in fast traffic with a clear idea of where I'd be in ten minutes, but the call was from Diane and what she had for me in the first sentences put me on the loop back to Oakland.

"I know him," she said. "He was French. He's the man in the newspaper, the mathematician at Berkeley."

The key here was don't get excited. Watch the road. Eye-witness testimony fails all the scientific tests of evidentiary fact-finding. Scientific detachment. Pushing on that door helped me relax.

"Are you sure he was the man? Is there a possibility the man you saw only looks like him?"

"He was with a red-headed woman. They were at the end of the hall. He was coming back from the ice machine. My door was open. I was playing telephone chess with Joshua. Joshua was in the office. This French fellow saw the board and he came in the room and said it was mate in four. He told me to take the pawn on f6 with my knight. I'd never seen him before."

"You talked to him?"

"I gave the phone to him. Joshua wanted to talk to him. That's when he got into French. I don't know French. They didn't care. They didn't ask."

"You had a good look at him?" I centered us.

"Joshua came around. It was polite for a few minutes, but not real polite, just decently behaved. Then this man went down to his room. He came back with a twenty and put it on his ice bucket. Joshua told him in English to knock himself out, and the guy took the pawn. Then they argued for a while about the money. The French guy kept waving it away."

"What happened to it?"

"Joshua ignored the knight. He left it there. He moved the rook pawn on the other side of the board to a4. The French guy reached for the knight and actually touched it. Then he jerked his hand back like the knight was red hot and he'd burned his hand."

I didn't say anything. I was approaching the 580. I was silent. It was still her call.

"He was stunned like a stone and all he could do was have this stare, putting a hole in the board—you can't describe it. His whole brain went into the chess pieces like a crazy person staring at the moon. Joshua wanted to give him a pass. After a minute or two minutes, I don't know, Joshua tried to get his attention in English. He offered the money back, but that didn't do it. We waited some more and Joshua told him to get out."

Then I remembered Brett. "Where was Brett?" I asked.

"Not here. This French guy left. He left the money on the ice bucket. I picked it up. What was I supposed to do?"

"What time was all this going on?"

"When? I don't know. It was Wednesday. I leave at eight, unless I'm playing Joshua. After eight."

Most of the year MacArthur is a wide, sun-drenched boulevard that you get onto off of 580. It crosses 580 again down past the hospital complex and gets you going all over, including a return to the 580 via the MacArthur Freeway if you got off by mistake. This is easy. The MacArthur Freeway is the 580. A strip of dirt and little bushes and paper cups divides six lanes. There is cheap gas and seven or eight inns on one side. The Starlight was the one right off the side I was on. It was two levels and a lot of evergreens, and not so sun-drenched down here.

"I'm in the parking lot," I said.

"Where?"

"Here."

"I'm at home."

"Oh, sugar. I'm at the Starlight."

"I have to go to class. I don't know much more. I know they had a game in Carmel. They live in Carmel. They set up the stakes at the motel. You can ask Mrs. Townes. She's in the office today."

I left my car at the forward edge of the red paint in the cupola. A family of five was signing in, counting the mother bouncing the baby in her lap and a boy and girl obediently bouncing on a sofa, kicking their feet, waiting for the prison of youth to end. A young couple was in an impatient patience at the counter. They had luggage, an hour's worth and using it up. The guy behind the counter was going over safety regulations in the pool area. In between instructions he answered the phone and got someone to hold the line.

Before I knew it I was up to bat. "I'd like to speak with Mrs. Townes," I said.

It was all I needed. I was surprised, as if someone had called ahead announcing my arrival. He took my name through the door behind the registration area. There was one tick and one tock, and he was back. He lifted the gate at the end of the counter, caught the door, adjusted the air, and left me very curious as to why, finally, the day was working like clockwork.

The room was built out into a garden from the back wall of the motel, windows on three sides, flowers and vines on each side, but each side touched up a bit differently, rounded in high walls plastered smooth in a hotel mustard tone.

Mrs. Townes had invested her waking hours in a chair, from which she sent no signals that she had intentions of getting out of it to greet strangers she hadn't never met, like me, and yet I was getting a better smile than I'd earned. And I wasn't sure myself why I was here. So she wasn't reading my mind. Who knows what makes people happy? Being sixty-five years old or so might have been what the doctor ordered.

A dark brown desk took up half the rug, a ten percent fraction of the room, and provided a platform for Mrs. Townes's right leg. A snapshot of Mrs. Townes from where I stood would frame a three-bowl fountain and a stone ball on a stone pedestal off her left shoulder out in the garden. Water trickling from a lion's mouth was something out there and not in here, in perspective, but in a two-dimensional compression, running just behind Mrs. Townes's right leg.

She put the cover on the ice bucket and blotted a wet spot with a napkin. Wet spots looked like bomb craters. Some were stains, some had etched through layers of mahogany stain. A congregation of them beyond her reach was old. The rims were white, bitten, chewed wood.

A sink, a refrigerator, and two shelves of bottles and glassware and linens and stuff were a short step out of a direct line to the desk from the door. She offered. I passed. Two chairs sat comfortably on the rug. I took the one farthest from her, but most turned to face her. I made it obvious I wasn't looking to bring up anything to do with her foot. It was all dressed up in survival gear with the perfect place to forget it.

"You look like you don't drink," she said. "What's the occasion?"

"I quit," I declared. "I'm celebrating."

She laughed like at a dumb Bob Hope joke.

"If you want to move back onto Satan's true path, the things on the desk here is what I'm having. Anything over there, help yourself. Aren't many reasons professionals drop in on my establishment."

"I didn't drop in," I said.

"I've been bumping into people who've been bumping into you since you arrived in our beautiful city, and now we've bumped into each other. It's all semantics. What can I do to get some self-revelation between us?"

"You have a neighbor over there on Piedmont at the furniture store. I drove all the way over this morning to ask a simple
question."

"And your GPS is broken, and you're here now and gone in
a few minutes."

"Renate Flyte-Simpson," I said.

"Ho, ho, ho, the plot thickens. Renate Flyte-Simpson," she
laughed into her glass. She poured a gulp and cupped it, mouth
open, with her head back. She gargled and swished her teeth.
When her mouth opened she let out the fumes like smoke rings.
She pulled a black-and-white checkered blouse off her chest and
grabbed a good hold and pumped air into the space. She let it
smooth itself down

"Renate Flyte-Simpson," she said in reference to the glass but
with a soft reverence, as if an artistic significance was involved.
She wiggled her foot. She liked to talk.

"Retrospectively," she said. She pointed me at the drinks.

"One night we were talking about the London Interbank
Offered Rate, and then we were talking about her, and then I
had something to do, and the next time we were talking about
her she was like the dead, she wouldn't be anyone I would ever
meet again; and like the dead you hear of breaking an axle in
jungle potholes in faraway lands, her saga unfolded over time.
Something about her was always percolating in our bunch.
Thirty pounds of cash had certainly concentrated our interest.
It was always the same story. You couldn't track many changes in
that story.

"Renate Flyte-Simpson," she said. "Subject A, right here at
this table in the garden of good and evil. Oh, man, did we have
a time." Her eyes darted a second at me on the other side of the
whiskey. You know who you're talking about?"

"The second Renate Flyte-Simpson?" I said. "A good guess?"

"There was no second. There was two firsts, and the second
first was Alix Sociedes. Born under that name, according to the
documents she carried."

She scooped two pieces of ice and got the right tinkle.

"Alix Sociedes. Well. Disappeared off and on, like Mack the Knife. The several sources claiming factually to contribute something of Alix's whereabouts didn't match, and in most particulars no two could be right. There were lines of speculation, a few plausible, as to what one expected to hear of Alix in any act of a dubious nature—they sounded right; nobody would quibble—and one of these started with the morning the old lady was knocked off the sidewalk where Columbus cuts off that triangle of Washington Square. One line came through a consular official in Florence, third-hand at least, mostly a knockoff of *The Roman Spring of Mrs. Stone*, from an Italian kid, Paolo, which kind of held together as gospel, as his subtext was *Venus in Furs*—but not where Paolo was concerned. There was this Austrian and a minor mountain castle in Graz and goings-on Paolo didn't actually witness, but this was Paolo's tale and, as I said, I was never going to see Alix again, and we all have a good time bending an elbow in a foggy diner in the City. Or where were we?

"Continuing: The old lady was on her back motionless the whole time Alix was on the phone, which wasn't that long, a scare anyways, though, registering so suddenly. Alix looked up from a pastry and a car was blocking the intersection. The driver had some fingers to the old woman's neck and phoned emergency, she guessed. Alix never heard sirens. The victim dusted herself off and got underway as far as the corner. She sat down and steadied a hand on the curb and made her own call. It's all Alix watched. She had to get to the travel agency to make arrangements for Ravenna. A colleague, name of Charlotte, from L.A., had proposed a threesome. A man with a name in film wanted their expertise on their terms. He would be the guy in the middle as two women meet in a divorce catharsis and fall in love. What kind of love he wanted was whatever happened with plenty of whips.

"The Ravenna brochure had happy attractions to ply her

with—the harbor on the seaward approach, the drive on the Via Della Fontana, a top-floor suite with a garden a stone's throw at one's pleasure, a marina that takes your breath away. Book an extra day. The eternal present. It's all about you. You don't ever get it back.

"She arrived for dinner in high-heel leather boots, a whip in her bag, the winning number in her eye, and she was late. An interval passed. Another interval, and a beautiful woman had been a party of one for a good hour. An evening in Italy had been embalmed. A national disgrace.

"She called her friend to check where their love was at, which was they were just down the street from each other. They had different numbers, which was nothing, but it was the way her friend pronounced Via Della Fontane that was not what Alix expected—but who speaks this proto-Italo dialect by the book? They were on different streets. The server said it was a different neighborhood. He called a cab. The cab driver knew what he was shaking his head about. The address. Charlotte had something extra wrong. It was definite. There was more wrong than right. Alix knew someone at the hotel to call but would he know better than a cab driver? Maybe it was a neighboring town on the Adriatic Coast? She called again. She asked her friend. Maybe she was closer to Venice? She heard a shrug. She was on the wrong coast. She and the client would leave Ravello when the bottle was empty. They could be together in six hours, make it, say, four A.M.

"There it was, Day One, the beginning, the middle, the end.

"Alix went to bed knowing. She was a bad investment. She owned it. There would be no togetherness in the morning. She had more than kicked a bankroll from under her plans. She had been racking up a base tab of thirteen hundred Euros a day, items now gathering on her account. The nickel-and-dime charges alone would be worth not having to consider. So what, though? She was loaded. She could cover a week, meet expenses as far as expenses. But who was kidding whom? The vanished per diem was a major disruption in self-esteem. What vexed her, lying under a chandelier in the missionary position in the dark, hinged on a principal. A real woman doesn't pay. It was hard to get out of bed, but stewing in one's juices, does this solve problems?

"Solving problems. What was a hotel for? Hotels opened doors. Not all doors. Some doors. Alix needed a job. Paying customers. Quality customers for quality services. Alix calculated. It was three steps from shelling out to raking it in. It was a gamble. An artist gambles.

"Alix felt an urge to see the lights with someone who knew where they were, a guide, a young man the hotel would vouch for unconditionally. Alix put out some seed money. Did she need to explain? The hotel provided a leather binder and a tranquil setting with a drink. Alix went through photographs checking off immediate availability. She nodded at a bronzed, black-haired gorgeous physique. Yes, he knew English. She would have many defining moments strengthening her regional vernacular. She had a glimpse of vivid hours ahead. It all came about perfectly. Even more so.

"When Paolo saw her, he could make no sense of it. His luck had fallen out of prayers he had for too long abandoned. He would absolutely vouchsafe her a visit of joy.

"There had been a short period, just past, when the most admired people in Paolo's life were American women who had hit the Rubicon and foreseen the future. On the other bank there was not much left to sit tight and wait out love on, not on the twelve-step plan—not that these travelers were open and fearless, but open for an arrangement with a companion who could discuss the odd poet. Each encounter had introduced a little bloop of perspective on life's depth and complexity, but the overall picture had remained steady. Paolo met Alix and let their friendship open on assumptions that had repeatedly proven their worth.

"As they strolled the afternoon, she told him about herself. He paid close attention to how much they had in common. How sublime are beachfront discussions. Linkages were invisible glances, adoring touches. The things that had happened to them as children had molded them into the people they were today. Alix was an entertainer. Alix had a business in San Francisco. Paolo had been to San Francisco. He knew the street where her business was located. He knew the Filbert steps, the Lyon Street steps, the mosaic staircase. He knew the steps in Corte Madera. Alix had friends there. It was all so effortless, and bittersweet that soon they must part, a tale of two cultures and something lost and something gained.

"The night arrived. Paolo was letter-perfect.

"A beautiful woman deserves love, but a beautiful woman designs her nights carefully in the broad encampment of her love of literature. They had fun with that, dancing, strolling, nibbling, substantiating in small steps how carefully a single woman sharing her mind might proceed. Paolo knew so much literature it was inevitable that Tennessee Williams would come up. They both adored *Streetcar*. At the foot of his bed was an empty space on a wall. A spark passed through Paolo's ambitions. Space for a Pulitzer. He would enjoy love there under a Pulitzer Prize.

"Unlike Paolo, Alix had never considered a personal Pulitzer. Like Ms. Dubois, Alix didn't have a husband but she wore a wedding ring. Alix had learned what she needed to know. Paolo knew things.

"At their table by the shore, Paolo mentioned an American consular officer in Florence whose position had conversational merits. He had an attractive profile. He could be blackmailed. Or so it seemed to a certain Austrian, Wanda, who had painted herself a pedigree, a countess. Nobody takes these bloodlines into the Holy Roman Empire seriously, but you make a claim and some breeding is expected. Sad to say, Wanda's motive was no literary entanglement—Masoch never arose. Hers was the shopworn flight from reality that attended to the routine commercial practice of pain.

"Alix laughed curiously, and the Wanda topic bounced

around all through winks and innuendo, light and breezy. Alix
was a lovely, voluble companion, readily distracted and readily
lost in complete sentences. Sudden shifts in interest, backtrack-
ings, loops forgotten and recalled were recycled through new
sets of data. Much was left out of focus, but there was always
the larger familiar vision, and Paolo had at his command the
wide range of responses that let Alix know she was never
misunderstood.

"Paolo stacked it all up, all the good will; he could cut it with
a knife. Wanda it was, Wanda it is.

"He talked about Wanda. Wanda was no good at it. It was
the word in Graz and Venice. Everywhere it was the same thing.
Dominance. Wanda had a poor feel for the concept. And not
the remotest feel for discretion. With the American she went
after the small score. She wanted a favor from him. The chip she
didn't wish to play, she said, was the call she might not make to
the American consulate where he worked. Blackmail never had
a chance. German was not the right language, for one thing. And
it was as funny as, 'I was just following orders,' makes the wrong
argument.

"In the laughter somewhere Alix had rolled her eyes, a simple
move Paolo recalled at the mention of a film. The title of a film.
That's what it was. Paolo swore it was the title of a film where
Alix's flame had gone out. She stared seaward in silence as if into
the realm of ideas. Like a think piece that coordinated a coming
to her senses, Alix sat sideways on the chair. She put her chin on
a palm and slid her hand under the table to occupy his attention. She cupped his manhood without the copious flourish, as if
driven by nonchalance in a vacant space, asking herself, 'Where
was I?'

"Recovering her voice, Alix mentioned that the boats seemed
to be decaying. She said this while opening his pants and with
no interest in how Paolo might respond. He remained ready if
needed. He throbbed delicately for her but thought she wanted
to recall something, such as a name of a character in a movie.

Perhaps Brando. She told him she had fucked herself, but in her stare was a threat from an interior in which she had been wrongly accused.

"Paolo ruminated in a guilty conscience that he now understood nothing she said to him. That the whole point of Ravenna, for example, should be a good time at someone else's expense, he had understood as a metaphorical statement. Alix dug herself out of one metaphor and flopped herself into another. Tomorrow noon she was into the hotel for three nights, but was any of this misunderstanding really her fault? Paolo had a nod that showed he had known hard times too. In this way he kept up, but only in the abstract, aware of the passing of time as in a classroom.

"He could now see that Alix had suffered famine young. She hadn't the genetics to come out of a scrap with hardship with the capacity to remain chipper over three or four drinks. She squeezed and said there is a time for everything. She had never done this before. Next time perhaps. God tells you when that is. It was time for brass tacks. Paolo listened. No doubt about it, active passivity was the professional move.

"Alix said good night. She had harvested a name, Joel Moncrief, the American. She had revealed historical-size chunks of herself for a name.

"That was, in essentials, most of version number one. It ended where we all knew what was coming. Paolo made some dough. A consular guy had his opposites reconciled and caught the tab. Alix was living in a castle in Graz."

Mrs. Townes stopped and thought. All talk and no drinking makes a dull Mrs. Townes.

"I mention an Alix sob story as a less credible version: The Mixup in Malta. A booze-cruise farce. It tapped into these screwy sagas of semi-epic vanishings that grew into a knowing laugh because they ended as somebody was coming out of the ever-receding past looking hopelessly for Alix, wanting her with the same puzzled expression. 'How did Alix become Alix?'

"Why do you want her?" She winked.

"She made some quality movies," I said. "She made them quite a while ago with a man who is now dead. The dead man had three of my books."

"I got sympathy. What were the titles?"

"*Speak, Memory; Plutarch's Lives; The Glass Key.*"

"He was buried with them? Dig them up."

"They're on a bookshelf. The house is in litigation."

"This is chicken droppings. Not a quality scam. You want to get to Alix, you show me a quality scam. Just summarizing my story."

"A man was in these movies. He was always on the periphery, a gardener, a street sweeper. I think he was the one who told me a Lady Lava had some operation up here on MacArthur. This involved a murdered man. The homicide gang might have asked you."

"Lady Lava," she said, too slowly with too much space between syllables. I was afraid of another chapter of the Italian saga in the garden of good and evil.

"Another woman was in some of the movies. I thought Alix might know where I could find her."

"This new all-water lunch you're on is good for you. Tell me the truth and I'll tell you the truth. How did you get to me? The homicide bureau didn't."

"Just floated in on a raft thinking about these Wednesdays."

"What about them?"

"You didn't ask me if the black woman was Lady Lava. You knew. So all I have to do is tell you the truth."

"Bring that down to earth and connect it to Wednesday."

"They're not connected. I would be surprised anyway. You just said to tell the truth. And what is that? You have a business in tourist rentals in Carmel, a nice, clean beach community. You get inquiries for space available. People who need special consideration know the password. I don't know how it goes after that, but hunches I can bring to earth. No more electronic connections.

Brett and Diane are part of the loop. They go down Wednesday night, come back Thursday morning. The furniture store is part of the loop. I also think it's part of the misdirection, but I could be making complications where none exist. I think some folks who register here have a password. And so forth. I don't care. It wouldn't fool the Girl Scouts, but the Oakland Secret Service wouldn't get it if you drew them a map."

"There's the Oakland P.D.," she said.

"How do they miss you? You should thank somebody. I think you could start with a higher-up in the city."

"I'd like to thank you, too. Is there a check I need to write?"

"If you're involved in Robert Lavoisier's death, make it out to the D.A.'s reelection fund. If not, there's Lady Lava."

"A lady. Oakland. Motel. Pick a name, make her a visit. And you were never here."

"She and Alix were once tight together?"

"Alix was tight with Renate Flyte-Simpson. She was Renate Flyte-Simpson. She needed a name. One Flyte-Simpson, why not another? Live in history."

"I need an address," I said. I made my interest vague.

"I need a drink for this. You'll need a drink for this."

"Suppose I take a vacation. I walk around the block. You have a drink. I'll come back."

She put her tumbler at eye level. "Here's mud in your eye, and love everywhere else." She asked her tumbler, "What were we talking about?"

"Another way to think of all this new age aesthetics."

"Yes. Medical exams. It was a growing industry. Plenty of medical females around who knew the procedures. Plenty of authenticity. Easy to add whips and stir. The word got out that the exams involved sexual excitement. There's a law against getting your health back that way, so she had to pay medical examiners, and they gave her anther fifteen minutes of fame, plus a client list."

"That's not an address," I said.

"It's a lie, too. You were almost there. You came here first. Smart. It's what I hear. That Elizabeth Cromwell didn't bump her head falling out of her crib."

"I bumped my head on that."

"Furniture store. Where you were going? You forgot. Ask there. Flyte-Simpson owned it. The nurses are moonlighting for somebody new. If it comes up, you never met me. You're just a good guesser, or you're old and it's a reasonably simple guess. That should be enough. Incidentally, what was the guess?"

"Art films, a few very old films. They pass through my library to rooms beyond. Flyte-Simpson had a film enterprise going. She put her name on it. A woman brought me a box of it. Then she disappeared."

"You know, a man who stops by Oakland once in a while, he didn't like you—not in the way you draw out that word like, as if you're tasting it."

As I shut the door behind me, I was sure she was telling me she wished she could like me. And don't come back.

] *Fourteen*

ARRIVING IN THE Berkeley area had always been at an
address beyond the Northbrae Tunnel, where Berkeley was
no longer Shattuck Avenue in my mind's arrangement of the East
Bay. The turns were just a set of reactions to landmarks. I had
come to the tunnel. The path that ran along the high ground to
the side of the tunnel came out on the Circle in North Berkeley.

The rise from here was narrow streets, twisting on ups and
drops, rarely following far along a flat, a lot of shade, one-story
and two-story places, fair size, nothing special in the great scheme
of things in the hills, but a feel of being somewhere that would
take a lot to uproot you voluntarily.

Where Kensington took over from Berkeley the road changed
names. The new name kept on trekking up, passing the edge of a
reservoir, to a large intersection. Across that it was uphill a block
more to where it leveled out at a little crossroads, Calvend Lane.
Crossing Calvend was Saul Road to the left and Old Spring Road
to the right, and it was thinner air.

Calvend was the ridge road above a canyon area. It ran around
a tight, skinny corner where the builders scratched their final
design out of the watershed of the hill. Andrei had the green unit
at the corner where Calvend turned sharply out of sight. The low
side of the road for two hundred feet was anchored on loose-fitted
stone, but solid. The higher side was washed seasonally by rains

but not washed out, just cut into deeper rivulets. Thin white poles defined a border around the turn at the head of a nature trail. Then a down and an up, and over the top of the up was another down and up to the high peaks. There were roads in the wild land. I remembered a Wildcat Road. That went through it somewhere.

I found 3715 Calvend. It was set deeper off the street than the next-door neighbor. It was small and it had a parking space in front bounded in elms and I backed into it. There was a car in the area of the front yard, the part of the land that fronted Calvend. No grass, no landscaping. Plenty of drought. There was a second car in a narrow driveway.

The hot, still air of chaparral hills, manzanita and eternal oak and the smell of nature, was the lure around here, if this lured you. I took a nature trail down and around a clump of boulders. The trail then hacked its way back up the loose earth to Andrei's side yard. There was a thin apron in back. Telephone poles stacked horizontally without gaps was the barrier that kept the backyards where they were. I wiped a layer of dust from a plastic yard chair with a handful of dead grass. The side of the house measured six paces, not trying hard. It wasn't small. It was little. On the front step I had the restive emotions that anticipate a reception finalized in the doorway as an honest mix-up. I heard a chair slide.

———

A TOUCHSCREEN was underneath a plastic shield. From the outside the front door was unlocked by a sequence of symbols. From inside there was an unlatching sound and an old-fashioned doorknob sound, which worked like they do. The door opened. He was in his three-piece outfit, cutoffs and sandals. I was checking my pockets to see if I hadn't dropped anything. I was too busy to be invited in. He said, "Hi." It was my turn. It might go pleasantly until he heard what I had to say.

"You busy?" I said.

He stepped to one side and pointed to my left, a "go that way" finger. I stepped inside. On a wall around the corner of the door were two buttons over two states, "on," and "off." The "on" was lit up in red, the "off" was off. He pointed again and I took two steps into a coordinated entity I'd call "this side of the house."

My mind behaved naturally. It blocked out a living room, dining room, kitchen, but it was all one area and no furniture, I mean no living room furniture, no dining table, no kitchen stools. At the sink lay a hard rubber mat over hardwood flooring. The ceiling sloped up from the front and back to a midpoint. The midpoint was a central wooden beam that carried track lighting and held the roof up. There was a panel on a short strip of wall at my left shoulder and sliding knobs imprinted with numbers, 1 through 6, and six cones angled from the beam that pointed in six directions.

A sliding glass door was half of a glass wall that looked out over a width of a dozen feet of flat irregular purplish stone. Beyond was the rolling canyon of nature scenery.

Andrei left the front door open. We hadn't gone far. He coughed twice. Get that over with.

"I didn't go to the university," I said.

"I would have been somewhere else," he said.

Along the far wall were two desks side by side, two high-backed chairs and a computer screen, a television screen, and a super-structure of many cubby slots assembled in a single joined piece like a mail sorting system. We faced off. I had something to say. I didn't say it at once, so he looked like he thought it was serious and he waited through a shallow breath. It was just a long, silent sigh without the sigh.

"I have something to worry about?" he asked.

"If you lied to the D.A. you do. It's not why I'm here."

"Okay."

"I have to see the D.A."

"Okay."

"Whatever we say in the next few minutes may come up in that talk."

"Why not see the D.A. and then we talk a few minutes?"

"We could. You want it that way?"

"You did it this way. So if we talk about why you did it this way, can you leave the subject of what you would tell the D.A. out of it?"

"You might have forgotten some things when you met with the D.A."

"I might have." He rubbed his chin. He was remembering as if he didn't remember anything to worry about. "It sounds like a pleasant conversation. You want to sit?" He got off a lean on the wall at the end of a bout of spinning a finger in his ear and closed the door. He came back and stood where he had been standing.

"Did you say to sit down?" I asked.

Looking at it from above, the desks were arranged in a large *E*. The lines of the *E* were tables at waist level. The vertical back of the *E* was against the wall. There were two computers on it and two chairs inside the horizontal lines of the *E*. The lines of the *E* stuck back into the room. These were platforms at the height of a normal table. They were tables. A table in the middle between the chairs formed a do-it-yourself amateur contraption of three plywood levels pegged on vertical blue two-by-fours. Two of these were pushed together for a double-length platform. The platforms outside the chairs were similar shelving units, real carpentry, not store-bought in look from where I was, but stained and fitted on invisible pegging. On top were sloped book rests and raised stops at the foot. You could stick three open books on these book rests simultaneously and compare what there was to compare.

Underfoot were colored plastic wires and boxy deals that regulated what went through the wires.

He waited for me to sit, I suppose. I didn't feel like it.

"I don't know if I want to talk about Robert," he said.

"You want me to go?"

"I don't know." He hadn't made a move that indicated he had decided what he wanted. His elbows were next to his ears. His fingers were locked behind his head.

"I was at the service in France," he said. "You think you know a language. We ate together. I had no idea what they were saying. It's a secret language to Americans. High school French gets you around the streets. You don't take the wrong bus. If they want to freeze you out, you're out. The eyes speak. I didn't deserve to clean his shoes. I think there were pointed hints I should get the hell out. Jacqueline was on my side, and publicly showed people I was not the Ugly American in her opinion. She's American, though, so I don't know. She touched my arm when I was leaving. Never did that before."

"Should I be here?" I said.

"Is this a mistake? I don't know. The police came here again. Two detectives. Two women. They wanted to see the premises. I showed them around. They were doing the me-and-the-wife scene again. I was in this room when he died. I hadn't seen him that day. They think I think I pulled a brilliant maneuver meeting Jacqueline, and it was undetectable. They were going to detect it."

He let his arms drop and walked into the kitchen.

"They haven't asked me to take a lie detector test," he said. "Can't figure that, unless they're afraid I'd pass it."

"They're not afraid of me."

"They're getting pressure. There's that failure motif. This sits on their records till they die."

He opened the refrigerator. He put a bottle of water on the counter and held a bottle up, yes or no. I said yes to a glass. He poured like a beer and put the glass on the counter and put his rear to the counter. I got the glass and backed off, facing him.

The kitchen had everything. There was a window to the outside. Light was coming through it. A short yellow wire ran under a bakery box from the stove to a stack of books next to the refrigerator. The bakery box had a cellophane window. To the side were four electronic gadgets and some notebooks. The top notebook was *Open Problems on Noncongruence Subgroups*. I lifted the cover and looked at a loose page in hand script. God only knows. I didn't touch anything else.

"Ice?"

"No."

I went through the loops, looking at everything there was to look at, maintaining a matter-of-fact formality. We kept the distance between us constant. I pecked some water for the taste.

"It's dry up here," I said. "I like your house."

"The one and only castle of Calvend Lane. My realtor said she couldn't sell it to anyone who could afford it. Ever seen a one-bedroom? Follow me."

Like the kitchen, the bedroom faced the canyon, with a glass door flush against the bed. The door could be used as a point of entry, but I didn't think it was. The bathroom facing the street was a larger room.

A washer and dryer were side by side, but weren't really. It was the spatial perspective in an odd color scheme, painted in a pure deep red and an orange that pulled the dryer and washer together. The toilet and sink were in a blue zone.

The garage was boxes and labeled collections. A red hand-push lawnmower stood on a red wagon in a space-saving arrangement atop sheets of packaging of something flat that balanced yard tools horizontally. There was a window high on the side wall, and a chair on pegs next to the window. This was the mate to the chair on a bicycle. Light seeped through the top crack of a door in the back. The knob was visible past cardboard boxes labeled in felt marker: COLLEGE; UNSORTED; P ≠ NP; LEGAL; QUIDDITIES.

That was the house. We went back to where we started. He swung his arm at two chairs, my choice. I took the heavy cast iron battle cruiser in pillows. It was soft and not bad in the back. You couldn't swivel it. And it faced in. The other faced out. I had caught the resolve that brings on the big next insight.

"Shouldn't we face each other?" I asked.

"I would like that," he said. He emphasized the thud with a

groan in the act of pulling the other chair to where we could stick
our legs at each other.

It was still bright at his desk. You didn't need a lamp with
your back to the window. But it would have been difficult from
my place at the farther desk to read a title of a book. We could
see each other fine, but anything facing the other half of the room
was dark. There were empty slots. I found a slot with space and
put my bag in it and poked the car keys in after.

"The way I see it, we'll dick around with the cops forever and
nothing's going to happen," he said. "And I'm going to forever not
know what it was, not ever."

I cupped my glass in my palms. I was drinking too fast or too
slow. I had to slow it down or speed it up. I wished I could do
something, but I didn't like how it sounded in my head. Some
half-wit Florence Nightingale. Like I owned him.

We stuck with another silence. They were becoming longer.
He studied the veins on the back of his hand.

An impulse to leave was rising. He caught the look, but I
don't think he saw past the look to the subject that made the look
what it was. I could say what the look was saying and lose him. I
saw Mavyn and Robert as everybody saw them, just a sociological
phenomenon, two people finding youth and beauty. He had to
find it. He could do the twelve-step program his own way, and
he would, eventually. I didn't want to be in the due diligence in
the middle of it. I stood up with my bag.

"I'm not much of a host," he said. He took me to the door and
we went outside and got tangled in a captive silence.

"I'm going to miss you when you go," he said.

"I'll miss you, too."

"How do we handle this? Do we like each other? Is tragedy
driving us together? Not romantic, is it? Shouldn't it be romantic?
You can't trust it."

"Why not?" I said. "What if passion drove us together and we
suffered a tragedy?"

He grabbed the space in front of his chest. His fingers curled inwards holding nothing. "He met someone who interested him. It could be a man. It could be a woman. It wasn't sex. Somebody was doing mathematics at his level, and they were working together. The police just can't comprehend what that means."

"Could they have met in a hotel?" I asked.

"Why they wanted to keep it secret, who knows? But it was big. It didn't matter where they met. Look at us here. An hour ago I would have said no way, but not impossible. And here we are. We see the explanation, but if someone drives along the street here, they look at us, having taken a piece out of it, then they can only explain it one way.

"Maybe the other person was in love with him?" I said.

"But who is out there at that level?"

"Was Robert good at chess?"

He gestured: so-so. "He didn't have the patience. It's more than brains in chess. I could hold my own with him. He didn't like it. It took up time. He had an aggressive style. He took risks. Speed things up. I knew I could wait him out. He knew I wasn't playing fair. He liked chess puzzles. He didn't like games with people, except he loved tucking his kids into bed. Jacqueline and I would listen to the three of them and laugh our heads off.

"He'd tell the children science theories, like there was something real about a DNA chain. It had a personality and could walk and talk. Then he'd pick at the theories. He made fun of the Big Bang. He'd jump up and yell, 'Bang.' That's how the world began. The kids would jump on their beds and yell, 'Bang.' He'd say their dog in France was a smart dog. The dog saw everything they could see. How the day started and ended. But could the dog imagine that we were on a platform that spun around? That's too crazy for the dog to believe. So even a very, very smart dog, like their dog, thinks the sun goes around us. We can't explain the Big Bang except as an explosion from a little place. Bang! And there's the universe. It's just like Genesis. Maybe updated some. Sophisticated, a lot of math in it. It's the same thing, in the beginning. It's how the stories start. The lesson is, we all have to find something we love to do, unless we want to understand the Big Bang. Physics people are very unlucky. They had a great century. Now it's someone else's turn. Math people are very lucky. But even he was tormented. He told them everyone is tormented, because people want something they can't have and it torments them. Kids want a candy bar as big as the Ritz."

"I wish I had met him," I said. "Strange, I almost did."

"He was hard to know. He and Jacqueline had a bond. She had what she wanted from him. He didn't play around. If you knew him, you'd know. I told the detectives. They looked at me. They've heard it."

"If he was seen in a room with a woman, then what?" I asked.

He knew why I was here. I was here to say something. Now he'd heard it. That was it. "How did you find out?"

"A chess player."

"The big old fact. It confirms what the cops already know. It doesn't matter. You have to tell them your fact."

We walked to my car. I didn't roll the window down. If he killed Robert he was good.

] *Fifteen*

THEIR NAMES WERE Shirley Grey and Nina Herring. They were the detectives at the interview I had had with the ADA earlier in the summer, when I didn't catch the names with any interest. We knew who we were, but during the exchange of names, I made a point to remember not to call Grey Herring, or the other way. They were forty-some, padded physiques, not much room for indulgences, about five feet seven or eight, distant eyes that gave us their full attention.

We were in a room at the U.S. Drug Enforcement Administration, a federal building. This is where they said to meet them. The president of the United States and the attorney general were on the wall. The boss of Drug Enforcement was as unknown to me as the man in the picture slanted not quite my way on the desk. Grey was to my right, her back to a door to another office. Herring was at the side of the desk opposite me. Andrei was next to me in the humorless crossfire. How it came about that he was included in the gathering I didn't ask, but the purpose of having us testify together had an obvious explanation, and the gist of what I suspected unfolded plainly. We all had the same oak chairs with short arms. I knew Andrei was unhappy. He couldn't sit still. He couldn't lean back.

Herring pushed the starter button on the voice recorder and gave the date and time and who was here and where we were.

She did the ready, set, go: "Ms. Cromwell, would you like to give your statement?"

I turned to Andrei. "I didn't know you would be here."

"I'm as surprised as you," he said. "They didn't tell me. Cutting corners, saving a bit of time, I assume. Just standard practice. See what makes anybody blink. I'm not sure what hangs in the balance. They've lost my trust. I'm not sure they care, if I have to sit in government-issue back-breakers like this."

Andrei stood behind his chair, and told Herring, "I can't sit in this."

Herring had the power in any confrontation. This instant she knew what to do with it.

"It's what's provided for all of us, Professor Andreyev. Have a seat, relax, take a deep breath. Smile, if you have one."

"I told you I had something important to tell you. I'm here voluntarily. I can leave voluntarily. If I do, a vital piece of information goes with me."

"Before you go, I would ask that you leave us the name of the killer."

"I told you I don't have it. I said I had a vital piece of information. I didn't know I had it till late last night. If you want me to keep it to myself, I can do that."

Herring, I assume, had the gift of gab. She and Grey agreed it would be that way during interrogations. Grey hadn't registered an interest in us that came with an emotion. This was another day, another dollar. It was a check at the end of the month. Herring did the talking is how she would earn it.

"You don't want the chair? Is that it?"

"That's it. That's not what we agreed to."

"I don't see what to suggest. If you come back and meet on your own without Ms. Cromwell, it will be the same chair. Or you could have her chair. What'll it be?"

"My choice?" he said.

She didn't say yes, but she didn't say no. Andrei sat on the floor with his back to the wall, opposite Grey. He stuck his feet out and crossed his ankles. He put his arms out, hands on the floor, like balance bars.

I got the impression that somehow he had threaded a needle. It elevated our meeting into a different realm. It reset my body clock. Herring waited. It looked like I had the floor.

I asked Herring, "Would you turn the recording off for a minute?"

She pressed the stop button and said politely, "What would you like?"

"I'm giving this statement because it relates to a murder. I have to include names. I asked if you would leave the people I name alone except as they are involved in this murder or in any serious crime. I believe I have your agreement, as best you can keep it. I've cooperated with various departments sufficiently often to come to rely on their word to allow people to earn a living as 'live and let live' describes it. I afford the same consideration to all public officials who seek my services. I see senators from red states who love their privacy. They get it from me."

The statement was too much by a big factor, but I felt better having said it. I nodded. Herring hit the button. I summoned a formal tone.

"Four days ago I spoke with a woman on the phone who recognized a picture of Robert Lavoisier as a man who had played chess with a Mr. Joshua Townes in a room at the Starlight Motel on MacArthur Boulevard."

Nobody stopped me. I went on.

"The woman's name is Diane. The man was unknown to her. She had never seen him before that night, and she hasn't seen him since. He was in a room with a person with red hair, though that may have been her description of maroon hair. Her impression was that the person with red hair was a woman. Joshua Townes is married to the owner of the motel, Mrs. Townes. They live in Carmel. Mr. Townes drops in occasionally at the motel. He is a chess grandmaster. He and Diane play chess. She seems to have become a regular at the San Francisco Chess Club.

"Previously, I had met a woman named Brett in a parking lot off Piedmont. I had met her once before. She was interested in the possibility of coming to work with me at the English Department. While we were filling in her background she mentioned her connection with the Starlight Motel. She knew Diane. Diane had witnessed a titanic case of bad manners. A guest had challenged Joshua Townes on a mating strategy in a game of chess he and Diane were in the middle of. The man with bad manners thought he was a great chess player. He worked himself into a lather in French with Mr. Townes, who speaks an island dialect. When I heard of a French guest with a woman with possibly maroon hair, I just thought, why not ask? I retrieved a photo of Lavoisier from the *Chronicle* and asked Brett to pass it along to Diane. She called me to say it was the man who took on Townes—and lost."

"Diane and Mr. Townes? Could you tell us how to reach them?"

"Yes" I said. "It is murder."

"And if it were not?"

"It all depends. In general, if I'm reasonably sure a crime has been committed, and I don't like the crime, there are departments I can call and let them know what I think I know. If the crime is something I don't want to be involved in, I make a note and let it go unless or until I have to change my mind.

"I saw a man for two sessions some years ago. He passed the interview well enough that I agreed to see him. In the third session he said he wanted us to explore his sexuality in a new fashion. He wanted to tie me up and tickle my feet. That was it. I didn't have to hear more. The instructions on my web page are explicit. The warnings are absolute. There are no deviations, and one of the warnings is don't ask twice for what I don't permit. I don't argue. I told him to leave, and he didn't.

"I pay a man for occurrences of this sort. He watches sessions from next door. I don't have to send a signal. He was outside the room as the man threatened to sue me for malpractice. When I heard that, I was pretty sure I could herd the guy to the street without any serious arguing. He huffed and he puffed, but he went.

"I was left with a strong sense of disparity between what he needed and what he thought he needed to hide of those needs until the right time.

"I gave his name to a cop I work with. If a man tells me he stole a car once, nobody hurt, I wouldn't bother. When I have reason to believe I've evidence of child abuse I report it."

"Spousal abuse?"

"Depends. Men confess to me. If a man says he hits his wife and needs to be punished, I raise the question, why not let her do it, though I know that's not the dynamic. He could be lying. He might not be married. He's living a story in his dreams. Usually I weed these candidates out in an interview. I don't take lawyers anymore."

Herring wanted this recorded for posterity.

"Why not?"

"Nothing is the way they want it. Life is adversarial. I don't whip them hard enough. They're not getting their money's worth. I advertise a false service. I'm a crook, a con, a cheat; they'll take every cent I'll ever earn. They'll see to it I die in a poorhouse. I don't need it."

"How are cops?"

"Women cops are much better than men. But...there are exceptions. Women aren't perfect. If you and Detective Grey were men, I'd find a way to soften that."

"You and Professor Andreyev know each other?"

"We met a couple times. I met him the second time at his house. Not like they meet in the Bible."

"What transpired that is material to the case?"

"After I was sure that Professor Lavoisier had been identified, I had some thoughts that it was Professor Andreyev who met him near his house and drove him around. He also might have picked up escorts for him. I didn't believe he killed Professor Lavoisier but I thought about it. Anything's possible. I needed a minute. He didn't do anything."

"You decided to call us, but why speak to the professor?"

"He has a belief. He put it to me so that I believed he believed it: that Robert wasn't meeting anyone for any purpose other than mathematics. What is equally hard for him to believe is that there is anyone in Oakland capable of even remotely interesting Robert in mathematics. I was caught in the middle of this whammy when I heard from Diane. I wanted to speak to the professor to say that I had to report what I knew, and he ought to know."

"That's not quite cricket."

"If I had to do it again, I would do it again."

"The professor puts us in a tough spot," Herring said. "Almost like nobody killed Robert. It didn't happen."

"What I understand him saying," I said, "is that it will be hard to solve. I do what I can."

"That's all we ask."

"When Professor Andreyev first contacted me he seemed to be thinking on a presumption, that I was a sex worker and that I'd been in close enough contact with Professor Lavoisier that I, or another sex worker I knew, had his laptop. He said that Lavoisier had the laptop with him at all times."

Herring pointed at the wall near the professor. "Why would he intimate that to you, if, as you say, he doesn't think that Professor Lavoisier would be in the company of a sex worker?"

"It's not a question I can answer," I said.

She looked at Andrei. I saw him shrug out of the corner of my eye.

"Would you care to try?"

I hesitated, digging in against their methods. I knew the methods. I knew the antidotes as well. "In the beginning I don't think he knew what he had to be certain of. Sex workers hang around bars. He found out I had called from right outside the bar, asking for Lavoisier. He had my number. He accused me of theft. It seems reasonable to me now. Nobody had the laptop."

"You take his side…against experience?"

"I have a trusting soul."

"Let an old hand help you out. Ladies with maroon hair meet their dates at motels. Usually. How did he get there and get home?"

"She might have had a car."

"Right. And she might have driven him the night of his death," Herring noted.

"That's exactly why I called you."

"You called Professor Andreyev first. Why bring Professor Andreyev into this, then?"

"Many possibilities open up, you know, anything can happen. I wanted to see what he said—and how he said it."

Herring slid her foot and I noticed Herring noticed I noticed. It took her a second to notice for herself. It acted as a prearranged foot noise when she noticed on time. Grey wanted to talk. It was against the rules. Herring stuck to the topic.

"Go on. How did he say it? Is this before you knew about your trusting soul?"

"He could have driven Lavoisier to the motel. He could have driven him any night. Why rely on what he tells me if I don't know him? I wanted to know him better."

"What would that help?"

"I could take his side."

Herring shrugged, like to Andrei, "Hear that? She takes your side."

"There's an explanation," I said.

"I'm asking for it," Herring said.

I didn't have it. I didn't have to say I didn't have it. If I had it I would have given it.

"Her hair wasn't maroon." Andrei's remark went over my right shoulder. I hadn't seen him get up. He was leaning on the wall when he said, "Her hair was magenta. I was coming out of the International House. They were at the corner talking. I didn't watch where they went. I saw her once before. It was magenta that time too."

We were all looking at him, as if we were accusing him of not knowing that it doesn't always have to be maroon, but he hadn't said anything to contradict that or to say anything we would get on our feet and clap our hands for—and he wouldn't have noticed. He was in his head. I'd seen this at his lecture. What was to come had been organized and stacked in units of digestible earfuls. This was zero hour.

He pushed off a shoulder. He went to the opposite wall and bounced off that, a caged lifer.

Herring said, "Why don't you calm down, Professor? That's what the chairs are for."

Andrei stopped at a wall. "This is complicated."

"If I need help, I'll ask you to get excited."

Andrei shoved his fingers in his pockets, indicating noteworthiness. "Yes, fine, but this is how it happened." Andrei squinted at something on the corner of the desk. He swiped the desk with a fingertip and studied the tip of the finger. Then I didn't see him. He was behind me. At the opposite wall, his fingers were back in his pockets.

"They were sitting next to each other in the cafeteria. There was a piece of paper on her table." He looked a long way away and came back. "It's in my car at the university. I brought it from home. When I left the office, I took BART. I forgot it. It's not important. I'll tell you what's on it. You asked me if I knew a woman. You called her Mavyn. You said she had maroon hair. I said I didn't know. Elizabeth just said a minute ago that Diane said that a person she thought was a woman with red hair was in a motel room with Robert."

He moved back to Grey's side of the room. "She didn't kill Robert. The guy she knew killed Robert. I think she's hiding for her safety—or—she's dead."

I thought it was only thoughtful to move my chair to the nearer wall. That removed a place he could bounce off of, and I could eliminate neck strain watching the show. I put my chair against the wall. One thing led to another. He picked his chair up and dropped it next to mine and got up and oriented it my direction, and stood behind it.

He spoke to me.

"I didn't know this when you came over. I didn't see it till last night, and then I didn't know what I was looking at. By this morning I could throw out what was wrong."

He said to Herring, "Robert and Mavyn were next to each other in the university cafeteria. I didn't see them. It has to be this way, though. That's when I called you."

He picked his chair up and looked at me. If he moved his chair, I'd have to move mine. He turned his chair facing Herring and sat in it, leaning forward, his elbows on his knees. He stopped moving and explained something. "I don't know why Robert was in that motel with her, but I'll bet one of two things: either they were waiting for a guy to arrive and he didn't, or he did arrive and she's dead. I think it's the former. I don't think Mavyn met him. He wouldn't let it happen, and it couldn't be an accidental encounter, not in a motel."

For a change he didn't get up. He even stayed still, like the theorem was done. There was no next week. The course had concluded.

Herring had been around the block. She hadn't gotten on a case of this importance without making a lot of good impressions. She had some places on her arm to pick at with a fingernail. In the middle of picking she looked at me for a clue as to what I used as a guide to choose men. I think she was apologizing she had put us in the same room in the same morning. But we did that on our own, too.

"All right," she said, "go back. Who is writing on a piece of paper?"

"Mavyn," he said. "It has to be Mavyn—and somebody else."

"I was thinking you were going to say that. People were writing on a piece of paper. And?"

"I found it in Robert's house in a desk with bills and scraps of things that the police didn't get time to find. When I was collecting the stuff to box up and send to France it wasn't anything to bother with. I noticed this yellow page because he didn't have a yellow pad. He worked on his laptop, or once or twice on single sheets of white printer paper. Across the top is French. It isn't his handwriting; it's a woman's. So I put it in a box. I could decide about that some other time. The French academy wants to honor him in a conference. They're very suspicious that the laptop is missing. They don't comprehend the circumstances of his murder. Sudden death conforms with French news accounts of crime in Oakland, but the poison is hard to fit. Anyway, my priority was to get his mathematics to the academy. There wasn't much without the laptop. That's what's hard to believe. It's missing. They don't believe what I tell them, I can tell you. You talk to them. They'll tell you.

"On the lower half right of the page is mathematics, but it isn't Robert's handwriting, so I thought somebody was showing him something and had to think in math, and they were in a hurry and it was quickly torn off a pad. The corner is missing. Down at the very bottom are some one-word questions. These are Robert's. A shopping list and daily reminders with underlining are on the bottom left. There's some French at the top, a couple paragraphs. These are in the same hand as the one that wrote the shopping list."

"I'd like to look at it," Herring said.

"I can mail it."

"We can drive you to your car. Could you take us there at your convenience, say after we conclude?"

"You wouldn't understand it if you had it in front of you. That's why I'm explaining, so when you do have it, you understand as much as it conveys. It's not the entire answer."

"Why don't you jump to the entire answer?"

"I can tell you what happened." He stood and walked off a few steps and stopped. It was a show, but it was coming at the end of twenty years of practice. It could be the best way he knew how to say anything. He had coordinated motion and thinking in an organized presentation in touch with the dull dreariness of logic. Five is a semi-primitive root of sixteen. I'd like to hear that again.

"It just happened," he said. "Robert was at lunch alone. His table is next to Mavyn's table. She's alone…eating and working at a laptop. She's put this piece of paper where Robert can see it at a glance. She's checked off the things she had to do. She had her car repaired—you can see '11:30 clutch,' and some crossed-out phone numbers are calls to do before lunch and she's done them. That's what the little checks are. After lunch she was going to toss it out.

"What does Robert see? He sees an integer. It's a one. It's the left side of an equation. It's equal to a sum of things on the right. These summands are functions. These functions depend on primes and a variable, *tau*. A greater-than sign indicates all the primes are odd. A squiggle symbol means the function has been transformed into a function in a new variable, *s*. This jumps out at Robert in an instant. These variables are standard notation in analytic prime number theory. The transformed equation is a zeta function. The equation before was a modular object. That's what the *tau* variable indicates.

"Because the sum at the top adds up to one, he wrote 'Partition of Unity,' with a question mark after a 'vs' that didn't mean anything to me.

"What I didn't notice was a vertical arrow after the question mark, so a 'vs' might mean 'vertical symmetry'. That would be new and Robert would see it and take into account the circumstances where he was seeing it. This really was going to puzzle him. He's never seen this woman in the department, but she might be a visitor.

"What he could work out, I don't know. I still don't see anything to this partition of unity. They're all over the place in math. But if Robert thinks this 'vs' is 'vertical symmetry,' he's going to go at it.

"This is what I was looking at last night for the first time. And I saw this, and I saw what happened, maybe. It's how it must have happened. He asks her about this equation. He might ask about the vertical arrow, and how is it related to this equation over here. She doesn't know, and she doesn't care. It's a pick-up line.

But he's French, a lively guy, good looking, well dressed, and he isn't saying things that turn her off. She says something back to him in French, and he starts in on the math in French—like who knew Berkeley has smart people you can actually meet at lunch? And she waves off her genius scribblings, like math is a nothing hobby of hers.

"That's when I started walking around last night making sure this could be right. Can I make it make sense? And I can, because she doesn't have to back this up. Somebody else wrote it. To know who, we'd have to know where the yellow pad was."

He got out of his chair like he was looking for where that was.

Herring interrupted. "Why can't she back it up?"

"Only two people on earth can high-jump eight feet. Are you going to meet one at lunch?"

"You're saying he met a woman who knows someone who can jump eight feet."

"Agreed. That's hard to believe. He could see that she couldn't. What she was seeing I don't know. She gave him the piece of paper. She sees he's very interested. She doesn't need it any longer. He's not trying to pick her up. She sees that. For some reason...I think...there was a mutual reason to get together again. That's what all this French stuff at the top of the page is about. Some mutual interest."

"She knows how she came to have this piece of paper," Herring said. "She and her boyfriend share a pad. They scribble on a pad together. They tear off pages. She needed the phone numbers and tore off the top sheet in a hurry. She knows this French guy wants to meet her boyfriend. You're saying her boyfriend can jump eight feet?"

We all looked at Andrei with the same note of "Can't argue with that."

Herring smiled. Andrei stopped looking like he would get up. He crossed an ankle on a knee. He spoke at his foot.

"I got a worse problem. Why does he kill Robert?"

Herring nodded. "It's what we've been doing for a month,

Professor. It's the same question every day. So far we've ruled out Polk."

"He couldn't be the one anyway."

"You mean beside the fact he was deceased?"

He got up again and squinted at Herring. "But not dead when Robert met Mavyn, assuming Mavyn is the one everyone says has maroon hair. I do. She was the exotic woman living with Polk."

"Wouldn't that mean Polk did this math?" Herring asked.

"Polk might be the boyfriend, but Polk didn't do this vertical symmetry," Andrei said. "I looked him up. He was in applied math at MIT, then Maryland. He works at Livermore. He didn't do this."

Andrei got up and walked around and leaned on the wall next to me.

"Did you find Mavyn?" he asked.

He looked up at the ceiling. "What is that, eight feet? You can jump over that? That's easier than vertical symmetry—if that's what it is. There's someone else. How does this guy know Polk? What do they talk about? Life is not good."

He was stepping on cracks in the floor talking to himself.

Andrei was stuck going around for a third time. "Why does Polk bother? What is he getting?" He hit his fist on his thigh. "What is Mavyn's cut?"

"Mavyn has Polk in bondage," I said. "She throws in Robert, a new trick. But why meet in a motel? And where does Mavyn jot a laundry list on a pad unless it's where she lives? The list is at the bottom of the page. Why leave the space above blank?"

"A phone was on the top half? Or a book? Or the bottom was in easy reach." He held his jaw and spoke. "That might be the proof. The French on top is something between them. It's in her hand. He's saying something, and she's writing it down."

I put my foot out. It authorized me to take a swing. "I was there. This pad wouldn't have been in the den or the living room. I know what those rooms are for. That leaves the kitchen. Who is scribbling math on a pad in the kitchen where Mavyn was living? You don't like Polk. Who then?"

"People scribble in the bathroom," Herring suggested. "Pads move," she added. "Who is scribbling where Mavyn is living if Mavyn doesn't know him?"

"We know Polk knew him and Mavyn didn't…if he killed Robert—and if Mavyn's alive. Why he killed Robert…it doesn't even slightly have a reason. If someone can tell me that, I don't have to walk around for five hours every night."

"Why was Robert in Polk's house?" Herring said.

"Why was I?" I asked.

Andrei seemed to be on his feet for good. He spoke at the floor. "The rest of the math is not in Polk's house, not four months after he died."

Andrei closed his eyes. "I may be way off."

"It's material to the case," Herring agreed, "in my judgment."

I put my chair back. Andrei was mumbling, "This guy can't know the whole thing."

Herring switched off the recorder. "What whole thing?"

"How it all works."

"How what works?"

"These crazy people."

"I'd like to say goodbye," I said. Nobody noticed to wave. I waved.

Herring said, "Why don't we split the difference, Ms. Cromwell? We'll all say goodbye."

] *Sixteen*

ANDREI HAD TAKEN BART and walked to the meeting. We left in my car and met Herring and Grey at the university. The yellow page was in an envelope. Andrei and Herring talked a while. It looked like Andrei was explaining something, but it ended fast. At his place we parked and met in the front yard on a quiet note that had its intricate hints in the looks we didn't give each other.

I accepted that all the hot clues we'd dumped on Herring and Grey had not tackled the essential problem of why Robert never saw it coming. A guy building his nights in the poetic devices of a suck and a fuck is a loser and deserves what he gets. It was all very shopworn. He was a sucker, which is the verdict the piece of paper attached to the pick-up at lunch. Worse, it kept constantly current a topic that made everything that bore life between us hard to access. I wanted to say I liked his little house, less riveting than acknowledging that his friend misplayed a game of chess in a dump.

We stood on the porch, perhaps to set up a touching zone.

"I never dreamed I would like a little house," I said. "A word doesn't do justice. I would imagine the realtor emphasized the immense backyard."

"The color scheme in the bathroom, she floated the insight it wasn't me. Some visitors from Norway chose the colors. I never cared till I watched you look at it."

"You've had a look at my web page," I said.

"I have."

"And?"

"You look so natural with a whip. You don't look like you're acting. The photo gallery of set pieces you've chosen to attract customers is interesting. The person I know of you is not in it. Not that I'm aware of. That's what I worry about. What's going on?"

"The me you see now is trying to attract you," I said.

"It's been working."

"I'm not looking for another customer. You sent me a note. You said you wanted to meet me. What do you need me for?"

"I like you being at my house. It doesn't take much to fill it up. It feels empty, though."

"I think we're afraid to go inside," I said. "Are you thinking the owner of the English Department will take over?"

"I can't see the owner of the English Department in a little house. I don't see what you would want."

"I'd want us to get another house. I'd want to keep this one. The owner of the English Department is sentimental already. It's a risk. I don't want to get too sentimental. So far so good. Men come to me to act out very circumscribed dramas. When they're successful it feels domestic. I've successfully confused the satisfactions with marriage, but I know what's missing. I have to be careful."

"I feel like I'm being interviewed," he said. "I'm boring. You may as well know that now."

"You live in your head," I said. "You've told yourself that's boring. Grey and Herring like you. I might even go further. Grey might even go further under the right circumstances. I don't think you noticed."

"I thought they liked each other," he said.

"You and I don't know what they like. The only thing I can say is that I would be very surprised if I was surprised. If I guessed,

I'd say they'll grow old and retire as they are. They might live together then. They might not. I don't want to grow old as I am now. When I received your note, that's what I was thinking. Let's see where this goes."

"I can think of a next step," he said. We looked in the distance, past the rise and fall and further rise to the hills, and looked everywhere for the next step. This was the time and place for it. He jerked his head to the street, and we took off for the trail. Right off we're alone in the chaparral, silent for a time, but moving against far-off voices somewhere ahead, and we ducked between two high bushes and dragged our feet in dry dirt making a decision. If not now, when? We put our arms around each other and pressed all the space from between us and he let his hands compose a future for our desire overlaid with the romantic instrument of restraint. And he said nothing. And I didn't. When we let go, we held hands briefly, and let go.

"Sex," I said. "There's nothing about it on your web page. It comes up in my business all the time." We were turning into a headwind. He was reluctant to push the topic. I wanted to peel off that layer.

"The discussion will be lopsided," he said. "On your web page you say 'no sex.' But they take their clothes off. You don't see that as sex?"

"There's a definition for what I don't do at my place," I said. "It's one of the ground rules we get into during the interview. No part of my body touches any part of their body. I don't take my clothes off. If they take their clothes off they wear a jock, or the equivalent. It's in case they ejaculate. But I'm not at my place. What's lopsided in your opinion?"

"I feel amateurish talking about it," he said.

"I can tell you how I feel talking about math. We could talk about that. We have time."

"We could look on the Internet," he said. "I can point at what I've done. I heard there were five hundred and some ways to fuck, defined as a penis in a vagina. There are hundreds of variations. I don't think you want to get into a list. I tried anal intercourse. An experiment. I thought I had to try. I don't like it. But I don't want to say what I don't want and find out you like it."

"It's much simpler than that," I said. "You like to fuck?"

"I'd like to fuck you."

"We're more than halfway then. Things are looking good. Before we share our love, we need blood tests. It's essential."

He was eager. "Sure. When?"

"You insist on a blood test with your sexual partners?"

It took him a few seconds. "No."

"You were lucky?"

"I feel good. I used to think that was lucky. I never married. Lucky? Yes and no. I'm not gay."

"That's good news for us," I laughed. You're forty-two, like me. You've never married, like me. What's wrong with us?"

"So far we've preferred to be alone."

"You can ask me anything you want. You're reluctant to push me. I like that. But I want to know you. I think we're going to fall for each other before I do. I met you cleaning up your friend's house. You have a strong sense of responsibility. Do you want children?"

"I'd like to get going. How about you?"

"I need to get going soon. I think it's that simple. I want a good father, a good husband. I've seen a lot of men. I have preferences. You're my favorite by far. I want it to work out. I'm afraid something will go wrong. It's not sex...unless there's something you're afraid to let me know about. Maybe I'll say no. Maybe you can live with no. We won't know unless you ask me."

"I could see a dozen variations of fucking. That gets us through a year."

My eyes went wide. "Once a month?"

"We could do each one twice. We could make it random. Draw balls from an urn, like bingo."

There were more voices now angling off somewhere nearer the mountains. It was the next step to take the trail. We picked up speed in the direction we'd been going. We soon cut off on the short loop back to the house.

"I've had experiences," he said. "In high school a girl challenged me to subdue her. She wanted to be wrestled into submission. It wasn't a gateway activity for us. She was intense and disappointed. I didn't want to go out where she wanted to go out. I was a bore. What there was was worth doing for a few weeks. She found someone else. It gave me some insight into myself."

"You were bored with her?" I said.

"I'm afraid you'll be bored with me. I am boring. It's a fact."

"Think what you want, but I'd like you to get off the boring kick. If I can trust you, you won't bore me," I said.

"I had an affair with a married woman. We were hot." I took his hand a second. He laughed. "I'm not bragging."

"I'm not stopping you. Go ahead and brag. It's what I've been trying to get at, but you won't allow yourself the pleasure of throwing yourself at my feet."

"What does that mean?"

"Surprise me. Tell me something I don't know about you."

"She was older than me by three years," he said.

"When's your birthday?"

"September fourth."

"I'm older than you by one week. I hope that's an attraction."

"Three years wasn't her preference. I liked her very much."

"But you broke up? What didn't go together?"

"Her daughter got in UC San Diego. Her husband had taken a position at Duke. She had no ties to Berkeley. A year after he left she moved with her twins to Oceanside. We sent Christmas cards the first year. I would assume her daughter is in her last year. She was a good musician. I don't know what happened."

"I haven't been horizontal with a man since I was a teenager," I said.

"We do it standing up?"

"I need to talk to a doctor," I said. "She and I have been

lovers. She's married, happily—not so fortunately—in for the two children, grandchildren, till death doeth its thing.

"I have a doctor in the university program," he said. "I picked a name. I've never been in. An appointment will take a while. A blood test takes time to process. Are we in a hurry?"

"Sex is a ways off for us," I said. Then I reconsidered.

"See my doctor. Just say, 'Elizabeth sent me.' She'll ask me. She'll want to look at you. Her office can expedite tests. I'll tell her you're coming."

"Tomorrow?"

"Tomorrow."

He stood in the street while I backed out of the front yard. I stopped and rolled the window down.

"I've never had a peek in a garage," I said. "I liked looking in yours. That may not sound like much to you."

"You can have another. Do you care for another?"

"I'll call you later, tell you how much it means to me. As good as a kiss."

"Am I losing you?" he said. "Is there someone else?"

"In a way," I said. "I want to tell her I like you."

"If you would, tell her I like you."

I dropped out of Kensington and made the turn to the freeway, aware that my brain had gone blank to resist any clear image of the future. But everything had changed—except I had to find a place to park.

] *Seventeen*

IT WASN'T BAD, QUICK, within expectations. I circled
through a four-block loop around Levi Plaza and found a space
on the first go-round. Every time I saw the plaza since the rede-
sign I showed up early waiting for Lieselotta on a new bench,
getting the park experience. She would drop a wink on the path
and I'd fetch it and we'd march as strangers on the way to our
lovers' loft.

It was summer and I could feel the spray of the waterfall on
my neck while following the circulation in the channel. I got off
my feet in view of Coit Tower risen over red brick. I had a deck of
willow overhead and I didn't have to watch my car as it was stolen.

A wiry fellow was in the middle of a pond where they have all
these granite piles. It's where the kids hop around defying calam-
ity. This guy was mid-thirties, long hair, the kind of long lump of
sinew that climbs tall buildings. He had put a box on a stone and
taken out two blue balls and tossed them up and caught them
same-handed, and I watched as I would watch a performance that
unfolded as diversion. But it was art, and the fair part of that art
was the way it was designed to sneak up.

He was looking at me. I looked around for pickpockets, not
really watching him till there was this glowing appreciation when
he had five balls going. I caught Lieselotta's hand as she poked my

shoulder, and we watched the balls caught in a regular rhythm, one by one very quickly. One rhythm would transform into another. He'd grab another ball out of the box and get that ball tossed in the air, and the new bunch would be back up to speed, and you had to be amazed. He had eight going when I was saying to Lieselotta at seven, "This can't go on." Even the kids stopped to watch. A couple with coffee cups were frozen. This was more than glowing appreciation. You wondered if life in the City was on the upswing. He had a go with nine balls briefly, then packed that up and started all over tossing two rings and catching them same-fingered.

Lieselotta was in a white shirt, open collar, a white coat with a physician's insignia on the pocket, black pen, and blue rubber-soled shoes. She was pale, northern stock, a light yellow hair that was fine and fell close to her skull and lay an inch on her shoulders.

She was upper-caste from a secluded enclave in Connecticut. She grew up aware of a struggle keeping her distance, remaining successfully circumspect in college, until mid-twenties she met a man whose family fit her family, and the announcement of the engagement was the last piece of growing up to fall into place. I met her in that period. We had started attending Amnesty International meetings at the same time and zeroed in on each other at the first dinner. We skipped the next dinner for a drive and a private dinner. Her fiancé was commuting from New York to be with her a few nights a month. There was a decision coming, where they would live and when they'd start a family. Our situation had come out of nowhere, unplanned. In the car she asked me to spank her with a strap. She didn't want to wait. She had the strap in her bag. We got in the back seat and managed, and agreed we would do it again. The next time she had it worked out where we would not have to look like prairie dogs poking our heads up all the time. That might have added a zing. Tucked in a curved drive on a private rise, we could strip in haste and take our time getting our clothes back on.

After the wedding she wanted our friendship to go on.
The agreement to settle in San Francisco far from family was a
hard-fought battle. She stood her ground. She wouldn't suck, a
bone of contention that came up in random disputes on anything
at all. She compromised by agreeing he could have it where he
could find it. Seeing me, and all the rest, somehow kept sancti-
fied her sense of self. She admired her ass and loved rooms with
mirrors angled so she could watch it get slapped silly.

She had two kids and had agreed they'd move east when the
oldest started school, and the oldest was now in the eighth grade.
The last battle is coming up. When we meet the circumstances
acknowledge the limits of her situation. Our get-togethers are
brief. We talk about what goes on with the children, and notice
in passing what is fading out between us.

We were partway around the curve of a grassy mound facing Battery, so I didn't have the immersion with the plaza center
that converts to a form of spiritual knowing. It was good enough.
We couldn't be seen by people going in and out of her building—which must have meant something—and nothing. There
were people going here and there, and we stood out in the com-
munal moods we enveloped ourselves in just lounging together
on a bench.

I had asked for her time when fifteen minutes had to be
shuffled hard to make an extra half-hour out of nothing, and
she knew something was up. She looked at me like I was there
to tell her I was dying. It was the goodbye look until I told her I
needed a favor. Then it was the goodbye look. I had found a man.
I wanted a kid. I was reassessing the English Department, which
had to do with the man and maybe not to do with him. I was having a dissociative reaction to life changes. I wasn't me anymore,
yak, yak. But I still needed a favor.

"He'll call tomorrow morning," I said. "He needs a clean bill
of health, say for when I meet him tomorrow night."

She relied on a small range of physician's knowing manners
with me, knowing that I, needy and fear-driven of the final split

between us, would hear her instructions as enlightenment, and ignore them.

"You want me to draw blood?" she said.

"I don't want to die."

"I should get him up and measure him?"

"Let me know what you think."

"What do you think?"

"We're both isolates," I said. "He sticks to himself. His best friend was murdered. The wife went back to France. He sees what his friend had. He wants a wife."

"I got married for a reason. Our families want a dynasty." She had a strong intake of breath. "In our family we do it that way."

"I'm forty-two, and he's forty-two, so you can make something of that," I said. "He was worth waiting for."

She put her upper arm along the top rail of the bench and dropped the side of her head on a palm so she could listen and respond judicially without moving.

"The English Department. You're selling? It's your life."

"I don't want to be alone anymore. We'll still meet."

"Foursomes? We don't do foursomes. We do tribes. Every kid in every grade has a birthday. That's just birthdays of classmates." She caught on. "You want a child."

"This year. Next couple of months."

"I knew this was coming." She looked away as if reminded of an example of how she knew. "I need the thought of you with me," she said.

I thought of the old conversations, and lately the challenge of the older daughter, the schools, the holidays in New South Wales, the in-laws. And now it was two uncoordinated schedules coming up, and down the road it was two families. I'd see her in ten years.

"If you need me," she said. "Anything else?"

"I want you to find a grudge to hold against me. We can share it."

"I hope my marriage survives. How about threesomes? And where do I drop my notes to you if you move? Think about me."

She turned her head and looked around in the vicinity of the juggler. She brushed her sleeves, straightened away from the lean of the bench, and stood on the motion, looking down, not perplexed, not giddy, not in a blithe spirit. She could do a Willy Loman quote, an observation on the poor me of anything, and stay glued tight.

As she went off into the sound of the streets in back of us, I reached for something on the bench, anything to touch, to retrieve, to pick up, to tuck away, to make vivid. I left a message with Andrei to call me. I took the path to the little gateway to Battery. Coming up to the gap in the wall was the juggler, sitting, a foot on the dirt and no box of balls.

] *Eighteen*

I N KHAKI SHORTS AND SHIRT, hiking boots and mud-colored woolen knee socks, he was a caricature of the comic cliché of Teddy Roosevelt: Man Meets African Safari. I smiled out loud where the mind couldn't help itself. I kept ninety percent inside and hoped the rest looked like admiration. I think it was.

He started the smile as I made the turn heading to the middle exit to Battery. I had ten seconds or twenty strides to look him over and pick another exit, or go as the crow flies and shoulder through the encounter—which might not be unpleasant, and might not be quick. He was a looker anytime. He had no right to be mythically handsome, not at this distance, not a man with a pith helmet under an arm, like a football coach on a lion hunt. It wasn't fair. I might have to stop and check my eyesight.

Great-looking did what great-looking knows how to do when introducing itself to a superior officer. He was at attention, motionless, and at the instant my eyes focused on the rest of the day beyond him he snapped off another quarter-inch to a military bearing, the free arm at his side. The man at the wall on the other side of the sidewalk was the juggler. They didn't look like they were together, just two park-dwellers incidentally appreciating a chick, best foot forward, maybe exchange hellos, winner take all.

"Hello, Ms. Cromwell," the incredibly handsome man said softly.

I stopped and looked at the circumstances in the street—were there more of them?—and turned to check on what was moving around behind me. The juggler was propped against the wall, legs crossed. He was making himself look irrelevant, manipulating a deck of cards one-handed, with that silent, coiled, primed pose. He could leap into action faster than I could leap out of it, and I kept an eye cocked on him, enough where I could get off a scream. The strangeness in San Francisco that is called "only in San Francisco," changes every ten years, gradually, until you see the new era. They mark it off, the change year. When this pair's era is gone, you've seen the golden age, uniquely a quality not being a quantity. Afterwards, the men aren't as good-looking as they were.

"Harold Hall, pleased to meet you." His head nodded right. "Martin Cartwright, over there, good man, the best, the one in a million, my chief of detectives."

The juggler was within hearing of a normal voice in the street. He got to his feet suddenly, as if he heard voices, but nobody was there. He went to a sedan double-parked just beyond the crosswalk. He took something out of the back end. The closer it got the more I recognized what Hall just might think he was here to talk about. Hall opened a box. Inside was a statue of a figure. It kicked points of light off its surface as he turned it. It was about eight inches tall. It would fit in a big hollow book. Hall said my name. He tapped the base. It was my name. I could have a look if I didn't believe him.

The statue was the duplicate of the statue I'd handled in Polk's house.

"All the while I was wondering what you were up to," I said. "And all the while you're as confused as I am."

"You're in the clear, Ms. Cromwell."

"I've been dying to hear that."

"In our end is our beginning: total confusion. Who dug holes

at the four corners of my estate and buried a statue of a woman
in each of them with your name on the base? Three more statues
are in my car. The state of the soil says this happened at least eight
years ago. But for erosion at the northeast corner, who would
have looked? How many times have we asked ourselves, 'Why not
ask Elizabeth why she put them there?' And that many times we
answered, 'We should be able to work this out.' Mr. Cartwright
is lost. Name anyone. They are lost. Ms. Cook is lost. The statue
in the book in Polk's house was our big break, we thought. Now
we'll know, we thought. This is a murder case. The full investi-
gative weight of Oakland is on the job, and once two loose ends
connect, the whole ball of yarn goes together. It solves itself. But
you found the statue and you went to the cops. And what else do
you have up your sleeve?

"Well, Ms. Cromwell, you see a broken man. I have no idea
why you gave Ms. Cook a video of a gang of moviemakers prowl-
ing around on my estate. It's an old movie. Fifteen years old. Did
they do it? Thank Mr. Cartwright for the kind word. He says you
have not one shred of connection with these statues, and what I
mean by that is I am wrong, and have been wrong, about you, and
I have nowhere to turn. I've tried money. I sent you a check for
ten thousand dollars. I'd like to encourage you to cash my check.
You're in the clear."

Cartwright had found his way back to a lean against a wall,
uncrossed his legs, and got a coin shifting through his fingers. The
coin actually was shifting itself, along the tops of the knuckles,
then underneath, then on top. Cartwright didn't dress as a chief
of detectives, but he might have been the chauffeur and gopher
and had talent and had time and initiative to develop this coin
thing, at which he was very good. As a reward, perhaps he got to
pick his own title. He looked happy, and the life without cares
suited him.

"You've seen him, Ms. Cromwell, many times. He's been following you for several months. You wouldn't know it. I am not
going to do so, but if I asked you where you saw him last, if you

wished to say anything to me, you would say you hadn't. That would be your opinion. He does a Cate Blanchett you wouldn't believe, but you wouldn't see that either."

Cartwright spoke to his coin, "Looked right through me." But the voice was Cate Blanchett in *Blue Jasmine*.

"Anyway, that's completely incidental. You don't know it and don't believe it, but Mr. Cartwright has in fact been very close to you. The two of you were having tea at the Golden Blossom teahouse in Montclair the night you met Mr. Lavoisier. That was a very tricky maneuver on his end, I've been told."

Mr. Cartwright said, "Very tricky."

"That was the last time that Mr. Cartwright saw Ada Tomek. Did you know she was following you? No? She was following you that night. She had been following you that morning when you cased the Polk house. She had her suspicions about something. We think she thought Mr. Polk had put a big pile of cash in the woods somewhere. Mr. Cartwright didn't know it then, but that's what we think now, and we think she suspected you knew where it was. The next day she's gone. And it wasn't you. You're in the clear.

"Tomek had parked on the cul-de-sac where you parked. She followed you over the bridge, and presumably through the alley. Mr. Cartwright figured he knew where you were headed and got his crate down and around and up on Elm, where he was sure to see you would come out of the alley, and that's what he saw. Then you screwed it all up."

"She sure did," Cartwright riffed.

"As I understand, you went into the bushes."

Cartwright said how he experienced my disappearance: "That threw me a monkey wrench."

"He had to decide in a hurry whether or not he had to act in a hurry. If you're in the bushes, where are you going, and will you come out a mile away? Up in the hills is anyone's guess. Then Ada came out of the alley a minute late, and she was a dollar short. She had no idea. So she sat on the grass at the top of Elm. She figured she had all routes covered. If you were returning with a sack of money she could intercept you before you got to the alley. If you were returning empty-handed, she can think about it.

"Summarizing: You're in the clear in the matter of the disappearance of Ada Tomek. The ADA is convinced. If she hadn't been, I would, in all candor, have had a dilemma in the dark night of the soul. I would, understanding most aspects of behavior, settle it in your favor. I would have asked that Mr. Cartwright testify on your side. And I would emphasize your innocence in the unlikely end of Professor Lavoisier. To suspect you is absurd."

I pointed at Cartwright. "He followed me?" I didn't care. "How do you know I met Lavoisier?"

"It's in the police report. You said so."

"Not to you."

"I didn't say you did."

Cartwright said, "Very strange night."

Hall tapped his pith helmet.

"When Lavoisier came out on Elm Street, who met him? Mr. Cartwright had stationed himself on Polk's street. He didn't see Lavoisier, and didn't know of his existence. Ada must have seen him and perhaps ignored him, perhaps because he would appear out of nowhere and might be assumed to have come from the party at the clubhouse at the corner. If he came from an unexpected direction, unconnected in her mind with Polk's house, would she notice the car he got into? Cartwright says a trained detective would. But Ada isn't here to back that up.

"No reason guessing, but who can help it? We all guess. It's the first step in the inquisitive method.

"Jumping to the last step, who killed him? Who met him on Elm? And how did Ada decide to go to Polk's house as you were coming out the back way and disappearing down the alley? She missed you altogether and left poor Cartwright with the haunting thought that he would never know what happened to her. He had to get to the intersection that you had to pass. The optics from there on are strange, but the thing to see had been on Elm."

Cartwright agreed, "Strange optics."

"From his mouth to God's ear. Is the course of history hard-wired? We think not, and then we ponder if we are not off the subject. And if we return to the subject, I would encourage us to relax."

"Sure. Encourage me."

"We have a table waiting at the diner—at the end of the street."

"I like it here," I said. "How did you know I was here?"

"It's what Mr. Cartwright cashes my checks for. We could go into that, but it's a non-starter if we're not having Irish tea. I'm afraid I'd lose your interest. The point is, you didn't put the statues on my property."

I stepped a step back to the edge of the brick walk. A man pushed a baby carriage ahead of a woman holding the hand of a boy. They were a young family. It was a nice place to take kids. Too bad they missed the juggler.

"How about a deal, Mr. Hall? Would it be possible to have some time alone with Mr. Cartwright? In return, I endorse your check to him."

Hall looked like he wanted to put his pith helmet on a finger and spin it, but there was an intermediate bother.

"Anything you say won't be confidential. Why not now?"

"I didn't get to tell him how good a juggler he is. He might blush."

Hall lit up a smile, like that was sure witty. He put his helmet on and adjusted the chinstrap, not caring a whit what continent he might look good on, and he did look good, if you could see through the goofy. That and money ought to get him more laughs than he was getting from the Battle of Kursk.

"I'll take the car," he said to Cartwright. He walked over to the car and got in and drove off all by himself.

Cartwright was playing fingers with a dime now. He was curious about something.

"You going to marry that Berkeley guy?" he asked.

"Not after meeting Hall," I said. "He's single, right?"

"No time for a mate till now, but he likes you. You could put in an application. I could make sure it gets to Kirsten's desk. Top priority. You want to hear your duties? You'd start easy. You'd be in charge of Soviet artillery to begin with. Then the northern counterattack. He doesn't need a pretty face around the house. You might enjoy what goes into your private account."

"I'd love to talk about it," I said. "You want to stay here, you want to drive around? What would be comfortable?"

"Ten thousand dollars goes a long way with me. You're the boss."

"Let's go," I said. I was quiet. See what happened.

"You didn't catch on," he said at the corner. "That's excellent in my business. Two months. You've looked at me four dozen times."

"You dress as women?"

"Mostly. Women don't follow people. And people don't interest you unless they're following you. I carry a quick-change bag, complexion enhancers, a new look often when I'm tailing close. I hired people for work breaks. Find out your patterns. You have an integrated neighborhood alert. If your lookouts don't understand what they're seeing, they don't see it. I found out your patterns."

The light changed.

"How did you find out about what I said to the D.A.? Pretend I'm naïve."

"If you weren't naïve, what would you think? That's how it gets done."

"What's going on in the ADA's mind?"

"You enter a house in secret and the poor professor leaves that house with a one-way ticket to the grave. They look into the extent of your contact with Lavoisier: nothing to report there. The one thing that kills their case? You weren't in the bar. You didn't drive him to the bar. They can't track your phone to the location of his car. In fact, you were having tea in Montclair. The server fingered you. You got the looks that create easy recall.

Where was Lavoisier before he died? They have more than your word for it. That's it."

"These statues. What do you think?"

"If you can't tell us, all I can think of is it's an art project, like that fence that guy put up. The amazing thing is he raised money, donations, hundreds of thousands of dollars, to string a useless spool of wire and cheap burlap twenty-five miles. You hear about it, a movie about a can of soup. A can of Campbell's soup. You want to be remembered that way? He had an obsession. Why four statues? We went over this with a fine-tooth comb. And still a mystery."

He pointed left. We went left.

"I'm Leon. Leon Cartwright. It's a stage name. Cook saw my act. Hall asked me to find his mother. She had a life-size bronze statue of a horsewoman set up on the mesa overlooking the house. More than a couple of bucks in that piece of bronze. She left the bill with the husband, Hall's father. He took off. Left the kid with servants and the horsewoman on the mesa. You're invited. You can see it if you want. Historical groups drop by. Mr. Hall put in a shaded parking area for visitors. Call Cook and make a date. She'll cater you a lunch up there you won't forget this lifetime."

"You're saying you wondered about me for months?"

"Not our preference. What else was there but to finally send you a check and see what you did?"

"I thought Hall wanted something I could provide."

"He understands the uses of money, and when it doesn't work his way, he quits."

"Did you find his mother?"

"Yup. A recluse in a trailer. Hall could have inherited a lot less oddness than his caretakers thought he would grow up with. He took off one day out his window at the age of nine, and ran a marathon, Thermopylae to Athens. Came in the back door and said he was falling dead. Leave him alone. It wasn't much more than a half a marathon even, but he was nine years old. I shouldn't give you ideas you can set your cap for Hall. You're not Hall's style. But you're somebody's style and you need to be careful. Two people are dead. Tomek is dead. That Campbell's soup guy, his girlfriend shot him. They're artists. You don't know what they're capable of."

"The police couldn't find Ada?"

"It's suspicious. Groceries in the refrigerator. Suitcase in the closet. She didn't say anything to anyone. Then she's gone. Her car is gone. She stumbled into something that didn't mean anything to her. You better know when you meet this guy."

We had gone a figure eight and didn't want to go another. I remembered I owed him. I could get Hall's check to him by mail, or we could drop by the office. I could drop him somewhere. He said goodbye. He was looking at a nickel crawling over the back of his hand. It sure didn't look like a trick nickel. Had a life of its own.

I thought of something else, and I thought I would never hear from Cartwright again and he was the one to ask.

"Why do you think there was a fifth statue?" I said.

"There might be more. You crawled through Polk's window. Where did you get the guts?"

"I didn't think of it that way."

"Cate Blanchett," he said. "I'm looking for a wife. I made her an offer. That took guts."

"She could watch you climb the Chrysler building. That would take guts."

"Wrong building, but it's the idea that counts, onward and upward."

"What do you think about the killer?"

He nodded thoughts along silently. He caught one and waved it away and pulled a new one in front of his face like he was washing a window. Loops shining the air. He pointed an index finger at the midpoint.

"I twiddle coins in my fingers and toes. I just missed not caring if I was a killer. I think I'd know him if I looked in his face, and he'd know I knew him. He can't pull a trigger. He's got an anger that can't be fixed killing people. Killing is an unavoidable incidental. He's not a serial outburst type on the road. That career missed him. He's playing with a blank life. He turns up a card and somebody dies. He was friends with Polk. I can't see around that curve. What moved his levers? The detectives on the case won't catch him. He's in a dream they won't get in even if he opened the door and put a mat out. It can be a mountain he has to climb, the north face of a mountain, the north face in January, a life-and-death dream. It doesn't matter too much if the dream is within reach or not, he keeps fixing it so that it recedes at least as fast as he needs it to. So there he is, inside view. That banish world ignorance?"

"How are you in the know?"

"The police loop? You playing naïve again? With Hall in my corner?"

"Cate said no?"

"Since we're using non-sequiturs, she didn't formalize the no. Now I'm asking you for your woman expertise. Do I try again?"

"Send her a movie of you as you were earlier, with that nickel. It's as good as a dime. Did I already say that? It'll work."

He opened the door, put his hand out. I shook and said it had been a pleasure.

"Not a lot of time left," he said through the window. "Call him up, tell your guy yes. I wish you well. I'm fifty-two. If you live, you will be too. I'm a bit surprised you're having troubles. Me too, if it comforts."

] *Nineteen*

I WAS INCHING ALONG the curve of the international terminal, making progress but not too much of it. I didn't want to get waved off and have to go all the way around again, and I had three minutes grace rolling invisibly in a low profile till Andrei came out of the revolving door or I would have to. Then he called to say he was looking at me. We were good. He was back from Paris.

He put his bag in the back seat and got in and had his hands on his knees communicating. It was nice riding next to me. I put my hand on his hand. I thought he was worth picking up.

We had the exuberance of going to where things would happen, but not the exuberance we could do no wrong. The boy–girl stuff carried for us the X-factor, the something that could happen, and the whole frigging business was beyond us, one of those things that couldn't be worked out, and then it just isn't. That was ahead of us too, and that had its slow caress.

He had moved the two cars into the drive, a hand's width between them. The dented fender sedan was Robert's. Andrei might not sell it. I got the place in the front yard. He dumped a backpack and a carry bag right inside the door and took my clothes off in a glance. The "I'm ready, are you ready?" was on the prowl between us. The appointment at Lieselotta's office was tomorrow morning, and we'd get the results in the afternoon. We had a pretty intense preexisting condition. A French kiss wanted to jump the schedule.

We'd ruled out the obvious theoretically, so whatever was left over was what was going to happen. We'd passed a Target on the way here, and that would have been a come-together activity. We could go back and shop for a second lawn chair. That would get some hot gears going sideways. I'd decided on discipline. All he needed was direction. I organized a posture that would alter the course of passion.

I had the routine in my hip pocket. Stillness. The strict stare. Get that going. Somebody's late and something ought to be done about it. He was getting a thorough going-over with it. If he kept perfectly still, it would come to him what it was.

"Well," I said. "How are we going to handle this hello that's hanging in the air?" A hand went on a hip while I tried out a deeply seriously stimulating dose of exercising an interest at his crotch. Technically timed oscillations can do the job of real rubs.

"Well?" I repeated. "Am I witnessing abstract detachment? Am I indicating I'm satisfied with let's talk it over, let's do this eventually? When might you decide I'm due a yes or a no?"

"I'm on the verge of dark sexuality?" He'd caught on.

"Taking all the factors into account, you're in a red zone," I said. "A decision is yours."

"Do we discuss rules of the road?"

"Would you like a booklet? You can look it over for a few hours."

"It's right now?" It took another two seconds. His smile included the evasive eye thing, wheels within wheels, but "Yes."

Just checking. "You're sure?"

"I'm sure."

"Too much emotional dust has been neglected. You agree?"

"I agree."

"We can do it right here," I said. I pointed at the floor in front of me and wiggled my finger to let him see where "right here" was. All the forces came into play now, or there were two directions and the two of us in two chairs with stiff shoulders. He stood where I was pointing.

"I like the response," I said. "I want us to think out loud, no crossed wires. I feel comfortable. How do you feel?"

"I feel comfortable."

"We have ourselves all to ourselves to do with as we please," I said. "We're on our way?"

I smiled. He had a smile, too. He might be thinking that's the attitude on which the scenario will pivot.

"I want to hear it," I said.

"We're on our way," he said.

"Would you like to shut the door? I don't want the neighbors to hear a laugh and listen for what caused it."

The front wall was bookshelves, five in a row, and a top shelf two feet over my head. Clothing was up there along the tops, and sacks. The middle structures obliterated the front window. The empty section of wall left over where the desks left off had some pictures of men in suits from olden days, some with beards, one bald guy without. Some photos were hung in frames, some were Scotch-taped. There were two ancient guys. One had an over-the-shoulder toga, one had a bare chest and a waist-high toga.

"These aren't relatives, I wouldn't think? Inspiration?"

"In school they were." A light illuminated the area of the photographs. "When I was a kid, Archimedes was someone I could almost go and visit someday when I grew up and had some money. I could ask him questions. The books said he was dead, so I knew the books were all there was."

"You have any pictures of family?"

"In a drawer in the bedroom. In a box."

I put a finger up indicating a place high on the wall beyond my right shoulder. "Who's in the big picture on top?"

"Riemann. Robert and I used to sit here in the evening and think he was getting to be the greatest of them all."

"I have a problem," I said. "I'd like the smaller chair over here, backwards. You'll go over that way."

"What if I want you?"

"I'm going out for a minute. You'll have me in a minute."

The bushes along a footpath that bordered the yard had what I wanted. I unscrewed a couple firm, not overly lengthy candidates for the screen test. I wandered around, the delay stirring a nurturing silence inside, all for the best of intentions. He might almost break, almost come to his senses and almost want to talk about it. I wanted him thinking himself to the edge.

When I slid the door shut his imagination was not his ally. I let a switch push its way onto the desk. I made a semi-circle of the other. I cut the air twice, let the air recover, and cut it again.

He relaxed his shoulders. His arms dropped. He rolled his eyes. Everything all of a sudden was—when. He got one hand on a button, and I said to wait.

"I like to watch clothes come off of good-looking bodies… slowly." I picked a point to point at. "Unbutton!"

The jeans fluctuated to his knees.

"Just kick them over there," I said. "Dump your shirt and let's talk."

I bounced the tip of the switch on his cock. "A mind of its own, I see."

He'd come to a head where I tapped. "You're punching a hole in those tight blue shorts," I said. "What do you think? On or off? I'd say off, but this is our first time. At this juncture, no further instructions. You're on your own."

One fell swoop and it was done. I cut some of the aristocratic steps, the hand kissing and the expressions of everlasting fealty. We hadn't practiced. "I want you to relax," I said. "This will be gentle. You can even have a dose of encouragement between strokes if you need it. I want you to make noises. I want to know where you are."

"What does that mean?" he groaned.

"It means you show me we're fine. And don't think about it. Do your best. Six strokes. You won't have to count. I'll count for you. I'll want the chair over here."

It took a minute to get the angles set mentally. I walked around feeling the freedom of a three-dimensional vantage. I had enough vantages to select approaches from various directions.

"Over," I said. "Knees straight."

I did a swishing hand motion at the top of the thigh, like I was dusting leaves. I was cluttering up the scene with diversions. I quit those at 3:15.

3:15:14 "Don't hold it in. Let me hear a yelp next time."
3:15:37 "Indulge me. Wiggle a bit. I like a wiggle."
3:16:14 "How are we doing? Good? I'm impressed."

I changed switches.

3:18:04 "You're doing great."
3:18:26 "One more. Let's get serious. Shall we?"
3:18:57 "Wow. Where have you been all my life?"

I ran my fingernail up and across a cheek. "This is the time when I say 'one for the road.' but we'll do that another time. Stand up. Face me."

He jumped out of his arch. "Strange," he said. "I had a doubt between two and three, but now I want to tell you I love you."

"I hope you don't let the feeling pass." I tapped his cock. "Tomorrow you get some relief."

"If I can inhabit the soft, sweet enclosure of your body."

"You might get dressed for lunch. It's not splitting hairs if you have neighbors."

We drove to town and made a list of supplies on the drive. We threw out shelves of dated items from the refrigerator and refilled the shelves, moving things in a back and forth, sack to sack, hand to hand, elusively, consciously, making more togetherness. I cleaned off counter space and set up fixings for sandwiches, and when I noticed he was gone, then there he was showered and changed. He had shaved. It was a new face all for me.

We set up a blanket in the yard with dictionaries on the corners. A box of books with a pillow is as good as a backrest. There was a plate of rye and wheat, sliced and toasted, bowls of gourmet prepared mixtures, and bags of exotic vegetables chipped and fried. We constructed sandwiches in the manner of late empire, cultivated Californians cross-legged.

It was sandwich time, and do-it-yourself sounds of fingerfuls of dip on chips between slurps.

Andrei spoke from a pleasing posture in another time. "My dream gift for a birthday was a smoothie machine. It's where I learned the value of a dollar. My father gave me a dollar. 'Go get a smoothie machine.' I had knowledge of how to get another dollar. I said I was using the dollar to take the bus to the museum to appreciate Klee. He was a Russian, I informed them. This was the right kind of culture they approved of. They usually fell for it. I got a smoothie."

"You were a good fundraiser."

"For a year it was where it got spent. When you're eight years old, a day without a smoothie is a tough day. In college I realized Klee was not a Russian."

He had changed to a light blue shirt with a pocket, tight on his frame, untucked in sections from jeans, sandals, no socks. It wasn't just a summer uniform. He wore a shirt with buttons when he went to France. Would I ever see him in a coat? He laced his fingers under his head. His black hair had short shoots of gray, but his face had a lot of child's consternation that the world had things yet to be unwrapped.

He slipped into the square root of minus one, and how in the beginnings there were just a few people who cared. Their ambitions weren't small, but they couldn't imagine how the subject would grow—eventually. I wasn't sure this is how I wanted to grow the conversation.

"There seems to be an afterglow," I said. I started my hand at the knee and went up inside the thigh. "Do I have that right?"

"I liked it," he said. "I wouldn't with anyone else. I guess they all tell you that."

"This time is a keeper," I said.

"There were so many little things."

"Like what?" I asked.

"Like sitting at a table with somebody who has this incredible expertise. She gives off expertise from how she is, but I don't know what it is. We talk about the weather. Then I go away, but somewhere I realize I've never heard about a barometric high that way." He rotated his head. "I want to hear it again."

"There's the advanced courses," I said. "No reason letting those cats out of the bag just yet."

"Can I ask a personal question?" he said.

"I've been waiting." I tipped over on my side. I put a hand on his arm.

"So." He said.

"Yes?"

"I've been processing what happened in terms of my life's analysis that I'm boring. I'm not going to ask if I was boring. That's as far as I got."

"The spirit moves in strange patterns."

He rolled on his side, darn close. "What should I take that to mean? Anything I want?"

I could wait for what might further be needed in some conversation someday. I got up. He followed, not quite sure what it all meant. I took two corners of the blanket. We shook out the blanket and bussed the area and washed and dried the good silverware. It was ever so slightly cooler when we dumped paper plates in the outdoor bin. In the last of the twilight we went back to what was begun and what could be cut off and begun again somewhen.

We cleaned the sink, put away leftovers and took standing positions against the counters. He spoke of Robert for the first time as a friend with feelings and weaknesses, a man past caring what anyone had once or would ever say about his qualities—a man of great talents, and a man now with fixed qualities.

"I was working here when his wife called to say he was dead and could I come over. Everyone is suspicious. The manner of his death doesn't go down at all right. That somebody is lying is taken as official. Murder. It's crazy, in the way the French have of saying it. Nobody could talk at meals. It was like the food had gone bad. The wine was vinegar. You wipe your chin with your shirt. A very sickening taste."

"They don't blame you," I said. "Not the ones who know you."

"Two of his sisters went to the authorities. The French embassy has their own investigation. I'm sad losing his family, losing their company. They don't want to see me. The sadness is all we share. They don't know why Robert gave me so much."

He placed his hands on his knees as he had in the car, and stood, pressing up on his arms. "They found out he was seen in a motel on MacArthur. The fact overwhelms them. Maybe he did meet someone. There's always a question. He was in a room with a redhead."

"I want to ask you if you'll do something for me," I said. "I always want to know you're safe—all the time. Hiding danger is not protecting me."

I put my palm on his and we had a deal.

I got a case of mineral water from the trunk and poked at an old loaf of nut bread and didn't get a bounce out of it and shut the trunk. It was warm still on the edge of the sage, and no wind when I locked up. The sun had gone over the hill, but there was light seeping from around the bookshelf in the front window, and that got me sitting on a pillow waiting to get the points of the stars around back. I already knew my way around in the night.

I'd left the sliding door open. I put the water on the counter and poured a glass, and surmised he would always have a thing to do. His hands were over a keyboard that was propped vertically on a backstand and propped underneath by a board. It put his hands up high at shoulder level and his face looking up intently. The screen was moving according to something going on in his instructions, or it was on its own. I knocked on the refrigerator. He looked over his shoulder at the right person knocking on his refrigerator at 11:13.

"You look like you need to finish a sentence. Could I use the shower?" I asked.

He stood up and reset the elastic at his waist. Fresh white shorts. Very fresh.

"You could finish a sentence for me," he said. "Let's see. How about: Whenever I walk in on a man in his shorts lusting for my body, I respond by asking him (a) where's the whip I left on the desk? (b) why isn't he in bed warming it up? (c) does he know how to wash a woman's back and not take advantage of her charms?"

I liked it that there would always be a place for me to sit while I was thinking. I sat in the swivel chair. It went back and forth a few times.

"How about washing my back, and I'll watch out for my charms. Oh, and, hello. You have an appointment tomorrow morning. The doctor is expecting you by noon. It's a walk-in."

"What are you thinking about right now?"

"I can see what you're thinking," I said.

"It's been a long time."

"Tomorrow and tomorrow and tomorrow," I said.

"Before we turn on the water?"

"Soap and water. It's slippery. It's a volatile mix."

"We'd be treading on very thin ice. Are we sleeping together?"

I raised two eyebrows and puckered my lips. "I could tie you down."

"I would get out."

"You want to try?"

He rotated his battle cruiser to face me, propped his chin forward on some knuckles and put fingers in his hair and scratched.

"What if we behave tonight and we get zapped by a neutralizing ray tomorrow and never do anything again?"

"That's not the way I see things will be when I walk in on you in boots and gloves."

"You ought to go first. I'll go second," he reasoned.

"But I'm a sadist," I countered.

"You aren't suffering?"

"I will someday if I fall for you. Let's see what I have to resist. Take your pants off."

It was one motion bending down and coming up, shoulders back and not finding it possible to hide that he was happy to think of having my company for a long time to come. Or he was proud it worked this way.

"Turn a quarter turn to the left," I said.

I didn't waste sentiments on just anybody. He was good material for sentimental arrangements. I was further into plotting than I thought I was before he stripped.

"Lock your fingers behind your neck and bend forward."

He bent forward and I couldn't decide. The switch was broken up in the bin. Drat.

"There is a switch outside. I know where I can find it. But. I don't know if I want to start something that at this instant I don't believe I want to carry through with. But. I do want to show you I have weapons that let me compete with that damn computer."

I sat and studied. I didn't have options. I had control, up to a point. He didn't mind that he was getting all my attention.

"I want clarity," I said. "I want hope without catharsis. I don't know what that means. This afternoon, when you were over the chair, I thought the area outside would be just right for a garden. I miss a garden. There's something they call the Holder–Kaplan effect, a thought that intrudes over and over after a vital life decision has been made. It blots out the decision, in fact. You become incompetent. You lose knowing what you know. You have an insight into a higher knowing, into uncharted territory. Theoreticians call this life solving itself. Does this make sense?"

"I'd rather you get the switch."

I took off my clothes while he let the water run to a soft steam. He looked at me convinced, but not of everything.

"We're getting in together?"

"Why not?"

"In for a penny."

"So I'm a pound, am I?"

I brushed past him, bumped the protruding points, and followed my hand into the warmth.

"At least wash my back. You promised." I rotated slowly a few times to get wet and glisten all over. I had my back to him and my arms up in the hallelujah part of the service. I did a rhumba move. I felt his eyes. I didn't feel a hand.

"Nature is not taking its course, I said."

He ran a bar of soap back and forth, and did car-washing swirls on my shoulder blades. He put the soap down and mashed slowly. The emphasis was do one area well and then another area. I made soft moans. He had the job.

When he got to my waist he said, "You wouldn't say below here is your back, I guess?"

"It's questionable. 'Backside,' I've heard."

"I could do one of them, half a backside. There's no word for that. It's like I haven't done anything. But then again, would you accept that in Scrabble?"

"I'd accept half-assed, but Scrabble doesn't have hyphens."

I picked up the soap and told him to face somewhere else and not to peek. I did the rest of me and took a towel around me into the bedroom. I sat on the bed and crossed my legs and let the grass grow awhile. He dried off, watching me watch him. He went into the front room. I heard the sliding door close and a lock snap. Then the lights went out from around the corner and then the light went out in the shower. He had fresh linen. We stripped the bed and worked opposite sides, tucking in corners. I changed the pillows. I dumped my clothes in with the sheets and started a load.

Passing into the hall I saw his figure leaning on the wall.

He asked if I'd like to go outside. We could lie on blankets and put pillows against the house. It was easier that way, sharing the panorama of nature and letting the fervor be out there with the virtue of patience.

A car occasionally passing along the next ridge turned down and away and shot a reddish film over the brush. The clear definition quickly silted over and lost its outline, merging in a long shadow under the streetlights from some street down the hill. Half an hour went by. Our excitements were peaceful, pleasantly of our own restraining. The bay had been under a dome that didn't want to move. A lot of heat stayed put. Some had escaped here at elevation by this time. My towel was nearly dry. In another half-hour it was dry, and I rolled on my side and pulled it over a shoulder and noticed out of the corner of an eye that the sky had changed colors. If I could touch it, it would feel like chiffon.

I extracted a piece of something in my eye and saw that it was bright now, the sun not over the mountains but soon. My clothes were folded on a blanket beside me. I got up on my knees and looked inside. His hands were poised over the keyboard. He was still communicating with the brain.

] *Twenty*

I WAS STABLE ON MY hands and knees, groggy, not in a permanent state of bewilderment but determined not to get any higher. I gave up and rolled on my back and shut my eyes and went to an involuntary state of investigation as to whether I was asleep or counting cars coming around the hairpin at the corner.

The sun had come a few inches up off the mountain. A swirl of dry air in the patio was warm and less warm, circulating a sense of before and a now. The temperature had gone up. The morning went slower out here. The get-up-and-get-with-it was resistible. I was a lifer now, a life of leisure. Was I retired? I forgot.

I shook my hair out, wrapped up, and became one with a chair inside. I looked at him, so I guess my slouch released the appearance of a listening person. We'd have to work that out. I had to get a new appearance to be understood in spite of appearances.

"You were tired," he said. "You got to hear the Riemann mapping theorem, but I had already lost you."

A baggy pair of cutoffs were inclined to hold low and gave up a half-inch of hip in motion. A large porcelain cup with a design that looked regularly irregular had the number 2014 and Seattle. He pointed at the pot. I nodded. He reached a cup from the cupboard. "How do you take it?"

I took it special. Milk and sweetener, fancy restaurant style, porcelain cup and saucer. He lifted a stack of paper from my right hand and looked around. It went in the slot under the table. I loosened the blanket on my shoulders and pulled it up over my knees. It was a house that warmed fast. A gap in the tall trees allowed a direct hit from the light at this hour in this season. A napkin and a little spoon filled out the get-up menu.

The phone rang. He looked at the number and he looked at me. I pushed air at the phone: take the call. I liked the looks that looked at me while he did business. The coffee was warming my skin. I opened the blanket more—more thigh, more chest, more looks, more appreciation of what he was getting himself into in these minutes. Very little had to be said sharing coffee in the morning looking at a good-morning body.

The day would come. No more looks. But not today. He hung up and left his eyes on me. The look was kind. He repeated a phrase to get a sound registered via talking to himself. He let it go. I didn't have to be in the loop. The things I liked were accumulating. Now if he's a good kisser, we could be there.

"You talk to yourself," I said.

"I live alone. I talk to myself in lectures. I tell them they don't have to write it down. It's already down. I tell them it's wrong. It doesn't matter. Is it on the final?"

"Last night I was saying something about eating cake with a plastic knife," I said. "What did I say?"

"You skipped some steps. The quickest quickie marriage from here was the county clerk's office. You heard about some cake shop in Reno. We could hop a flight out of Oakland to the Chapel of the Tinkling Bells arriving by wedding cab. We consummate in the back seat. Then the big decision, cake-eating utensils."

"I'm glad I didn't meet you at the office. It would confuse me."

"I'm not sure what we're into," he said.

"I could define success."

"I have baroque sex fantasies about you."

"If we were married, I could say not now, I'm tired."

"You're hard to resist."

"It's why I didn't marry a younger man before forty. If I need to go to sleep fast I can ask about the Riemann mapping theorem."

"If you get really interested you'll never sleep again."

"Marriage is risks."

"You don't eat cake with a fork? So we don't need forks. That's a saving."

We got dressed and got going. I turned onto the street by the side door that Dr. Lieselotta Trigg used to come out of to pass through Levi Plaza.

I reminded him. "You're already pulling rank. You don't need to ask questions. An eye will peek at you through a one-way mirror. Call me when you're done."

I got a call way out on the Embarcadero as I was working my way back onto a street parallel to Battery.

"I'm done," he said. "I wait for results."

He was where I'd let him out, but eager now and on topic. "What would you like to do?"

I hadn't thought about it. Driving a car doesn't pass as a substitute for an armchair.

"We should eat," he said. "You want to tell me something?"

"Yes, we should. Yes, I do."

I headed for the bridge behind a dead-end caption. A woman my age was just ahead of us in a puce Mercedes. It might not have been her car. But she might be married to the owner or, worse off, he did her thinking. It was her one true thought.

I O NOBDY.

I referred to the license plate. "There's the life," I said.

"Four wildebeest survive lions three hundred and thirty-one days," he said, pointing at 4 WSL 331.

"Two bogus Korean translations of one hundred and fifty-two poets," referencing 2 BKT 152.

"But does that catch me up?" I asked. "I like yours better."

He described a floor plan of a house with rooms and doors.

"Can you go through every door once and only once and end in the same place you started? It's why I love math."

"I was trying to change the subject," I said.

"But the will has its way."

"BTWHIW," I spelled. Could anyone guess how happy we are?"

"I'm glad you brought it up. There's a house for sale around the corner from mine. Your books want to live near us?"

Over the bridge and off 101 was the scenic way to what had been a frequent destination. Homes had been added over the years, and it was a new drive every year, but they still had a gully or two of separation, and it was still rustic. The simple grandeur of California coastal sage was where I had wanted to live, where I had bought a piece of land and sold it for reasons I could kick myself for. We arrived by the long way to a drop into Tamalpais Valley. At a country crossroads was a place from before the Dust Bowl called the Last Chance Burger Joint, which provided a bit more these days. You could buy a Lotto ticket.

We had them do salads in orange shells you could eat if you wanted building material in your system. I liked to chip pieces off and see if they fit back together while I talked. We sat opposite on a picnic bench. I looked at my stub.

"Seven, seventeen, thirty-one, thirty-three, forty-nine, fifty-two."

He rubbed his lucky ear. "We should wait here till it pays off. It's not advisable to carry a ticket away from its place of origin."

"It's not recommended in the lottery manual of winning procedures?"

"Breaks the enveloping lines of force for true wealth."

"To true hearts." We clicked plastic cups.

"The guy who sold me the ticket," he said, "he does marriages."

"Lucky marriages?"

"If we sit here on the bench the rest of our lives, what could go wrong?"

"Buying Lotto tickets? We could starve to death."

"Passersby would call it true love."

"A couple of skeletons. We'd be a lesson to their children: get rich quick can't be done."

I was spearfishing lone onions, one by one disappearing in a diminishing return on effort. I pushed my plate to the side. We cleared our space and pushed a week's crumbs through cracks and looked in each other's eyes and looked away for words. A ranch house on a hill wasn't far, but the road down and around and over and around was a lot of turning getting there. I thought it was time.

"I need to tell you something," I said, asking for tolerance. A summary of who had had my heart was on its way. His body shifted to absorb the details and give back a carefully expressed "I understand," in view of whatever images of me in affairs he understood and whatever monotony he would endure with the confession.

"The doctor, Trigg, you met her?"

"I noticed a doctor. I don't think she noticed me."

I came off my arms. I folded my hands under the table. "She noticed you. A hundred office visits, get one free for a friend. We've been meeting for fourteen years. I figured I could call in a favor."

His eyes followed my eyes, like I could go slow.

"Her husband is a surgeon," I said. "He loves attending the NFL draft. He loves maple syrup in Vermont. His heart is with the Patriots. They're a professional football team. Soon there will be a line drawn. Do they move to the east or stay? They've drawn the line twice. Her argument has carried twice. The older the kids get, the stronger his family asserts its position. One more win and he'll discover a woman who would love home games in New England and have a family of her own."

It took me a while summarizing what was available in a nutshell. "The husband knows about me. They have had an understanding. It was stable up till now—now being yesterday when I told her about you. Yesterday, I wanted her to meet you. We've talked about the day I might get married. She said she would be curious to meet the man she was getting dumped for.

"We haven't met in bed for two years. We've been meeting on a park bench once every three months. The bench might happen once more if she leaves—which is what I think has been coming. Yesterday our separation became legal. We're divorced."

I set out a moment for him to comment. After a long pause he gave me a turning point. "I was fairly hot under the collar on the phone with you that day when I thought you had the laptop. I had put two and two together—you were the thief. You were incredibly cool. If you hadn't been, I never would have heard the Lieselotta history."

"You want to know if there's more?" I said.

"You were monogamous. Did I get that wrong? Nearly monogamous?"

"There was a man before. He was the man of the moment everywhere, and knew it. I was highly flattered he wanted me to coexist with him, as I had no money and no place to live. He could do role-play, boy he could do role-play. A writer/playwright/essayist. You would know the name. A big movie hit, or three. A ragged life, biographically powerful. He provided a place for me to live in Malibu till I was seventeen."

Andrei took his time on that. "You were with Lieselotta a long time."

"What drew me to her?"

"Either," he said. "You stayed together. You didn't have to."

"She laughed in my face when I told her I was an eighth-grade dropout. I put her over my lap. I gave it to her good, and she kept laughing."

"An eighth-grade dropout? It's not on your web page."

"I was the reason she didn't go home. She's deep blue among the bluebloods. You want to hear the clash and clang of battle? The husband says the son goes to Exeter, she says no.

The son has agreed. He wants to be a blueblood. She is seeing the light.

"I ran away from home. I read a book and I told a man I read books, and he gave me his books, and it went on and on. I wanted a thing and I got it. I'm coming out of a profession barely civilized. I still have a figure. I'm still worth a fee, good for a session. I hope you want something I can give you. That would feel very good to me."

"Backrubs," he said. "Last night, what was that?"

"If you married me and you couldn't love me I couldn't stand me."

He reached my arm. I was looking through a mist.

"This could turn into a small torrent," I said. "I've been with her fourteen years, Andrei. When I saw you I saw a man cleaning the home of a friend's wife. You could have been having an affair with the wife, true, and you were cleaning up for all those rolls in the hay. Whatever. You were acting responsibly. You were there at the moment. I was vain enough to think you couldn't help admiring me. I could do with that what I wanted. When I got your note I wanted to see.

"The sun never sets on a truth-teller."

"A stitch in time wastes time," he added and winced. "That's no good. Three stitches in time?"

"I may have the wet eye," I said, "but I quit crying if I have to think out of the box."

"But the box faces east," he said.

"We need help."

He unhitched a leg like it would be the first step from the table, but he straddled the seat for a wider view of both sides of the ground, and then got up. He seemed to stand on a resolution to give it up, and that was the end. I would have thought that if I hadn't watched this absentminded maneuver before. He did a loop-the-loop and sat down calmly, much too calmly.

"Let's keep it that way," he said.

"What are you saying?" I asked.

"I'm saying what you're saying. You're stuck with me. I want more than fourteen years."

"In fourteen years I'll want what I want now. I've met you, and it's not too late. I know you enough. I don't want to wear a mask. I'm saying I would like us to go to my place so I can think about what I can bring to your place and live with a bit more luxury than a one-night stand. I can carry one suitcase. I might bring two."

We digested a moment, each on the verge of making a remark, and letting it go. He seemed to want to consider how to respond in kind, sort of level the field. I could have asked about Mrs. Lavoisier. I was curious about that. I could wait.

The call arrived on the approach to Fulton. Lieselotta's assistant had some terrible remark to say about cholesterol, a joke, to get some innuendo into the data. She never found a guy not worth a few vicarious stabs at life with. He asked her to send me an official note that he was marriage material. Then he watched the park go past until we were past it, and it was getting time to tell me himself.

] *Twenty-one*

I STUCK TO PROCEDURE with goings and comings from and to the English Department. I called Mr. Liu fifteen minutes ahead of an estimated arrival time to speak with him regarding updates on the neighborhood. The facts on the ground were fairly constant, so our regular updates were less security related than about how life was treating us. The irregularities were conversation.

Mr. Liu and I had, for twenty years, been on the friendliest of formal terms. I dialed and he started. It was always the same warm welcome home.

"Hello, Ms. Cromwell," he said. "Welcome back."

"Thank you, Mr. Liu. How is Mrs. Liu?"

"Very fine, thank you."

"I have someone I would like you to meet. Could we drop by in a few moments? If it isn't convenient, we could stop by another time."

Mrs. Liu had been cleaning the house. It smelled of cleaner. If we could wave from the gate, he would see us. I stopped in the middle of the street. We got out. I got a tight hold on Andrei's arm.

"This is Andrei Andreyev, Mr. Liu. He is my fiancé."

Mr. Liu bowed his head and said that he was happy for me,

and he asked if I would want any updates. Should he save them for later? Better now, I suggested.

"The man in the brown suit was on the street again today."

Mr. Liu transmitted a clip of a man of an average description, mid-thirties, a brisk even stride, apparently not in possession of a whole lot of time to go around the block and come past the alcove of the English Department three times before work. That's what he did, though.

"This was seven thirty-five, Ms. Cromwell. He was back at a quarter after twelve, about sixteen minutes after, if it's important. He parked on Elliot Street. Travis had him with Massachusetts plates. You have the license number in a text. This is the fifth day. Same routine. Not this evening at five. Today is different."

"Well, the heart is a lonely hunter, I hear. He found it somewhere else."

"Why doesn't he call you?" Mr. Liu asked. "He is confused."

"It's a philosophical debate, Mr. Liu. Smarter minds are confused. You have a wife who wants you. You are the one percent."

"I had Mr. Ward run the plates. It's a rental—a week yesterday, which was a Tuesday—to Joel Moncrief. He arrived SFO; point of origin, Florence. I referenced your mail. He wrote. I am forwarding two messages from Moncrief. He is at the Fairmont, room 414."

"Please give my regards to Mrs. Liu, and have a nice evening."

I transferred the messages to the reader. A woman's monotone spoke the words in the order Moncrief wrote them. It was standard business. I have a library. My holdings include upwards of 200 one-of-a-kind items, and growing, on top of 15,000 items, eighty-three percent books, sixty-six percent hardcover, twenty-eight percent of which is no better than porn in my librarian's estimation. Moncrief enquired what I would consider a fair offer for the four volumes of the *Memoirs of the Renate Flyte-Simpson Society*. I assumed he was referring to the *Minutes of the Renate Flyte-Simpson Society*.

The machine dialed the Fairmont. I asked for Mr. Moncrief in room 414. He was expecting my call.

A man's voice said, "Moncrief here, yes."

"This is Elizabeth Cromwell. I have your note."

There was a Shubert piece he had to get his head out of. It stopped. The silence was silence. It could have been heavy. He had a moment to decide. He was taking it.

"I received your letter," he said finally. "You've changed your mind?"

"You've cruised the English Department a dozen times. What's on your mind?"

"What I said. I would like to buy the *Memoirs of the Renate Flyte-Simpson*. If you wouldn't sell them I was thinking how I could steal them."

"Any second thoughts?"

"I can beg. I would love to have them."

I recalled a passage in his letter. "You describe a young man who innocently gets himself on a rough patch with a strict, beautiful woman on a train from London. You asked for a session to recreate the situation. What's that about?"

"You didn't answer the first letter."

"Ah, yes," I summarized. "You have a mixed motive. You were tricking me."

"I want to lay my case before you. Whip me—whatever pleases you. Is a session a condition to discuss this?"

"You're at the Fairmont. Where are you from?"

"I'm in the U.S. Consulate in Florence. I want the *Minutes*. How do men meet you?"

I glanced at Andrei. Don't say it.

"You have my sympathy, but I'm in a hurry. Here's what we can do. I'll check with my librarian, and he'll give me a number and I'll give you the number and I'll put them in the mail."

"I would like to leave tomorrow," he said.

"We're talking about something that will take at least a month, perhaps a day or two less. Collectors want my books. I'm not in the book business. I'm not set up for it. I would be putting blood and tears into this, parting with a treasure."

"Can we meet tonight?"

"Tonight? I can mail them to Florence. Good night, Mr. Moncrief."

I parked in the alley on gambler's luck. In the trunk was a bag of cardboard flaps, a felt pen, and pleas on the tip of my tongue for the occasion.

LOADING HERE 7:57—GONE 7:59
THANKS, ENGLISH DEPARTMENT

The stairs from the basement came through a trapdoor to a hall between the office and the living area. I picked out a suitcase that would fit through the trapdoor and spread it open on the bed. I took a selection from each drawer in two bureaus and a night table and stacked it. I took off my shoes and put on different shoes, wrapped the old shoes in a new bag, and packed them. I bagged some things I would have had to stop for at a Walgreens. I grabbed a little umbrella. You never know. I went in the library and looked up the address of the *Minutes of the Renate Flyte-Simpson Society*. I did once hear them called *Memoirs*. Close enough. Couldn't find them. Knew I had them. Positive. Struck my forehead. No time for complex confusion disorder. I know my way into the mind of my librarian. I tried *Renate Flyte-Simpson Society, Minutes of*, and got a ladder and got them to the floor next to the suitcase.

I waved Andrei a kiss and went first down the hatch. Andrei followed partway, handing down the books and suitcase, gripping an overhead rail one-handed. He got in the driver's seat. I went back for a couple health bars and water. I tossed the cardboard flap in the back seat and shut my door and stopped.

"What am I forgetting?" I asked, squinting.

"We can do it now," he said.

"I have a checklist. Lights, water, refrigerator, computer... and there's something else...lock the door, did that."

He backed out into an uphill and pumped the brake down the hill to the turns that led to the few blocks that went under 80, and the final left to the on-ramp east.

"He was sly," Andrei said.

"Moncrief? I get requests all...the...time. From...all... over: *Song of the Riding Whip*, 1956, hardcover. Name your price."

"Why would he bother?"

"Florence, I guess. The cradle of Renaissance stuffiness. The *Minutes* will find an ornate backrest to lean on."

"You have a good memory. You have a heck of a library."

"The *Minutes* were a gift from a client. They were phony. He ought to know. He said there wasn't any Renate Flyte-Simpson Society. The *Minutes* are a reconstruction of events in Piedmont that never happened. When we got going we worked our scenes off of some of the wife–husband punishment scenarios...very old-fashioned. I don't get much call for them exactly as they are described. Customers want a lot of extras now, which I don't do. Instead of lugging the books around, he left them here, and when he had to say one day that it was our last day, as an afterthought, he said to take them."

I was getting side-glances that could have come with remarks but didn't. I'd seen this to notice. He was expert in nonchalance. It provoked responses, and he let me talk while he was minding his own business.

"Come to think," I said, "a lot of scenes had a Society-appointed disciplinarian."

He took a hand off the wheel and pushed the fingers through his hair. He left the hand at the back of his head holding it off the headrest.

"It's hard to see," he said. "Moncrief comes halfway around the world after you didn't answer his messages. Could they be valuable?"

"The atmosphere of those scenes is rare in dominant sessions now. Today it's more brutal, more invasive, more gender rever-sal, more variation in fetish-wear. I don't see there's money in

nostalgia, not that kind. I might be a few hundred dollars stupid."
I ran a hand down his thigh. "Maybe not so stupid."

I was looking at the time and temperature in Berkeley coming off the bridge. I dialed Kirsten Cook. She didn't remember my voice or she remembered it was late for a call.

"I see your name," she snipped. "How do I know you're Elizabeth Cromwell?"

"I was with Mr. Cartwright and Mr. Hall, not too long ago. You can ask Mr. Cartwright what we talked about. Then I can tell you what we talked about. It's as good as DNA. Is he there? I'd like to speak with him."

"He's not here."

"Could I have his number?"

"Of course not."

"Would you ask him to call me, please? I have a man who wants to buy my books, name of Joel Moncrief, which seems to be legitimate. Mr. Cartwright will know if it is."

"Just a minute." I was on hold. I heard nothing. Then a click and contact, not to put too fine a point on it. "He'll call this number. Be available."

Seven minutes later I called her again to find out if Cartwright might have forgotten I was available.

"He doesn't want to do it," she said. "It's not legal. Also, the system knows when a name is accessed. There are fingerprints. Those would be his. Also, if he does this once, you'll ask again. His life isn't wonderful, but he thinks he has a wonderful life."

She hung up. No mention of the times we had across a table face-to-face working together for the common purpose. Whatever I was to her, it was set in stone before I was in the clear with Mr. Hall.

I had a snow globe in the pocket between the seats. It snows for an hour when you turn it over. Under it was a free coffee coupon and another two hundred coupons like that. I turned them over and peeled one off the top. It was from 2006. The

Bean Bag had been enclosed in plywood and reopened as the Bag of Beans, and that transitioned into a computer repair joint. I doubled a rubber band around the lot and the rubber band broke.

I put the globe back on the stack and let it snow. I put my hands on my face and felt the stuff they call old age creep up under the skin. It makes the butter melt and the joints stiff and you know you've seen all the sunsets you need on this side of the divide. The memories are the part of the snow I was watching when the phone rang.

The name was Leon. I picked up. I didn't say anything.

"Are you there?"

"I'm here," I said.

"Something you ought to know. I got it off the daily incidents reports at the station. They're cheaper reading and more interesting than newspapers. They're free for private cops with some backing. We are authorized from upstairs to poke our noses in the door and chat. Just thought you might want to know there was a guy at a Catholic girl's school here in Oakland. Called the librarian and asked if he could look at some yearbooks from twenty-five years ago. The librarian got a sister to be there when he arrived. She could help out. She was in the class of ninety-two.

"Well, the guy didn't want help. He didn't want to say what he wanted beyond generalities. The more this sister offered to help in particulars, the more this guy had to tell her he wanted to do it himself.

"This is a Catholic institution, seething in a secret underground imagination. They're true to form. They dream the dreams of sinners. Everybody suspects evil, but evil is hierarchical and you don't investigate evil above your pay grade. Sisters don't investigate superiors. They can't beat students anymore. They can't torture fallen girls, but a stranger is fair game. Our sister of divine suspicions called in the head honcho and put together a case of devil worship against this fellow and called it in to the Oakland P.D. And what would you think?"

"Moncrief," I guessed. "In a rental with Massachusetts plates."

"And he said he was from Amherst and he was a Frost scholar and he was looking up a possible descendent of Robert Frost."

"To get her off his back?"

"You don't get a nun off your back once she's climbed on. The priest is Irish. The sergeant is Irish. He's a graduate of the school over here that turns out these sterling quarter-wits that line up for their life of service settling in on the public dime. It doesn't just happen in Oakland. It's still a birthright.

"Moncrief is tough to find culpable for probable cause. They can't quite ask him in for a little of his time. He lied about Amherst. Must have got the idea from the plates. They ran him through all the Rolodexes. He's a Pennsylvania boy. He's an officer in the American Consulate in Florence. He has no good explanation for why he's looking at pictures of girls in a Catholic school. He's unclean, but as of noon they can't touch him. Makes a nun want to chew her sandals."

After a while I was wondering why we had so much to talk about.

"Now, if you and this nun want to pool vindictiveness, I have her name and number. She may have the last laugh. The cops answered a call, a dead woman in a shack in a backyard of shacks on that area you can catch crossing the freeway, big old house on Ellis Avenue. An Evelyn Iges, Berkeley girl, Ph.D., drug overdose, and everything to live for. Somebody saw a man go in the backyard around two o'clock. The plates weren't California. The color matched Massachusetts. The man could've been her dealer. Not too likely. Nobody has ever seen him and three descriptions put him between a hundred and fifty pounds and a few cream puffs shy of three hundred, but he looked like a white dealer, and they don't have those on their street. What else would catch your interest?"

"He's been showing up on my street breakfast, lunch, and dinner, dinner being about five, but not today," I said.

"Checking in on a dead chick at two o'clock could be why he skipped you. He finds a dead girl and decides he might turn in his car at the airport and take off, especially suspicious if she graduated from the Catholic school and she knew an Evelyn Iges."

"He's at the Fairmont," I said.

"Could be innocent. If she's a grad student, not likely a graduate in 1992."

Leon knew what I had almost said and he said good night.

We parked in the front yard. Andrei put my suitcase in the bedroom. He had turned a chair to the screen and had a knee on it, comparing images, flipping windows. He still had his hand behind his head. The *Minutes* were at the end of the desk, stacked. I put them in reverse order bottom to top, picked at the volume on top, the most recent, not ready to look under the cover. I had to say something.

"The first two volumes were typed on a carbon, in different eras," I said. "Once there were six books. I got the carbon copies, too, and gave them to a client who saw a dollar in the individual predicaments and had the scenes chopped up into short stories. Godawful Press did those in the seventies and eighties. They weren't porn, and they were straight, and superior to the manuals, *Ideal Marriage for Idiots*, so you could sell them off the rack in smoke shops. They made the sales quota, so he came to me for the other two volumes. The amazing thing was how the author never repeated himself, like Sherlock Holmes."

Andrei unlocked the sliding door, shut it behind him, and disappeared in the area off the edge of the window. He was looking at his phone. In a minute he came to the door and left the screen shut. He held the phone up as if to say it was a call for me.

"He doesn't know everything," he said. It wasn't vaguely expressed, but it was vaguely a talking out of some dispute with someone in his head. "If he'd left out the dead woman, what's changed?"

He went out into the yard again. I heard him talking. The tone sounded like he was still talking to me. I went outside.

"Who are you talking to?"

"We should call Herring. The dead woman isn't Evelyn Iges. The cops should have caught up with Moncrief by now, but they hadn't by the time you spoke with him. Look at the neighborhood. She was living in a shack. They won't bother until next week. Herring won't hear about it. If she notices the report, she won't notice anything to notice."

"What should she notice?"

"I'm not sure yet. I may know when they get here. I'll know most of it."

"You want to say that to them?"

"Blame the murder on Moncrief. If he's innocent, why did he call you? You're involved in another murder. That makes him involved, and if things work out, he answers that, and possibly more."

He looked up Herring and put the call on speaker. The call went through to the night number at the Oakland P.D., not the emergency number, so the desk was closed and he could leave a message. He called the emergency number and calmly related the circumstances that would lead him to think that this was a police matter and Oakland was involved, and if he could be put in touch with either of two of detectives, Herring or Grey, they would be up to speed with his concerns.

I stood around a while in front of an open refrigerator. I walked the four corners of the kitchen. I was leaning two hands on the counter when his phone buzzed. There was no identifying I.D. but Herring's voice was soft and patient and encouraging. Why had he called?

"I don't know if I should worry. Perhaps I'm in danger," he said.

"Did you call the Berkeley police? You're calling from Kensington."

"They'd ask what you're asking. They'd ask why I'm worried."

"Why do think there is reason to worry?"

"A woman was found dead today in the back of a house

on Ellis Street," he said. "I think she was murdered, today or yesterday."

"Who is that?"

"I was given her name, Evelyn Iges."

There was a pause, and mumbled talking. When she returned she verified, with Andrei's assent, that he was at 3715 Calvend Lane, and asked that he remain there. They would be right over.

I was on the edge of the drive at the street when they got around to shutting off their lights. A hippie travel wagon sat in the street, an older off-white V.W. camper, and two dark shapes in the front seats. A flash hit me, went up and down, and went all over the house and grounds. The passenger got out and walked off to where the street turned the corner, pushing a light along the edge of the road. The driver passed me to have a look along the side of the house and then off into the night beyond, making mental notes about maybe this was a great area to retire. I came to be with her. I stood next to her.

"We've met," I said to Herring.

She swung her body in my direction. She didn't ask who I was. "You were inside?"

"I saw a car coming. I watched you drive up."

"The front door is closed."

"I came from the back." I pointed.

She carried alertness, and threw it around everywhere she looked. The search seemed like procedure. Know the environment. She was in dark slacks and a flowery short-sleeve that was coming untucked but no hem showed. Her shoes were leather dress shoes, laced, not for hiking, not for long walks. She walked around the car in the front yard.

"This your car?"

"There's no room to park in the drive."

"The owner of the house called us. The owner isn't here now?"

"He went outside. He took a walk, I guess. His phone's here."

"What do you think happened to him?"

"He was curious."

She asked if we could go inside. She followed me inside and took a few steps and waited standing at the desk area. She asked what was down the hall, and I said look around. I heard the light switch, steps, nothing, a light switch, a door open, nothing, a door close. She bent over for a close look at Andrei's phone and what could be read on a sheet of paper. The computer had gone to sleep. The kitchen light was on.

"Whose suitcase is in the bedroom?"

"Mine."

"You moving in or out?"

"I just arrived."

"The professor was expecting you?"

"We arrived together."

"Have you touched his phone?"

I held ten fingers out to show how I hadn't touched anything, and I said so. It was a quiet neighborhood. Something had her going. Her head stopped regularly and listened.

] *Twenty-two*

THERE WAS ONE VOICE and three words and two different sounds of footsteps at the open door. Andrei took himself through sideways. Grey spread her legs slightly in a standing vigil, watching, everybody at arm's length. Nobody moved any chairs, not this time. Herring and I put the four of us at the corners of a pinched-in square. Andrei might be inclined to tell us something important by the look he had, like when he broke the chalk at the blackboard before his lecture. I was annoyed.

"Where have you been?" I jumped at him. "You were going in the back."

Herring broke that up. "I'd like to speak with the professor, Ms. Cromwell. We'll get to you."

"You called us," she said to Andrei. "Ms. Cromwell is worried. What does she have to be worried about?"

He put his arm out to indicate some manner of support for a forthcoming claim that he could show us on the computer, but it meant more. "She's in danger if she's with me. She doesn't know it."

Grey and Herring exchanged a whistle with their eyes. We'd established a baseline sanity with them at the last meeting, in my opinion. Also, Andrei had put the murder way out there in higher learning. He was believable to himself, which was infectious

when he'd put his mind on something serious. He'd been pas-
sionate, but overdone. His enthusiasm held together enough to
get them here. I assumed.

Herring nailed it for me. "Danger? From whom?"

Andrei's T-shirt sported a stain from lunch, and that cost him
some gravitas. A walk in the dark wasn't much time to prepare
what he was going to say to them, and he had these off-the-cuff
manners that looked like a load of inner turmoil was all there was
to it. Cops must see this all the time.

"I gave you a piece of paper the other day," he said to Herring. "You remember what was on it?" He took the direct look
off Herring and calculated a decent thinking period on the floor
between them.

"Just tell us about it. What's dangerous?"

"It was evidence," he said. His interest in evidence was
strong. What Herring doubted didn't interest him.

"All right. So remember, there was some mathematics on it,
and that wasn't Robert's. There was a bit of some other math and
a question underneath, and that was Robert's. The other writing
on the other side was a woman's, and I know whose that was now.
The last time we met I didn't know. And I couldn't understand
how anything got going between Robert and the woman. I saw
a step, maybe two, but it had to have a reason to feed off itself
from her end, getting something worth what she was giving. And
I see most of that now. We might get the guy who killed Robert,
and he might not be far off. He killed the woman in the shack.
I'm scared for Elizabeth. But she has a barrier the woman in the
shack didn't. Elizabeth doesn't know him. If I find out, I don't
have that protection.

"This woman didn't realize she needed to get away till he
killed Robert. After that I think she was hiding out. She didn't
realize how far away she needed to get. She thought the shack
protected her and never learned why it didn't. That will connect
him to something about her, and we have her information, the
facts of her life.

"Evelyn Iges was not the woman in the shack. I can show you."

Andrei sat at the screen. What should interest us was highlighted. He expanded an image. He put his finger where Herring could see what was to see. I leaned on my hands from the other side of the table. Andrei sat so we could all see.

"There." He pointed at a face. Next to the face were some people in a room. The caption put a Berkeley scholar on the cusp of a book deal.

"That's Evelyn Iges eight days ago in New York. She's turning her thesis into a book. She was one of three doctoral students who won best thesis this spring at Berkeley. She's in art history. The thesis is brilliant."

His chair didn't turn unless he was in the mood to make the effort. He twisted himself to look up at Herring. Directly to her face he asked, "When I gave you that paper, I showed you that 1. That 1 was equal to that sum of those symbols. Those were functions. I said it at the meeting. It's just a term, a partition of unity, which is just saying in words what the formula is saying. But that's what it is, a partition of unity."

He brought up another page, a list of phrases like film titles. We read where he pointed: *Partitions d' Unité*. It was the title of Iges's thesis.

Andrei sat silently. Grey was noisy in her silence, curious. Andrei got out of his chair. He went back to the window. Herring watched her night being wasted.

"Who wrote that thesis?" he asked. "I'm going to get a copy tomorrow at the library. But I don't have to. I know who wrote it, and I know why, and…and we all know why. This is what she got from Robert, an art history thesis. He can toss this off in any subject. Look in the *Times* article. It's all about the brilliant observations…in brilliant French!"

Andrei looked at Herring in an "I told you so."

"I can see them at the two tables," he said. "Robert glanced over. She was at a laptop. She had pushed some things into a stack next to her, outside her work area. There was a piece of paper with the modular stuff and steps that hook it all into an argument for horizontal symmetry. Robert knew this stuff. It's ancient. But there were those arrows. He might have thought about them because they're never there. But there they were. Also, the transforms are not really an argument for horizontal symmetry. Certain symbols don't go back where they belong under the transformation. That makes the vertical arrows interesting. They go with the new ingredient that's different.

"Robert is going to ask about those arrows. She's going to say she doesn't know. I think…as her laptop was open…he reads the stuff she was writing. He asked and gets a smile, and he tossed off some remarks. She asked him to repeat something, and he blithered on for a minute or two with a lot of fancy French stuff, and perhaps he offered to translate it, but she said not to bother. She knew French.

"He pressed her about the arrows. He saw the math was not her handwriting. He asked about it, and she might have said she would have to ask, and she wasn't sure when she could get him an answer. He pressed more and she said if he gave her his name she could get back with him. But it was up in the air if they would meet again.

"And here…it's hard to say…but it has to be something like she goes to her thesis advisor, and the thesis advisor flipped out and said to keep this new stuff coming. So there's her motive for staying in contact with Robert.

"Remember, when we met before that was one of the things I didn't know. Something like it had to be there, the thing that would interest her in meeting Robert. It can't be her bothering somebody for math in exchange for hotel stuff. I knew that, but the thing itself, I couldn't say. Now we know."

"And then they get in contact," Herring said. "Assume she talked to her math friend. Why would he give Lavoisier math?"

"Remember that function I showed you on the paper?" He spoke to me. I understood. That was enough. He brought up a page on the computer and highlighted that function.

"That function! The guy was looking for places where that function is zero. I don't think he found them."

"Lavoisier found them?" I asked.

"No, but they were both looking, but they didn't know how to find them. This is what I think. Robert could see the other guy was ahead of him. He was onto a new approach. Robert was very intrigued. At some point the other guy was told about Robert. He was intrigued with what Robert could make out of the steps he had.

"Iges gets the answer from Polk, but remember, it wasn't Polk doing the thinking. Polk was in the middle, and he got stuff from someone else and gave it to her."

"What happened when Polk died?" Herring asked.

"I don't know," Andrei said. "If I take Polk out of the middle, then there's a direct transfer from the guy doing the math to Evelyn Iges. That's not possible, or Iges would be dead. Robert was going back to the house four months after Polk was dead and four months after Iges—who we've known as Mavyn—had to find a place to live somewhere else."

"The professor was meeting with the killer," Herring said.

"Sounds logical if you want to think somebody gave away brilliant ideas to people and then killed them."

"He could have needed what the professor gave him. Then he killed him."

"We're stuck with that," Andrei said. "But there's the woman in the shack, and that means we don't know something."

Andrei studied Herring. "We do know Iges didn't talk to you after Robert was killed," he said. "And she had to know." He looked at Herring with the question, "Unless she did?"

"We're interested in what you say," Herring said.

Andrei knew Herring knew he knew he was on the sardonic end of detective stuff. He flopped his hands. "If you want me to not bother you, fine. You came all the way up here. I'm sorry. But I'm sure the woman in the shack is not Evelyn Iges. When I saw Evelyn Iges, I saw Mavyn. And I saw the answer to two questions that came up earlier. I don't have all the answers."

Herring liked Andrei. I still thought so. No detective surrenders a case, but they're perfectly willing to let anybody think they are. It's all grist for their mill. Herring knew Andrei knew Herring knew he knew to get over it and not waste her time with what everybody knows.

"Help us out here," she went on. "You say that Iges didn't write her own thesis. I want to hear about how she repays Lavoisier for all his kindness."

"Look up Iges," Andrei said. "She has a web page now. She's a celebrity. She was born in Paso Robles, but she's local, raised by a grandmother. It's in her bio. She went to a Catholic school in Oakland, and then UCLA." He pointed at the screen. "The French in her thesis alone won a prize. This is her eight-foot high-jump. The woman in the shack must not have had identification. What connection she had to Iges, besides the thesis, would be good to know."

"Why does the man who put the math on the note use go-betweens? Can you figure it out for us?" Herring asked.

"I can wonder out loud if it's someone in the math department, but then that wouldn't happen. It can't happen. That's what's crazy. Who is this? And that's what's dangerous. You don't know how you're going to bump into him following up on Iges. A good lesson is the woman in the shack. He's not going to warn you."

Andrei opened his hands holding a warning. "Two people are dead, or three, or who knows?"

"How did you find out about the dead woman in the shack?" Herring asked. "I've been meaning to get to that."

I said, "A man called me. He knew."

"You have a name?"

"If I gave you his name he could dry up as a guy who trusts me. If you find out his name, you can't do anything about it. He's connected way up in the clouds, where he hears things."

Herring let go with a sigh that would come back with the same question whenever. She'd been making faces with Grey.

She stepped it up. I didn't try to see what Grey said. They had a heck of a signal, unless they always agreed.

"What does the D.A. think?" Andrei asked.

"You mean that meeting when we met with her about vertical symmetry? She thinks you're a bright fellow who likes to play detective. The FBI is involved because the deceased was a big wheel in France. What you've told us tonight is something to think about. I give you that. We'll definitely think. As far as the D.A. goes, the Iges case belongs to the FBI, no matter who turns up deceased,"

"What if it's the same poison?" Andrei asked.

"They'll let the FBI think about it. They have the resources to invest in these chemical killings. What are you two up to on the next stage of this case, not including the thesis at the library?"

I asked Herring, "Did you want to ask me anything?"

Herring looked out the window with a wooden fixation on leaving us alone forever.

"I called you when we heard," Andrei said. "We haven't even eaten."

Herring topped that. "We're supposed to be at home watching TV now. Your call forces us to think carefully about what you're telling us in the middle of the night in Kensington, out of our jurisdiction."

"They're not simple questions."

"But that's the way you can repay our kindness. Make us think our time is valuable. This is a Berkeley case. You people put it in Oakland. When people kill people in Oakland, other people see it. We get on them. We make the case if the people who see the murder are willing to say what they saw under oath. Even if they're too smart to believe we can protect them, the case is solved. Professor Lavoisier's killer thinks time is on his side. He may still be in Oakland. In Oakland all lives matter. We want justice to prevail as much as you do."

She looked at me like she wanted me to see what was coming.

"You were thinking about protecting me from people in high

offices, Ms. Cromwell. How about I take my chances? I'd like the
name of the guy who told you about the woman in the shack. I
don't want to run through your phone log. Couldn't you just save
me the time?"

"I'll tell you what I tell everybody who insists I do what they
tell me: I'll think about it."

"But we'd be missing the background of the call. You could
help us."

"Suppose I give you the background?"

"That would make us feel good about coming up here
tonight."

The four volumes of the *Minutes* were on the table in front
of me. I put my finger on the top volume.

"A man wanted to buy these books. They're part of my library.
I don't want them. I just didn't get around to bothering with
boxing them up. He offered to come in for whatever I wanted
to do to him. He was willing to put some skin in the game. He
was motivated. My librarian saw some money in this. I put him
off. Well, he didn't go away. A man had been casing the English
Department—ostentatiously, like he wanted to be seen and he
wanted his license number checked out. He hoped I would call
him and ask what his problem was. He was the one who had written me about those books on the desk here."

Herring asked for the volume on top. I handed it over. She
made a space for it where she was. She opened the cover and
read the title page. She let pages slip past a thumb. She asked
for a second book, opened it in the middle and took a minute.

"The guy who wants this comes all the way from Italy?"

"I told him I'd get back with him in a month or so. I needed
to see what I wanted for them."

"And his car was seen earlier on Ellis. Not the best place to
be seen. It means we have to see him."

"He's at the Fairmont," I said. His name is Joel Moncrief."

"Just curiosity. How do you know so much?"

"I have employees who get names from license plates. When

I need more I ask around. Moncrief is in the consular service. That seemed peculiar enough to find out what else he might want to tell me. We talked."

"This man who called you to say there was a dead woman in a shack in Oakland, does he know how he connects with vertical symmetry?"

"Vertical symmetry didn't come up."

Herring followed up with Moncrief. "What if we put the books on the table under his nose and say a hundred thousand? What do we get?"

"I'm not a book dealer. I was tempted to toss a thousand-dollar sales tag at him, see what happened. This was porn before we were born. The world has moved on."

"These books don't look like expensive items. I assume you weren't asked before?"

"Not to sell them," I said. "I used them for scenes. It was known I had them."

"Moncrief asked for just these?"

"Just these."

"Where did you get them?"

"I can't tell you."

Herring let a second of silence sink in. This wasn't dodgeball.

"I went over before with you how we conduct an investigation. I asked you a question."

"I'm trying to get that across to you being polite. I'm not telling you."

"Why does a perfectly cooperative meeting always end this way?"

"You get to see I have clients who believe I can be trusted."

"I might want to hear that at the station."

"You met my lawyer. I'd get to call her. She'd remind me I don't have to answer your questions. You can charge me, a charge that goes head first to a wastebasket as you explain how you get a call with an offer of cooperation from two people who want to find out who killed Robert Lavoisier. And you think you need to push three times your weight at me. You'd look petulant, and worse, you'd look like a dumb detective wasting the taxpayer's trust."

"We decide what's material, Ms. Cromwell. That's how it works."

"It does if that's why you're a cop. If so, get out of this house now, or take me in. We'll see how it works."

It was the first smile I'd seen on her. It did something for her system. I couldn't see her temperature go up. I got up and pushed the chair an inch for the grate of iron on wood.

"Where are you going?" Herring asked.

"Wherever I want."

I went to the bathroom and splashed water on my face and came back to the front room drying my face with a towel, making the point that this is where I live. It's late. Herring had rid herself of a smile. She didn't seem on the verge of taking the cuffs out of her belt. She might put a bullet in me. That was always the third option. I knew what was wrong. It wasn't failure, not just failure. It was failure as far as the end of days. All she was getting out of a genius was vertical symmetry and a thesis. I'd given her statues and *Der Mann Ohne Eigenshaften*. She thought it was fair to take one stab on her own. It could be worse. But it was failure.

She asked Andrei, "How do I get Iges back in town if she tells me she's busy?"

"She's Mavyn," he said, "the woman who lived with Polk. She was in a motel room with Robert Lavoisier. They met—regularly, I don't know. I'm fairly positive. I guess you'll need to drag her in from wherever. If you need me to speak up in person, I can be there. She'll hear at some point that a woman was murdered reading her thesis. She might know she needs protection. I don't think so. She'd be dead by now. But she might not agree."

"What do I ask her?"

"Who did Polk hang around with? She won't know who put the math on the note. She can tell you what she knows about Polk but more likely her lawyer will tell you to take a hike. You won't be able to knock her around. She can afford lawyers. You could try to leverage a charge of fraud. Robert wrote her thesis. But Robert's not here to say he did. It's a problem."

"What do I do with Moncrief? Ms. Cromwell suddenly adores the Constitution."

"You might hit him with a name," I said. "Not right away. Mention the Catholic school and the dead woman. Wait until he thinks he knows what you're after. Bring up the name Alix Sociedes in conjunction with Renate Flyte-Simpson. I heard they're the same. She's in a rumor with a man working in the consulate in Florence. Call it a 'report.' Someone's going down. Tell Moncrief it doesn't have to be him."

Herring gave me a blank look. "And then what?"

"Does he want the *Minutes*, or does someone else? I like that idea you had of a hundred thousand dollars. If he doesn't laugh, he has to call his banker. Tap his phone. The Constitution is a scrap of paper in Philadelphia."

"Alix Sociedes," Herring said. "Any other name we ought to know?"

"I don't know what gives with Moncrief," I said. "I passed an hour with the owner of the Starlight. She had Alix on her mind that hour. It would be good to be careful. Someday you're driving around, and the next thing I read is you're the poor woman in the shack. You're the news."

] *Twenty-three*

THE ADDRESS ON MY driver's license was my place of business. The address on Andrei's license was where I lived. It was the explanation the clerk would need. We had been living together for a day is what I could tell her. That entitled us to a confidential marriage, which meant we didn't have to have a witness.

Andrei was tearing a box open. I went to the sliding door and said I had an idea. I sat in the swivel chair and swiveled. I was suggesting I was available. I didn't want to seem counterintuitive.

But it took a moment to see where things would go before we got the table and the canopy and the chairs that caught the summer sun before it was hot, around ten in the morning in the open door. And the birds singing and all that. It felt good. And it got better. He knelt next to me and lifted my top and put his lips on my nipple. He was a good kisser. I pushed his head to where it would do more for my sense of time and place. Kiss there, kiss some more. And he worked my pants down and I damn straight helped out holding my hips high and getting my hand under his shorts, so the nipple on the side he was kneeling on was getting all his attention. When I got a stroke going on his cock that was the clincher. He was going to give me all the help there I could ask for, and he was not going to change this position, so the one nipple and the clit was the zone that had all the prosperity, and

] 214 [

I went up the ladder and grabbed the top rung, and doubled tightly into the explosion. I hadn't made those sounds in anyone's presence, not even for the movie version of the greatest boom of all time. Clients want to pay for the sounds that their suffering brings me off. Now I knew what they were missing. I could have faked for them up to a grade-B performance of *Gone with the Gasp*, but it just didn't fit the parameters for Lady Thwackham. Oh. Oh. Oh. That was nice. And he said thank you. So I did too.

We recovered later, after we'd come back from an ice cream and a recreational looking-in-windows. We could use a second cabinet in the bathroom. I was telling him about it, putting him off guard. I had him against the wall, interlocking fingers, and I twisted his shorts into a jockstrap that was in real time a gag on his cock, and for the stupid symbolism I lost it. You can eroticize and chew gum at the same time, but you throw a lot of spit in the air and make an impression that the sources of pleasure are sometimes too much and you can't take it anymore. I put my arms around him.

It was that moment that I parted with bothering to make fetish a commercial ceremony. This moment he was what was going to happen for a long time to come, and I put his back to the wall and urged and urged until his legs were spread way far apart so he was low enough that I could press against him and get him inside me and I went at it till I felt, well, in a few weeks I'll know if I need to think of remodeling.

Andrei said that when he bought the house, a chair that had been there had gone over into the canyon in a storm, and so he couldn't use the patio anymore. It was too much. I gave him a couple strokes for that and learned I had to be careful. It acted like true love, and he made it tough for me while I was making anniversary cupcakes. I didn't yet want to have to say no. I was too new at this to know exactly when to turn things off as spice for later. We didn't have our cupcakes till after midnight. I will have to pick my shots. I saved a cupcake in the freezer.

We bought the expensive outdoor lounge that extends. We

bought extra pillows and doubled up on one of them wasting a lot of room at the end of the pad. We were keeping our hands on and off each other when he was talking about a vacation, and I asked him what it meant. He said he wanted to take me to Lake Maggiore. I thought we were going to Leningrad and Helsinki.

"It's a shrine the tourists don't know about," he said. He opened his laptop, stuck it between us, and brought up a view from just above some red terra cotta roofs well up a hill overlooking a lake that went off the page on both sides, a big lake.

"Riemann. He's the one on the wall you asked about. His mother died, then a sister and a grandmother he was living with, and a brother and his father and another sister, or two others, one blow after another. He toured Italy twice. It seemed to buy time between enormous mathematical discoveries at Göttingen. As the Seven Weeks' War came along he went to a little spot on the lake with his wife."

He opened a map covering a section of the lake. "He died somewhere in this area." He traced a *via* up to a tight turn and took his finger around and up and down to a name, Biganzolo. "There's the church here for this diocese, and down around a turn in the road is a cemetery. Robert was there every year. You could see his kids getting bigger year by year, standing against the same entranceway by the Riemann plaque. Riemann was buried here. There's no grave to look at. The cemetery has been reorganized. I guess they had to free up some room for dead locals."

I read the inscription.

"He didn't make forty," I said.

"Everything he touched turned to gold. He was the heavyweight of the century he shared with Gauss. He was one of a few who developed a subject called 'complex function theory.' It must have come to him one day that the theory was capable of performing a miracle. You could count primes in terms of the zeros of a function. Gauss would have loved to see that. Just missed it. He died a few years earlier. That happens a lot. A mathematician spends his whole life on a problem, and then passes away and just misses the solution. Chebyshev just missed the prime number theorem. And that came directly out of Riemann's idea. The whole push for a long while was inspired by Riemann in a paper that everybody knows by heart.

"It was a short paper. There were arguments for statements that were filled in after Riemann died. One statement is still open. Robert kept a lot of his time available for that problem. He would ask his kids to calculate primes when they went to bed. Is 2017 a prime? And what's a quick way to tell? They divided by primes up to the square root of 2017, and that got the answer. They wondered if there was a quicker way. His girl is a prime this year. She was the perfect number, six, last year; but don't despair. She would be perfect one more time, and they worked that out, what year that would be."

"The Riemann hypothesis" was the title at the top of a page.

"Is there a version for idiots?"

"We're all idiots."

"Do you want to prove this?"

"I'm too dumb, or I'm not that dumb. No way."

"How smart would somebody have to be, if after all these years it hasn't been done?"

"Smart hasn't done it yet." He set up a screen. "Here, I'm going to let you tell yourself."

He brought the screen to my lap and opened a document. He highlighted a collection of symbols assembled in a tight unit that I accepted as an expression in math that worked for him as a set of instructions for making numbers. That last part is what he said verbatim.

"This is the zeta function."

He highlighted a series of expressions that started at the top of the page, and went down line by line.

"This is a collection of transformations that modifies the appearance of the zeta function into this different-looking function at the bottom. The values are the same, so the function at the bottom is zero exactly where the function at the top is zero. The function at the bottom is the one we work with."

He highlighted a space between two vertical lines. A horizontal line that crossed them was the real axis.

"This is the critical strip. This vertical line in the middle is the critical line. Let's start with where the real axis crosses the critical line. That's one-half. So we put one-half in this expression, and you push that key."

I pushed the key. A long decimal appeared with some symbols at the end.

"This decimal on the screen is a fraction, but that's because the computer can't give you the exact value. The value it gives you is accurate to twenty-three decimal places. We could increase the accuracy, but not arbitrarily. There is a limit. A more powerful machine will provide more accuracy, but it will have a limit. It might be a fraction. But we don't know."

"What do you notice?"

"Some fours."

"That could be important. Another thing is the negative sign in front of the decimal. Let's try fourteen."

"That's negative too," I noticed.

"We'll try fifteen."

I pushed the key. "This time it doesn't have a negative sign."

"It's positive. It's negative at fourteen and positive at fifteen. What do you think?"

"In between it will be zero. How do you find that?"

"Try something in between."

I put in 14.5. It was positive again. The same for 14.4 and 14.3 and 14.2. But it was negative at 14.1 and positive at 14.15.

"That's how you do it, you keep trying in between positive and negative values?"

"At the moment that's the only way anyone knows how to do it. That's how Riemann did it. He stopped at 14.13. Then he got a two-decimal approximation to the next zero.

"Here. Push this key."

The value at 14.134725 was very small and negative.

"That's accuracy in seconds that would have amazed Riemann. There are tables that give a thousand places of accuracy. You can go on until the calculation takes longer than you want to wait. Riemann preferred to get more zeros rather than home in on one zero, but he could have done both. He was the first person to see this, so he was the first person to assert that you would only find zeros on this critical line."

He opened another page. He put dots at the two opposite corners of a rectangle. "We'll consider a rectangle. We'll say the corners are at (0, 14) and (1, 15). You want to push the button?"

I pushed the button. "It's a 1."

"There's one zero in that rectangle, and we know it's on the one-half line between height fourteen and height fifteen and we found it to six-place accuracy. We'll make another box with corners at (0, 15) and (1, 20)."

Where the one was before was now a zero. There were no zeros between height fifteen and height twenty.

"No zeros. We have to go higher. We'll try (0, 20) and (1, 30)."

"Two," I said.

"That's about the way it works. The experts have refined the search procedure. We amateurs put numbers into this expression and follow this plus-and-minus routine. You tell it to stop when two consecutive values are within some range you've prescribed. The values are approximations to the zeros. Then you tell the computer how to check if there are no zeros between the new zero and the last one you calculated. You then have all the zeros up to that height. The values are approximations to the actual values, although someday they might discover a decimal that repeats. They would keep trying for more accuracy, but only get repetitions and go out of their minds."

"How would they decide if they are in their minds doing something like this all day and all night?"

"Couldn't care less. What's happening fits expectations."

"You don't know what to expect."

"True. Riemann found his numbers as the zeros of a function. Somebody someday will discover them in some other way. He'll be checking the average displacement of the upper corner of a building in a wind over fifty years and he'll see 14.134725 millimeters, and he won't be able to shake the idea that that's a stupid number, but that he's seen it somewhere, and he'll put it in a table of stupid numbers and there it is. But it has nothing to do with displacements."

"You expect that?"

"It will have to have a bit of ingenuity in it. I'm sure that's what happened to Robert when he saw that page I showed you. The sense of falling into a strange new set of properties of the zeta function fell on him."

"You said it's impossible Polk did this."

He shook his head yes, it's impossible. "I think Robert went off and couldn't believe what he was looking at because of where he found it. Nobody in the math department would waste their time on a prank like this. Fifty years ago, if a proof had been found, you would have expected to hear the discovery came at some place like Princeton or Cambridge, but now it could come from anywhere. And nobody would come up with a new idea like vertical symmetry and then leave it on a pad."

"That's all he needed? That's all he saw?"

"I said vertical symmetry, not Robert. He never mentioned it, but around Halloween he was agitated. When I collected his papers to send to France, there was only the one page with a section of zeta-related work. It was something I could ignore, I thought. What Robert thought he was seeing at that first meeting with Iges, I don't know, but he saw what I would not have."

"Why wouldn't he show you?"

"He wouldn't talk about it. That's what I was saying before. He doesn't talk to people for inspiration. Between us he would toss off some ideas. If I could figure them out, I'd write them up and show him. If he had more that could be added, he'd say so. Then I'd send it off. If I had ideas that got us into a back-and-forth, invariably the final result—if there was one—spun out of some deeper analysis. My idea was just a portion of what was true. He'd see the whole truth. But he was cryptic. Often I'd try to write up what we had talked about, but I'd get stuck and then discover what a technical aside he had been concerned with was all about. Then I could see what he was hung up on and how he got past a difficulty. We rarely talked as if we were connecting the same things. He saw the difficulties and got them straightened out and went on to another problem, but he wouldn't punctuate a conversation, stop, pause, go."

"He could fall for Iges for other reasons." I could guess.

"I guess."

"You don't guess, though."

"Iges was getting *crème de la crème* on a silver platter."

I read the statement of the Riemann hypothesis and looked at the picture on the screen.

"I don't understand infinitely many zeros," I said.

He went into a stare, and muttered, "A function that is zero infinitely often. You can't keep pushing a button. Eventually you have to think. It will be done. Until it is, there will be doubts. Some think it can't be proved, but it doesn't have that undecidable look. Say it takes a thousand years; that would be seen as an indictment of human intelligence. Mathematicians would really feel bad. Maybe a large gang of researchers, an army of peasants pooling brains, will do it. It would really be a blow if computers did it. The people with money to spare have offered a million dollars to the human who finds the proof. They may not have to pay off. The ultimate race might be humans against fate.

"Say the Riemann hypothesis is proved and the next day the world ends. Have we put our brains into the right questions, supposing we have some control over the end of the world? Mathematics is like the arts. Good taste may not equal survival. Survival might not be fun to work on."

] *Twenty-four*

I'D COME TO THE CITY to meet Brett. I had a reason for coming in early. Ms. Cook had left a message. That guy with the shovel in the tape I'd given her had generated follow-up. Hall had had a dream linking the wealth of Croesus and the luck of a simpleton. He got a shovel and dug in the middle of the night. By the light of the moon he'd found another statue. Now he had five. How many did I have? Don't worry. I could catch up and forge ahead. I have many tapes. Dig where the guy has the shovel in the ground. They weren't porn tapes. They were maps of where statues had been buried. Don't ask. It takes all kinds, and then some.

I was going through the tapes when Brett arrived. I had a map of San Jose on the desk. Some of the Polk tapes I'd seen began on Coral Crescent in Piedmont, and then went down 880, so I could fast-forward to the particular exit the car took from 880, and follow the trail from there to where the car passed the guy with the shovel. I was putting black dots at those locations. I had eleven of them finished and fifty to go, and I was beginning to entertain the notion I was seeing patterns.

That was one puzzle. Then there was Brett.

Back when Brett and I had said goodbye in the parking lot on Piedmont, when working with me had all the future prospects of one of several second jobs, it had been easy to imagine us turning the lights on at the English Department and strapping it on. You know, show up and start. She'd followed up and suggested "next week." That's when it hit me: next week what? On the phone, things had occurred to us, two *sine qua nons* on her side. I didn't have to get into mine. She had a partner. She didn't need another partner such as me coming at her. Stay on my side. I'd heard that, but no harm running it by me again. Also, if the world of girl bands took off, and her group hit it, she would take off.

I'd breathed a serious sigh of relief. I was sorry. I thought we'd ended on a sad silence absorbing the nature of being true to one's dreams, when she said she had to grow up; she had to confront the reality of what that statement signified. It seemed she'd made a one-eighty on a dime, and with that out of the way, we were back to my thoughts. I said I'd meet her, but I'd emphasized the real likelihood that I couldn't say yes. I had an upholstered chair for visitors. She fell into a slouch, and dared me to hire her.

Brett had found places to sleep with the name Brittany Lawford. The people who had hired her in Oakland had run a background check on the name. She had brought with her their report, the essential Brett, which any investigation would come up with running the name. She put a manila envelope on the desk. I opened it.

It was a diploma-looking page certifying she had been a member of Mensa in Pasadena. Her IQ was 155. There was a photograph of her at nineteen. It was the identification there was.

"You drive a Jeep," I said. "You don't have a driver's license?"

"The Jeep belongs to Diane. I don't drink. I don't do drugs. I keep my mouth shut. I'm punctual. I'm worth more than I'm making. I want my own place before I'm thirty."

"It's illegal to drive without a license," I said. "You were telling me over the phone you were thinking of growing up. Where'd you learn to sing?"

"I did a lot of singing at home. My mother encouraged me to try out at talent agencies. Everyone said I'm good."

She was in lilac pants and short-sleeve flowery shirt and orange tennis shoes. I was getting used to seeing young twenties women, apparently single, in orange shoes, not often, but enough to notice there was a group of them. She was still five foot ten and a hundred and fifteen.

"The people you work for," I said, "they're not legal. It's given you a false impression."

"Hoops? I have to jump through hoops? I never would've thought. It's a profession. It's why it's called professional dominance. Sexual dominance doesn't do it a just description for the long hours of dedication to craft. I get asked for everything you can take a picture of. They try stuff with me. More than illegal. You wouldn't have the slightest idea what impressions I have."

She got on her feet and braced her hands on the desk and leaned forward. She twisted her neck to catch the map of San Jose from several angles.

"What's this about?" she asked.

I opened a drawer. I handed her a photograph of a statue with my name on the base.

"Looks like you." She put the photograph on the table like she was sailing a single-wing paper airplane.

"I think a statue like this is buried at every one of these dots," I said.

She picked up the photo and flopped herself in the chair with it. "Erotic statues," she said. "As a layperson, accepting my definition of erotic, I wouldn't think this is going for much more than the price you can get melting it into ingots. This could be a publicity stunt. There's some money. An art gallery is opening. In San Jose?"

"No clue," I answered.

"What are you getting out of it? And better yet, how many people do you split with?" She took her phone out of a back pocket. "Here's a dead Austrian, Bruno Zach. He did women in flimsy outfits holding a whip behind their backs. Is that erotic? Sure, of course it is. Twenty-six inches. A hundred and fifty-six thousand at auction. Just a year ago." She let me see. She reversed her phone and stuck it at me like a badge.

"You were saying," she said.

"A man named Polk died in March," I said. "At least ten years before he died, he and some people made art films. They're in this box on the desk. Videotapes. In each film a man is standing with a shovel on end. It might be that a statue is buried where the point of the shovel touches the ground."

"I have ten questions I don't want the answers to."

"You want to run a background check on me?" I said.

"I would like to see the premises—if you're going to ask me to think about working here."

The office was small. The foyer was small. Just to the right through the door to the library was a small changing room. I skipped that and the bathroom. I led her through the center aisle of free-standing stacks. We emerged into a small open area in front of a raised platform, curved at the back. It made a small stage for readings. The catalogues were around the perimeter on both sides of the stage. I'd modeled it on a seventeenth-century design of the monastery in Joanina in Portugal. I'd had the ceiling removed. Lights hung from the ceiling of the room above the room that was now empty space. The long cables caught the immensity. Some details in the woodwork was fair imitation of centuries-old Portuguese work. I expected the library to take her breath away.

"You took down your web page," she said. She made small turns and made remarks at each turn. "It's quiet in here. I like that. It has class. I admire what you've done." She looked up at the catwalks on the floor above. "The salons are up there?"

I led the way up a spiral staircase of two full turns of dark oak and maple. There were ornate mahogany handholds where you stepped onto the walkway that went around three sides. The fourth side was used to run beams to anchor the stacks below. There were twenty-two hundred volumes on the walls up here. At the turn were three small rooms, three themes, three differ- ent views of how one found excitement in the theatricality of discipline.

Brett practiced tapping a toe and looking strict and unim- pressed with bad behavior. She had a middle finger on her lower lip and a forefinger playing around on her cheek. The thumb went under the jaw. The little finger jiggled. She talked it over with herself: "They strip downstairs, and you walk them up here. I like it. You thought this out pretty good. It gives them a long time to chicken out. The condemned upper-class twits of Eton and Harrow. Of course they never had the choice to chicken out."

We went back to the office. It was time to start the long haul. I began to distinguish the freelance conditions she enjoyed in her limousine appointments versus the courses she would need to complete before we settled on an arrangement. The health safety course was one of them, and the fee was not insignificant, so before any medical instruction went into her schedule, we had to discuss an initial outlay, and what I could help her with. While I was jotting a list, she put her finger on a map. There was another map on the desk. She asked. I said to have a look.

"This is Capitola," she said. "Why is a dot here? All the rest are encircling San Jose."

"Who knows why dots are anywhere?" I said.

"Why don't we find out?" she said. "Isn't this unusual, a dot in Capitola?"

———

THE Capitola tape showed the Polk bunch had curved off High- way 17 onto Highway 1 south, exited toward the ocean to a couple zigs and zags northwest past a lake on the right. On the way we bought a shovel. I pulled up behind a rusted sedan on the side of a road that ran parallel to the beach. The ocean was on my left, a lake on my right, a heavy cover of beach ice plant on both sides.

I got the shovel out. "You think you're a dominatrix," I said, "and then one day you have to think again."

A beach dweller was on the other side of the road leaning elbows on the rail of a bridge over a sluice that continued from a pipe that went under the road. He looked at us like he knew what was what; "You want to dig, you get to dig."

A hundred feet ahead of my car a barrier blocked a private road that ran perpendicular off the beach road, away from the beach. The first four structures across from the lake were rental apartments with lettered parking places. These hadn't been in the film. Before they were here there had been dunes. Where the curve of the road ended were three homes in place of the two in the film. I was two hundred yards off. The spot I was looking for was up there at a house in sight.

We went along a public path up the north edge of the lake inside a row of immense eucalyptus. We left the path and came out on the paved road that ended in front of the house. A boulder the size of a washing machine was at the corner of a lawn area. I took bearings from one tree and then a second, and went to where the bearings crossed. There was a fitted stone drive. That was new, but a drive was in the film, and that put the digging place a long step from the street and a short step from the drive, on somebody's property.

I stood in a long silence searching for the words, "Who digs?" I put the point of the shovel against the pavement, stacked my hands on the end of the handle and put my chin on my knuckles. I said, "I should explain."

"If you want to keep this a secret," she said, "don't bother with it."

I went to the location I'd fixed a minute before. I put my foot on it. "About here. I want to dig a hole right here. About three feet deep. Perhaps four feet."

"Don't think about it too long," she said. She looked past my arm. "A tall thin man is standing at an open door watching. Could be Nick Charles. He's drinking."

"Let me do the talking," I said. "I'll offer you to him. While you're at it, I'll get the statue. We'll meet at the car."

She led the way to the porch and introduced herself. He was six foot three and pretty thin. It was the scotch diet. He didn't hold out his hand, but he was pleasant about admiring us. He was an active-looking eighty.

I pointed at the point of interest at the corner of his yard. "I have reason to believe someone buried a valuable statue over there. Would you be aware of that?"

"I was wondering what you were going to say. I couldn't imagine what you two were doing with a shovel. Makes sense now. Don't tell me. Let me think about it. An ancient Native American artifact? I pay you to go away and not tell anybody?"

"Not even warm," I said. "Modern. Bronze. About eight inches. A figure of a woman, half naked, looks like me, and has my name at the base."

"Thanks. I never would have got it. How much do I give you that makes it worth your while to say something like that?"

"Absolutely nothing," I said. "I just dig a hole, get the statue, and fill the hole up."

"How deep?"

"Three feet. I hope."

He smiled a nice warm smile. "You can't dig in that ground. Too many rocks. I'd invite you two in, but this is too past my naptime." He stepped inside the door and wished us a nice day, and shut the door.

We reassembled in the street. "You going to leave him the shovel?" Brett asked.

"I own it. Why would I?"

"No reason. You want to wait here?" She went back to the house and used the knocker. The door opened. They spoke very briefly, like a question and an answer. He didn't shut the door. They kept on talking. A minute passed. The man looked at me. Brett came back. She asked, "What was Polk's first name?"

I yelled, "Burleigh."

The man pulled the door shut behind him and joined us in the street. "I knew Polk died," he said. "Why didn't you say?"

"I didn't know I was supposed to," I said.

"Polk was my thesis student at MIT. He didn't bury a statue here. It would take a long time to dig three feet in this ground. That's the first thing. The second thing is I won't let you. I own the two houses next door. I have enough. Who are you two?"

"We are professional dominants from San Francisco. I'm Elizabeth Cromwell and she's with me. You want the shovel? It's free."

"Nothing's free. You should know that. Come to think of it, you could leave the shovel against the stone wall at the house next door. I could use it there."

We stopped for gum and chips on the approach to the highway. It was two o'clock. I called Andrei and said I was in Capitola, leaving now. I thought I'd be digging all afternoon. I was dropping someone in Oakland. Could we meet for dinner? Talk later.

I didn't want to lead her on. Earlier I'd blocked out a list of things to let her think about. She had been ready to hear what I had to say then, and ask questions and answer questions. We had been on 880 for a while, and except for a sneeze she hadn't said a thing, just looked out the window, certainly indicating a preference by not facing me. Maybe she saw my reflection. "You didn't say you loved him."

I didn't answer.

"Let me ask you a question," she said. "Suppose I bury statues around a city. What does that say to you? Seems like he wants to fence it in, possess the city, claim it's his."

I didn't feel like talking about it.

"It seems like you're not living at the English Department now. You took your web page down. You're taking your books with you?"

"Keep the twenty-five hundred books I plan to read before I die somewhere else? I'm thinking about it. You want a free area?"

"You don't use long whips?" she said.

"I'm asked," I said. "Am I putting you in the position of explaining the concept of capitalism to me?"

"The clientele is out there overflowing."

I got off 880 and headed up to Lake Merritt and went around the north side on a guess till she suddenly pointed, "I'll get out there." When I made the U back to Berkeley her back was to me. Her head was down. There was something impeccable in the figure. She was a beauty, and she was a great shot in the mist and tragedy of some movie I'd seen. A pack of gum was on the seat.

Twenty-five

ANDREI WAS WAITING at our table outside in the corner. I took a seat and we blew puffs. It's been a hard day. My puff was bigger than his, so I got to lead off with a look saying it's been a hard day and you don't want to know about it, and give me a chance to catch my breath and I'll tell you. He put his arm on the table up to the elbow, palm up, and it was good to feel that soft finger caress and an exploratory wandering around to a grip on his middle finger. I won't say it doesn't get better than this, but within a comparison to anything an hour either way, this was as good as a long sweet kiss in the sheets.

He got his coffee, a big roll, a house bagel, three jams, two forks, a knife, and I picked off this and that from his plate onto a napkin and dragged the napkin my way, and said, "There's a bird's nest up there," and when he looked, I popped a morsel off his plate to where it would taste good. I told him about the fifth statue.

"A lot more where that came from," I said. "They're buried all over San Jose, a few farther out. Brett and I went to a house in Capitola. She wants a job."

He went inside for more napkins. When he came back his math was bad.

"A two-and-two-is-three day," he said.

I wasn't into any understanding there, but I pretended and said, "Oh, yes indeed."

He lifted his plate and studied closely the space underneath. He had a search going, deadpan. "Some of my bagel disappeared."

"Should I call Herring and Grey?" I asked.

"I wouldn't get excited about re-establishing rapport," he said. "You still say Herring adores me? What is this secret signal women see other women send?"

"Adore is too overwrought. Do you like her?"

"I like the strategy they've come to. Grey does all the not-talking. They have to live with each other. They talk to a thousand suspects a year. They would avoid this 'sorry for interrupting, you go first' etiquette. That would drive a wedge. Better their way for reading vibes. One shakes, the other watches what comes loose."

"You think you can read people?" I asked.

"I don't try. A kid comes in and says his grandmother died, and he has to take the final late, I just do it. I can read Herring and Grey. They haven't absorbed the implications of vertical symmetry. It's a laugh between them."

"Do they care?"

"A timely query. I have something new to show them."

He hauled a briefcase to the table, removed an accordion folder, put the briefcase next to the table, pulled a stack of loose sheets of white paper from the folder, and squared off the pile of paper on the folder. He moved his plate and cup to the side.

"It's an article," he said. "The second page had a drawing. It looked like a drawing in a math paper I'd seen. It was written by a psychoanalyst in Sacramento in 1997."

He turned the title page: "*Les Diagrammes Enfantins* of an Adolescent Schizophrenic."

The next page was a collection of orbiting doughnuts around a dumbbell, which was two blobs of tightly wound squiggles and a thin string attached to both, but not attached like it had any carrying capacity. You could break the string with a breath of air.

The doughnuts had curved lines between them. These did not connect. They had arrowheads on one end and tail fins, indicating some idea that you were to see something of one doughnut going to another. There was more than one arc between two doughnuts. A doughnut could connect to itself.

The next page was another drawing, like the first, but not the same. He turned page after page to show there was page after page of these. They were complicated drawings of a kind I'd never seen, not like paint-dripping art. This was made out of highly structured pieces, drawn by a child.

"These dots at the top of the page," he said, "mean there are infinitely many doughnuts that the page can't hold, but it is clear how to make a chart, and you can add to the chart as long as you want, like you know, point-three-three-three-dot-dot-dot means one-third. You can't put in all the threes, but you can put in the dots to indicate you intend an expression with all the threes.

"I was searching online under 'partitions of unity' trying to put myself in Robert's mind. What was he seeing? I came across this paper. Here, look at this one."

There were seven doughnuts about the same size, printed as if copied from a hand drawing.

"This configuration is associated with the rational number two hundred ten. You can start with infinitely many doughnuts, and you can work it down to finitely many by a process this guy calls, 'boiling down.' You can boil down some configurations to simpler configurations. You can find the definition on the third page of the paper, if you can understand it. The dumbbell is a partition, and the configuration is the unity, which is how the psychoanalyst says this adolescent puts the halves together. Each end of the dumbbell is a blob. Each blob has its own characteristics, which can be added. Together they generate a unity of two blobs. The unity is expressed in the shape of the orbiting doughnuts. That unity is, by definition, rational, if it boils down to finitely many doughnuts.

"Matt Bollinger is the name chosen to identify the patient

for the sake of the article. Matt Bollinger might have been a girl. Regardless, he's the subject of the paper. The partitions of unity was his idea. The analyst got it down, as best he could, I assume. In my opinion, he did a bang-up job, a lot better than what I would have expected. It's really sophisticated. The whole point of the paper is to expose schizophrenic thinking. Bollinger shows that the two halves of himself do not make a rational unity. The argument is arithmetical and topological. The analyst says it doesn't make sense except to Matt Bollinger. You can read his introduction. He says it's a roadmap into the mind. He implies it's a waste of time for a sane person to try to make sense of it as a thing in itself. He never comes out and calls it a 'crazy idea,' but what is schizophrenia if it isn't crazy?"

I looked at the paper upside down. There was underlining in red ink and blue ink. Several doughnuts were circled in green ink.

"You have fun going crazy?"

"Once you get there, what do you have to lose? Strange, I like the paper. I never heard of it. The funny thing is the title was split into French and English, like he was trying to unify those languages.

"It's almost a universal theory of psychological integration. In an appendix, there's a description of the unification of Matt Bollinger and another person, X."

He opened the document at a plastic paper clip and turned all the pages in my direction. He removed the top page.

"This blob is Bollinger, and this is X, as labeled. The dumb-bell is the sum of the two of them. Now, here is an odd thing to see…well…I won't tell you."

"A lot more red than green," I said.

"That's one thing."

"It's not the right thing, though?"

"It's right, but there are other things right. Look at the top of the drawing. What's missing?"

"No dots?"

"No dots."

"The two of them together are rational?"

"The collection of doughnuts boils down to finitely many doughnuts. I'm positive they're elliptic curves, over various fields, but I would have to bring that up with Herring to be sure."

"You've had a hard day," I sympathized. "My car's here. You want a ride home?"

————

WHEN I woke it was ten after four. I was sure I had been asleep, and sure I had heard "Jesus." It's why I think I woke up, but it felt like I had gone back into a slumber and couldn't get any bearings on him running a hand around under the covers. It wasn't warm. He hadn't been in bed for a while. It's what woke me up.

He was at the window desk, naked, in the swivel chair, and when I came in he was looking in my direction. He had heard me coming. I didn't receive the look that he was excited to see me. In honor of the extreme sensitivity of some claim, he said in a calmness of spirit entering an inner sanctum: "He proved e plus pi is rational."

I sat and blinked. "Who did?"

"That psychoanalyst. He killed Robert. There is no Matt Bollinger."

I could see this couldn't wait for the morning. He saw the question in the leaning posture in my shoulders.

"You were asleep," he said. "Can you go back to sleep?" He was holding a pen. He had been writing. Pages were spread in an overlapping jumble on the table directly under the computer screen, as if his work and the mind of the computer were linked. A blue bar was moving on the screen. He glanced at it.

"I thought I left quietly."

I was silent.

"I don't know," I said.

He gestured at the screen. "This is how you do this boiling down."

"You want some coffee?" I asked. My panacea. I got a pot going and called, "Jelly and toast?"

"It's cold," he said. "It's colder than last night." He had his shirt going over his head. I heard, "Yes. Please."

He went to the bookshelf and found what he needed. I put a plate out for us, toast and jelly and peanut butter. I put a knife on a napkin and made mine, and he made his.

He looked at the screen. "It finished. It added two thousand seventeen and forty-two. It's what I thought it would be. It's amazing."

"What are you going to do?" I asked.

"I was going to sleep on the unity surrounding e. It's in the paper. It just happens that e has a unity you can work out, almost in your head, and I was convinced that Bollinger had done that right. And you want to know something odd. The name of the psychoanalyst is John Hermite."

"The John Hermite?"

"The one and only."

"Who's John Hermite?"

"Charles Hermite proved e is transcendental in eighteen seventy-something."

"John is a descendent?"

"If he is, he's as clever, maybe more." He got up and walked into the kitchen and appeared with a salt shaker containing a sugar-cinnamon mix. He shook some on his hand and licked it.

"There's a small problem in this. Just publish the math. Why bring this schizophrenic into it? Matt Bollinger died in nineteen seventy-six. It doesn't say he's a suicide. These people disguise who their patients are. Is this a disguise? Why go to the trouble? He proves e plus pi is rational and puts that in a paper about partitions of the human psyche? Who's crazy around here?"

He shook sugar-cinnamon in his coffee, stirred and licked his finger.

"It can't work. There's no Bollinger. But why?"

"I wish I could tell you," I said.

"This boiling down is an incredible idea of combining elliptic curves to express the addition of two real numbers—which is utterly beyond anything I could dream of. A psychoanalyst that smart? If he's that smart, he's crazy."

"He had to know Polk," I said.

"This is what got Robert. He must have seen this. When he saw it, he knew. But why show him?"

He brought up John Hermite on the screen. He was seventy-eight, had all the credentials, editorships, awards, family, hobbies, plug-ins, a member of the NRA. That was a tell. That could be it.

I plucked some factoids:

"He says his favorite song of all time is, 'Fascination.'"

"Never heard it."

I sang: "It was fascination, I know, seeing you alone with the moonlight above."

"He can love any song he wants. He proved e plus pi is rational. Robert knew he wasn't talking to the celebrated man in the street. This guy did it. And he lives in Sacramento."

He walked to the window, maybe attracted to the dawn, maybe just dazed.

"A proof like that comes along once in a generation—if that."

"He doesn't know you know," I said. "You're to keep it that way."

"We're the only ones," he said. "He's safe...we're safe... the cops are safe...we're all safe. If this were France the cops would listen. It's the style there. It's not that they're smarter than Anglo-Saxons. It's a willingness of the continental mind to plumb abstractions. They like theories."

"You don't believe that. You're trying to tell me you want to be a detective," I said.

"Somebody living in Sacramento leaves a trail killing people in Oakland. The night Robert was killed is a day that pins this man down. He must be a big wheel. He has to be places, say at a grandchild's birthday in San Diego, but unexpectedly he's occupied with an emergency. And he can't back up the story he gives his family."

"A detective can turn up evidence that you are not going to bother with." I put a hard edge in the tone. "There must be a thousand analysts who can't get their story straight the night Robert was killed. What action would you expect Herring to take?"

I was making a new topic. "Did Herring say if they reached Iges? She might have seen the analyst."

"They didn't call. We can ask."

I had tried to confuse him. I went in the kitchen and started some hot water and two settings. While I was making tea, I asked him to look at it through a single peephole.

"Is a seventy-eight-year-old psychoanalyst going to poison a French mathematician in a bar in Oakland? Don't answer right away. Wait for tea."

We went out on the patio and put our backs on pillows and listened to the jackrabbits sleep. I listened to sipping thinking, which is a good kind. It brings on the sleep I'd missed.

"When you rule out the impossible," he said, "you know the refrain."

"Which one is impossible," I asked. "And what can you do?"

"Technically, nothing. I'm a big-mouth kind of sleuth."

"Would you consider speaking with a detective I know?"

The dawn passed and the day went a long way before Andrei and I had another chance to go over the *e* plus *pi* argument, which didn't make anything fit the rest of reality, but we had to have something to say to Cartwright other than we would pay his fee. He would like to arrange in advance what he might call a successful mission. Between me and Andrei, short of a murder confession, we ourselves couldn't get together on a definable task other than "see what you can find." That's what we agreed to. Andrei had a lecture. I would meet Cartwright and put the problem in my own words.

] *Twenty-six*

THE FIRST BIG HILL on the Hall land, entering from the
south, was an artificial plateau with a garden of trees and
bushes inside a waist-high stone wall that had a sign that said not
to sit on it. You saw the sign where a steep, narrow grade leveled
off between a couple pines. This is where the access road ended
and where I set the brake and got out. A fellow in agricultural
clothes with rainbow suspenders parked my car. The garden had
two higher levels next to the parking area. We took a step up to
a crushed brick path through barrier hedges to the other end of
the plateau, which was not exactly a short walk because we made
four U-turns. One place looked like another, but when you come
out the other end, boy, you catch your breath.

The patio was a purplish grouted stone. From the wall the
immediate world was the Hall vista, everything east of the Santa
Inez Forest, and lesser hills that bumped far off into the line of
Highway 280. The dining area was tented under movable canvas covers that let the sun fall where, at any particular time of
day, it was wanted, and you could do that for yourself pushing
buttons. Iron-frame chairs were against the wall out of service.
Arching flower arrangements met above the center of the table.
Two places were set.

Tents and smoke and kitchen racket were beyond a hedge on

the other side of a goldfish pond. In the pond was a three-tiered fountain. A central jet fell into a catch basin and overflowed into another. It was a pleasant racket, and a lot of it.

Beyond two stone columns through an open section of wall was a small landing where a brick walk began its descent to a macadam road that passed between hills and led on to a bricked receiving area. A high pole fence gave the assemblage of structures a mildly garrisoned look, not a walled fortress, but a bunch of buildings of different shapes protected from coyotes. The big building at the corner was the hacienda and nerve center. Walks radiated to all the buildings. This arrangement had been copied all over California. Some of the gated communities copied the garrisoned look. Way off in the distance, beyond the outer bordering hills, was activity, people on foot and tractor-like vehicles.

At a single-story house, a window in a wall of windows opened. A man with something going on with his hand closed the window behind him and moved toward the hill in long steps, but the staircase was a hike of its own, and it took some time.

We met at the gap in the wall. There wasn't a drop of sweat on him. He was in a black long-sleeve shirt tucked into light green pants with black pockets along the thighs. We sat at the table. I put a napkin in my lap. Cartwright held his hand out flat.

"How many do you see?"

There were eight small steel bearings.

He futzed around with them with his hand out in plain view. No tricks. He stopped his hand.

"How many?" he said.

"Seven," I said. I couldn't possibly have expected anything else.

He went through it all again. This time there were nine. So much for that theory, and I didn't have a theory. He put the bearings on the table.

"It's in the spell," he said. "I cloud their minds and they count wrong. There are always eight. You want to do it again now that you know the secret?"

A box of push-buttons was on one shelf of a mahogany stand. Cartwright pressed one. Our server appeared. I glanced around for a menu. Cartwright saved the moment.

"If I might be so bold, let me recommend the BLT on toasted pumpernickel, sprinkled lavishly in house chips and garnished with house pickles. Today is a day you will never forget where you were."

"I'll have ice and a little water," he said.

"I'll have what he just said." I pinched my sides circumstantially. My belt was loose, but I wasn't fooling Cartwright.

"How do you think I keep my figure?" he asked. "Still get into a size six and look too stunning for words in the mirror. The question then is, will I need a six? Do I have to follow someone?"

He raised his glass. We clinked. "To a profitable relationship," he said. "I charge according to a circuitous logic."

It had been the Bay Area stop-wait-and-stop drive on the way here. I didn't feel rested, but the chair was incredible. I wouldn't forget what I was sitting in today. I got going on a summary as Andrei and I had agreed, a psychoanalyst in Sacramento, John Hermite, murdered a mathematician in Oakland. The mathematician was visiting a Berkeley mathematician, Andrei Andreyev, from Paris, his home university, and so and so on. The evidence was open-and-shut according to Andrei's way of seeing it, but the police wouldn't agree, and so on.

"I thought you might have advice for us," I said.

"I know the case," he said. "Herring and Grey have a fair opinion of the professor. He believes sincerely anything he says. You impressed. You didn't give them my name, and they tried. You can draw some credit on that. Also, you brought the case to me and not to them. They will extend their gratitude when I inform them of your consideration for their time by themselves by the pool. As for what you want from me, you might think about my preferences in detection. I love following cheaters.

I love photographing cheaters. I get off getting closer to cheaters than they can believe possible. A case of murder or grand theft auto, yes, but only yes if Mr. Hall needs the service. Otherwise I wouldn't be interested. But regarding advice, it's a beautiful day in the neighborhood. And you do have need.

"Whether he was one or not, the murdered man had the characteristics of a cheater, but as the victim he wasn't the kind I can follow. So I was never interested. My job was following you for Mr. Hall. In that capacity I also followed Ms. Tomek, who has vanished. She was a detective, and I don't like to see things like that happen to a detective. That's where I would take some of your money. Could she have seen who drove the professor to the bar? If so, would that be a psychoanalyst hanging around nights in Montclair with time to dispose of a detective—not just to poison someone, but to fit into the schedule the added bother of getting the crime out of sight? I don't think so. The woman in the shack was left in the shack, and she owned a house a block from where Mavyn rented, so to speak, from Polk.

"I'm guessing the perpetrator lived near her. I might mention that she knew when to get lost. She knew him.

"Your killer lives within two or three blocks of Polk. You can go to Sacramento, but you're not following leads. This fellow Andrei is clever, and clever is clever. I wouldn't take that away from him. I just wish he would try juggling three balls in the air once in a while. Be good for him. It would bring him down to earth."

It was a fine sandwich, fine water, and a pickle that accented the bread. I bagged the chips. I had to say no to cheesecake I would never forget I said no to. They gave me a commemorative box of it, so I wouldn't. When I got home the cheesecake went in the freezer where it would be unearthed when its time had arrived to forget it. I left the chips on the counter for an hour and went into town for supper fixings.

When Andrei drove up he walked over to the nature trail and put himself somewhere into it for a moment, leave some unresolvables out there and come back to them another day, if he could find them. He came in the back door and set a backpack on the floor and had a look at me like looking at me was the truth, the whole truth, and nothing but. I told him I had been there, done that. He didn't ask how it went. I was happy I could have him at home. I had opinions that supported the sensible thing.

"I love cornbread," he said. It was on the rack cooling. I went to him and pushed his shoulders together and said I loved him and hoped he liked monster salads. We ate on the patio and, as is our habit, washed up and went outside with the dishes in the drainer. He rolled on his back and pointed straight up.

"The psychoanalyst didn't do it," I said.

"I agree," he said.

I waited for the bell to ring.

"I promised you I would never put myself in danger. If you want to ask me if I meant it, please do."

I indicated in silence that once was enough.

"If this Hermite has nothing to do with anything, there's no danger peeking into his inner world. I'm sure your detective agrees, even though he doesn't know what he's talking about. I need to know where you are."

He looked at me, no haziness in between.

"Where am I?" I said. "I'm saying no."

"You're scared I'll make a fool of myself."

"I'll get a gun," I said.

He rolled into a laugh. "Thank God. We can shoot our way out of Dodge."

"Why are we going to Dodge? You agreed Hermite didn't do it."

"He didn't write the paper. Somebody collaborated with him, somebody who wanted to bury a brilliant idea in a professional paper among professionals who can't find the axioms of consciousness. Why Hermite agreed is covered in this two-minds-in-one claim. The collaborator knew what Bollinger was claiming. The analyst wrote what he was told to write."

"You think accusing him to his face will make him collapse like in a Perry Mason show?" I said.

"I'll have the drop on him."

"He wants to confess? Get it off his chest? I know a little bit about this. Are you confident you can break him with a stare or something?" I said.

"He'll know I know."

"He might say, 'Go to the police.' He's in his rights to call and claim you're nuts."

"Elizabeth, with me he won't have the illusion of innocent until proven guilty. He published the proof. Nobody noticed till Robert saw it, like I found it." He stopped speaking to me. "Maybe he found some clue that took him to the collaborator. Or he stumbled into the collaborator…but that sequence doesn't work. Hermite comes first."

He stood up and put his hands behind his neck. He paced off steps getting a back-and-forth right. He pointed at me.

"Robert reached him through e plus pi. Like us. It has to work this way. He doesn't need Iges or Polk. This collaborator doesn't have to come out of his cave." He wandered through the kitchen, moving silverware to its right places. "But why help Robert? He's just another bright guy, so why say hello when he can stay in his cave? He doesn't have to come out—unless…and this absolutely has to be right—unless the Riemann hypothesis is killing him and Robert understands the vertical symmetry, or understands it a step further than he received it. Our collaborator puts a toe out of the cave."

"Robert found the proof?" I said.

"He would have acted differently around me. He would have acted the way he acted with you. He found a step, something to consider. Not the proof. Robert sent something back via the Silk Road beginning with Evelyn. She can't intervene between them. The code cuts everybody out. The people in the middle can't add anything. Robert and the cave guy know they're passing their Wagner through an organ grinder."

He went in the kitchen again and rearranged the silverware. He came out not liking something. "The cave guy killed him. Why? He wanted the answer for himself?"

"You have to tell someone," I said.

He stopped and wondered what was percolating in my tricky mind. "You want to walk or what?"

"Let's walk into town. There's cake in the freezer. It's for you."

I put a sweater around my middle, locked the back door, and caught up with him.

"Why meet night after night?" I asked.

"Robert's first step must have knocked the cave guy very hard. He saw stars. He takes Robert's idea and thinks he can do it now. But that runs its course to the brick wall again, and he sends a note back. What's in that note is a good question. It might be an acknowledgment, a salute."

"Another step?"

"No. It can't work that way. Another step would finish it. He starts hand-waving—suppose you do this, then I can do that— that kind of stuff, like ordinary dopes who know the worst: they're both stuck. But they're all they have. But that's what I absolutely would hold up on this for. Robert sees the answer. He tells the guy. He doesn't see this guy doesn't want the world to know. It's a kind of greed."

"Robert would tell the world?" I said.

"He would. He'd have a tough time keeping *e* plus *pi* under his hat, too. The cave guy is into cryptic expositions, speaking among people who do not know what they're hearing. He sits there patting himself on the head knowing nobody knows why. It's a twisted motivation. I've never seen it in math. Of course, I wouldn't."

"He wants to be left alone," I said.

"He wanted the Riemann hypothesis more."

"We can't tell the police. They won't listen."

"We have to make them listen. Wherever he is, I'm too stupid to talk to him. I have to talk to Hermite."

I pointed at him this time. "I won't let you be locked up without me."

It was the Dunning-Kruger effect. The talents we didn't share were pretty much identical to the talents we needed to see why we didn't have what the other lacked, and so kept us from knowing how to patch the deficit. Of course we could try the utterly superficial and experience how little control we had over fate. And the next day we did just that. We were rubes blessed with a talent for collecting an ounce of knowledge from any two points of view, opposing or not.

] *Twenty-seven*

WE WERE TEN MINUTES out of Vallejo, coming up the twist on 80, gaining elevation. Down on the left was the Death's Door water slide at Water World, where I was thinking of taking a kid, where I would never have thought I would trod a sophisticated foot. On the other side of the divide the first bug splattered the windshield, which I passed off with some thought it wasn't worth it to ask Andrei to clean it off. We had gas. We weren't stopping. We weren't rethinking this, so I rode with my eyes shut to keep from seeing what happened to the bug.

I felt a hand on my shoulder about when I expected to open my eyes to the sight of Vacaville slipping past, but we were going over the Sacramento River.

There was a doormat of artificial grass decorating the space where you would stop to read a wooden sign that said that the brown two-story wooden building behind it was the Darwin Fawn Psychoanalytic Institute of Sacramento. A strip of California poppies had taken root around the grass and blended with a fence of inverted horseshoe-wire stakes. A portico at the front door came out to the sidewalk. Across the street was the high embankment of the Capitol Expressway.

A car was coming out of the driveway at the side of the building. A lot was back there with space available, it would seem, but Andrei didn't bother with it. The Institute was on Orange

Street. On Orange there was no parking. The next street going west toward the center of Sacramento was Apple. In between was Chestnut Alley. He drove around the block to Apple and came back and turned into the alley and had a look at a fried chicken outlet, a doughnut outlet, a Christian bookstore, a dry cleaner, an electronics shop announcing a blockbuster going-out-of-business sale.

A tall, rust-colored stake fence enclosed a row of parking places, triple what was needed for the volume of business they were doing, and ran the length of the alley. Across from the doughnut shop was a gate and a spring that pulled the gate shut. At one end was a faded billboard. Young teen representatives of the world's ethnic backgrounds were jumping over soccer balls in the same pants.

The gate was the point of back entry to the Institute. Andrei held it open. He was in his natural state. There was a lot of eye contact that looks deeper than is necessary to find out what's on my mind. We were nervous coordinating who does what. I hesitated as his foot moved to where I ought to be vacating the spot where my foot was. I got a shoe bump in the leg, and I did a hop and a skip. A short path through yellow grass led onto the Institute lot. It was divvied up into named parking and patient parking. "Dr. Hermite" was the name on a cement block at the head of a dark blue Volvo. From building C was visible a back door to building B, an unlettered door. On the other side of the building, separate from A, was a door with a B, which opened to a deserted waiting room full of music with no rise or fall to it. It made a pleasant background.

It was 10:40. Straight ahead was a door to an office that must have let out through another door in back to a patio and the parking lot. There was no polite way of putting my ear to the door to find out what was what. Of course, who knows, silence was a lot of the communication. The waiting room was split in half. On either side wall a sofa, a magazine table, an end table, a lamp, a trash receptacle looked on the same arrangement on the other side. Magazines addressed to the professional addresses of Dr. John Hermite, Dr. Rose A. Lagarde, and Dr. Adam Perelman were available. Soft track lighting lit the room from where the walls met the ceiling. We sat on the same sofa, which, from the end cushion looked down a hallway to a second office and a bathroom. We'd see what happened at 11:00.

At 10:51 two voices in conversation came from outside, close, somewhere in the lot. Andrei opened the door. Two women were talking about a road closure on H Street. In the next ten minutes I heard motors coming up the drive, and I could see foot traffic to and from the back of building A. The low murmur of greetings exchanged in the change of classes was in progress when a door opened to the second office in the hallway. A woman went in the bathroom and locked herself in. Five minutes passed. The woman came out of the bathroom, ready to hit the rest of the day dabbing an eye. She was an attractive married woman in her thirties in high heels and dressed for a lunch at Luigi's if she was in Rome.

The door to the office we were watching didn't move.

After the front door shut, a door in the hallway opened but didn't close. A fiftyish man with a Mephisto goatee, passing to the restroom, absently looked to his right and noticed me. A moment later he recrossed the hallway from the bathroom, and a door shut. At 11:06 a man with a tennis racket entered the waiting room from the outside, knocked on the door in the hall, went in and shut the door. Andrei selected a magazine and tossed it where it didn't belong. The door in the hallway opened, and the man with the goatee came to the head of the hallway and made it clear either of us could answer.

"Are you here to see me?"

Andrei was on his feet. "We were waiting for Dr. Hermite."

He looked sorry for us, but not puzzled.

"There's been a mistake. Check with the receptionist. She can fix anything."

"His car is in his parking place," Andrei said.

"And that means what to you?" he asked.

"He can answer a question about this paper he wrote." Andrei was holding a manila envelope. He jiggled the envelope.

The man thought about something. Then he said, "Dr. Hermite isn't here to answer your question. Our discussing the subject isn't going to change that. It's a question of critical thinking. What's the paper?"

"*Les Diagrammes Enfantins* of an Adolescent Schizophrenic."

"Great paper." He reached his voice out, "I'm Adam Perelman. And you are?"

"I'm not anybody. I'm interested in this paper."

"Everybody is somebody."

"I'm not. We saw his car."

He looked at me and frown-smiled tolerance. "Are you anybody?"

"I'm not anybody either," I said.

"Two nobodies from nowhere. Business is picking up." He took a second. "Dr. Hermite had a stroke. He comes in occasionally for seminars. His parking place has been temporarily reassigned. As far as Dr. Hermite is concerned, nobody on the premises today is anybody who is seeing him. Can you accept what I am saying? He's not here."

We went back to the car. I looked up John Hermite. I had his address. It was available online. Andrei gave me the keys. I put the key in the ignition and plugged in 132 Brent.

"He had a stroke," Andrei said. "He's been dropping in occasionally for seminars. He had a stroke. He can't drive. He doesn't park. I should have thought of that."

"He said the paper was great." I said. I got into the swing of this. "Maybe they're all in cahoots, they're all murderers."

"I had a teacher in college with a goatee like that. A history teacher." Andrei imitated an erudite lecturing style.

"'They say Schliemann found Troy I and destroyed the Troy he was looking for, Troy VII.'"

"Erudite," I agreed.

Brent Street was white picket fences, yards watered rarely,

canopied by trees maybe four stories tall. It was noon and hot—Sacramento hot. The people who settled here got going right away on trees. Not a drop of sun anywhere in the neighborhood of the Hermite residence. Andrei said he didn't want to bother me with walking with him all the way to the front door. I said calmly try and stop me. I wanted to hear.

The front door opened slowly, and stopped opening when a woman took up the narrow space where the door opened to rainwear on hooks and a staircase to the upstairs. A wrinkled but emotionless face waited to hear why we had rung the bell.

"Is Dr. Hermite at home?" Andrei asked. The woman looked to the right, past the door, and kept on looking, while the sound of an apparatus made its way to the door. The woman backed up and a stooped man with sparkling black eyes and a welcoming smile received us as lost strangers in a strange land. He said it was wonderful that we wanted to see him.

Andrei introduced himself. He opened the flap of the envelope and pulled a bunch of pages out, and turned the paper so the doctor could read it.

"You didn't write this," Andrei said.

I heard a faint groan like this day wasn't like yesterday. A series of expressions converged to a breath. Then the man caught a deep breath and said, "No, I did not."

"Who did?"

"I would ask you in, but my wife tires easily. I don't know who. I don't know why. Once I accepted credit I couldn't go back. Who are you?"

"A friend of mine was murdered. Whoever wrote this paper killed him."

It was an awkward silence. Nothing could be added to his initial statement if he was telling the truth. What Andrei's fact meant to him—if it was a new fact—was visibly unsettling to the extent that any distant tragedy was terrible, but distant, a tragedy he could do nothing about.

"Of course you have been to the police. They haven't been here. I can't tell them any more than I've told you."

"You didn't write the paper. I don't see that you reported that. The police won't know any more than you know. Or was that the point, that nobody should know?"

"It's a much-cited article," Hermite said. "It's brilliant in its way. Why give me the credit? I never understood. If you find him will you let me know?"

Andrei asked, "Was there a Matt Bollinger who killed himself?"

"There was. It could have gotten me in trouble. There was a Matt Bollinger twenty years before the paper was written. The boy died in November 1976, they say the twentieth, but it might have been the twenty-first. He was found in the Sacramento River. My reputation covered my explanation. I would never reveal a client's identity. Privately, I investigated. After the boy died, the family moved. They lived above Eureka. I heard the father died."

He seemed to feel he owed somebody an explanation. He wavered unsteadily without moving a foot. He used his arms to keep his balance holding the door. He was tiring. I didn't see an expression of relief or fear that the truth was out. It was another stage of life. Andrei almost left it at that.

"One more thing. Was Bollinger a gifted mathematician?"

"I wouldn't know."

We got in the car. I put my hand on his arm. "What will you do?"

"I don't know. There was a chance. I don't know." He put the back of his hand to his mouth and said, "Just a minute. I'll be back." He went to the door and waited. The door opened and he and Dr. Hermite spoke until Hermite backed away. When the door shut Andrei nodded at me. He got in and left a foot dangling outside, and scratched his hair. "Robert was here."

He pulled his foot inside and shut the door. He asked if I would drive to 98 Clover Lane. Hermite knew the address. It wasn't far. It was twelve minutes if we stuck to the speed limit. After a few turns Andrei told me what they had spoken about. "They spoke French. Hermite was born in Paris. He said he thought he was speaking to a count. He lied to Robert, but he knew that from the way he lied, Robert knew he'd lied, so it wasn't really a lie. It was an aristocratic lie. Robert didn't ask about Bollinger. He was ahead of us."

Clover Lane was in another old part of town, not as old as Hermite's, but still had a less modern attitude to suburbia—no fences, some stucco places, waist-high hedges, trees well under-way, big and shady but not fully overarching. There was a sliver of sun on 98 Clover Lane. The house was up from the corner. We parked on the cross street. A car came by, and then a minute went by. We got out and walked a few blocks and encountered no one coming the other way.

We came back to where we started and went the other way, past where the Bollingers had lived.

Andrei looked at addresses. "You want to pick a house? Somebody might remember him."

"What would they remember?" I asked.

"Ask if he was good at mathematics."

We split up but kept in sight, working in parallel along oppo-site sides of the street. We were a couple of Christian missionaries wanting to talk math. Not many doors opened. People talked through mail slots. Dogs barked. One man said to come around to the back fence and kiss his nails. We turned ninety degrees and worked the cross street. We turned another ninety degrees and did another block. I met Andrei at the corner.

"There's a widower at the house over there," I said. "He says the Bollinger boy was friends with Richard Shoemaker. Rich-ard Shoemaker was brilliant. The Shoemakers used to live a few streets over, on Essex Street. Mrs. Shoemaker took Richard out of school in the sixth grade and sent him to the library to read any-thing he wanted. When he was fourteen she wanted to be able to discuss philosophy with him in French. Social services wouldn't accept the arrangement, so he entered Sacramento State. He preferred math."

We got back in the car. I presumed Andrei wanted to be chauffeured to Sac State. I set the compass. On the way Andrei looked up Richard Shoemaker. There were fifty-eight to put through the sieve. Every few seconds or so Andrei said, "No, no way."

I said, "The neighbor also said that Mrs. Bollinger wouldn't let Matt visit Richard. They were getting too close."

We found visitor parking. I asked Andrei how long we feed the meter for.

"Well, this is the guy. I know what will happen. I go in there and find someone who remembers Richard. They remember they couldn't teach him anything. He dropped out. Or maybe they sent him to Berkeley. I could ask around. I haven't heard the name, but it was a long time ago, if he was there, and there have been plenty of these prodigies since. And what do I find out? He was brilliant and he dropped out."

"The magician I met, a fellow who works for Hall—Leon Cartwright—he says he bets the one you call Richard Shoemaker is living close to where Polk lived. That narrows it down to where I don't want you to go near."

"Can we call that guy?"

We headed back down 80. I called Leon. No answer; leave no message. I called Cook and left a name, Richard Shoemaker, born about 1962, a good bet in Sacramento, lived on Essex Street, Sacramento. Where is he now?

"I wonder how he did that? He published a paper in Hermite's name. He intercepted the incoming mail to Hermite and answered the queries of the publisher. He was a patient there. Maybe. It must be."

I agreed in silence.

"Why kill Robert? He asked himself.

We pulled onto the front grass on Calvend Lane about four o'clock.

] *Twenty-eight*

T HE FIRST FEW SUITCASES to Kensington were the things I would have grabbed in any emergency and lived out of fairly comfortably, short of showing myself at a wedding or a funeral or opening night at La Scala. For a couple of months, while I picked up a shower cap and grabbed a box of Band-Aids and built up a collection of trash can liners in four colors, living with Andrei was not much more than a daily purchase, scarcely more than an afterthought in front of a Walgreens that amounted to a collection of items that were used up and replaced at roughly equal rates. It was a life that breezed along like marriage, like it was supposed to. Once in a while an acquaintance from what were becoming the old days would see me and offer congratulations, and we'd know a name who'd dropped off the ends of the earth, and we too hurried off to distant points of our lives with a sort of pang that it was what it was, not much of a goodbye. But there it was. I got a note from a Mistress Alexandra who had put up her shingle in my time. She was cross with me that she hadn't been remembered for the bachelorette bash, but there hadn't been one.

I was separating piles that were going to Kensington or getting boxed and donated. As I went through the upstairs chambers, a whip seen on edge against a saddle got me thinking of putting together a handy package. I wasn't going to run out to the canyon all hours for a switch when the basics were available in all degrees of vivid experience.

The saddle, shaded from direct light in the hall, began to layer outlines of a body that clicked in a name: The Gawdawful Press.

The saddle had been the favorite of a pornographer who had seen how to break up the Flyte-Simpson *Minutes* into a collection of cliff-hangers, the Oakwood Domestic Saga. Would Mr. Wilson get it at high noon Saturday, or after services Sunday? Would Mrs. Wilson have him grab his ankles, or bend him over the laundry basket? Serialization was the force-multiplier for the bottom line. Sex was absent from the saga, so it was carried in commercial bookstores in the relationships sections, and the series turned a profit. The first few installments advertised the rest. The author rented my two cents' worth to make whole the bimonthly version of a Ms. Wilson. I'd read the scripts and worked some matriarchal manners into a focus that gave him the angle, and he'd dash off a book of seventy-five pages, typeset it, and run off the copies he thought he could sell. Horse stables provided his best-selling scenes, and the saddle was the lap of luxury in his own imagination.

While I was on the road I was aware of taking on a fateful decision—was I going to reread *Lair of the Lash*? God! I was thinking of the Gawdawful Press—and simultaneously detached in a kind of reverie where a house in the distance would suddenly return a title, as of a movie or a play, my thoughts absentmindedly at a work that, in its triviality, camouflaged itself, wondering where I'd seen this or that phrase. My memory struck a phrase in an annual best erotica anthology. It came to me: I was thinking about Sullivan. He was usually represented. For over twenty years he had appeared in collections. When I got to the office I looked him up in the card catalogue. I had his story, *The Woman Over There with the Lunch Pail*, off the shelf and on the desk, and as I was getting ready to lock up, I opened the cover and saw the dedication to Mrs. Richard III. It could be psychoanalyzed

seven ways from Tuesday. One of them was me, or the me
Sullivan saw.

I reread the story over the weekend. It was a journey into a
woman. She was a dominant, professionally. It begins on the day
after Labor Day at the ferry dock in Sausalito, and a man waving
a newspaper at a seagull brought himself to the woman's attention
as if she had opened her wallet and pulled out his photograph.
The man, the average man of the era, was in an open collar. He
handed a cup of coffee to a well-dressed woman arriving at the
dock, and took her suitcase and hustled her off, as they do in
Sullivan stories, to the inn. The dominant waited with no idea
why she wanted to see the man again. It had to do with some
quality of herself at that moment that made her susceptible to
an act of liberation. She never saw that man again. But her crisis
was underway.

I didn't get to the crisis. I'd read it more than once before.
I called Sullivan. He had disappeared when we understood we
would never be a couple. I wanted to see him if he'd see me. I
thought I could recall our last meeting.

The English Department had been a speakeasy during Pro-
hibition. There were eight rubber mats in the basement. There
were Chinese characters on seven of them, the days of the week,
and a trapdoor under one to a sub-basement, a still lower level,
which was not in the floor plans of the structure I purchased in
1997. There was no indication of such a space in the paperwork
at escrow. I assumed it had been the emergency exit, and to cure
my curiosity, I had a fellow torch the metal seal on a plate and
cut it open to a corridor that came up through another trapdoor
into a narrow stairway on the other side of the alley. Today the
stairway leads up to a rear door of the women's facilities on the
third floor of a restaurant on the next street over.

The top hats eat up there, at The Balcony. Not on the bal-
cony, but at The Balcony, sparkling even on a gray day in low fog.
You were three flights over a street where they had watched the
Tong Wars. Meals came up in a dumbwaiter. Lieselotta entered

the English Department this way once and freaked out. We would be trapped, locked in each other's embrace, and never found. At lunch, Sullivan and I slipped to the cavern for quickly administered behavior adjustments and went back for espressos.

I was waiting with my legs crossed when Sullivan arrived. It started like that, in a strict posture.

A curtain parted and our server, a severe Asian lady in a silk sheath, regarded us indulgently with professional patience. Sullivan announced he was five minutes late and asked for five strokes of the cane, a request marginally relevant yet meaningfully correlated to the two of us who might carry out the sentence. I was trying to look elegant. I was a known commodity up here. The server quit the nonsense. She left a wine list. She didn't say she would be back.

Sullivan stood behind his chair at attention, perhaps on tiptoe. He was average in appearance in all but the eyes. A life of self-examination had taught him: take no responsibility. His eyes twinkled. I knew I was on. We were smiles all around.

"I was late, madam. It shall not happen again," he began.

"Oh, gosh. Again? Please. What does a poem mean?"

"Simple and frank speech, if I'm not confused."

"And am I hearing poetry, Sullivan?"

"Perhaps misses the profound."

"Stick to what you know, Sullivan, and remind me—poor French?"

"Whipping didn't do the trick."

"May I then suggest a subject for today, Sullivan. Pornography."

"Pornography, mistress?"

"If I might be so forward. Complaints, Sullivan?"

"None, mistress."

"Begin, if you will. Attempt a definition, in the abstract, without examples."

"Should I limit my definition to writing?"

"And why wouldn't we do that, Sullivan?"

"Well, Beethoven's violin concerto. I forget the number. Well, one of them, anyway, it arouses me."

"Sexually?"

"Yes, mistress."

"You are weird, Sullivan. I believe you know I know that. Incidentally, why did you stop coming to the English Department? I haven't seen you for years. How many, Sullivan?"

"Too many, mistress."

His shoulders rounded. "At attention, Sullivan. Answer the question."

"Permission to speak frankly, mistress?"

The curtain opened. Our server asked if we were ready to stop fooling around. Sullivan ordered a whip and wrist restraints. The curtain closed.

"Sullivan, let's clear this up. Where were we? You were prepared to tax your wits. Press on, Sullivan."

"You're too beautiful, mistress."

"What mischief are you up to? Three additional for the attempt, whatever your sneaky habits are up to."

"None, mistress. You're too good for me. I don't deserve your instruction."

"That is the point, Sullivan. If you were too good for me, then what? Remember, you were speaking frankly."

"I met someone."

"There we are. Continue. Wait. Excuse me, better than me?"

"I'm wondering why we're not clearing up the five minutes, mistress?"

"That, again? Am I not humane, Sullivan?"

"You are, mistress."

"You were telling me of a dominant of superior qualities. Go on."

"Not as beautiful."

"Of course not, Sullivan, but to you, Sullivan, what is the quality straining for expression on the tip of your tongue?"

"She is a pure cane mistress."

"What in the world have I been all these years?"

"Baudelaire's complications are in your image. You're a product of a background that goes back to immigrants, straight-laced, striving, too hard on itself. Why else pro dominance? A dignity in the mix of your traumas is extracted and trimmed back appropriately to earn a living in perfect instruction as a redemption. In your image is the enveloping aura of dignity and a lofty melancholy always magisterial."

"Care to sum that up, Sullivan?"

"I was beginning to care, mistress. It hurt too much. Love, you know, I didn't like the feeling. A circular firing squad."

"Shall we?" I said.

He left a rose on the table and cash, and we took the street to my office. The oak chairs were still worn thin. It was a half sad, half sort of exciting jolt of remembrance running his hands over the old arms that pulled him back to the crazy hours of working to scripts of Sally Spankbare, where the afternoons stood still and yet ran off into a goodnight pinch to grow an inch and then back to the sweatshop on all-night deadlines for the next edition.

"We were on the clock," he said. "No time to think of our place in literature."

"The woman you met, the 'pure cane mistress,' as you describe her. It's an autistic phrase. I don't want to explain that. It means something special to you. You wouldn't understand it to explain it to me, but you made use of it in *The Woman Over There with the Lunch Pail*."

"What's bothering you?" he asked. "My writing? I don't recall jealousy."

"The story was good. It was well padded, more than what I would have expected from a direct reading of the corresponding story in the *Minutes*. You saw something in her you liked, and you took it. Is she the woman you met?"

"I saw her for a year. I didn't want to know her. Likewise. It gave rise to an odd snobbery between us, good for the discipline. It didn't do much for my writing. We lived intensely for a time. She didn't show up one day and I knew I loved her. When I could function as an ex lovesick dolt, she was back, still a pure cane mistress—and I, stuck with an inability to profit from previous despair, was in love. That's the forensics of canings in the morning."

"Go on with that," I said.

"She came back to me. She was in a crisis. A man she had met. She was fascinated with him. He was standing at the doorway of an investment house counting his money. He had just made three thousand dollars on a hundred-dollar investment in twenty-four hours. She went to lunch with him. She wanted to know how he did it. He told her, and she couldn't understand a word. She asked if she could meet him again. He said he was going to drown himself that night, so they ought to meet for an early dinner. At dinner they talked about his upcoming death, and also, where was his money? He had given it back to the investment house. He reinvested. He said he would lose most of it in six months. He knew the market. He played the market to verify his calculations. Money came and money went. He was uninterested. What he wanted was to own the Bay Area. He wanted to be a king. He decided this was impossible. So why live an impossible dream?"

"You remember her name?"

"She was a hybrid, Flyte-Simpson. Sounded phony, but it tripped off my tongue as her subject."

"Renate?"

"You know her?"

"Heard of her. Her crisis was money?"

"Slipping through her fingers, like...what should I say... water?"

"She promised you lust eternal."

"She delivered. In my book you could take every dominant in San Francisco and stack every bit of their talent in a heap and it would be like a kid's scribble against...I don't know what...Renoir, if you think he's any good. She knew her advantages with me. I had to have her. I have no pride, no talent, a mediocre neurotic."

"So you reaped the joy of lust. What did she get? Don't answer. She got stories. You wrote stories to keep the suicidal man alive on hope, a hope that the stories would come true."

I didn't look like I wanted to interrupt. He went on.

"It worked for a year. I had the idea of the Spanish governor of the San Jose territory who deeded the territory to President Polk. The deed went home with Polk when he left office. The deed was forgotten. Polk didn't want San Jose. No descendent of Polk ever claimed the land. Finally, a Polk arrived. You know the rest. I got the idea from *The Baron of Arizona*, average grade-C flick, a Vincent Price vehicle. He wanted Arizona. Renate had a Polk under her thumb and they worked out a happy-ever-after story for this other guy. He made good profit for her in the market. She kept him alive on the Caudillo of San Jose scheme. You can't make this up."

"I'm not sure what you're making up." I said. "How does it end?"

"How would I know? It had been a year of my life without porn. We all wake up. I went back to the true and the worthless. The dirty bang for the dollar."

"You're too modest. *The Woman Over There with the Lunch Pail* was...do I dare say it?...superb in its conception. The Flyte-Simpson character was impeccable. I knew her as if I'd known her all my life. Only money got her out of bed—put the gas in the tank."

"God and present company excepted," he said, "she had one fine grasp of the Ten Commandments."

"You got her nature in every syllable. The main character in the *Minutes* became the man who lost his shirt in the crash, and married the seamstress. He was terrified of having money. He was Dostoevsky's gambler who had to lose it. The wife realized she would have to become the blackjack dealer with the whip. Anything he earned, she saw to it, he lost it to her. She understood the need. She kept a statue of a goddess on her dresser. The goddess with the riding whip.

"Did I do justice?" I asked

"O. Henry stuff." He sniffed lovingly.

"Funny, after all these years, we are hearing the voice of a man who went through the crash. It's all in the *Minutes*."

"You hear who wrote it?" he asked.

"The man I got it from was the third owner," I said.

"*Debasement and the Good Marriage*. A working title. The combination has some neat scenes."

"Why would anyone want the *Minutes of the Renate Flyte-Simpson Society*, other than you and me and all the aficionados?"

He bent forward, one hand squeezing the other.

"It's old tripe. Nobody would ever do it the Flyte-Simpson way again. There was a pleasure to be found for the inhibited. Repression could still be our ally and best ghost."

"A man came to see me from a faraway country," I said. "He was willing to pay for the *Minutes*. What say you?"

"How much you get?"

"I gave them to him."

"Renate would not approve. And I, too, would say you took a bath. It was good writing. He didn't try to hang on to his people. They got up to their own enactments. A hack like me was happy to have the crumbs off his table. Why that form—the minutes of meetings in a basement in Piedmont. Good as a castle in Transylvania. Beautiful stuff. How does he come up with that? The forgotten man. I looked up Bram Stoker. Wrote tons of garbage. Out of nowhere comes the vampire industry."

"If I might incur three strokes for changing the subject, what's bothering you?"

"He was willing to pay," I said. "Thousands? I didn't ask."

"Sounds like a woman over there with a lunch pail. You have no idea what you're seeing."

"Renate?" I asked.

"If she's part of it, she's the mastermind. You got took. But I know you, you'll live."

"Speaking of your genius, how did I come out as Mrs. Richard III?"

"The mystery of Mrs. Richard III had me on the edge when I did the winter-summer soliloquy and you were across the room. I saw Richard's wife, and if she had meant the world to him beyond his ridiculous ambition, if he could forget his hump and his short arm and his crippled spirit…and I thought, well, suppose he can forget. Put a fork in Shakespeare. What about that woman across the room? She has this wall to stand against where money or some other commodity with power over her needs guides her to interpret a role she's requested to play. And I wrote it as it was, your struggle with me. How honest was I?

"You made me hold your ankle and dared me to lie," he said. "I paid you back. I wore unmatched socks. What sweet revenge. I could see the marriage on paper in a vagueness conjured out of thin air. I was a head-banger. I remember the first time and what you said to me:

"'I'm reaching out to you. Don't take me for granted. You can't hurt me hurting yourself. You can turn out less than you promise. I like you enough to give of myself to let you know me as much as you can make out of these expressions of mourning and terror. Speak to me of your own if you wish.'"

"I kicked you in the leg," I said. "I could do that again."

He started to roll his pant leg up and let it go. "It's still there, the scar. It's comforting. It's eye-catching. I have this chair I vacation in with dinner in my lap, my feet on a pillow about eye level, passing judgment on life passively, usually aware of not wanting the day back, usually pretty happy there's nothing in the night ahead more than take all the time I want studying the lights on my apparatuses. And I have my scar. I worked with Elizabeth Cromwell on something like equal terms."

We left by the front gate and took a few steps on the up route to the corner of Stafford, which would have taken us around the block to The Balcony and to the beginning, and we risked the feeling that's hard to control, wanting the other for the feel of life that was once spontaneous, the life in which desire for life came into an awareness of the first thing that gave contentment and… frustration…deciding…we were never possible…

] *Twenty-nine*

FOR A FEW WEEKS Andrei and I studied lists of properties within a short walk of Polk's house for hints about where Richard Shoemaker might be living. If he was at an address in there, it would fill in the opportunity part of means, method, and opportunity to kill Robert, though we didn't think he did it, but thought he knew who did do it. And that was hard to believe. The burden of proof against him, based on the concepts Andrei had used to find his name, was still a tough analysis, only a bit less given the discovery that a woman who had lived a block over on the next street above Polk was the dead woman in the shack. Another coincidence: she and Polk died from the same kind of poison.

And then one day Richard Shoemaker walked into the Annals of Screwball California. It was one of the classical instances of man bites dog, and it might have caught a paragraph below the fold in the local section of the *San Jose Mercury News* if Gail Sanchez had had her second dose of morning Dexedrine. She had returned on Monday from an L.A. weekend. She could talk while asleep, and she could listen for long stretches. It didn't matter if her retention that day was short-lived. Shoemaker seemed to be saying he was submitting an application for ownership of an area of California once known as Rancho San Jose, and he was leaving it off with Gail at the lost-and-found desk of a San Jose Home Depot.

He placed a statue of a woman with a whip on the counter in front of her window. The name on the base of the statue was Elizabeth Cromwell. He opened a map. If one drew a convex polygon connecting the x's on the map, this is the region he claimed. At each x was buried an identical statue to the one he submitted as to his bona fides. The region was more extensive than modern-day San Jose. Documentation consisted of four items: (1) a death certificate for a Burleigh Polk; (2) a last will and testament dictated to Matt Bolllinger, a longtime friend—everything bequeathed to Richard Shoemaker; (3) a thirty-four-page article, a second-person account of events from a hundred years before; (4) a cover letter, the testimony of an unnamed eyewitness to a proof that $e + \pi$ is rational.

When Gail returned from her morning break the Shoemaker material had not yet been shelved. Shoemaker had left an address: Cloud 9, Parcel, 9^2, Plot, 9^9. It was unlikely he would find his way back, nor could he be found even if anybody had wanted to. Friday was Gail's last day with Home Depot. She took the statue home with her that night. The rest of it could sit on a shelf forever.

Hector Ruiz had met Bonnie Seal through Gail, whom he had known since high school. Bonnie and Gail had shared an apartment for over a year. They were on a second lease. Hector had been coming over for a few months. He had been dating Bonnie. Gail and Hector would have a beer while Bonnie was getting ready to go out for the evening. The statue was an interesting item. Gail had discovered there were no Elizabeth Cromwells in San Jose, nor any around the Bay. The statue looked historical to Hector. He found an Elizabeth Cromwell in history, the mother of Oliver Cromwell. The statue could be worth something. He called around to pawnbrokers and curio shops. An antique dealer asked for photographs. Hector set the statue against a ruler. It was a good eight and one-half inches of erotic art. The woman was mostly naked. She had a whip. She possibly had been royalty. He got a provisional offer of eight dollars, perhaps more when he brought it in. Gail might get triple that on eBay. Hector offered her five bucks. Gail decided to keep it on the bureau, at least for a while, to see how it grew on her, or didn't.

Two weeks went by. Gail had started a new job with a chain of seafood restaurants. She and Bonnie had decided to relocate to another apartment, including a third roommate. While wrapping a set of teacups in newsprint Gail saw a picture of a man in the *Mercury*. The man had unloaded a shopping cart of cardboard and assembled the sections into a homelike structure. A sign taped to the portico declared the residence of El Caudillo de Plaza de Cesar Chavez de San Jose. He would not levy taxes on his citizens, nor raise an army. In his pockets the police found a one-hundred-dollar bill and a sock with about five dollars in coin. Temporarily, San Jose owned him. He was placed in a shelter until he was recognized. The man had no tattoos or scars, no distinctive facial features, but Gail was sure this was the man who had given her the statue, and she called the tip line of the *Mercury*.

A reporter, Anne Knudsen, called her back. She met Gail the next evening after work. The interview was on deep background, as Gail had facts that she wished kept out of the record. She produced a statue from the bedroom. The homeless man had brought this statue with him to the lost-and-found at Home Depot, where she had worked. The name at the base, Elizabeth Cromwell, might refer to the mother of the Lord Protector of the Commonwealth of England, although the Caudillo title didn't conform to that title. But she did remember there was a map with *x*'s, and the man had said there were identical statues buried at the *x*'s. It came back to her that the man claimed the land inside the *x*'s, although she also thought that the man had found the statue and map in the store. He was not turning it in for himself. She gave the information to Anne. It was confusing.

The Home Depot where Gail had been employed was open

till 10:00 P.M. and Anne Knudsen stopped by. She spoke with Dan Fricke, who could open the lost-and-found office, which was closed till the next day. It was routine to be asked for identification and asked for explanations. Anne provided press identification and the purpose of her visit, the possible identification of a homeless man. Fricke made a copy of her I.D. and had Anne sign the copy. Materials that seemed to have been shelved with the map were placed together on a desk. It was hard to see how this stuff could have been mislaid or forgotten at Home Depot, and Dan decided to keep it in his office until authorized to release it. Anne Knudsen took a few notes. She kept Gail's recollections of Richard Shoemaker's remarks to herself. The few x's not within the convex polygon of land claimed were places to start her search the next day.

Ralph Konrad was not too surprised to open his front door to a young woman with a bronze statue of Elizabeth Cromwell. Anne showed her press I.D. and Ralph took her to where two women claimed that a like statue had been buried to a depth of three feet at the corner of his front yard. She asked if he was familiar with the names Richard Shoemaker, Matt Bollinger, or Burleigh Polk. Of course; Polk had been his research student at MIT. He had died recently and tragically at the height of an exceptional career at the Lawrence Livermore labs. The other two he didn't recall, and he could offer no reason why Polk would leave Shoemaker anything. He believed Polk had no family other than a foster mother in Wisconsin somewhere.

He could throw some light on the two women who had a shovel to dig up the statue. They said they were professional dominants—jokingly, he thought. One of them was an Elizabeth. She called herself Elizabeth Cromwell from San Francisco, but he found all Internet references to her were erased. She might have moved away. He thought she had omitted to give the other woman's name. As for Polk, he was a good student, but the reports of the extraordinary advances he made for the Department of Defense just never fit the work Konrad thought Polk was capable of. Konrad's letter of recommendation for Polk received considerable criticism.

Anne's editor at the *Mercury* submitted an application to a data agency for information on two subjects, a Richard Shoemaker and a Matt Bollinger. The editor thought a homeless man in San Jose, a man in his late fifties, might be Richard Shoemaker. He was claiming an inheritance from Burleigh Polk, which, in his mind, included a region once known as Rancho San Jose. Matt Bollinger might have been a colleague of Burleigh Polk at Lawrence Livermore. He might also have known Richard Shoemaker. The editor included the serial number of a one-hundred-dollar bill in the possession of the homeless man.

The editor received confirmation that a Richard Shoemaker and a Matt Bollinger were born twelve days apart in July of 1963 in California. They had lived three blocks from each other for nine years in Sacramento. Matt Bollinger died in 1976. Richard Shoemaker's parents were dead. He was declared legally dead in 1998. He could have recovered more than three million dollars' worth of unclaimed assets, which included stocks, bank accounts, insurance policies, and property settlements. His mother's estate went to his father's brother, who died in 2012. The one-hundred-dollar bill in the possession of the homeless man had been tracked through the banking system fourteen years earlier in Santa Cruz. It had been a bill in a five-hundred-dollar withdrawal by Ralph Konrad.

Anne Knudsen would attempt to uncover further information on Shoemaker. The editor hoped he would have updates reasonably soon.

Roman Zdrojewski was the assistant features editor at the *Mercury*. He spoke with Spike Davidson, West Coast manager of Home Depot. By now the homeless man was being referred to as Richard Shoemaker. Davidson said the Shoemaker material had been sent to Sacramento. He didn't know if a copy had been made. If so, he'd send that to Anne Knudsen. Anne sent a request for the Shoemaker material to the controller's office of the State of California. Two weeks later the State of California sent Anne a stapled collection of thirty-four pages of a first-person account of some proceedings of an organization called the Renate Flyte-Simpson Society. Included was a claim that someone had proved that $e + \pi$ is rational. Polk's last will and testament was not included, nor was the death certificate for Burleigh Polk.

Anne looked up the mathematics department page of San Jose State University. A Scott Phelps taught a course on rational and irrational numbers. Anne left a message with him that a homeless man, possibly emotionally impaired, said he had seen a proof that a number $e + \pi$ is rational. Is this result known, and would it be of any interest?

At ten after the hour Scott called and said the result was not a conjecture, not even a guess, but a possibility and the least likely possibility. People had, no doubt, claimed they had proven it. They weren't all attention seekers, necessarily, but they were way out of their depth. This kind of thing was not uncommon in mathematics. Even serious people made mistakes. It happened once in a while that buried errors remained undiscovered for a long time. Some might still be, but a proof that $e + \pi$ is rational is not a part of mathematical lore he was aware of.

Shoemaker was nuts, but Anne's instincts caused her to wonder if his disorder might have a peculiarity born of real events. A story written by a man named Grant Sullivan contained elements that might have supplied an incomplete background to the origins of Shoemaker's spurious claim of rightful ownership to San Jose.

In June of 1917 the U.S. Army was looking for land in the West Bay for a training center. A tract in Los Altos was in a legal dispute that had been unresolved by the courts. It was sitting there. The dispute went back to the overlapping claims of Edward Greenfield and Maxwell Hall, and like most such disputes at the time of California statehood was not covered in the broad strokes of the treaty of Guadalupe-Hidalgo. Both Greenfield and Hall could bring powerful influence to bear on individual judges, which kept pushing off the proceedings in search of a solution in which no reputations were sullied. This was responsible for a sequence of judges who had thought best to pass the baton. And then Greenfield was wounded in the Spanish–American War, and his service and recuperation was another delay. Then he died and the transfer of property to a Randall Polk, who was married to Greenfield's daughter, and divorced, held things up. Most of the Hall people and Polk people had come to treat the dispute as the way life worked, and the lawyers went along. Nobody pushed until the Army insisted on a quick fix between Andrew Hall and Reed Jenkins Polk—which was that the Army got use of the land for the duration of the World War, and would then give it back to Polk and Hall after the armistice. At the end of the war the Army changed its mind and kept possession in perpetuity on a provisional ruling of 1883. Reed Polk was a colonel in a division that saw combat in France. His protest was honored. In 1921 the Army said they were satisfied if Polk settled on a land transfer from Hall near Eureka, and cash, and Hall got the Los Altos land.

How Reed Jenkins Polk connected with Burleigh Polk was not available, which made the proceedings strange as a document put forward by Shoemaker, even on a crazy claim. But then the proceedings got crazy. A lawyer, William Dade, acting on Polk's behalf, had married an assistant, Gladys Wilson, in Arizona, an arrangement that Mrs. Polk contested in California, as she was already married to Dade. The disposition of that subsidiary case was hard for Anne Knudsen to believe. It seemed to enter the jurisdiction of some legal entity within the Renate Flyte-Simpson Society, although the case was not a legal case. The issue of the complainant, Mrs. Dade, was emotional distress. She gave her side of the matter to a jury of three women, who found in her favor. William Dade was sentenced to a dozen strokes of the cane on the bare buttocks before the assembled membership of the Society. Dade appealed in writing. The appeals group agreed to hear his side in person, but ruled against him and increased the sentence to fifteen strokes, which was specified by the jeopardy clause in the appeal process. Dade had known about it. He then wrote a last appeal to the high priestess, a woman with a secondary title, Mistress, otherwise known as Renate Flyte-Simpson herself.

This stuff went on and on, and culminated in a verdict of two dozen strokes, and Anne Knudsen was beginning to think Dade was asking for it. She began to suspect she was reading pornography, although how the material might account for sexual arousal was beyond her.

One of the x's on Shoemaker's map was a cross of two different colors, as though Shoemaker's pen had run out of ink midstream. It was within four other x's, and so did not denote a boundary point. She called a number at the Harold Hall estate and spoke with a Ms. Cook. She related what she knew of Richard Shoemaker and asked what Ms. Cook could tell her, which basically was that Ms. Cook knew about the statues found on the property, and these could be discovered from a visual code within films made by the Renate Flyte-Simpson Society. The Elizabeth Cromwell on the base of the statues referred to such a person living in San Francisco. Not only had she met this woman, but she knew someone who had her private number.

Anne called Elizabeth Cromwell. When Anne arrived at the house in Kensington she met Elizabeth and a professor of mathematics at U.C. Berkeley. They had set a third chair in the room. They said she was going to get the story of the month. It had legs. She might wind up at *The New York Times*. The professor got a story, too. All along he had been positive that Richard Shoemaker had killed Robert Lavoisier. But it could not be so. And it wasn't that way at all.

] *Thirty*

A MANUSCRIPT OF a proof of the Riemann hypothesis was in the Wednesday mail addressed to Professor Apostopoulos at the University of Athens. The professor had written a book on the subject. A manuscript claiming to be a proof was not unusual. An assistant opened the envelope, wrote the title and the name of the author, Cybele Hallas, in the day's log, found no reference to the author in a worldwide mathematics directory, clipped the contents to the envelope, and dropped it on a stack of set-asides.

Professor Apostopoulos had a look at the week's mail log on Friday. The Wednesday proof had been the only proof received for several weeks. He looked at the list of references. His book was not referenced. This was unusual.

That night he and his wife had dinner out and followed up with a French film at a cinema. It had been a love story that hadn't taken his interest, and during the film he recalled that the paper in his office that claimed it was a proof of Rh was written in French. He hadn't seen misspellings or extravagant language or other telltale signs that signal a crank, but the return address was a district of Athens he would avoid, at night certainly.

After the film, he went home intending to put in an hour catching up on things to do before bedtime. He had copied a formula for the nth prime from the first page of the manuscript. He hadn't seen anything like it. He took the formula from his briefcase with an intention to have a look at it insofar as it would give the right asymptotic result—or that if it didn't, that would be that on page one. An hour passed just running things around in desktop calculations. There seemed to be no good stopping point attempting to verify that the series of terms converged. He couldn't even see how two terms might effectively combine into a like term. An integer was notated to indicate that it was represented differently in each term, but he had assumed he wouldn't have to bother with that. That aspect of the calculation came later in the paper. The bare bones of the formula for the nth prime that appeared on the first page was therefore missing essential instructions. He would have to get into the paper, and that would have to be in the coming week.

On Monday evening Apostopoulos had a longer look at what he was up against. There was a section zero of the paper. It laid out the structure of the argument within a sequence of statements to be considered in the body of the paper. The presentation looked very good. An overall survey of contents more than held his interest. He almost wanted to hold on to the awe, and leave it at that. The individual lemmas—the helper theorems on which the structure of the proof was built—were models of poetic brevity, and technically challenging, beyond the wherewithal of even a professional mathematician to cut and paste from book reading, so the manuscript, although the product of an unknown, and certainly containing an error, couldn't be ignored until some error materialized, pure and simple. That was the goal. Find the error.

An error embedded in an argument at this level of sophistication now and then repaid analysis. There could be new mathematics. He was fifty-one percent inclined to think that the proof contained insights within its individual claims. If one of them was right, Hallas could take a bow for a serious attempt at a problem that hadn't been cracked in the entirety of the twentieth century. Unlikely as it might be, a mistake in a lemma might be fixable—regardless that the argument as a whole would expose a misconception. Subtle or not, the proof would fall like a stone.

As things stood, the technical troubles took shape in the first lemma. A new subject had to be mastered. The proof of the lemma relied on tools not yet written up in the literature, not that Apostopoulos knew of. Even if they existed in print, each of these tools involved substantial results that required a lot of preparation. His current work would have to be shelved to get up to speed. The Hallas style assumed that the interested reader would create from ignorance the new methods as he read along. Assuming statements to be true didn't help. The reader was expected to understand how one got to the statements.

At the end of the first serious round with the paper, Apostopoulos found himself on the verge of being dragged into a project that felt like a turn into a new life. So far he had nothing, not even a few general remarks for a case of fraud. He was well acquainted with the appearance of obscurity for its own sake. That each statement in the lemmas was inaccessible without an enormous effort did not constitute proof of fraud. If he was up against a house of cards, he still hadn't kicked a single prop out of the thing. A week in the library didn't help, except he could measure further effort against accomplishment, and that assessment kicked the ball into another court. He didn't own the theorem. Let somebody else tackle the nth prime formula.

By itself, the nth prime formula was not the pushover he had taken for granted, and it was not a concrete statement, as one had to track the interaction of a given integer, n, with the integer index of a term in the series that defined the nth prime. That threw you into the depths of the so-called argument. So he couldn't send out the formula alone—it would be worthless—but that's what he did.

Apostopoulos got a couple same-day replies with cursory interest in the identity of Cybele Hallas, of which Apostopoulos hadn't any guesses. But they were tepid takers—thank you and "I'll have a look at it" type of responses that segued into changes of subject. No further requests for information on Hallas arrived in the next few days. He had a copy of the full manuscript transferred to a disc, and copies sent to three colleagues. He had recently returned from a conference at Oberwohlfach, where he and a Professor Temmler had hung out some, as was their custom. Temmler was staying put at Göttingen for the fall. Apostopoulos shot him a copy.

He heard from Temmler by phone the next morning as the Internet lit up. The nth prime formula had gone around the world. In eighteen hours an international ad hoc discussion had unmethodically become the output of a giant brain. A discovery had occurred, possibly in Athens, but a quickening of echoes had put a dozen experts under the microscope as the one true source, and everywhere it was a bright new day of speculation.

Temmler had a reputation for careful assessments. He was coming to Athens. Get Hallas at the blackboard. As usual, Temmler was invited to stay at Apostopoulos's mother's place, but this was a considerable commute in Athens. He would bunk on a cot in Apostopoulos's faculty office. No hotel check-in time-wasting.

Temmler bumped into a three-person ensemble from Warsaw at the Athens airport. They had had the same response as Temmler: get to Athens, locate Hallas, and invite themselves over. They met Apostopoulos, put a security team together, and caravanned to a door that opened to a room of several young children and an old lady. The old lady said she would accept the million-dollar prize in some universal currency. Precious stones were acceptable, preferable to gold. Cybele was unavailable until delivery. No banks needed.

They were on their own.

Göttingen was where the story started. In a day's march it looked vanishingly unlikely that, in Athens, it would have its final phase, but Athens was where the five of them stared into a decision that night. A fraud of this cunning was a masterpiece standing alone. They hadn't the authority to hold onto the result of the encounter with the old lady. The little they knew went out *urbi et orbi*.

So there wasn't a center from which announcements about

the manuscript would radiate. Temmler was lost in the shuffle of what the big shots would begin to set down as the procedural framework formalizing the world response, which, in less than two weeks was already an undertaking many steps behind the wave. There were claims for new proofs, better proofs, generalizations, translations, and plans for celebrations. The deepest insight was there was no Hallas, but a Greek philosophy cult living in Pythagoras' cave. They had skipped two thousand years, waiting for the end of the world, although nobody could see the arithmetic significance of 2017.

(Apostopoulos wrote *The Last Ten Days of the Riemann Hypothesis*, and I've taken the liberty to put down some of his remarks here.)

Andrei and I had made an offer on a house a quarter-mile along the continuation of Calvend Lane around the bend. Brett and I were hauling books from the English Department to a storage space I'd rented. I'd floated some ideas where to put them when we began discussing the décor in a second house, but the few discussions on that subject faded out. That would be a discussion for later.

We went to bed around midnight.

] *Thirty-one*

A COUPLE HOURS BEFORE DAWN Andrei received a call that the Riemann hypothesis had been proved to a moral certainty. The New Thing was there. God had opened His book. The hand of God was all over the proof. The author, Cybele Hallas, was in hiding. She was waiting for a million dollars in precious stones. I didn't know this for ten minutes. Andrei had gotten out of bed and walked the call to the backyard. There was a "Fuck this noise," several times, each coming out in a rough and ready eagerness to get in the car and go somewhere and fight. Somebody was egging him on. That got me up to get coffee going and wait for him in the front room. He saw me in the kitchen, and must have forgotten why he had shifted the conversation outside. He didn't come in till the call finished.

He shared his thinking about what came first and so forth, but there was only one thing to do. The decision to give a talk had been a spontaneous impulse to action in the first minute of the call. A friend from Caltech was in Ulm. The proof he had received was in its initial hours of investigation, but the paper had arrived with an aura of bewilderment. The friend was calling around. His frank reaction was that the proof had been stolen. Some cult was involved. Andrei had told him his instincts were right. Just hang on.

That claim of clairvoyance from Berkeley was received in Ulm as a spooky stamp of omniscience, the other hand of God.

Andrei reserved a lecture room for two o'clock at the Math Sciences Research Institute in Berkeley. An announcement went out to the campus community that a special lecture would be given by Professor A. Andreyev in honor of Robert Lavoisier. Of equal honor would be a recognition of the mathematical achievements of a Richard Shoemaker. Other matters of interest would be included.

In the main lecture room a panel discussion of the Cybele Hallas proof of the Riemann hypothesis had been underway since one o'clock. We pushed through a crowd in the hall watching a live feed. There were seven speakers—a panel free-for-all in progress on the screen. All previously scheduled lectures at MSRI had been cancelled. Everybody's schedule was swept up into the sheer pleasure of pandemonium remaking the mathematical universe. The press was interviewing; anybody and everybody was their expert. The human presence was the contribution to the moment that would penetrate deeply in history, the Woodstock of a before and after. No one would forget where they were this St. Crispin's day.

Anne Knudsen of the *San Jose Mercury News* poked her head into our room as Andrei was rolling chalk in the chalk tray. I had called her. She and I sat next to each other by the door in the front row. She had come with a camera crew. They had arrived early. Some instinct in the breed told them to follow the action. They had set up shop in the main lecture room. I had left a message for Herring and Grey, as soon as the time and place of the lecture had been set. They were at my back.

Two men had sprinkled themselves in the second row to my left on the other side of a center aisle. They were silent in an end-of-time vigil. The room had a backwater somber feel, as if mourning something or other that hadn't gone according to the prophecy. Andrei shut the door.

Andrei was in a maroon T-shirt with a dress pocket on the left, jeans and sandals, no socks. I had dropped by a Target for a new pair of sandals for him. They were in the trunk. When I remembered, it was too late. He started by passing out flyers announcing a proof that $e + \pi$ is rational. It had been submitted for publication several hours earlier. The author, Richard Shoemaker, was in the care of the State of California. He had no institutional affiliation.

Andrei said, "Okay?" The response was no response. It was okay to start. He was in the final step attending a speck on the board when the door opened. A man burst through the doorway as if onto a bus he'd been chasing. He looked more than winded. He had bones to pick with all of us.

"What's going on in here?" he accused us.

Andrei pointed at the wall, indicating something relevant to read was over there. "There's a flyer on the bulletin board."

The man stepped around the corner into the room and inspected the wall in a beleaguered defiance. "There's nothing there!"

"The bulletin board is outside. You saw it as you approached the door."

"I was invited," the man said. "I'm a speaker."

"Not here. I've reserved the room."

"They won't let me in."

"Just sit down," Andrei advised. "You're in."

The man was drawn to the noise in the hall for a moment, but came back. "Who is Richard Shoemaker?"

"I'm about to tell you."

The man found a face on the other side of the room. He lifted his nose and spoke past my head, "Why are you here?"

"I read the announcement, Harry. I decided this is what I wanted to hear."

Andrei said, "If you're visiting the Institute to participate in an analysis of a proof of the Riemann hypothesis, you're in the wrong room."

"I'm on the panel," Harry said. Harry had been socked with strange fresh facts.

Andrei provided him an option: "You want to go join the panel, no hard feelings. Honest."

"I can't get in. Standing room only—and that's all used up. You can't even sit on the floor. That's gone."

"Find a lap, Harry," was suggested from a voice in the second row.

Harry pulled a suitcase to the wall by a window. He folded a coat on a desk, and stacked a computer carrying case on it. He looked back to say "Hi, Norman." The other man stood and introduced himself as Goro Mochizuki. Harry sat, raising his hand in peace. "I apologize," he said. "I just don't understand what I have to apologize for. Excuse me." Nothing happened for two seconds. "I'll sit here and shut up."

Andrei twiddled chalk behind his back two-handed, and started speaking while placing it soundlessly on a small table in front of him.

"If you care to stay, you're welcome to join us in honor of the authors of the Riemann hypothesis—Robert Lavoisier and Richard Shoemaker."

Harry raised his hand to grip his forehead. "Who is Cybele Hallas? Somebody please tell me."

Andrei lightly thumped the table for order. Harry decided to let go of his head. He threw his hand at the air, and flopped it on the writing leaf of the desk.

Andrei said, "I'll be done in fifteen minutes. To those who crave epiphanies, how much of your life are you betting with to throw a quarter-hour of it on the table?"

"If you put it that way," Harry agreed.

"It's all I ask," Andrei said, "a little enthusiasm. So if we're okay, I was going to say this will be the first of many assemblies to honor Robert Lavoisier and Richard Shoemaker. In time we'll know a great deal more of the steps in the truly remarkable collaboration that produced their result, which consists, I'm certain, of a full resolution of the problem of the primes. I'll come back to this in a bit. I've had a few hours to read the Lavoisier-Shoemaker paper. It's in French. I'm sure there are those who knew Robert who already recognize his hand. They must be very confused.

"Due to circumstances that I will not have time to explain, Richard Shoemaker cannot be here today. I would hope that someday he will appreciate his contribution to a work of art in a field of art that is beyond comprehension but to a few. Perhaps he already does. Perhaps he believes we're all screwballs, splashing in our petty ponds.

"It strikes me this moment that it was Robert's nature that attracted Shoemaker to work with him and share a camaraderie in an obscure arrangement of circumstances. I suspect they hadn't the same awareness of what was at stake. The title of a paper—half French, half English—may also express a basis for a most amazing friendship.

"Other things first. Unpleasant things.

"This morning early my wife and I were awoken to the news that the Riemann hypothesis had been proved by a woman calling herself Cybele Hallas. I believe she is known, at least some of the time, as Alix Sociedes, and at other times has called herself Renate Flyte-Simpson. The contact address that was given to Professor Apostopoulos in Athens is merely a drop for one million dollars. Alix Sociedes murdered Robert Lavoisier. She murdered at least one other person, and is involved in other murders—and all, to all appearances, for money, which is not a reason I would call rational."

Norman said, "I've never heard the name Alix Sociedes. You've accused her of murder. This is a serious accusation."

"I have, and it is. The authorities will take the appropriate steps in the event Ms. Sociedes is a victim of slander."

"He died in a bar alone, I heard. How did she kill him?"

"It's all a series of stacked guesses," Andrei said. "They fit."

"This could be scary," Harry said.

"I can tell you how it happened," Andrei said. "You tell me if it's scary."

"Getting killed for a theorem is silly," Harry decided.

A voice from the second row: "You can get killed for a quarter in Oakland, Harry. A million dollars might save your life."

"There are a lot of things to worry about," Andrei said. "Getting killed for a million dollars is what I don't have to worry about. Getting killed for a quarter, I don't know. I see the risk."

Harry's risk was not knowing. "Who is Shoemaker?" he demanded.

"I never met him," Andrei said. "The proof of the Riemann hypothesis is the product of a collaboration between Robert Lavoisier and Richard Shoemaker. This will be verified fairly quickly. I can tell you that a cloud of unreality pervaded the murder of Robert Lavoisier. A false frame was put up around him to box up his life so that it might be unpacked by the numbers for a ready access to the reasons for his murder. I knew the box was unreal, but I have been mistaken on several hunches, hunches that I knew what was going on at one time and learned afterward that I did not know what was going on. This is the third try.

"As for Richard Shoemaker, an intense friendship of two boys ended somewhere on a November night in 1976. At the age of thirteen Matt Bollinger drowned in the Sacramento River, falling out of a rowboat. His friend, Richard Shoemaker, left Sacramento with his mother within a year. He left his mother sometime later. When he left is not known. Where he went afterwards and what he did is not known, but in 1997 he reappeared, and when he did, there is no doubt it was he who had appeared and had, at the same time, remained unknown, as he left a signature that could not be counterfeited and could not be recognized. It was a signature that was left as an identifying marker on a scholarly paper of a quality that appears perhaps a few times in a century.

"Richard Shoemaker's achievement might have remained undiscovered. Why it didn't is the story of one million dollars and how money made a proof of the Riemann hypothesis possible.

"Richard Shoemaker published a paper in a journal of psychoanalysis. The paper contained the strange diagrams of an unusual adolescent. The diagrams were used to show how two parts of

Matt Bollinger were united within the interaction of infinitely many orbiting objects. These objects were not Matt Bollinger's exterior. The whole person was this solar system. At the same time, the union of two orbiting systems could show how Matt Bollinger and Richard Shoemaker could unite as one organism. To mental health professionals the paper made visible the syntax of a disturbed mind, where the syntax itself, being crazy, had no worthwhile function. Richard Shoemaker guaranteed his paper would be accepted for publication by writing under the name of a psychoanalyst, who, after much confusion, simply let the situation ride. The paper was his paper, and Matt Bollinger was the cover name of his patient. That's the way it was until 2017.

"As far as anyone can say, Richard Shoemaker was content to allow the circumstances of 1997 to remain forever fixed, and the authorship of his paper to remain as he signed it. His design was the proverbial nest of mysteries. The design is itself so hard to believe that any word I can come up with doesn't cut it. Call it not believable.

"What was not suspected was that the paper indicated a manner in which two real numbers could be added, the way 19 and 23 are added to give 42. The addition is not done in the way you and I do it.

"And you and I cannot understand it without much effort.

"Following the breadcrumbs of the oddly resonant phrase 'partitions of unity,' I was inclined one afternoon to read a psychoanalyst's paper. My friend, Robert Lavoisier, had been poisoned in a bar in Oakland, a fact in itself that amounted to a collection of impossibilities—less impossible for the French to accept, given that impossibilities regarding violent death in America are not seen in France as they are here. The paper, as a paper on the structure of the human mind, was about the unification of two entities of the self, called 'blobs,' the union being a 'dumbbell.' Given the characteristics of the numbers e and pi viewed in a Shoemaker diagram, it was possible to wonder that an argument was available there of the statement that the sum e plus pi is

rational. I can say my reaction was much as the experience How-
ard Carter would have had, had he found *A Tale of Two Cities* in
Hebrew on King Tut's sarcophagus. The paper that was published
in a psychoanalytic journal seemed as far removed from mathematics as the theory of object relations is to the law of quadratic
reciprocity.

"In the investigation of Robert's murder, to every appearance
the middle-aged soul of Robert Lavoisier had taken a sojourn in a
familiar rut. Many nights he ditched his wife, covered his tracks,
and disappeared into an excitement so well understood that it
was not questioned, except by someone who knew him. That e
plus pi is rational cracked the right door more than enough for
me to know, axiomatically, that there was another explanation
for Lavoisier's behavior—only one other explanation. Lavoisier
had found someone who could speak with him in mathematics
at his level.

"A mind at that level was suggested in scribbles on a sheet of
paper that I found in Robert's desk. In that scrap of mathematics is a formula that could be easily understood as a previously
unseen type of expression called a partition of unity. Certain
phrases indicated that the author, Richard Shoemaker, a name
then unknown to me, had found unknown symmetries in the
Riemann zeta function via these partitions. These symmetries
were perhaps only guessed at by Shoemaker, but their existence
was detected in Shoemaker's scribbles by Robert.

"I was sure: the psychoanalytic paper, as distant from mathematics as Dickens from King Tut, had to connect to Robert
Lavoisier. It gave evidence of an intellect that had the capacity
to interest Robert, evidence that had only shown itself to me in
Robert's movements as an abstract attracting force.

"The paper jumped the investigation in my mind over and
beyond a passing discovery. The 'how can this be' impossibility
was the sheer blank wall facing me. The paper removed it. Whatever evidence there was that pointed elsewhere had to be wrong.

"The piece of paper was also a first connection between

Robert and a doctoral candidate in art history. The impact of that piece of paper, bearing the image of a partition of unity, pushed me to several conclusions, some right, some wrong. My argument, regarding partitions of unity, on the Oakland police produced, very naturally, tolerance. I would guess they saw that I had lost a friend, and, guided by undigested emotion, I denied the obvious for the mathematical answer.

"My wife, Elizabeth, argued that a further statement to the police, that *e* plus *pi* is rational was the direction the investigation must follow, would tip a benign evaluation of me into a hostile confrontation. From then on, she and I were on our own.

"We began with two unlikely possibilities: the psychoanalyst was crazy and he had given some enormously clever mathematical discovery to Lavoisier, and then killed him. In a hierarchy of impossibilities, that was too unlikely. That the analyst did not write the paper was less unlikely. If he didn't, who did?

"And what put Lavoisier in harm's way? It was the oldest motive in the book: money. An American mathematical group had done what an American group with spare cash does. They put a bounty on a thing called the Riemann hypothesis. As a justification, it worked. The downside was Robert's murder. It's how the bounty on Robert's head worked. For a brief moment, probably for less than an hour, Robert had what he wanted in mathematics, a proof set in stone of the Riemann hypothesis—and much more. The world is verifying that now.

"The unlikely steps that brought Robert and Shoemaker together will never be known. It's a miracle they did come to know each other, though I suspect they never met. As I have said, what started their association was a piece of paper. In between them were three people—Evelyn Iges, Burleigh Polk, Alix Sociedes, and a third woman, somewhere off to a side, whose role is vague to me. She was also murdered by Alix Sociedes."

Andrei stopped. A glance behind him caught the clock.

"This may be a good time to stop. What I've said here I said this morning to someone else. There's an intention to have a conference in Robert's honor in Paris. I don't know when. There will be a conference in Shoemaker's honor here at the Math Institute. There will be many conferences. The purpose of this talk has been fulfilled. Any questions?"

Harry said, "This is unbelievable."

"I meant to say that." It was over now. Andrei stuck his palms in his front pockets and waited.

Harry insisted on getting to the bottom of the mystery man. "Where is Shoemaker? Why isn't he here?"

"I'll accept the question in the spirit I'd accept the question if I asked it."

"Could you rephrase that? Please."

"It means he doesn't belong to Facebook. He doesn't belong anywhere I've ever existed. I have to say who he is under those circumstances. He is *der Mann ohne Eigenschaften* in the sense Robert Musil meant the phrase to describe himself. He lacks the qualities that allow him to interact with the world."

"How do I ask the right question, then, so that if I did ask the right question, I would get an answer to the stupid question 'Who is Shoemaker'?"

Andrei took a piece of chalk to roll in his fingers for support. "The stupid answer to me will not be the stupid answer to you."

"If you're not as stupid as me, I won't understand. If I'm not as stupid as you, the explanation will be stupid."

"The number *e* plus *pi* is rational. He proved it."

"So he is not without an extraordinary quality of brilliance. What does that have to do with *Der Mann Ohne Eigenschaften*?"

"I wondered about that too long and too hard. I came to the conclusion the title of the two-volume set—which had been hollowed out to accommodate a statue of a woman—provided an insight. Why would Shoemaker hang around with a man named Polk, who made art movies with two women? The four of them would drive around burying identical copies of these statues. Why? The answer is the satisfaction afforded to people without qualities. Shoemaker got a satisfaction from digging holes in the ground and putting these statues in them. I think that one of the women, Alix Sociedes, also had a satisfaction making the same movie over and over again. I'm inclined to say they all shared an uninhibited, unashamed delight. I don't think she shared the belief that she could claim ownership of San Jose based on the location of these statues. I think that amused her, though."

Harry shook his head. "I have no idea what you're saying."

"Where do I get Shoemaker's proof?" Norman said.

"I just submitted it for publication. You can get hard copy in the math office. The paper will get Shoemaker accepted as Robert's co-author. We all know Robert's papers. They are extremely tough reading. He invented mathematics in his expositions. He was hard-nosed about it: It's a free country, read it or don't. I feel a bit sorry for the poor souls down the hall. The proof of the Riemann hypothesis was written by Robert. I wish he were here to watch."

"Did Robert bury statues, too?" Harry wondered.

"No. But he spent some unknown amount of time alone in a house communicating with Shoemaker electronically. Robert had time to case the house. The Musil volumes were on the shelf, English and German versions. I'm sure he looked and found the statue in the empty volumes. When my wife crawled through the window to the laundry room, he was inside, and he knew she was looking for the statue."

"Your wife?" Norman looked at the four of us women. He picked me to settle a question on. "You're his wife?"

"I am," I said.

He retreated into a puzzled expression, as if too many possible questions dried them all up.

Andrei looked at me. "Did you check the back door?"

"I didn't think it would be open," I said. "Maybe I did. I think I did. Robert locked it."

Andrei turned to Norman. "I'm going to skip a few of your questions."

"I feel very fortunate. Thank you. Jumping ahead, then, your wife does not share in the proof of the Riemann hypothesis? Do I understand that much?"

"I can see you want the nitty-gritty." Andrei was going to a larger canvas. He went counter-clockwise around the four of us. "My wife, Elizabeth Cromwell; Anne Knudsen, of the *San Jose Mercury News*; detectives Herring and Grey with the Oakland police department. Norman was Norman Shapiro, retired, of the University of Pennsylvania. Goro Mochizuki was at Reed.

"The night Robert was murdered, my wife passed Alix Sociedes in an alley in Montclair. What saved Elizabeth's life is that Sociedes thought she was on her way to a dance in the neighborhood. Instead, my wife accidentally ran into Robert in a house. In a final transmission from inside the house to a receiver somewhere nearby, Robert had obtained Shoemaker's permission to publish the Riemann hypothesis. Robert was exultant. And we have Elizabeth's testimony to a remarkably uncharacteristic reaction to her presence: he invited her to a bar. I knew Robert. This is proof positive of a celebration of a lifetime—to me."

Norman addressed me. "You were on your way to a dance—without your husband?"

"It just looked that way to Alix," I said.

"I don't want to get into all the circumstances." Andrei said. "I didn't know her at the time. I only would stress a doubt here, that Robert asked Shoemaker about his *e* plus *pi* paper, as that would involve a personal loss of a treasured friend, very painful, an event that has haunted Shoemaker since he was thirteen.

"I also want to mention that I believe that if the manuscript submitted to Apostopoulos is examined carefully, they will find evidence of tampering. You can be sure the original paper was written in the language of a collaborative work. Alix had to convert the text to a single-author format. I mean you can't have sentences that say, 'we decided to,' and the like." There will be pedestrian phrases, like rubber bands, holding together segments of a magnificent suspension bridge."

"Is this Sociedes woman in custody?" Norman asked.

"Not that I know of," Andrei said.

Harry gave up in a long sigh. "I get a call this morning; the Riemann hypothesis is proved. Be at MSRI at two o'clock. I get to Las Vegas. I get out of Las Vegas. I can't get to San Francisco. I can't get to Oakland. I get to Sacramento. I rent a car and I get here and *e* plus *pi* is rational and your wife crawls through a laundry window and meets the proud new owner of the answer to who solved the Riemann hypothesis."

"Your whole world is crashing," Norman commiserated.

"It gets worse," Andrei added, "the square root of two is a normal number."

Norman groaned, "I don't believe this. Shoemaker?"

"No. Andreyev. I made it up."

Harry stood and got his coat in a fist. "The questions are two steps behind anything I want to know." He pushed his glasses down his nose, off his eyes. What he saw, or missed, checked his decision to leave. He sat and held his coat threateningly in his lap. He looked at me.

"Climbing through a window suggests illegal entry. Are you out on bail for this talk?"

"I'm in the clear," I said.

Andrei raised his voice a notch. "Her meeting with Robert was accidental. Without the information she gave to the police, we would never have known of Richard Shoemaker. We wouldn't have the proof of *e* plus *pi* rational. You'd be paying off Cybele Hallas in diamonds."

"And the square root of two would still be up in the air," Norman said.

"We owe Elizabeth our gratitude," he said. "I would like to finish with a few other remarks."

Harry folded his coat again. There was a pause. Andrei took five seconds to verify compliance. Not a perfect predictor, but nothing happened during the pause or immediately after in the next pause.

"The last half-hour of Robert's life begins with the meeting with Elizabeth in the laundry room. Robert looks at her, surprised, but pleased to share his happiness. He goes outside and tells her, through the window, she can meet him at a bar on Grand Avenue. Robert believes this is where he will finally meet Shoemaker. Sociedes is waiting for him in an alley. He is excited. She offers him a cognac. He accepts and they drive away. A detective, Ada Tomek, is in a position to see Robert and Alix in the alley. It's why she's dead. She's been following Elizabeth. A detective following Tomek does not see what Tomek has seen. It's why he's alive. Alix leaves Robert off at the head of some steps on an adjoining street to Grand Avenue. He cuts through by a pedestrian walkway. He goes to the bar and dies waiting for Shoemaker.

"Alix planned to persuade Robert to leave his laptop in the car, but he refused. It didn't matter. Alix watched from the street and didn't see the laptop come out with the police or with the medical people. She decided she could come back and claim the briefcase on some identifying marks or labels when they opened in the morning. It didn't happen that way. The laptop came out in the night after everyone had left. A character named X had hidden under Robert's seat. Apparently, it happens in restaurants more than people know. I never knew it. He stole the laptop and destroyed the contents trying to get in. So Shoemaker's copy was what there was. The police told me this much. They know the identity of X."

Norman asked, "Is the variable X in the room? I'd like to hear his side of the story."

"I can't say how it is that Robert and Shoemaker came in contact, except to say again that it would not have happened had it not been for the existence of a one-million-dollar prize for a proof of the Riemann hypothesis. Alix Sociedes was the gatekeeper. It took time for the penny to drop in her tin cup to realize what Robert was interested in talking to Shoemaker about, and, most importantly, that the subject was an investment opportunity. She worked out a method by which she could have it all."

] *Thirty-two*

KARLOFF'S IS A SANDWICH SHOP in San Rafael. A diner in a plaid shirt and string tie at the window watched me, didn't recognize Andrei, didn't care to indicate he knew him from Adam. Not a clue. He was into the Riemann hypothesis like he was into pheasant under glass. Herring and Grey had beers going in an exterior space enclosed in a plastic awning that expanded and contracted as the door to the kitchen opened and closed. I took the chair next to Grey. We shook hands. Andrei shook with Herring and leaned a hand across the table to Grey. Then Herring and I.

As we might never see each other again, Herring had invited us to a farewell banquet, but didn't intend a smile to convey any misconceptions. "You better be right this time, Professor."

"If I get life, friends are appreciated. Bring a hacksaw."

"You'll do soft time in a federal ping-pong playpen. You won't want to leave."

I caught the server. "Two bottles of water that overflow when you unscrew the cap and two Reubens, two slices of swiss, one thin slice corned beef, light Thousand Island dressing, hold the butter, sauerkraut, and whatever else. He and I will share a dill pickle. Yes, chips, one plate."

The server waited silently on Herring and Grey. They had an

eye-contact version of how are things? I'm fine, thanks. How are you? They wanted the usual.

"What's the draw over here to get out of Oakland for burgers and fries?" I asked Herring.

"Shirley Temple ate here. If there's a shoot-out in the kitchen, it's somebody else's mess. The burgers sit well in cheesecake."

"Tell me, Professor, with your powers of cogitation, where do we *not* look for Alix?"

"An Austrian castle in the mountains above Graz will have a naked lady in the window of the turret sticking through the mist. Don't go there."

"What if she doubles back to Oakland?"

"Too clever. You have as much of her now as you'll get. Could be a famous cold case in twenty years. I don't believe Alix killed Polk, but the sex was unusual. A best-seller."

Herring drifted into self-revelation, "The thing we love: consult for a television series."

"The guy who hides in a cupboard under the seats in the Grandstand, he's your star. How do you explain that guy?"

"Eyes and ears on the payroll. Code name: Hazel. He crawls around in the attics of hotels on MacArthur. He sees what he wants to see. We tell him what we want him to see."

"How did you think to connect him to Robert's computer?" I asked.

Herring kept her beer in the corner of her eye. She twirled the bottle in little twists, till she could get a thumb on the label. She had a gulp and let it settle.

"We have regular get-togethers. He didn't remember Lavoisier and a redhead. Wasn't his night at the Starlight. There were some other matters. We had reports of thefts that had to have happened at the Grandstand, but there was no proof they had. Things were disappearing from purses. He didn't have anything for us on those either. When his helpfulness is slow, we don't always believe him. In the past he'd worked grift with restaurant help. We perused his phone log. Sharon's number was here and there, and in particular, it was there on the nights around the murder, and then nothing. The day after the murder he and Sharon ceased communication.

"When we talked with him he had a story about their time together. It was a very romantic fable and well presented as a tragically doomed love, so from an abundance of experience we knew he and Sharon had some game going where she worked. We reminded him murder was our red line. We asked again about a Professor Robert Lavoisier. Forget the redhead this time. Lavoisier had lost a laptop among other misfortunes. If Hazel was at the Grandstand on the night in question, it explained how the laptop disappeared. We explained his future to him if he had taken the laptop and lied and we ever found out. And we were going to talk to Sharon about him being her accomplice, and he should hope she didn't give him up."

"Then it was his turn to talk?" I asked.

"It was him or Sharon. At once we found out about the cubby he hides in underneath a row of banquettes along a wall. Sharon chats up a customer and Hazel slides a panel open. He has nothing to do with the menu. He still thinks she killed Lavoisier. Accidentally slipped him too much jungle juice. It wasn't intentional."

I cut a pickle. I pointed. Everybody. I'm sharing. Herring split off some fries for anybody. Grey minded her own business. She had cut a burger in half. A lot of ingredients lost contact and fell into finger-cleaning tomato-and-chili goo.

I had noticed the sentimentality in Herring's voice, a melliflu-ence I heard as a fondness for Hazel, but she was aware of the consequences a dim bulb could have on history.

"He made a mess when he tried to open the laptop. We had him fetch the remains from the attic in the Maple Inn. The technical people whistled. Lavoisier knew how to keep a secret. Insides burned to a crisp."

"The secret almost died with him," I said.

"Would Lavoisier have solved the Riemann hypothesis alone?" Herring asked Andrei.

"When he was in his teens he was sure he would. He was mystified in the years when he was convinced the proof was right around the corner. Time went on. He found cities of gold, but the corner wasn't in those cities, and he became forty and even got older. He became the man to talk to about the mystery."

"You gave a nice talk, Professor. A man comes from Phoenix to hear another talk and has to settle for yours. And he lucks out."

"You didn't like the talk. Do I get that right?"

"I don't run the world," Herring said. "It was your talk."

"We should keep our murders at the university where they belong?"

"I just said you better be right this time. I said that when you sat down, and you thought I was kidding."

Herring unwrapped her lips from the distaste of saying what had to be said.

"Lavoisier parks his car a couple blocks from his house and leaves his cell and keys. Iges meets him. They go to a motel. He doesn't tell his wife. And you explained how all that can be explained so that Robert gets into heaven, but if I don't forget he wrote her thesis, because he's so brilliant, I don't see why Iges doesn't kill Robert. All I hear is Alix would have killed Iges if Iges knew what she didn't know. That's nice to know. Come again, how you figured that? Oh yes, you knew Robert. That's what I keep forgetting to forget, why they didn't meet at the library rather than a motel. It's what we detectives call a theory in a hole. We wouldn't let Hazel have the last word on a story like that."

"What was I supposed to say, that I didn't know him?"

"You have to say Sociedes killed Lavoisier. We don't have to."

"She didn't? Who's Cybele Hallas? Iges is meeting her publisher in New York."

"Someday a guy is going to run a deal past us, and the deal is he remembers the plate of the passing car that shot at him and missed and killed a woman two blocks away. The plate belongs to Iges. The point being you don't know Iges from Ma Barker."

"What was I supposed to do?"

"You keep asking. What would you suggest?"

Grey made a throat-clearing sound that resembled an intention to speak. Andrei lost his answer to Herring. Grey put her concerns in the center of the table.

"Suzanne Oliver worked at Livermore with Polk," she said. "She's the driver in the films. From something she becomes aware of, according to you, she comes to a conclusion Alix is a danger to her. She hides in a shack from Alix, but the shack offers her no protection. Why does she think it does? She was poisoned. Assuming Alix found her, how does Alix get her to go through some reunion greeting that results in her death? If Moncrief was Alix's accomplice, why not kill Moncrief?" And another thing. If Shoemaker is photographed digging holes, who was the photographer?"

"You're not saying Cybele Hallas?" I said.

"I'm not saying she's not, Ms. Cromwell. She's another name we would talk to if we dropped in on a misty Austrian castle. We listened to the professor today. We hear all sides. We talk to people who know what they know, and they're so convinced, they don't care if they convince us."

"A lot of loose ends is a good hiding place," Andrei observed.

"We could hang Hazel. He fits all the loose ends. His life is the example of the 'wrong place at the wrong time' parable."

Grey leaned on her elbows and watched her fingers flick thoughts. "We don't care if Lavoisier and Iges had a relationship. We're not judgmental. But if we bring your story to the D.A., she's going to ask these questions, because she's wondering how we know Iges didn't drive Lavoisier to the Grandstand the night of the murder. And we don't know why it wasn't her. And Lavoisier was desperate—Iges has the key he has to have. Why meet in a motel? To write a thesis? Question marks stick to questions like that."

Andrei suddenly looked relieved.

"Tell the D.A. it's too simple to waste her time on. All the way up and down the line, Iges doesn't fit. Alix ran that gang. If you're going to blame it on the photographer, don't bring me into it. I don't have an answer. But if my hooey goes to the D.A., please let me do my own talking. I told you how Iges and Robert got going. Robert had a look at her screen, which surely was her thesis, and Robert adds a few remarks, which she fills out in a few more pages. She takes this stuff to her advisor, and the advisor comes out of his head. He wants more of this. Forget the other stuff. So Iges and Robert have needs to realize of each other, but it's not in her interest to introduce Robert and Polk. She gets pushed out in that event. She has to milk this."

"But Polk's too stupid," Herring noted, emphasizing some core fact about Ph.D.s from MIT. "There's nothing to milk."

"If Robert meets Polk—which he didn't—he knows exactly that in ten seconds. But none of that matters. Robert saw vertical symmetry at the first encounter with Iges, which was around the middle of October, judging from his behavior. It was enough. Small talk after that wasn't the same. He'd gone underground alone. When he came back from France after Christmas he had worked out all the steps of the argument. He wouldn't write anything down until that was done."

"This your latest guess?" Herring asked. "How about if Lavoisier puts questions for Polk on cue cards? What happens if Iges asks Polk about vertical symmetry in the Riemann zeta function?"

"She'd know more than Polk." Andrei studied a potato chip. "You told me the D.A. is working with the Iges attorney to come in for an interview?"

"It's developing."

"Iges will know something, not much. Start with Polk went to Alix with the cue card. Alix thought about why they should bother Shoemaker with vertical symmetry. That talk gets them to the Riemann hypothesis. Polk thinks he heard there was money in it. They look it up. A million dollars for a proof. I don't know how long this took, but that changes things. Nobody needs Iges now. There was a week—at most—at the beginning when Robert thought he needed Iges, and they met to work out how she was going to set up the connection with the vertical symmetry guy. Iges knows from Polk he's out of it, so she thinks she can't deliver on her end, but right at the beginning, she's all Robert's got. For a time, Robert is willing to wait. The motel might have come under that heading. A library is no good. She doesn't want to be seen with a guy telling her what to type into her computer. It looks good meeting a guy at a motel. Everybody understands what's going on. Robert could go twenty-five pages of prime quality art history a night at a dartboard. Multiply that by four or five, and a thesis is done. *Voilà*."

"French men give a woman the shirt off their back," Herring said in Grey's direction. "Maybe we knew that."

"Why didn't Alix get Shoemaker to solve the problem by himself?" Herring asked.

"In some sense she's a normal person. It must have knocked her for a loop that Shoemaker could make a million bucks just looking at the ceiling. She asks him. He smiles. Remember, he's a loon. Maybe he drools. What happens next, I don't know. I don't have a feel for him. I'm fairly sure he was stuck. Something didn't work."

"Alix has to bring in help?" I said.

"Looks that way. Once she's worked out her cut, she's going to make sure a joint effort takes shape."

Herring said, "You're saying Iges and Polk are out of it. Alix introduces herself."

Andrei nodded. "That would have been fun to see. Alix is feeling out Robert on a merger, playing up her dedication to scientific togetherness, all the while thinking out the steps in the endgame. Robert already knows the proof. He's working out why he's lucky and who was responsible. He'd have had suspicions regarding the math department, but they didn't materialize. He'd get the name Polk from Iges, while they're rolling along in the fourth chapter of her thesis. Polk would shock him."

"Thinking it was Polk, then discovering he's an idiot at Livermore?" Herring mused.

"*Exactement,*" Grey punctuated.

"I see it so far," Herring said, "but if Lavoisier has the proof, why play along with Sociedes?"

"If you don't mind an old-fashioned word: honor. It's something about mathematics that enforces an incredibly conservative way of thinking on the practice of the believers. Robert knew he never would have guessed that peculiar property sitting inside the zeta function that expressed the equations that nailed down the primes. You can see in the paper that he dropped the zeta function. The vertical symmetry goes over into combinatorial-type lemmas that eventually bring out the zeros of the zeta function, but not by way of analytic manipulations. It's not analytic number theory, at least not as it was done in books up till then.

"So Robert has to find the vertical symmetry guy. He's dealing with one strange *monsieur*, but they are co-discoverers. Robert will have to meet him. Robert needs his permission to publish, and Alix is the one to chat up, and she's going to be Robert's love interest. Alix is cagey squared, but she wants something. That makes her needy. That makes any secret that she's stashed away vulnerable in a conversation that has to be charming, especially as she is unaware of Robert's motivation."

"Alix was meeting Robert?" Herring said.

Andrei gestured with his hands: Yes.

"In time Robert put two of her words together, like 'Hermite' and 'schizophrenic,' and he had the psychoanalyst's paper, and that gave him the name of a math prodigy who had vanished. The words could have come out on different days, or different weeks, but Robert was at the crossroads. He doesn't need Alix as a go-between with phony cue cards anymore. He needs Richard Shoemaker. He wants to talk to him. He wants to express his admiration. He doesn't send any more cue cards until he has her cooperation. That's a fatal step with Alix—and it was his fatal step. The one mistake he made: he thought he had a step on her.

"Alix is fast on her feet. She gets Shoemaker to set up a signaling system to Polk's house. That's why Robert was there that night. He was in direct contact with the prodigy. He would need to know he was talking to Shoemaker. Shoemaker would give him a rational number. Boom. It's the sum of *e* and *pi*. Nobody else can do that. Shoemaker says yes to a joint paper."

Herring said, "Sociedes knows what Shoemaker will say. She will make sure he asks for a copy of the proof. Robert meets her. She shoots him. She has his laptop."

Andrei locked his fingers behind his head. We waited. He said nothing.

"Let me come back to that." Andrei unlocked his hands and rubbed an eye.

"In a minute," Herring said. "Why not shoot him and take the laptop? What's the poison in the bar all about?"

"I can give you an answer. It might not be *the* answer."

"I like answers. If you get to them."

"Go back a little before the shooting. Robert is communicating with Shoemaker from Polk's house. All of a sudden Robert gets an urge. He wants to look the discoverer of vertical symmetry in the eye and shake his hand. That much I know for a virtual fact. Shoemaker says yes. They agree to meet in a bar. They exchange brief goodbyes, see you soon. When Robert meets Alix, she is thinking at speed. She has spoken with Shoemaker. She agrees. But first she insists on a celebration, the culmination of an historic whatever. Robert has a cognac.

"So Shoemaker has called Sociedes," Grey said. "He tells her about the meeting with Lavoisier. Okay. But how does Shoemaker get there?"

"The woman in the shack lives close?" Andrei suggested.

"Yeah, it could happen," Grey nodded. "They made movies together."

"And Shoemaker gets to the bar and changes his mind. Or

somebody changes his mind. Robert walks right past him. He goes inside and waits. Elizabeth shows up. She talks to Shoemaker. She drives home. Robert is the loser."

"How does Robert forget to mention the fourth party, Elizabeth Cromwell?"

"Until I knew how it could be that Robert could be so excited at the moment he met Elizabeth, I couldn't believe he invited her to join him at a bar. He decided in seconds. Just before he sees Elizabeth, Robert had come to agree with Shoemaker the proof was done and they should publish a joint work. Robert's system has had such a jolt that he wants to kiss the first girl he meets, like the moment Paris was liberated in 1944. It's not like any other moment he'll ever have again. It's maybe the first five minutes of the existence of the proof. This is simple. I see it. As soon as he leaves the house, he forgets Elizabeth. The soldier who kisses the girl in Paris takes off."

"The perfect crime. Alix can have it all." Herring nodded approvingly at the workmanship. "We have a lot of those in Oakland. I recommend the forget-your-affair ice cream. Four kinds of nuts, four kinds of chocolate chunks. Either chocolate or vanilla."

The server brought two bowls. They shared theirs, we shared ours. Shirley Temple had survived. It got us through.

"They had all made movies," I said. "Polk, Alix, Suzanne, Shoemaker, and the photographer. They were together a long time till Robert arrived. Why stay together?"

Herring smoothed the paper tablecloth. She worked the crease, but not perfectly. "You wouldn't call them a happy family, would you? It's easy to see Alix and Polk and the fetish. Shoemaker and Alix in the same box? I don't know."

"Alix would hear Shoemaker's dream, and sense the payoff in it somewhere." I said. "He gave off brilliance that can be used. The ruler of the Bay was Shoemaker's guiding vision. That had scam potential way up there. Alix had seen a story about a land-grab in the *Minutes of the Renate Flyte-Simpson Society,* and she saw how to scale Shoemaker's claim to realistic proportions. Just go for San Jose and the rivers. She must have come up with the idea of the art films that hid statues."

"It looks like Shoemaker loved it," Grey said. "His kind of loopy dame. Alix sees this guy doesn't fool around in small units of wealth."

"She introduced him to Polk or Polk was there with her at the meet," I said. "Polk mentioned technical things of weapons systems half-done, half not done, not understood, and Richard tossed solutions off and created new technical things not dreamed of. And the Polk–Shoemaker connection blossomed. She sees what he can do for Polk. She has known bright men, big dreamers, big talkers, but not bright like her Richard."

"I think that dots that," Herring said. "I still can't take it upstairs."

] *Thirty-three*

THEY HAD DELIVERED one million dollars in counterfeit gems to the old lady's house where the precious stones were supposed to be delivered, and covered every which way Alix could pick them up. They were prepared to shoot down pigeons on crutches or flying rats. After two years waiting for her, nobody who had studied her past behavior as indicators of what she would do in the future expected Alix Sociedes to show. She had caught on to her colossal misjudgment getting mixed up with the Riemann hypothesis, and cut her ties with a fatal investment, disappearing into one of those places where charisma is so much dark matter. She had owned the Riemann hypothesis for thirty-eight days. And gave it away. The hole in the world she disappeared into should have been evident. And it was when she was found.

One afternoon a Canadian banker newly stationed in Paris acted on a tip that had spoken for itself without eliciting any comments. The tip led to a meeting in a farmhouse with inexpensive tapestries on the walls. The woman he met said her crazy brother lived in the attic. It's how she explained the noises.

She arranged interviews, and she was the first of several such. Under favorable impressions, an exchange of fictional identities and alter egos would follow, and the principals were on their way.

The banker watched films. At once he had had a problem. He was usually quick off the mark choosing a companion from screen performances, from which, so he prided himself, he could identify the finer hints of the discriminating experience. It was a curious half-hour. He felt nit-picky, fussy, on the lookout for disappointment. The candidates were physically adequate for the role of professionals acting as strict married women on the go for an anonymous connection, but several acts had rambled on and on in the half-Herculean, half-cringing stubbornness of the newer perversions. They all lacked the ingredient he knew as "tone"—the camouflage of ordinary encounters that most attracted him.

Overall, it was all a wash. Tone, or whatever you call the substance of the classic tradition, was not there. The modulations of authority, the verbal expressions of the governess, that she alone illuminates a superior understanding of the deportment of young males, had been more evident on random occasions when he had been asking for traffic directions. The nervous fearful ecstasy, the majesty conjured out of thin air in Victorian tradecraft, was missing; the Gothic shadows entombed, ignored, drowned. Any three pejoratives could take their places. Time passed. That he couldn't come to a decision was not it at all. To an expert, he had. He needed to be taken in hand.

A Svengali strictness in the conduct of the interview had awakened the banker. He was experiencing a desire—he wanted what he couldn't have. He wanted the interviewer. While she was merely selling a product, she had set free the erotic syndrome she knew like the time by her own watch. He hadn't met a woman like her. She didn't have to get into that. She would modify her line—fill in for a performer. He would submit on command. He was far away from home at loose ends, inhibited, undisciplined. She opened an armoire and set a whip on the desk. She understood these phrases. She returned in an outfit that made it quite clear the banker was in for it. His investment paid off in a storage shed.

Alix was coasting now. She was the master of first steps, land-ing on her feet in a down-at-heels farmhouse disguise, descending into an orbit where regular helpings of fantasy were stuck onto the human condition. It wasn't just a matter of getting along on special effects. In her company had once been the thrill of a love letter, when you shared with the other the poetry in your head: "I was there in your presence when you were the one and only one to be with." Of course, it all wears out down the road where life goes south, but the banker had been unexpectedly pleased getting acquainted.

His tastes established, there were regularities to be coordi-nated and peculiarities to be agreed upon. They could be fixed with a contract sealed on a kiss, so to speak. It would be a quar-terly arrangement, once every two weeks, with a payment up front: five thousand euros on the follow-up visit.

The banker's name was in a list of ancient names in a book. Some of his ancestral family had escaped the Terror, and had settled in Russia. His line had returned to rejoin society in France at the end of the Second Empire. From there a third son had taken a final step to Montreal.

Money had never been a problem. The banker left Alix a thousand euros and another five hundred, a good faith gesture. When he returned to the bank and had made his way through the rest of the day, he had dinner and went to a show at the Crazy Horse. He started through the girls until a shimmy in a hip caught his eye, and he stared at her the rest of the performance. The next week he discovered he had decided the buy-in with Alix was a bit steep, and he had the power of the purse. When he went back for his scheduled appointment he let her know of his revised think-ing on their contract. She didn't mind. She offered him a cognac and a toast to great experiences to come.

He had the blood of an aristocratic line that had an instinct for keeping their heads on their shoulders. He offered her his glass, and she tossed it back with a look—he didn't know what he was missing. There might have been a veiled wink too deep in too many layers that he failed to understand. At the end of their meeting she poured another round and drank hers. He had seen something to fear, but he had formed judgments on a skewed sample. Country club ladies had let him get away with what he thought he knew about women. Not only did he not get a second chance with Alix, he never had a prayer. He drank up and said *Au revoir*. He was arriving in Paris when she died.

Andrei had remained a day at the math institute in Paris. They filled him in on Alix. She had become a name that would always come up in retrospectives in the annals of mathematics. She had knocked off one last guy. His name was the answer to a trivia question in mathematics. He lived long enough to appreciate the arc of life in his last hour.

We had had an apartment in Paris and split up. Our daughter, Catherine, and I rejoined Andrei at the airport in Malpensa for a change of direction motoring into the lake scenery. For several years the three of us had been showing ourselves annually on Lake Maggiore. We included a stop on the western shore of the lake where Robert had taken pictures of his family. We'd pay our respects and head to a bed and breakfast midway up the slope. We'd been staying there since I was carrying Catherine.

I was holding her on the drive. She was awake. We could talk. We were going over what Andrei had picked up on Alix.

"The guy who had been in the consulate in Florence made the visual I.D.," Andrei said. "They didn't believe he didn't know where she was. He had been looking for her ever since Oakland, and he made it look like he was leading the cops to all the wrong places. He made quite a scene when they pulled the sheet back. He broke down like a life without her would last forever. It was a convincing act. They transported him to a hospital and kept him under a watch"

"I was thinking they would never find her," I said. "She could have gotten away. I can't see that she had to take her own life."

"She might have suffered a regret," he said. "She had Polk and Richard and Oliver and the photographer, whatever the

name was. They were her gang. They all lived in the same neighborhood. Hung out together. Then Robert comes along, and
suddenly there's the opportunity to score, and she couldn't help
herself. A million dollars had always looked like a birthright. She
hadn't experienced what it meant to lose something substantial
to get it. She didn't kill Polk."

"That was a scatterbrained guess?" I asked.

"Less than that. It's a reminder to think it through someday.
Not to leave a stone unturned. His death might have broken a
delicate balance."

"Why kill the banker?" I asked.

"She had set up a business. It would have carried her. She
meets a banker, but the old magic hadn't the zing it once had.
He stiffed her. It had failed with Robert, and that might not have
been easy to look back on. Robert had needed her, and she had
always known what to do with that. She might have expected
some appreciation on the side with him. She'd lost Polk. They
had had something. Robert would oblige her with some deep
talks, roll out the ecstasy of mathematics routine, but he'd keep
his shorts on. If she caught sight of herself in Robert's eyes, she
could have been nicked a bit. He made a few pretensions with
her, but it amounted to letting her cheat herself. All he thought of
was going around her. And then he has the proof, and he hardly
sees she's there. Robert and Shoemaker had what can't be broken
into. She got it her way, and it cost her what she couldn't buy
back.

"The banker was the last nail. She was waiting for him or
someone like him. Her career as an erotic thoroughbred had
picked up one too many doubts. There was a lot of career left,
but how much of a diminishing resource was worth wasting on
bums nickel-and-diming her?

"The banker fell sick during a meeting. He knew what happened, and hoped he had time to fix it. They had to retrace his
steps in a hurry—and determine an antidote—but it was too
late. All he had at the end was a glimpse of the Medici standard

operating procedure. Then it was easy. Her DNA matched the DNA they got off the Riemann manuscript."

Catherine had been walking for over a year, and then one morning at the age of two she refused to wear shoes. The ground had these hard stickers that blew everywhere in the wind. We had left the stroller in the apartment. One of us had to carry her. It was Andrei's turn. We were in the courtyard where Riemann's plaque was on the wall. We looked in reverence in a silence that didn't outlast Catherine's budding impatience. We went out and followed the wall around in back of the courtyard to the flowers in the wild area on the hillside. That was her first big word: "flower." Missing the second letter. Couldn't say it often enough. She had just the other night pointed at the silhouette of the moon and said "cloud" and somehow found the second letter, so someday she was going to win the international worst first sentence contest.

Andrei walked a narrow path that followed the curve of the hill and frequently bent Catherine close for the experience of this brief age to touch with her own fingers a "red flower" and a "yellow flower" and a "blue flower" and I was sure next summer it would be "two flowers and two flowers is four flowers" and the year of emotional descriptions would be over and they'd be exchanging flowers hand to hand and calculating who had how many and their backs were to me and they were getting farther away where their voices carried off in the wind and I thought now this is my family and words will never be what I see.

] [